70000000318480

"Oh, I'm so sorry!" Brianna automatically apologized, stepping back and trying to collect herself.

She felt slightly flustered, but did her best not to show it.

"No, it was totally my fault," Sebastian said, annoyed with himself. Drawing back, he'd automatically reached out to steady the woman he'd nearly sent sprawling. He caught her by her slender shoulders. The next moment, his vision clearing, enabling him to actually focus on the face of the woman before him, he dropped his hands from her shoulders, stunned.

At the same time, Sebastian's jaw dropped.

The one person he hadn't wanted to run into at the reunion was standing less than five inches away from him.

Looking far more radiant than he ever remembered her looking.

TEN YEARS LATER…

BY
MARIE FERRARELLA

First published in Great Britain 2013
by Mills & Boon, an imprint of Harlequin (UK) Limited,
Eton House, 18-24 Paradise Road, Richmond, Surrey TW9 1SR

ISBN: 978 0 263 90118 4
ebook ISBN: 978 1 472 00493 2

23-0613

Harlequin (UK) policy is to use papers that are natural, renewable and recyclable products and made from wood grown in sustainable forests. The logging and manufacturing processes conform to the legal environmental regulations of the country of origin.

Printed and bound in Spain
by Blackprint CPI, Barcelona

Marie Ferrarella, a *USA TODAY* bestselling and RITA® Award-winning author, has written more than two hundred books for Mills & Boon, some under the name Marie Nicole. Her romances are beloved by fans worldwide. Visit her website, www.marieferrarella.com.

To
Patience Bloom
and
her Sam,
who were my inspiration
for this story.
Thank you.

Prologue

"Maizie, may I speak with you?"

Maizie Sommer looked up from her desk and watched the approach of the sweet-faced, heavyset woman who'd just entered her real estate office.

She knew that look. She'd seen it before, more than once. Not in her capacity as a remarkably successful Realtor with her own agency, but in her role as an even *more* successful matchmaker.

What had begun several years ago as a determined plan to get her own daughter—and the daughters of her two best friends—matched up and married to their soul mates had turned into a calling.

Since the first time she had gone down this path, Maizie, along with Theresa Manetti and Cecilia Parnell, all three best friends since the third grade, had never encountered failure. Strong gut instincts had guided the three women as they played matchmakers for friends and relatives, unerringly pairing up their targets, not for profit but for the sheer love of it.

As they amassed one triumphant pairing after another, their reputations grew. So much so that at times, their businesses were forced to take a temporary backseat to what Maizie liked to refer to as their "true mission."

"Come in, Barbara," Maizie said warmly. Rising, she turned the chair in front of her desk so that the visitor could easily take a seat. "So tell me, what can I do for you?"

Barbara Hunter, whose fondness for rich, good food was evident, sank down into the proffered chair. The retired high school English teacher sighed wearily. This was something she'd been wrestling with for a long time. Coming to Maizie for help amounted to a last-ditch effort before she completely gave up.

"You can tell me how to light a fire under my stubborn son."

Maizie looked at the other woman, puzzled. "I'm afraid I don't—"

Anticipating her friend's question, Barbara elaborated. "He was supposed to come home for his high school's ten-year reunion, but now he tells me that he doesn't have time for that 'nonsense,'—his word, not mine—and that he wants to save that time and put it toward his Christmas vacation so that when he *does* come out, we can have a nice, long visit."

Soft brown eyes shifted imploringly toward Maizie. "Oh, Maizie, I had such hopes for him…." Barbara's voice trailed off, lost in another deep sigh.

Maizie, meanwhile, was busy cataloging information. "Remind me, where's your son now?"

"Sebastian is in Japan, teaching Japanese businessmen how to speak English. He's really very good at it," she interjected with visible pride. "When he skipped his five-year reunion, he told me that he'd attend the next milestone reunion 'for sure.' His words," she said again, more bleakly this time. She looked like a woman clinging to the last vestiges of hope and trying to make peace with the knowledge that it was slipping through her fingers. "I was hoping he'd go to this one and maybe even get together with Brianna."

The name seemed to just wistfully hang there. "Brianna?" Maizie prodded.

Barbara nodded. "Brianna MacKenzie, the girl Sebastian went with during his senior year. I have this beautiful prom picture of the two of them," she confided, then added with feeling, "A lovely, lovely girl. I really thought that they'd wind up getting married, but Sebastian went off to college and Brianna stayed behind to take care of her father. The poor man was involved in a terrible car accident the night of the prom. She literally nursed him back to health and was so good at it, she went on to become an actual nurse."

Barbara closed her eyes and shook her head as she felt the last nail being hammered into the coffin of her dreams.

"I had hoped..." Her voice trailed off, but it wasn't hard to fill in the blanks. "Now Sebastian's apparently changed his mind again. I'm beginning to think that I'm never going to see my son get married, much less hold a grandchild in my arms. Sebastian's my only boy, Maizie. My only child. I've tried to be patient. Lord knows I haven't interfered in his life, but I don't have forever. Do you have *any* suggestions?" she asked, clearly counting on a miracle.

The wheels in Maizie's head were already turning and she was lost in thought. "How's that again?" she asked, focusing intently.

"Do you have any suggestions?" Barbara Hunter repeated.

But Maizie shook her head. "No, not that. What did you say just before that?" she coaxed.

Barbara paused and thought. "That I don't want to interfere in his life?" She had no idea what Maizie was after.

Maizie frowned, shaking her head. "No, *after* that," she stressed.

Barbara paused again, thinking for a moment longer. "That I don't have forever?" It was purely a guess at this point.

Maizie smiled broadly. "That's it."

Barbara looked at her uncertainly, completely lost. "*What's* it?"

The pieces were all coming together. Maizie almost beamed. "That's how you're going to get Sebastian to come home—and incidentally, to attend the reunion."

Barbara struggled to follow what her friend was saying, but it wasn't easy. "I think that Sebastian already suspects I'm not immortal."

"To suspect is one thing—we all know no one lives forever—but to suddenly come up against that jarring fact is quite another." She watched Barbara expectantly, throwing the ball back into her court.

Barbara came to the only conclusion she could. "You want me to tell Sebastian I'm dying?" Even as she said it, it sounded surreal.

"Not dying, Barbara," Maizie corrected gently. "You're going to tell your son that you had 'an episode.'"

It still didn't make any sense. "An episode? An episode of what?"

"Well, definitely not an episode of *NCIS: Los Angeles,*" Maizie told her with a patient smile. "If I remember correctly, Bedford High is celebrating a graduating class's tenth reunion in ten days, right?"

That her friend had this sort of information at her fingertips caught Barbara off guard. She knew that Maizie's daughter hadn't gone to that school and knew of no reason why the woman should be aware that the high school was throwing another reunion party.

"How do you know?"

"How do I know that?" Maizie guessed. She loved being on top of things. "It just so happens that Theresa Manetti was talking about landing the catering assignment for that party just the other day. But never mind that for now. You just call that son of yours and tell him that you don't want to alarm him but that you might have had a minor stroke, and that you'd really rather not put off seeing him, 'just in case.'"

"But I'll be lying to Sebastian and that's a bad lie," Barbara protested uncomfortably.

Maizie looked at her innocently. "Then you *do* want to put off seeing him?"

"No, of course not. That part's true enough, but I haven't had a stroke, light or otherwise," Barbara underscored.

Maizie quoted a statistic. "Did you know that, according to a report I recently read, some people actually have strokes and never realize it?"

"No, I didn't kn—" Barbara held the information highly suspect. "Maizie, are you stretching the truth?"

"No, not stretching, Barbara, but you of all people must know that communication is all about how you use your words. It's not what you say but how you say it," she told the other woman with a broad smile. "You have to be ruthless if you want your son to come home."

Barbara still seemed uncomfortable about the untruth. "I don't know, Maizie...."

"You don't know if you want to see your son happily married and starting a family?" Maizie asked.

"No, of course I do," Barbara said with feeling. And got no further.

Maizie could feel her adrenaline beginning to surge. She *loved* a challenge—and this had the makings of a really good one.

"Good. Then let me look into a few things and I'll get right back to you. With the reunion so close, we don't have that much time. In the meanwhile, you get that son of yours on the phone and tell him that you *really* want to see him now. That you'd rather not wait until Christmas—just in case. Understood?"

Barbara nodded. "Understood." She only hoped that, in the long run, Sebastian would find it in his heart to forgive her.

Chapter One

Sebastian Hunter felt exhausted as he and the three hundred and twelve other passengers packed closely around him ended their eleven-and-a-half-hour international flight by finally getting off the plane at LAX.

Concerned ever since he'd gotten off the phone with his mother a scant two days ago, he'd been far too wired even to catnap on the flight, which had covered more than five thousand miles and had taken him from the heart of Tokyo to Los Angeles.

It didn't help matters any that there was a sixteen-hour time difference between the two cities, not to mention that he felt as if he'd been traveling backward. He'd left Tokyo early on Saturday morning only to arrive in Los Angeles late Friday night, which technically made it the night before.

And he wasn't done yet.

There was still customs to go through, despite the fact that he had brought nothing with him to declare. He'd packed hastily, informed his employer of the family emergency that necessitated his presence and arranged for a leave of absence. And now, perilously close to fraying his very last nerve—because airport security had the passengers as well as its staff on edge—he was forced to pretend he was cool, calm and collected. Otherwise, if he allowed any of the tension he was feeling to show, he might just find himself detained far longer than it would take to queue up for a random search. Tense passengers were regarded with suspicion.

He struggled to curb his impatience, although he was losing the battle.

C'mon, c'mon, how long are you going to spend going through her underwear? he wondered irritably as the customs agent rifled through a young woman's suitcase.

The process seemed to take forever. Where were Dorothy's ruby-red slippers when you needed them, Sebastian thought darkly.

The phrase echoed in his brain, startling him. God, he had to *really* be punchy if he was thinking about donning the fairy-tale footwear just to get him home.

His mind was going—and that was in part thanks to his lack of sleep.

But he wasn't in a hurry because of fatigue. He was in a hurry because, for the first time in his life, at the age of twenty-nine, he had become acutely aware of mortality.

Not his own. The thought of not being around someday didn't bother him in the slightest. What would be would be, as his mother always liked to say.

However, somewhere in the back of his mind, he'd grown comfortable with the concept of always having his mother around. His image of her had stabilized somewhere between what she'd looked like when he'd last seen her and a little older than an actress she had always admired, Barbara Stanwyck, playing the matriarch of a large family. To him his mother was—and always had been—proud, determined and incredibly capable.

He knew the image wasn't eternal and certainly not realistic, but he couldn't entertain the idea that his mother would someday decline and eventually cease to be. Nor did he want to.

He would have traded in his soul to be able to break into a run, make time stand still and miraculously appear at her side the moment he hung up the phone, ending the unexpected, unnerving call he'd received from her.

And now it seemed as if it had been forever before Sebastian was finally standing outside the terminal where he had deplaned, signaling to the closest taxi driver that he needed a ride to get to his final destination.

He hoped, because the hour was so late, that for once he would be spared having to deal with an infamous

Los Angeles traffic jam. But it was also Friday night, which meant that everyone was out on the road.

Being as sprawled out as Los Angeles was, nothing was ever close by and thus necessitated obligatory travel from one point to the next, which in turn, like as not, resulted in gridlock.

"Business or pleasure?" the gypsy cabdriver asked him as they found themselves inching along the San Diego Freeway.

Preoccupied, trying not to worry about his mother, Sebastian barely heard the question. Looking up, his eyes met the driver's in the rearview mirror. "What?"

"Are you here on business or pleasure?" the man repeated, looking to kill some time by striking up a conversation.

"Neither."

How did you categorize flying halfway around the world to ascertain whether or not your only living relative, the mother you loved, would be around to welcome in another year? It still felt very surreal to him.

"Oh," the driver muttered in response, obviously taking the answer to mean that his passenger didn't want to be communicative.

Sebastian thought of saying something inane to show the driver that he wasn't trying to be rude, but decided if he did that, it might leave him open to an onslaught of conversation. He allowed the silence within the vehicle to continue by default.

Outside the gypsy cab, the typical sounds of engines, horns and vehicles whose drivers were impatient to reach their destinations echoed through the night air like a bad symphony.

Sebastian tried to relax.

He couldn't.

Despite the fact that the house in Bedford where he had grown up was located only forty-five miles from the airport, it took him over two hours to reach it. But eventually, Sebastian could finally make out the silhouette of the familiar two-story building.

In his hurry to get out, Sebastian gave the driver a fistful of bills he'd pulled out of his wallet. The man's pleased grunt in response told him that he had probably well exceeded the amount due, even when taking a generous tip into account.

Pocketing the money, the cabdriver jumped out of the vehicle, quickly removed the carry-on luggage and set it on the sidewalk. In two seconds, he was back behind the wheel and driving swiftly away, as if he was afraid that his fare would suddenly change his mind and take back some of the cash.

Alone, Sebastian stood and looked at the dark house where he'd lived for all his formative years.

The relentless sense of urgency that had dogged his every move throughout the five and a half thousand miles slipped into the background, pushed there by a very real, gnawing fear that once he was in his mother's company, he would hear something he wasn't prepared to hear.

He knew he wasn't being realistic, but as long as the details were not out in the open, he could pretend that they didn't exist, or at the very least, that they were better than he'd been led to believe.

Sebastian frowned in the dark.

Since when had he become such a coward? he silently demanded. He'd always gone full-steam ahead, hiding from nothing, consequences be damned. His philosophy had *always* been that it was far better to know than not to know. That way, he felt that he was always prepared for anything.

Yes, but this is your mother, your home port. Your rock. The cornerstone of who and what you are.

He was, he realized, afraid of losing her. His mother had always been the one steadfast thing in his life. She was why he felt free to roam, to explore the depths and extent of the possibilities of his life. As long as she was there to anchor him, to return to, he felt free to fly as high as he wanted.

But if she wasn't there…

Grow up, Hunter, Sebastian ordered himself.

He left it at that, not wanting to follow his thought to its logical conclusion. Instead, he made up his mind that if his mother needed him, he would be there for her, no matter what it took, just as she had always been there for him.

From the time that he was five years old, it had been just the two of them. It was time that he paid her back for that. For all the support, emotional and otherwise, that she had so willingly, so freely given him.

Exhaling a long breath, he braced himself. Sebastian

slipped his hand into his right pocket, feeling around for a moment.

His fingers curled around a very familiar object.

His house key.

He always kept the key on his person—for luck more than anything else. But now he held it in his hand, intending to use it for its true purpose: to get him inside his house.

For a moment, he considered doing just that. Unlocking the door, walking in and surprising his mother. But given the fact that she had suffered a recent, mild—God, he hoped it was truly just that—stroke, surprising her like that might bring on a heart attack—or worse. Most likely not, but he was not about to take a chance on even a remote possibility of that happening.

So he took out his cell phone and pressed the second preprogrammed number on his keypad. A moment later, he heard the phone on the other end ringing.

Two more rings and then a sleepy voice mumbled, "Hello?"

Why was he choking up just at the sound of her voice? He wasn't going to be a help to anyone if he kept tearing up, he admonished himself.

"Hi, Mom."

"Sebastian!" Besides instant recognition, there was also an instant smile evident in her voice. "Where are you?"

"I'm right outside your front door, Mom," he answered.

"My front door?" she echoed, suddenly wide awake. "Here?"

"You have another front door I should know about?" Sebastian joked.

She sounded great. Just the way she always did. Maybe there'd been some mix-up, he thought hopefully. Maybe she hadn't had a stroke. After all, her blood work had always been good.

So good, in fact, that it had been the source of envy among her friends.

His mother had always been the healthiest woman he'd ever known. Which made this news so much harder for him to accept.

Barbara didn't answer her son's question. Instead, she said, "Well, don't just stand there, Sebastian. Come in, come in," she urged.

Before Sebastian could pick up his suitcase and cross from the curb to the tall, stained-glass front door, it all but flew open. His mother, wearing the ice-blue robe he'd sent her last Christmas, her salt-and-pepper hair a slightly messy, fluffy halo around her head, was standing in the doorway, her arms outstretched, waiting for her only son to fill them.

Sebastian stepped forward, ready to embrace his mother. But when he reached out to her, he almost wound up stepping on a very indignant gray-and-white-striped cat that was weaving itself in and out between his legs.

The cat was not shy about voicing her displeasure at having to put up with an intruder in her well-organized little world.

Sebastian pretended to take no notice of the feline as he bent over and hugged his mother. Relief surged through him like unleashed adrenaline.

"Come in, come in," Barbara urged eagerly, stepping back into her living room.

As Sebastian took a step forward, the cat again wove in and out between his legs, narrowly avoiding getting into a collision with him.

When he almost tripped on the furry animal, he frowned more deeply. He looked down at the offending territorial creature with sharp claws.

"When did you get a cat?" he asked. His mother had never been one for pets, and he had grown up without one.

"Don't you recognize her, Sebastian?" Barbara asked in surprise.

He shrugged. "Sorry. You've seen one cat, you've seen them all," he tossed out casually.

"He doesn't mean that, Marilyn," she told the cat in a soothing voice. Turning toward her son, she said, "That's the kitten you gave me before you left for Japan. She's grown some," she added needlessly.

"Grown 'some'?" he questioned incredulously, looking back at the cat. The cat looked as if she could benefit from a week's stay at a health spa. "She's as big as a house."

"Don't hurt her feelings, Sebastian," his mother requested. "She can understand everything that we say about her."

A highly skeptical expression passed over his face.

As much as he would have liked to humor his mother, there had to be a line drawn somewhere. He fixed the cat with a look meant to hold her in place for a moment.

"Get out of the way, cat." The feline didn't budge. Sebastian grinned as he turned to his mother. "Apparently not everything."

"Oh, she understands," Barbara maintained good-naturedly. "She just chooses not to listen, that's all. Not unlike a little boy I used to know," his mother concluded with affection.

Sebastian brought in his suitcase, leaving it next to the doorway. He closed the door, then paused and took full measure of his mother, after she'd turned on the lights inside the room.

"Mom," Sebastian began, partly confused, partly relieved, "you look good. You look *very* good," he underscored. "How do you feel?"

It was then that Barbara remembered she was supposed to be playing a part. For a minute, seeing her son standing there on her doorstep, every other thought had fled from her mind. As she considered what she was about to say, the deception threatened to gag her. But then she recalled the afternoon of coaching she'd undergone with Maizie. The matchmaker had seemed so sure of the outcome of all this.

She *had* to give it a chance.

"I don't feel as good as I look, I'm afraid. Makeup does wonders."

Now that was a new one. "Since when do you wear makeup to bed?"

"Since I had to call nine-one-one in the middle of the night," she answered primly.

"You do realize that when they respond, they're here to possibly take you to the hospital, not escort you to a party," he told her.

"I didn't want them to have to see an ugly old lady," she said simply.

"You're not an ugly old lady, Mom. You're a pretty old lady," he said, tongue in cheek.

"Remind me to hit you when I get better," she answered.

That had been the test. Had she taken a swipe at him, the way she had in the past when the teasing between them had escalated, he would have felt that perhaps there'd been a false alarm, that she was really all right.

But her restraint told him the exact opposite. That she *wasn't* all right.

He pressed a kiss to her temple. "You're not an old lady, Mom. You know that. You look younger than women fifteen years younger than you are."

She smiled at him, grateful for the compliment, even though she knew it was a huge exaggeration.

"Nevertheless, a lady should always look her best," she maintained.

He shook his head, but unlike the old days, this time it was affection rather than impatience that filled him. That was his mother, determined to look her best no matter what the situation. He had to admire that kind of strong will.

And then he realized what she'd just told him. "You had to call nine-one-one?"

This was just going to be the first of many lies, Barbara thought, even as she reminded herself that it was all for an ultimate greater good.

"Yes. But it wasn't so bad, dear," she assured him. "The young men took very good care of me."

There was genuine regret in his eyes. "I'm sorry I wasn't here for you, Mom."

She patted his hand, the simple gesture meant to absolve him of any blame. "Don't give it another thought. You have your own life, Sebastian. And besides, you're here now and that's what counts," she added.

"So tell me everything," he urged. "What did the doctor say?"

"We can talk about all that tomorrow," she told him, waving away his request. "Tonight I just want to look at you. You still like coffee?" she asked suddenly, then turning on her heel, she began to lead the way to the kitchen. "Or have you decided to switch to green tea now?"

"I still like coffee," he answered.

"Nice to know that some things don't change," she told him.

Yes, but most things do, he thought, following behind her.

As the thought sank in, he could feel his heart aching. He should have come home a lot more, he upbraided himself. Even if coming home reminded him of all the things he'd given up and all the things he still didn't have, he should have come home more often.

"Sure you're up to this?" he asked his mother, concerned.

Barbara turned on the overhead lights, throwing the small, light blue kitchen into daylight.

"Putting water into a coffee urn? I think so," she deadpanned. "And if for some reason I can't, as I recall, you can."

And then she paused to hook both her arms through his for a moment and just squeeze him to her.

"Oh, it's so good to have you here. You're just the best medicine I could ask for."

Her words both gladdened his heart and pierced it with guilt. He switched the topic.

"Marilyn, huh?" The animal in question had followed them to the kitchen and had now positioned herself directly by the refrigerator, like a furry sentry who wanted to be paid in fish scraps. "Why Marilyn?"

"After Marilyn Monroe," Barbara answered without any hesitation. "Because when she crosses a room, she moves her hips just like Marilyn Monroe did in *Some Like It Hot*."

Sebastian pressed his lips together, knowing that his mother wouldn't appreciate his laughing at her explanation. All he trusted himself to say, almost under his breath, was "If you say so, Mom."

Turning away to look at the cat, he missed seeing the look of satisfaction that fleetingly passed over his mother's face.

Chapter Two

"You look pretty, Mama."

Brianna turned from the full-length mirror in her bedroom and glanced at the slightly prejudiced short person who had just uttered those flattering words. Sweet though it was, it wasn't the compliment that had warmed her heart; it was what the little girl had called her.

Mama.

She wondered if she would ever get used to hearing that particular word addressed to her.

Certainly she knew that she'd never take it for granted, especially since, biologically speaking, she wasn't Carrie's mother.

But there was no denying that presently she was the four-year-old's only family. She and her father, who, mercifully, had taken to the role of grandfather like the proverbial duck to water. He liked nothing better than doting on the curly-haired small girl and, in effect, being her partner in crime. Not only was Carrie precocious and the personification of energy, she also possessed a *very* active imagination.

"Least I can do after all you've done for me, Bree," he'd told her when she'd commented on the unusual dynamics their family had taken on.

"You are my dad," she reminded him, dismissing the need for any gratitude or words of thanks. "What was I supposed to do, just walk away and leave you to fend for yourself?"

He'd smiled at her. Brianna had never been one to take credit for anything. "A lot of other kids would have," he'd pointed out. "And not many would have postponed their education—and their life," he emphasized, recalling everything that had been involved that terrible summer when she'd stayed behind to nurse him after his horrific car accident.

An accident that his doctors insisted would leave him totally paralyzed, if not a comatose vegetable. Brianna had been his one-woman cheering section, refusing to allow him to wallow in self-pity or give in to the almost crippling pain. Instead, she'd worked him like a heartless straw boss. He gave up every day, but not Brianna.

She'd kept insisting that he was going to walk away from his wheelchair no matter what his doctors said to the contrary. She took nursing courses and physical therapy courses, all with a single focus in mind: to get him to walk again.

And during whatever downtime she had, between working with him and studying, she'd pitched in to help run his hardware store, working with his partner, J.T., whenever the latter needed to have some slack picked up.

By Jim MacKenzie's accounting, his daughter hadn't slept for more than a couple of hours a night for close to three years. The day he'd taken those first shaky steps away from his wheelchair, he remembered that she'd looked at him with tears in her eyes, a radiant smile on her lips, and declared, "Looks like I can go to bed now."

Brianna now looked at the little girl who was sitting on her bed, waving her feet back and forth as if channeling out her energy to the world at large.

"Thank you, baby," Brianna said to the child she'd come to love as her own.

"She doesn't look pretty, Carrie," Jim informed the little girl as he left his post in the doorway and walked into the room to join the two women in his life. "She looks *beautiful*."

Brianna's eyes met her father's. A knowing smile curved her lips. "I'm onto you, you know. You're just saying that because you want me to go to this silly reunion."

In his own way, her father was as stubborn as she was. He didn't believe in giving an inch. "I'm just saying it because it's true—and because I want you to go out and have a good time."

He was up to something and she knew it. "Then let's go to the movies," she suggested. "The three of us. My treat," she added to sweeten the pot.

"Number one—" he ticked off on his fingers "—the movies aren't going anywhere—they'll always be there. Number two, even if I said yes to going, I don't need you paying for my ticket. I'm the dad. I get to take the two of you out."

Brianna seized the moment. "Great—let's go."

His eyes told her he wasn't about to budge from his position. "But not tonight," he continued, remaining firm. "Go, catch up with your friends," he coaxed, then predicted, "It'll be fun."

Brianna sighed and shook her head, her light auburn hair swirling about her face like a pale red cloud. "Spoken like a man who has never had to attend any of his high school reunions."

Carrie puckered her small face, a sure sign that she was trying to absorb the conversation around her. Given a choice, the little girl always preferred the company of adults to that of children her own age. She knew that adults occasionally even forgot that she was there, but she didn't mind. She was content just to sit there, listening to them talk.

She was truly a sponge. Soaking up everything, her curiosity constantly being aroused.

"What's a higher reunion?" she asked, looking from her grandfather to the woman she thought of as her mother.

"High *school* reunion," Brianna corrected. "That's

when a bunch of people who used to go to the same classes together hold a party every few years so that they can pretend to be successful, making people jealous of them while they're checking who got fat and who lost their hair."

Carrie was quiet for a moment, then observed, "Doesn't sound like much fun."

Her point eloquently stated, Brianna looked at her father as she gestured toward Carrie. "Out of the mouths of babes."

Carrie's lower lip stuck out just a shade as she protested, "I'm not a baby."

"Maybe not," Brianna allowed, giving the girl a quick hug, "but you're *my* baby."

"And you're mine," Jim informed her firmly, but with the same underlying note of love. "Now, shake a leg and get to this thing before it's over."

Brianna grinned, pretending to weigh the thought. "Now, *there's* an idea. If I take my time getting ready and move really slowly, this lame reunion will be over by the time I get there."

"I hereby declare you ready," Jim announced, taking her by the hand and drawing her to the stairs. Carrie was quick to grab her other hand and follow suit, her blue eyes dancing. "I'm all set to babysit and you look fantastic. You have no excuse," Jim concluded, his words firmly declaring that the discussion—or argument—was officially over.

Giving in, Brianna allowed herself to be led down the stairs. Once on the ground floor, she raised her hands in semisurrender. She gave her father her compromise.

"I'll go—but I'll be home early," she told him.

He wasn't through bargaining. "You'll be home late and like it," he countered. Putting his wide, hamlike hands to her back, he aimed her at the front door and gave her a little push. "Now *go*."

This time, it was an order.

With a sigh, Brianna gave in. In the long run, it was easier that way. Kissing Carrie and then her father goodbye, she left.

Her CR-V, the car that J.T. had left to her upon his incredibly untimely death, was parked in the driveway and she crossed to it.

According to the very short will, J.T. had stated that the vehicle was an inadequate thank-you present. Though it wasn't spelled out, Brianna knew he was thanking her for saying that she would be Carrie's guardian in the event that something happened to him.

And then "something" had.

A week before their quickly planned wedding, J.T. had died in what amounted to a freak boating accident.

All throughout the funeral, she couldn't help thinking of the old adage J.T. had always been fond of quoting: If you wanted to make God laugh, tell Him you've started making plans.

She certainly hadn't planned for it to be this way. She had a daughter—and a CR-V—and no husband, no shot at attaining "happily ever after."

It was the second time that had happened to her.

Was that it? she wondered suddenly. Was that why she kept attending these damn reunions?

Was that why she'd let her father talk her into attending this one?

Because deep down inside, was she hoping that the first man who had made her yearn for a "happily ever after" before it had all turned to dust might attend this reunion?

As she drove down the brightly lit streets, she reminded herself that Sebastian Hunter hadn't attended the last reunion. Why in heaven's name did she think he was going to attend this one?

And even if he did, a little voice in her head mocked her, *are you going to rush up to him, throw your arms around him and say, "Let's pick up where we left off"?*

"No, of course not," Brianna said tersely, defensively, giving voice to her thoughts out loud.

Brianna took in a deep breath and unconsciously squared her shoulders as she came to a stop at a red light. Annoyed at the path her thoughts were taking, she reminded herself that she was made of sterner stuff than that. She hadn't cracked up when her father had almost died in that car accident—she'd stuck by him and done what had to be done.

And she hadn't cracked up when the guy she loved more than anything on earth had left her behind to go to college, emotionally stranding her and growing progressively more and more distant until he'd finally just completely disappeared from her life.

She hadn't even given up and booked a ride on the SS *Catatonic* when J.T. was killed.

Instead, she'd faced each and every one of her challenges, emerging whole on the other side. Moreover, she knew she would continue to face her challenges, determined to come out the victor no matter what dragon she was forced to battle.

Raising her head up a little higher, Brianna drove on.

Sebastian frowned behind his near-empty wineglass. He still couldn't believe that he had actually wound up here, despite his determination not to set foot into this sad little affair.

He was here because his mother had begged him to attend. Face-to-face with those incredibly sad eyes of hers, he found that the word *no* just refused to emerge.

Sebastian was far from happy about this unexpected turn of events.

But it was all his own fault. He couldn't blame anyone else for his being here right now. The blame rested squarely on his own shoulders. He'd been so desperate to do anything to please his infirm mother, he'd made the mistake of saying as much—and this, *this,* was the only thing she asked of him. To attend his high school reunion—and then come home and tell her all about it in the morning.

Except that there wasn't all that much to tell, he thought, slowly looking around and taking in the various little cliques gathered together throughout the large room.

Apparently the "mean kids" were now "mean adults," and the "nice kids" were still their targets, even though they were now, for the most part, "nice adults."

And, he noted, the ones who went on to make something of themselves and become successful had skipped the reunion entirely.

Just as he should have done.

Just as he had intended on doing until he'd been informed of his mother's stroke.

Okay, so he was here now because he'd promised his mother he would attend. However, he hadn't told her how *long* he'd be staying, so the duration of this Chinese water torture was strictly up to him.

Sebastian glanced at his watch. Nine o'clock. As good a time as any to declare that his stint in hell was officially over.

Draining the last bit of punch from the glass he'd been holding on to for the past hour—at least the food and drink had been excellent—Sebastian put the empty glass down on one of the side tables.

Time for a swift exit.

He looked neither to the left nor to the right, afraid that if he accidentally made eye contact with anyone he might be forced to spend an extra few minutes engaged in stilted, polite conversation with a person he would only pretend to remember.

It was exactly because he was avoiding making any sort of possible eye contact that he didn't see her.

Not until they had collided.

At that point, they were just two bodies with definite goals in mind and gaits that resembled slightly disoriented gazelles attempting to flee their unwanted location.

"Oh, I'm so sorry!" Brianna automatically apologized, stepping back and trying to collect herself. She felt slightly flustered, but did her best not to show it.

"No, it was totally my fault," Sebastian said, annoyed with himself for being so preoccupied that he'd been oblivious of where he was going.

Mercifully, at least there were no small, half-filled glasses of red punch to christen the unplanned collision. He really didn't want to remain here one more moment than he already had. So far, he hadn't really run into anyone he knew and for simplicity's sake, and the sake of a clean getaway, he wanted to keep it that way.

Drawing back, he reached out to steady the woman he'd nearly sent sprawling. He caught her by her slender shoulders. The next moment, his vision clearing, enabling him to actually focus on the face of the woman before him, he dropped his hands from her shoulders, stunned.

At the same time, Sebastian's jaw dropped.

The one person he hadn't wanted to run into at the reunion was standing less than five inches away from him.

Looking far more radiant than he ever remembered her looking.

Maybe he was wrong.

Maybe it wasn't her.

"Bree?" He cleared his throat and this time managed to say her full name. It came out in the form of a question. "Brianna?"

And even as he said her name, he tried to convince himself that he was mistaken. That he had just bumped into someone who merely reminded him of the girl he'd left behind.

The girl who had, in effect, emotionally stranded him, leaving him adrift.

Brianna could feel her stomach sinking—and fervently wished that the rest of her could go, too. Straight down through a hole in the ground.

But the floor remained solid even as her stomach twisted into a knot, making it hard for her even to breathe.

Her chin shot up as she squared her shoulders, looking for all the world like a soldier prepared to face certain death.

"Sebastian?"

The way Brianna said his name had always made him smile. Half lecture, half prayer. That much, he thought, hadn't changed.

But everything else *had,* he silently stressed. He'd gone on to make a life for himself abroad. A very good life.

If it, coincidentally, was also a solitary life, well, that had been his choice, right? Had he stayed behind or at least waited for her, instead of beginning to cut ties practically from the start, maybe life would have turned out differently.

But there was no way of really knowing just how

things would have gone, and besides, he had no *real* regrets. He didn't *allow* himself to have any. He'd chosen to leave Bedford and grow, rather than to remain here and stagnate.

"You look good," he heard himself saying to her.

God, talk about inane lines. But his mind had gone blank. Either that, or abruptly missing in action.

But she did look good, he had to admit. Maybe even *too* good. He didn't remember her figure being quite this curvy. And he was in a position to know. The last day they had been together, he'd shared the last dance at the prom with her. It had been a slow number and he'd held her to him for what had felt like an eternity.

Maybe you would have held her for far longer if you had actually remained in Bedford.

He blocked out the voice.

"You, too," Brianna was saying.

Her mouth felt dry, as if it was incapable of sustaining or uttering a single word without her tongue sticking to the roof of her mouth.

She cleared her throat, searching for a graceful way to end this awkward moment. A moment that *shouldn't* have been awkward at all.

Sebastian had been her first love, and her first lover.

Her pulse was racing. That couldn't be good, she thought.

"Were you just leaving?" Brianna finally managed to ask. *When at a loss for words, go with the truth,* she told herself.

"No." The denial was purely automatic. Relenting

just a little, he murmured, "Maybe." But that was obviously a lie. So he finally admitted, "Yes."

The fluctuating answer amused her a little. "I thought multiple choices were only for exams. Am I supposed to pick an answer from the above three?" she asked him.

Sebastian shook his head. He needed to go before he made a complete fool of himself.

"I was leaving," he confirmed, nodding toward the door behind her. "For some reason, my attending this reunion seemed to mean a great deal to my mother, so I told her that I would go. But I'm *really* not comfortable here." He looked around at the sea of mostly unfamiliar faces. "Being here kind of feels like putting on a sweater that used to fit but doesn't anymore."

"Because you've outgrown it."

It wasn't a question. She knew exactly what he was saying, because he'd described exactly the way she felt about attending this reunion.

Rather than nostalgia, what she'd heard in the various conversations she'd either taken in or overheard was the longing of former gridiron stars and ex-cheerleaders talking about the past, the scene of their glory days. For most it had been downhill after that. Hearing them talk just made her sad.

"My father made me come," she admitted.

"Your father," he echoed. That was right—he remembered his mother saying something about the old man's miraculous recovery. His mother insisted the miracle came in the form of Brianna. "How is he? I heard he made a full recovery, thanks to you."

She could feel color creeping up to her cheeks. Brianna quickly shrugged away his take on the story. "I don't know how much I really had to do with it, but my father did recover and he's doing just fine. Thanks for asking."

There were a thousand things to ask—and nothing left to talk about. He needed to go before the situation grew any more awkward. "Well, tell him I said hi."

"I will." She reciprocated and told him, "Say hi to your mom for me."

She'd always liked his mother a great deal, but after Sebastian had left her life, she couldn't make herself remain in contact with the woman. Being around Barbara Hunter reminded her far too much of what she had ultimately lost.

"Will do," he answered. "Well, I guess I'll see you around, Bree." He had no idea why he'd just said that, since he would be leaving for Japan soon.

"See you around," she echoed with a quick nod of her head.

"Well, what do we have here? Sebastian Hunter and Brianna MacKenzie, the king and queen of prom, together again!" Tiffany Riley, the official reunion coordinator, gushed ecstatically as she came up to them.

Chapter Three

Before she had a chance to recover from Tiffany's suddenly popping up, or to come up with a polite way to deny that they were "together," Brianna found herself being abruptly ushered to the center of the room, as was Sebastian. He seemed just as stunned by the former head cheerleader as Brianna was.

Aided by the element of surprise, Tiffany had brought them both over to stand before the band. The five-man group appeared to wait for some sort of signal from the woman.

In a voice loud enough to be heard not just across the populated gym but all the way across the street as well, Tiffany continued doing what she had always done best: talking and manipulating.

"Hey, everyone, what d'you say we get our king and

queen of the prom to re-create that last magical dance for us?"

She definitely did *not* want to go there, Brianna thought.

Especially not with everyone staring at them. It stirred up too many memories, too many feelings. Memories and feelings she wasn't sure she would be able to contain once aroused.

She slanted a look at Tiffany, who had a very smug expression on her face. Why? In high school, Tiffany had done everything she could to try to win Sebastian back. He'd dated the blonde cheerleader before he'd become *her* boyfriend, Brianna recalled, and although he'd once told her that he'd never considered himself and Tiffany to be a couple, Tiffany obviously had.

So why was Tiffany bringing attention to them now? Brianna wondered, feeling decidedly uncomfortable. This made no sense.

"No, I really don't thin—" Brianna began to beg off.

"I haven't danced since—"

Sebastian's voice blended with hers, but it was as if neither one of them had spoken, for all the effect it had on Tiffany. She apparently had decided to turn a deaf ear to both of them, focusing only on getting them to dance.

For just the slightest second, a smirk crossed Tiffany's full lips. She was enjoying their discomfort, Brianna realized. *Still hateful after all these years.*

"Aw, they're shy. Looks like they need some encouragement," Tiffany mocked. "Okay, give it up for

Sebastian and Brianna," she cried, beckoning for the attendees to applaud or chant the couple's names. Or better yet, both. The crowd complied immediately.

Tiffany's smirk turned into a look of satisfaction. "Music, please, boys," she called out to the band, then tossed a final, somewhat condescending bone to the audience. "And, for those of you who don't remember, that last 'magical' song they danced to was Etta James's 'At Last.'"

Tiffany, a commando in bright lavender taffeta, narrowed her eyes as she appraised the couple she had hustled to the center of the dance floor. The look on her face seemed to say, "So, what are you waiting for?"

Sebastian was far from happy about this turn of events, but the last thing he wanted was to cause a scene. The thought that no good deed went unpunished crossed his mind. If he hadn't come here to please his mother, he wouldn't be going through this now.

"Tiffany's going to bully us into dancing to that song. You realize that, don't you?" Sebastian whispered to Brianna, barely moving his lips.

Brianna did her best not to shiver as his breath slid along her bare shoulder. A wealth of old, repressed sensations and feelings came cascading down on her before she had a chance to block them again.

She focused only on what Sebastian had just said, not on what she'd just felt. "Bullying comes naturally to Tiffany," Brianna whispered back, recalling several instances during her high school years. Tiffany had always been obsessed with holding court and being the center of attention. The cheerleader had been utterly furious when she'd lost the bid to be crowned prom queen, especially to someone who hadn't lobbied to win the title.

Despite the fact that, the whole time she'd been driving here, she'd done her best to anesthetize herself against Sebastian should she run into him, she could feel that old thrill trying to break through.

It had just about succeeded when Sebastian suddenly took her hand and said, "One dance can't hurt."

A lot you know, she thought grudgingly. *Nobody broke your heart the way you broke mine.*

Brianna pressed her lips together to keep the words back. If she was lucky, they'd have this dance and then he'd leave.

If you're luckier, you'll have this dance and he won't leave.

The thought startled her.

Out loud she said, "Guess not," as she forced herself to smile broadly up into his face—strictly for appearances' sake.

The strains of the classic song filled the carefully decorated gym. The next moment, someone had the bright idea to dim the lights. And just like that, Brianna felt herself being teleported back across time and space until she was right there, at the prom, with the last song surrounding her like a soft, warm wrap.

Before she realized it, or could do anything to prevent it, her body was blending together with Sebastian's.

Just as it had that night.

The whole world had been at her feet that night. Everything had been fresh and new and it had whispered the promise of such wonderful things to come.

As it had turned out, it was the last time that she had felt sure of anything. The last time she'd felt secure. It had been just hours before her entire world was upended. While she was dancing with Sebastian, her father had been involved in that awful car accident, when an underage driver had jumped the light and plowed right into him.

Her whole life had changed in a matter of seconds. Instead of going away to college with Sebastian and beginning a new chapter in her life, not only going away to college but also moving in with Sebastian, she'd opted to remain home and help her father recover from the accident.

She'd thought her heart would literally break as she watched Sebastian leave, even though she had been the one to encourage him to go.

Was that really all those years ago? she wondered now. It seemed like just yesterday, especially with all these old feelings ambushing her.

Maybe her father was right. Maybe she really did need to take a short break from everything. From constantly shouldering problems that weren't always just her own. Her ability to empathize helped her be the kind of nurse every patient wanted, but at times it wreaked havoc with her own life, continually draining her.

So just for tonight, she decided abruptly, she was going to allow herself to reminisce, to go back to a time when she'd believed that her life was going to be absolutely nothing short of perfect.

"You still wear that perfume."

Sebastian's voice, low and still incredibly—and unintentionally—sensual, crept into her consciousness, catching her off guard.

It took her a second to play back the words and understand them. It took her another second to realize that she'd laid her head on his shoulder.

The way she had that last night.

Blinking, Brianna raised her head and looked at him. "What?"

"Your perfume," he repeated. "It's the same one you wore that night." He remembered how it had eroded any defenses he might have had and had made him want her in the worst way.

"It's the same one I wear all the time. I guess I'm not very exciting," she confessed with a slight, careless shrug.

Exciting or not, she was still her own person. Her own person who was committed to going her own way whenever she had to and helping others whenever she could. Being a nurse wasn't just what she did—it was what she *was*.

"Oh, I wouldn't exactly say that," Sebastian told her.

Maybe it was the combination of the perfume, the song and the fact that, for the most part, he'd led a fairly solitary life overseas. There were more than a few times when he'd felt alone in the crowd for these past few years, despite living in one of the most crowded cities in Japan.

Whatever the reason, holding Brianna like this, having her perfume fill his senses, managed to stir up some old, treasured memories. Memories that nonetheless felt a little misty, because time had a way of creating holes in the fabric of life as it began to stretch out.

The memories allowed him to suddenly feel as if he had been transported back to the past. To the last time he'd held Brianna in his arms. Then his head had been full of dreams for both of them.

He'd made love to her for the first—and only—time that night.

The wave of nostalgia that hit him was almost overpoweringly strong.

Brianna was undergoing a struggle of her own—and losing.

Talk, damn it. Say something. Something vague and neutral. Before you wind up making a fool of yourself and melting all over him.

Desperate, Brianna hit on the only topic she could actually think of. "So, how is your mother doing these days?"

"Not as well as I'd like," Sebastian admitted in an unguarded moment.

Ordinarily, he wasn't given to voicing his concerns or feelings. The years had made him far more stoic than he had been.

Less than five minutes in Brianna's company and he was regressing, he thought, annoyed with himself.

The concern he saw entering her eyes surprised him. "What do you mean by that?"

A simple excuse occurred to him. One that was, ultimately, a lie. But he had never been able to lie to Brianna. To start now just seemed wrong.

So he told her the truth. "The doctor said she'd had a minor stroke—reminded me just how fragile life really is. I was planning on having a lengthy visit with her over the Christmas holidays, but once she told me about her condition, I rearranged my vacation plans and flew out as soon as possible."

He paused for a moment, debating his next words. It exposed his vulnerable side, but then, this was Brianna, whom he had once trusted implicitly. He supposed, simply because old habits were hard to break, part of him still did.

"Mom made me realize that putting off the visit home might not be the wisest thing to do. If something had happened to her before I got a chance to see her, I'd never forgive myself."

She knew he wasn't being dramatic. His mother was a wonderful woman whom everyone absolutely loved. Including Sebastian. And her.

"So here I am," Sebastian concluded.

The wheels in her head had instantly begun turning at the first mention of his mother's illness. The nurse in her was never off duty.

"Has your mother ever had a stroke before?"

"No, not to my knowledge." He came back at her with his own question. "Why?"

Her shoulders rose and then fell in a casual shrug. “No real reason. I’m just trying to pull some facts together.”

He’d been so caught up in the moment—and trying not to be—that he’d completely forgotten. “That’s right. You became a nurse, didn’t you?”

Brianna nodded. “After my father got well, there was this tremendous feeling of relief. But at the same time, there was also this feeling of ‘what do I do with myself now?’”

“The words ‘relax a little’ come to mind,” he told her.

She smiled as she shook her head. “Not really in my nature. Besides, going into nursing seemed like the natural progression at the time. I like helping people, like getting them motivated and helping them realize that the only thing holding them back from achieving their goals—no matter what those goals are—is themselves.”

Sebastian had grown quiet and there was a strange look on his face now.

She flushed a little ruefully. “I’m talking too much, aren’t I?”

She was even prettier than she had been when he’d left, he thought now. Her looks were enhanced by a confidence that hadn’t been there when they’d gone together.

He found himself having to struggle to keep from being drawn in.

“I don’t think so,” he answered honestly. Who would have thought that the feelings he had for her were still there? That they hadn’t disappeared but had just gone into hibernation? "When my mother asked me to attend this reunion—"

"She *asked* you to attend?" Brianna echoed in surprise. That sounded so much like what her father had done, she was struck by the odd similarity.

He nodded. "My coming to the reunion seemed to mean a lot to her. Why is beyond me," he admitted. But then, the workings of a female mind mystified him. "What?" he asked when he saw her mouth beginning to curve. To his knowledge, he hadn't said anything funny.

"Don't act as if you came here kicking and screaming," she told him, amused at his protest. "The Sebastian I remember never did anything he didn't want to do."

The shrug was careless, even though he didn't take his eyes off her for a second.

"Maybe I've gotten more thoughtful in my old age," he speculated.

"Twenty-nine only qualifies for old age if you happen to be related to a fruit fly," she countered.

Sebastian smiled in response, a slightly self-deprecating expression on his face. She'd forgotten how easily that could get to her. Several more couples had joined them on the dance floor, so it no longer felt as if the two of them were putting on an exhibition strictly for Tiffany's amusement.

When Sebastian stopped moving about on the floor a moment later, she looked up at him curiously. "Why did you stop dancing?"

"Because the music stopped playing," he answered simply.

Damn it, how could she have missed that? Had she

been *that* mesmerized by him? That couldn't be allowed to happen.

"Right." Embarrassed, Brianna stepped back, dropping her hands from his. "Well, I guess we've fulfilled any leftover obligations from that last prom."

At least the obligations to strangers, she couldn't help thinking.

"Oh, no, you two aren't planning on ditching us already, are you?" Tiffany gushed, suddenly coming up to them again. "Maybe for a little secret rendezvous?" she asked with a laugh that threatened to turn Brianna's stomach.

Like an unwanted guest who was oblivious to any attempt to get her to leave, Tiffany hooked one arm through each of theirs, placing herself strategically between them. Her smile was as fake as it was wide.

"Is that it?" she pressed. "Do you two *really* intend to make up for lost time?"

He knew that telling Tiffany it was none of her business just made her more curious—and more determined to prove that she was right.

So he deftly avoided a direct answer. "I guess I can stay for a little longer," Sebastian told the former cheerleader.

Without meaning to or being totally conscious of doing it, he glanced in Brianna's direction to see if she'd been persuaded to remain for a while longer as well.

Or, he supposed, strong-armed into it.

He had to admit that he expected to see fireworks between the two women at any second. His money was on Brianna. Of the two, she appeared to be in far better shape—not to mention a lot feistier than Tiffany.

"Wonderful," Tiffany exclaimed, clapping her hands together. In what seemed like an afterthought, she looked in Brianna's direction. "And you, Bree?"

There had always been something condescending in her voice, Brianna thought, no matter whom she addressed. It used to intimidate her, but she'd had to shoulder so much in these past few years that the snide attitude of one small-minded woman no longer bothered her in the slightest, the way it might have at some other time.

She supposed that, as Sebastian had already said, it would do no harm to hang around here a little longer. After all, after tonight he would most likely go back to his work, which she'd heard was out of the country, and she would go back to hers. And their paths would never cross again.

So she awarded Tiffany with a carefree smile and said, "Sure, why not?"

"Great." This time, because they both seemed so willing, the word sounded a little less than upbeat. "This way, please," Tiffany told them, leading them to another part of the gym.

Sebastian stayed where he was for a moment longer and asked, "And just what's 'this way'?"

It was obvious to both of them that Tiffany didn't like being questioned or having to explain herself. She was, as Brianna would later tell her father when he asked how things had gone, a control freak in search of her own country to rule.

"Why, a photographer, you distrustful man." Tiffany laughed as if she had just said something exceedingly witty. "We're trying to put together an album of former students. You know, kind of like a 'where are they now?' sort of thing."

Sebastian looked at Brianna and asked, "You okay with that?" The display of concern toward Brianna irritated Tiffany no end, even as she continued maintaining her completely artificial smile.

"Sure," Brianna agreed. "I've got no problem having my picture taken."

"Thank you." Tiffany's gushing tone had been abandoned. What lay beneath had definite touches of frost to it, as did the glance she shot Brianna's way.

But the next moment, Tiffany once again reclaimed center stage and wound her expensively manicured fingers around the microphone, and the wide, shallow smile had returned.

"Attention. Can I have your attention?" she requested in a voice that grew louder with each passing syllable. "The photographer's been making the rounds to your tables, but now it's time for all of us to stand up and come together for group shots," she announced. "We all thought it might be fun if we did it the way the yearbook was done—pictures taken in our old clubs. Those of you, like myself—" unable to stop herself, she allowed the superior smirk to pass over her face again "—who belonged to an endless number of groups will be forced to have your picture taken in each and every one of them. Just remember, this is ultimately for the good of the student body."

"Is she for real?" Sebastian whispered the question to Brianna. He'd turned his head away at the last moment so that Tiffany wouldn't be able to overhear him.

Brianna took a quick survey of the woman at the microphone. As far as "real" went, she highly doubted it. Tiffany had obviously had her nose shortened, her chin reinforced, not to mention that her cup size had been increased by a multiple of two. Her hair was neither her natural color, nor, from what she remembered, actually hers. Her hairdo was comprised of elaborately woven extensions.

"Not as far as I can tell," Brianna quipped.

Sebastian suddenly had to bite his lower lip to keep from laughing.

Brianna saw the contained laughter in his eyes when he looked at her and that old feeling, the one she was desperately struggling to block, rose up and found her again.

She reminded herself that this was an isolated evening, one with ties to the past and absolutely no ties to either one of their futures.

With that understood and taken into consideration, she allowed herself to react to him, but only as long as she kept in mind that all her tomorrows would be without him, just as so many of her yesterdays had been.

Tiffany beckoned over the photographer, a tall, balding man who had a camera hanging from his neck and another one held firmly in his hands.

"All right, Alan, let the snapping begin," Tiffany declared as she turned her body three-quarters toward the photographer, her hands on her hips and her head thrown back.

She was posing for him.

To her chagrin, the photographer turned his camera toward Sebastian and Brianna and began shooting shot after shot.

Tiffany collected herself and stormed away.

Chapter Four

"I think you've got more than enough photographs now."

Something in Sebastian's voice must have told the photographer there was no room for argument. Resigned, the man nodded and lowered the camera that he had been firing at them in rapid fashion.

"Yeah, I guess maybe I do," the photographer murmured.

The next moment, he was turning his attention toward other alumni, his camera once again shooting.

Sebastian became acutely aware of Brianna beside him and the silence that seemed to seal them into their own private bubble, despite all the people and noise around them.

"I guess I should have asked you before sending that guy away," Sebastian said.

For old times' sake, Brianna decided to absolve him of any guilt, especially since, unlike Tiffany, she had absolutely no desire to be digitally captured and immortalized pretending she was still a teenager.

"He was getting on my nerves, too," she confided to Sebastian.

"Good to know," he murmured, feeling more awkward and at loose ends than he could recall feeling since…well, since more than ten years ago when he'd initially walked up to her and struck up a conversation. At the time, he'd tried hard not to trip over his own tongue because he thought she was just so genuinely pretty, without resorting to any of the usual enhancing beauty aids that the other girls used.

He took a long breath. This was the part where he took his leave. He'd say a few vague, noncommittal words, something generic and nonspecific about it being nice to see her again, or it was fun catching up, and then he'd get the hell out of there as fast as he could.

The fact that they hadn't caught up wasn't really supposed to matter.

Except that it did.

This was the girl he'd left behind, the one who "got away," as his mother had told him more than once over the past ten years.

Not that Brianna had made a single move that took her out of his reach.

No, *he* was the one who had made all the moves. *He*

was the one who had left Bedford alone after they had initially made plans to leave together.

But the plans that he could have sworn had been written in stone turned out to have been written in tapioca pudding. He had gone on to the college that had accepted them both, while Brianna had staunchly remained at home, nursing her father back from the jaws of paralysis to become the healed man he was today.

In a word, she had just continued being Brianna.

And now he was here, trying to collect himself after just having held in his arms the only woman, if he were being truly honest, who had ever mattered to him in that all-important way.

And, yes, damn it, he was experiencing regrets. Very real regrets. Something he'd *thought* he was finally beyond having. He was an intelligent, successful man and that meant he'd moved on.

Or at least he'd *thought* he'd moved on.

Except that now he wasn't so sure. "Moving on" didn't have the painful, gut-twisting feeling attached to it, the one he was experiencing now.

Did it?

And, if he'd genuinely moved on, he wouldn't have heard himself saying this little gem: "Listen, would you like to go get a drink somewhere, or maybe go out to dinner sometime? I'm in town for at least another week…."

Abruptly running out of steam, Sebastian let his voice trail off.

Another week. Seven days, and then he'd be gone

again. He would be here just long enough to rip open all her old wounds and then he'd go again, his job here done.

Say no, Bree. For God's sake, save yourself and say no.

Her problem was that she never listened to that little, all-important inner voice, the one that always made such sense.

The one that had urged her, ten years ago, to go on with her life. To hire someone if she could for her father and get her degree the way she'd planned for years, instead of standing there with tears in her eyes, telling Sebastian that she couldn't just leave her father with strangers.

That same lack of common sense—as well as lack of self-preservation—now had her saying to Sebastian, "That would be nice." It was a phrase that opened up the door to a world of possibilities she *knew* she wasn't emotionally equipped to deal with at this point.

Too late now.

"How about tomorrow night?" Sebastian asked, even as he told himself that what he was actually supposed to say at this point was "Good. I'll call you," or even "Great. I'll get back to you about details." And then leave it at that.

The *last* thing he was supposed to do was get specific. And citing a date like tomorrow didn't give his common sense enough time to kick in and talk him out of this extremely rash move.

Why am I nodding? her little voice demanded.

Worse, she thought, why was she asking Sebastian, "Is six good for you?"

Six is terrible for me. I misspoke. How about we change that from tomorrow to the twelfth of never?

The handful of lifesaving words raged in Sebastian's head, helplessly caged and unable to break free in order to slip off his tongue.

So instead, what he heard was his own doom being sealed, his death knell sounding as he responded—rather than saying, "No, no, a thousand times no"—"Perfect."

"All right, then I'll expect you at six tomorrow."

"What's your address?" Sebastian asked, piercing a hole in the rubber balloon of her desperate thoughts.

Brianna blinked as she looked at him, her mind a sudden blank. "What?"

"Your address," he specified. When she still looked at him as if he was using a foreign language, he added, "So I can come and pick you up."

The fog lifted. "Right." The smile she flashed at him was bordering on anemic. "I still live in the same house," Brianna told him. "Never had the time to move out," she added.

The smile he saw on her lips was fast—but lethal nonetheless.

Just as lethal, he realized, as it ever was.

Perhaps even more.

Time had been very good to her. The pretty little high school senior was now a strikingly beautiful woman.

"That'll make it easy for me to find." As he stood

there, drawing out the conversation when he knew he should be running for cover, he had a sudden, strong and nearly irresistible urge to kiss her, despite the fact that approximately half their graduating class was milling around to bear witness to his insanity.

He called himself seven kinds of a fool. It was enough—for now—to stop him.

"I'll walk you to your car," he finally heard himself volunteer.

Panic vied with a surge of pulsating excitement. "You're leaving, too?" she asked.

He nodded, glancing over his shoulder. He spotted the former cheerleader looking their way. "Thought I should make good my getaway before Tiffany comes up with something else."

Brianna nodded. "Tiffany's married to a doctor now. Well, a dentist," she corrected, not because she thought of one career as being superior to the other but because she wanted to be accurate. "Actually, it's rather lucky he is a dentist." Sebastian raised a quizzical eyebrow, waiting for an explanation. "They have three kids and all three are in braces. When they smile on a sunny day, the glare could blind you."

Brianna heard him laugh at that and found the low, sensual sound oddly comforting. She tried to persuade herself that his reaction one way or another didn't matter to her.

She reminded herself that she had come a long way since she'd been that heartbroken, starry-eyed girl who'd cried into her pillow every night for a month.

Right now, though, none of that could get her to change the way she was responding to him. Couldn't erase the warm glow growing inside her, created by his nearness.

He'd always had that sort of effect on her, she recalled.

"She never forgave you for dumping her, you know," she told Sebastian.

The protest was automatic—and with feeling. "I didn't dump her."

She was only telling him what she knew that Tiffany believed. "I think it felt that way to her."

He wanted to correct the record, strictly for old times' sake, he silently insisted, not because it mattered to him to be blameless in her eyes.

"To dump someone, you have to be going with that person to begin with," he reminded her. "And we weren't going together."

"She certainly thought that you were going together," Brianna dutifully pointed out, recalling the vicious looks she'd been subjected to by Tiffany and her circle of friends.

They had begun walking toward the exit and he found himself quickening his pace just a little. The conversation wasn't on a path he wanted to take.

"I can't help what she thought. I just know that it wasn't anything I said to her—or even alluded to. To be honest," he continued as they walked out of the gym and down the empty, dimly lit hallway, "Tiffany kind of scared me."

He was kidding, right? "She weighed all of ninety-eight pounds to your one-eighty." Brianna knew that, because back then Tiffany was forever bragging about losing weight and hardly ever allowed herself to eat anything of substance.

"Her weight had nothing to do with it," he maintained. "A stick of dynamite can blow up a barn. And irrational people are capable of doing some really very scary, unhinged things.

"Where's your car?" Sebastian asked, abruptly changing the subject.

The last thing he wanted to do was talk about Tiffany and the past. He didn't really want to dwell on the past at all, because if he allowed himself to do that, then he would start to remember just how much he'd once loved Brianna and how irrationally hurt and cheated he'd felt when he was made to choose—not in so many words but in actual fact—between the woman he loved and going on to pursue his dreams.

Brianna was supposed to have been part of those dreams, not an alternative choice.

But looking back now, he couldn't help but wonder, if only for a brief, unguarded moment, if his choice had been the right one.

Sure it was. Don't start second-guessing yourself. You see? This is why you should never have come back to Bedford.

Except that he had to and he knew it. To willfully not come back when his mother had made it so clear that she needed him would have been, if nothing else, incredibly selfish on his part. And that didn't even begin to take into consideration the fact that if something had actually happened to his mother, he would have never forgiven himself for not seeing her one last time.

Especially since she'd made a point of requesting it.

It was that moment, as this thought began to sink deep into his mind, when for the very first time he actually understood just what Brianna must have gone through all those years ago. Understood how she felt when her father had survived the accident but had been given the prognosis that he would never walk again, never function independently in any manner, shape or form.

Never be the man he had been until that terrible accident.

Now he understood how very torn she had to have been between following her conscience, which bound her to the man who had done everything to give her the very best possible life, and following her heart and going away to college with him.

Sebastian looked at her and, before he could think to stop himself, he heard himself saying to her, "Bree, I'm sorry."

They were out in the parking lot now, walking toward the spot where Brianna had parked her car. His words, coming completely out of the blue and cocooned in such heart-wrenching sadness, left her utterly confused.

She needed an explanation. "Sorry about what?"

By then Sebastian's instincts of self-preservation had

finally kicked in, the same ones that told him there was no purpose in revisiting the past.

They supplied the right words to get him out of this verbal grave he had managed, so quickly, to dig for himself.

"Sorry if I was a bit rusty back there. You know, on the dance floor," he added, knowing this had to be up for an award somewhere as one of the lamest excuses of the decade, if not the century. "It's been a while since I've done any dancing."

She had a hunch that wasn't what Sebastian had initially alluded to with his apology, but she just couldn't see the point of making him twist and turn in the wind.

What on earth for?

So instead, she just shrugged it off and said something equally bland.

"Really? I would have never known. Not that I'm exactly a double threat on the dance floor myself, but you seemed pretty smooth to me back there."

To be honest, having him hold her in his arms had effectively destroyed the ability on her part to take notice of *anything* else.

Sebastian laughed softly under his breath, another group of memories popping out of hiding and scampering lightly across his brain in toe shoes.

And then he smiled at her. "You never did find fault with me, even when I said it was okay to, did you, Brianna?"

She shrugged again, the movement more deliberate than careless.

"Life's too short to nitpick," Brianna answered. Suddenly aware of where she was in the parking lot, she stopped walking. She'd almost walked right past her vehicle. "Well, this is my car, so your escort service is no longer needed."

Nice going, Bree. Could you be more awkward sounding? she upbraided herself. She was never an out-and-out wit, but she also never sounded as if her tongue didn't quite work right, either.

His attention drawn to her car, Sebastian looked at the light blue vehicle and recognition set in. "Hey, isn't that—?"

"Yes," Brianna answered, anticipating what he was about to ask. "It's the old Toyota my dad gave me as an early graduation present just before the prom." At the last minute, she'd decided to leave J.T.'s CR-V behind and drive this car instead. It seemed more in keeping with the evening's whole nostalgic mood. "It still runs like a dream—well, close to a dream, anyway," she amended with a nervous little laugh. "But I really don't see the need to get rid of it just because it's an old model and the paint could use a little freshening.

"I guess I just tend to stick with things," she added.

Too late she realized what that might have sounded like to Sebastian: a rebuke for choosing to move on, to shed the city he'd been born and raised in.

The city where she had remained.

Pressing her lips together, Brianna searched for the right words to help her fix what she'd just done.

When none occurred to her, Brianna fell back on a

tried-and-true excuse. "But that's just me, I guess. Just an old stick-in-the-mud."

"Old sticks never looked so good," Sebastian murmured with appreciation before his mind had a chance to filter his words.

He was developing a serious case of foot-in-mouth disease, he upbraided himself.

Sebastian stood back as she unlocked her car door on the driver's side. Then, reaching past her, he opened it and held the door open for her as she slid in.

The skirt of Brianna's street-length dress rose up on one side, climbing up rather high on her thigh before she had a chance to pull it down again.

She still had the best legs he'd ever seen, Sebastian caught himself thinking.

Some things, fortunately, never changed.

And then he forced himself to focus on making his final getaway. "Okay, then. Tomorrow at six. Your place, right?"

"Right."

She had no one to blame but herself, Brianna thought. She knew she could still change her mind, still act on the second thoughts that she was now experiencing at a prodigious rate. Act on them and come up with some kind of an excuse.

Plausible or not, Sebastian would have to accept whatever rationale she gave him. After all, he couldn't exactly *force* her to come to dinner with him, now, could he?

Of course not.

Brianna was still thinking this as she drove away, watching Sebastian get smaller and smaller in her rear-view mirror.

Chapter Five

With a sigh, Brianna stepped out of the latest dress she'd just tried on and tossed it onto the growing mountain of fabric on her bed.

Why didn't anything look right on her?

This was getting serious. Her frustration doubled and grew by the nanosecond.

When she'd pulled back the sliding mirrored door of her wardrobe in her bedroom, approximately forty-five minutes ago, Brianna was fairly certain she knew exactly what she was going to wear to this dinner, which she should have never agreed to. But once she had put the dress on, it just looked all wrong, so she had gone on to choice number two and put *that* on.

It met the same fate.

As did choices number three through five.

And, at the same time, with each discarded garment, the butterflies in her stomach multiplied.

Exasperated when yet another choice seemed woefully inadequate on her, several disparaging, less-than-flattering words rose to her lips, poised for release. But she remained silent when she saw Carrie curiously stick her head into her room.

The old soul trapped in a child's body looked at the ever-growing pile of clothes that had accumulated on Brianna's double bed. After a moment, the blue eyes shifted from the bed to her.

"Why are all the clothes out, Mama? Are you cleaning?"

"No, honey. I just can't find anything to wear," Brianna answered, doing her best not to allow the growing despair to surface in her voice.

Why had she ever agreed to this? And why hadn't she noticed before tonight that *nothing* she owned fit her the way it was supposed to?

Her response confused her ordinarily unflappable daughter. Carrie gestured toward the bed. "Sure you can, Mama. It's all right there, on your bed. *Lots* of clothes," she emphasized.

Ever the practical child, Brianna thought with affection.

"What I mean is that everything I tried on just wasn't... pretty enough," she concluded, finally settling on the right word to describe her dissatisfaction.

"Clothes aren't pretty, Mama," said Carrie, the picture of endearing innocence. "You are," she insisted definitively.

The child should be bottled as a tranquilizing agent. "You're right—clothes *aren't* pretty." In the back of her mind, she wondered if she should be recording this conversation, saving it to replay when her tiny soul-of-logic turned into a sullen, typical teenager experiencing out-of-control angst over having a wardrobe that was too dull, too boring or just plain no longer sufficient for her current needs.

Brianna took a deep breath, trying her best to center herself. Maybe the solution to her problem was just to let a neutral bystander pick her outfit.

She glanced down at her daughter. "All right, what would *you* pick out to wear if you were going out to eat with someone who had once been very special to you but who you haven't really seen in the last ten years?"

Rather than dive into the piles of clothing strewn all over her mother's bed, Carrie turned toward her with a question of her own. "Why didn't you see the special person? Was he hiding?"

Maybe. Maybe I was, too, Brianna thought. Hiding from the pain, from the fact that her heart felt as if it had been literally broken in two. Someone you loved was supposed to support you during a crisis, not go on with his own life and ignore what you were going through.

"He went away to college," she told Carrie.

Carrie looked at her with wide, caring eyes. "And you couldn't go?"

How was it that this child could always strip everything down to its bare essentials, making the situation appear so simple, so cut-and-dried, even when it didn't feel that way?

"Grandpa was in a big accident—before you were born," she qualified when she saw the question rising in her daughter's intense blue eyes, "and I had to take care of him."

Carrie nodded her head. The little girl was probably merely taking in her words, but it almost felt as if Carrie was giving Brianna her own seal of approval for what she'd done.

"And he's all better now," Carrie noted with no small pleasure. She beamed at the only woman she had ever known to be her mother. "You did a good job taking care of him, Mama."

Brianna returned her daughter's smile, feeling heartened. Everything always seemed better, brighter, more hopeful whenever Carrie was around.

"I did, didn't I?" For some unknown reason, Brianna felt better now and was more confident.

Grateful, she kissed the top of Carrie's head. There were times when she couldn't help wondering exactly who was taking care of whom.

What she *did* know in her heart was that she would be utterly and completely *lost* without this unassuming girl.

"Okay, Carrie, you tell me. Which dress should I wear?"

This time Carrie *did* turn her attention to the clothes

haphazardly heaped on the bed, a thoughtful expression wrinkling her small brow as she studied the dresses.

After a moment, Carrie walked around the bed like a half-pint judge at a county fair pie bake-off contest, slowly regarding each "contestant" she viewed before her. Once or twice, she touched an article of clothing until, digging through the tallest mountain, her slender, small fingers closed over a scrap of bright blue fabric.

Pulling on it, Carrie managed to draw out a simple dress that had been thrown onto the pile without the benefit of having been tried on. Brianna remembered dismissing the garment out of hand as being just too plain.

Carrie held it up for her now. "This one," the child pronounced.

Brianna regarded her daughter's choice. "That one? You're sure?"

Carrie nodded her head enthusiastically. Still, the dress didn't really spark her imagination, so Brianna reached for another, far more formal, dress.

"How about…?"

She never got any further, because Carrie just moved her head from side to side, summarily vetoing the new choice.

Instead, she deliberately separated the dress she'd selected from the others and now held it up for her review.

"Try it on, Mama," she coaxed.

With a shrug, Brianna slipped the dress on, wiggling into the soft, short skirt and allowing it to glide lovingly over her hips. With short, focused movements, she smoothed down the fabric.

The moment the dress was on her, Carrie's smile grew wider. "You look really beautiful, Mama," she declared with satisfied finality.

How could she bring herself to argue with that? Brianna wondered fondly.

"Well, if you really like it that much, then I'll *have* to wear it," she told the little girl. Maybe it wasn't all *that* bad.

Just then, after rapping once sharply on the unlocked door, Brianna's father peered in.

"You ready yet?" he asked with just a touch of impatience in his voice.

She was just freshening up her makeup. "Just about, Dad."

Jim MacKenzie shook his head in absolute, mystified wonder.

"I swear, it took less time for Michelangelo to paint the Sistine Chapel ceiling than it does for an ordinary woman to get ready," he mumbled under his breath—but it was still audible. "Your mother, God rest her soul, was just the same way," he admitted, allowing a fond note to slip into his voice. "She started getting ready on a Thursday for a party she was attending the following Saturday."

"We take a long time because we want to look good," Carrie piped up.

Her father did his best not to laugh out loud, while

Brianna declared, "What she said," with complete approval.

Jim shifted his eyes to look at his daughter. "Well, I guess it would be worth his wait—if this guy were waiting in our living room for you," he added with a smile.

Startled, Brianna glanced at her watch, then at her father. She'd lost track of time and it was getting late. "He's not, is he?"

"Nope. By my calculation, he's got about ten more minutes. Unless he believes in being early—" As if on cue, the doorbell rang. Amused, Jim nodded. "Speak of the devil." With that, Brianna's father stepped back into the hall. "I'd better go let him in before he thinks you've stood him up."

Maybe it would be better that way, Brianna thought as the tsunami in her stomach rose to a record-breaking height. For now she kept that to herself.

Glancing over to where Carrie had been just a second ago dispensing her little-old-lady wisdom, Brianna realized that the girl was no longer there. She had just *too* much energy.

"Where's Carrie?" she asked, turning toward her father.

As if caught off guard by the question, he looked over toward the corner where he'd last seen her.

Pointing, he told her, "She was just right here—" And then he sighed. The girl had more moves than three-week-old puppies. "Probably answering the door," he realized. Carrie was *nothing* if not a challenge to keep track of. And he knew that with each passing year, it was only going to get worse. He sighed now, as if mentally bracing himself. "Don't worry, I'll go get her."

"No, we'll *both* go get her," Brianna said, grabbing her shoes in her hand rather than pausing to put them on. Right now, her temper was at the end of a dangerously short fuse. "I told her a hundred times she wasn't to open the door by herself."

She was such a smart little girl in all other ways—why did she insist on disregarding this most important of rules?

Okay, they lived in a very safe neighborhood, but that didn't mean that someone who was less than trustworthy couldn't just come in at will and ruin their lives by abducting Carrie—or worse.

At that exact moment, Carrie had reached the front door and was presently yanking it open. The door was not unduly heavy, but neither was it light, and the determined girl had to use both hands to budge the front door from its frame.

"Hi," she declared brightly upon achieving success. She was visibly checking out the person standing on the other side of her doorstep.

Expecting to see someone near his own height, or thereabouts, Sebastian had to lower his eyes before saying, "Hi. Is Brianna around?"

After appraising him, the little girl nodded. Then, turning her head ever so slightly so that her voice would carry inside the house, Carrie raised her volume and called out, "That guy is here to see you, Mama."

Mama?

The simple, two-syllable word completely knocked the pins right out from under Sebastian.

When he'd seen her again last night after such a long absence of contact, it really hadn't occurred to him that Brianna had gotten married, much less that she'd had a child.

"She's your mother?" he heard himself asking the child as he struggled to keep his voice steady and lofty sounding.

Even to his own untrained ear, Sebastian was forced to admit that he hadn't exactly succeeded.

"Uh-huh." Large, luminous blue eyes regarded him. "Are you the guy my mama thinks is special?" she asked.

The question took him completely aback and more than a little by surprise.

Special?

Did Brianna really think he was special, after all this time had passed? Or had the very pretty little girl with the rosebud mouth just gotten her facts rather confused?

"I really don't know," Sebastian replied quite honestly.

Before he had to face answering any more questions from the pint-size interrogator, he saw Brianna hurrying in, looking equal parts flustered and absolutely gorgeous. And she was headed for the girl.

"Carrie, what did I tell you about opening the door when you're alone?" she demanded.

"Not to," the little girl replied dutifully. "But I'm not alone," she protested in the next breath. "You and Grandpa are here."

"But we're not close enough," Brianna reminded her.

Carrie cocked her head. "For what, Mama?"

"We're not close enough to stop someone if they wanted to grab you and take you along with them."

In utterly logical fashion, Carrie glanced up at Sebastian. "You didn't want to take me with you, did you?" she asked Sebastian.

"I'm here to take out Brianna—your mom," he tagged on.

And why would she have agreed to see him, to go out for dinner, if she was a married woman?

Unless…

He looked at Brianna. "Is she yours?" he asked. He already knew the answer to that, or thought he did. He was trying to create a starting point for himself and then go from there.

Brianna smiled, one arm going around the slender child and pulling her closer.

"She is that," she acknowledged both fondly and firmly.

"Hello, son," her father said heartily, coming in behind his daughter and addressing the young man he'd known and watched grow ever since he was four years old, as Carrie was now.

Clasping Sebastian's hand with both of his, he shook it warmly.

"Nice seeing you again, sir," Sebastian replied with equal feeling. "You're looking really well," he couldn't help adding. The man really did seem better now than before Sebastian had left Bedford.

James MacKenzie looked hardy and healthy and, except for the shafts of silver that were woven through his once dark, thick hair, he didn't look a day over fifty—even though Sebastian knew that he was.

"That's all Brianna's doing." Jim more than gladly gave his daughter the credit for saving his life, and for all but bringing him back from the dead. "She makes a great little dictator as well as an incredibly fine nurse," he said fondly. "And if it weren't for her, I don't mind telling you that I'd be pushing up daisies right this minute."

"Pushing them from where, Grandpa?" Carrie asked.

"We'll talk about that while Sebastian takes your mama out for a nice dinner," he promised. Not possessing a subtle bone in his body, Jim all but shooed the couple out the door. "You two better be going," he prodded, "if you want to get a good table. They go fast this time of the evening. And you *don't* want them putting you by the kitchen."

"We're going, Dad, we're going," Brianna assured him, knowing her father was afraid that she would find a reason at the last minute not to go.

As much as she wanted to come up with an excuse to bow out of the evening, she had a feeling that it would just be postponing things. This way, she'd endure the evening and then it would all be behind her.

After that, she thought, Sebastian would be on his way back to Japan or wherever and she could go back to living a quiet, normal life—such as it was.

"Don't hurry back," her father called after them as

they left the house. "I've got everything under control here."

I only wish I did, Brianna couldn't help thinking as she turned to wave goodbye to her daughter.

Chapter Six

Holding the car door open for her, Sebastian automatically looked down at Brianna's left hand as she slid into the passenger seat and then drew in her legs. He paused before closing the door.

Confusion mingled with a touch of relief when he saw that her ring finger was conspicuously unadorned. He wasn't sure exactly what made him look at her other hand, but when he did, he saw a small, tidy-looking diamond ring on the third finger.

Well, that answered *that* question, he told himself. Or so he believed.

"Change your mind?" he heard Brianna asking.

Caught between two streams of thought, Sebastian looked at her quizzically. He wasn't sure what she was referring to.

It hadn't gotten any clearer by the time he came around to the driver's side and got in. He glanced at her before buckling up.

"What?"

How did she tactfully word this without making it seem as if she was criticizing him? She gave it her best shot.

"Well, you were just standing there.... I thought that maybe you'd changed your mind about our going out for dinner."

Belatedly, he realized that he'd just frozen for a moment while she'd not only gotten into the car, but while she'd fastened her seat belt as well. He'd managed to close her door after a beat and had rounded the car to his side like a man trapped in a dream.

She'd probably thought he had turned into a village idiot, Sebastian upbraided himself.

"No, sorry, I guess I just got caught up in a thought."

He'd been staring at her and something was obviously either bothering him or distracting him. Either way, she wanted to know what this was all about. Otherwise, the awkward moments would only continue to pile up on one another.

"Something you'd like to share with the class?" she prodded, tongue in cheek.

For a second, he thought of just shrugging it off. The idea of saying something inane about needing to call his immediate superior in Japan crossed his mind as well. But any hastily constructed excuse would only be entrenching himself in a lie, and lies had a way of coming back and either biting you or blowing up on you when you least expected it. If nothing else, lies were hell to keep track of and usually became far too complicated to remember.

He had no desire to be caught in a lie. It was a long way back from that sort of thing.

"I was just looking at your ring," he told her, nodding at her right hand as he reached behind himself for the seat belt and buckled up.

At the mention of the ring, Brianna glanced down at her right hand. The engagement ring that J.T. had slipped onto her hand when he'd proposed to her had held such promise for her once. Now what it held was the memory of the man and what had almost been.

It also served to remind her that, for whatever reason, she just couldn't seem to get to the "finish line," couldn't even get to first base in that mystical land of "happily ever after."

Get a grip. He wants to catch up, not watch you sob into your salad.

Since Sebastian wasn't following up his statement with either a question or an observation, she felt obligated to say something herself and push the stillborn conversation along a little further.

"Carrie's father gave me this ring."

"Were you married long?" he asked Brianna out of the blue.

The question took her aback for a moment and she said the first thing that popped into her head. "No."

Which had to mean that her ex was a piece of work,

Sebastian concluded, because he knew Brianna. She wouldn't have just shrugged her shoulders and walked away from her marriage at the first sign of trouble. She was and always had been a fighter. He would bet his soul that she had tried to resolve whatever it was that had ended the union.

"I hope the divorce wasn't a drawn-out, nasty affair," he said with sympathy. "Those can really be hard on a kid, although your daughter does seem as if she's a very bright, well-adjusted little girl."

He was babbling now, Sebastian realized, and couldn't find the right place to stop without just abruptly shutting his mouth. He chastised himself for ever beginning the awkward topic.

"Sorry," he murmured. "Forget I said anything. It's none of my business."

The light ahead turned red and he brought his vehicle to a stop. That was when he became aware that Brianna had raised her hand and was waving it like a student.

"Yes, the girl in the front row," he responded, calling on her the way he would if this had actually been a classroom scene.

"I thought I'd rescue you before you wound up going too far in the wrong direction," Brianna told him.

Rather than clear anything up, she'd just confused the issue even further for him. "Too far in the wrong direction?" he echoed. It made even less sense to him when *he* said it than when she had. "What wrong direction am I taking it in?"

"There was no divorce—"

"You're still married?" he asked, stunned.

No, Brianna wasn't the type to step out on a husband, he told himself. And yet, how else was he to interpret her words? Was there a second husband? Taking what she'd said into account, did that mean that Carrie's father was an ex-husband whom Brianna had left behind? Some man she'd found too difficult to put up with and had gone on to shed before marrying someone else?

Or…?

"Light's green," she prodded just before the driver behind them lightly beeped his horn.

Sebastian quickly took his foot off the brake and put it back on the accelerator. As they drove down the next street, Brianna bit back a sigh.

"If you want the full, accurate story, you're going to have to let me talk in something a little bit longer than just sound bites," she told him.

He opened his mouth to protest, then realized that she was right. He *had* cut her off more than once. "Sorry. I guess I am jumping to conclusions," he allowed.

"More like you're pole-vaulting to them," she corrected. She searched for the most concise way to summarize the past few years. "Okay, to give you just the brief headlines—one, I'm not married—"

"Currently," he tacked on as if the word was the bow on the present.

"Okay," she allowed, letting him have his way for a second if it made him happy. "Currently. Two," she continued, her next words completely surprising him,

"I was *never* married. Consequently, three—since there was no marriage, there was no divorce."

He was still, he realized, utterly unenlightened about the state of her life. "Then are you still seeing Carrie's father?" he asked, becoming acutely aware of the fact that the thought of Bree being with another man, of seeing that man and creating a child with him, disturbed him far more than he'd thought possible. He knew, logically, that he had no right to feel that way.

She laughed softly to herself, despite the absence of humor in the situation.

"No," she answered, "I'm not seeing him. Not unless I'm doing a great deal of drinking. And just in case you're wondering, I don't drink more than a glass of wine at any given occasion."

Sebastian frowned in utter frustration. "I don't follow you."

"I'm not still seeing Carrie's father because he died in a boating accident a week before we were supposed to get married. I guess I'm just one of those people who's not meant to walk down the aisle."

There was a touch of ironic resignation in her voice. She'd grown up just assuming that a husband, marriage and children were in her future. Who knew she'd been assuming incorrectly?

He was putting together the pieces as fast as he could, but there were still edges that didn't fit. He had more questions. "And you had the baby after he died?"

"What baby?" she asked.

Were there more children? Children she hadn't introduced him to? Just how much *had* she changed in the past ten years?

"Carrie," he prompted.

He still hadn't gotten it straight, she realized. "I think that in order to get the right picture, you're going to have to do some more listening, Sebastian. *Silent* listening," she emphasized.

He turned right at the end of the block. "Okay," he agreed.

All right, from the beginning. "To start with, J.T. was Dad's partner at the hardware store. After Dad's near-fatal accident—" she still felt a cold shiver down her spine every time she thought of that "—J.T. ran the store all by himself, putting in eighteen-hour days. Dad would have lost the store if it wasn't for J.T." There was no mistaking the gratitude in her voice.

Was that why she'd gotten engaged to the man? Out of a sense of gratitude? Sebastian caught himself wondering. He realized that gratitude worked far better for him than thinking she'd done it out of love.

"Once I finally got Dad to the point that he decided he *was* going to recover, I took a second look at the store and knew I needed to pitch in.

"I guess J.T. and I grew closer. Couldn't pinpoint when or how, but we just did. He was a shoulder I could cry on, someone who would let me vent when I had to, and he never asked for anything in return." As far as she could see, the man was totally selfless. "But I sensed that he cared about me. A great deal. And then he had to deal with his own tragedy. He lost his wife in childbirth. I guess I helped him through that. He'd bring Carrie to work with him and we'd take turns taking care of her while one of us ran the store."

When she paused, he saw his opening. Sebastian couldn't help himself—he had to ask. "So then, is Carrie yours?"

"Yes."

There wasn't even a micromoment's hesitation on her part—because the child *was* hers. Carrie was locked away in her heart, and though she and the little girl didn't share a drop of the same DNA, they shared love and there wasn't anything she wouldn't do for Carrie.

"But not in the sense you mean," she added. "Carrie's mother died giving birth to her. She was an infant when J.T. and I became engaged. At four, I'm the only mother she's ever known, although I did tell her about her birth mother. She knows I adopted her."

He couldn't imagine how to start a conversation like that with a child. "Isn't four a little young for that?"

"Possibly," she allowed. "I do know that four is too young to be lied to," she told him. "I thought that if Carrie knew about her birth mother from the very start, she'd just accept things the way they are and not be bothered by the fact that she was adopted."

Brianna knew that she didn't owe him any kind of explanation, but she could sense that unanswered questions crowded his thoughts, so she proceeded to give him as much information as she thought was needed.

"When J.T. was killed, there was no next of kin to step up and adopt Carrie. She would have just been absorbed into the system, and I knew that J.T. wouldn't have wanted that. Hell, *I* didn't want that. J.T. did so much for my dad, I felt that adopting Carrie was the least I could do for him.

"So I petitioned to be allowed to adopt her. I held my breath for a whole year," she readily admitted, "putting up with unannounced spot checks where social workers would swoop down on their brooms, night or day, and just commandeer the premises. I had to stand back, let them go over everything with a fine-tooth comb and hope that I met whatever lofty requirements were in place at that particular time. I have no idea what they were expecting to find. Maybe they thought I was running a brothel," she speculated with a dry laugh.

"But in the end, you passed their inspections." It wasn't a guess on his part. No matter what else might have changed, he knew that much about Brianna. If she set her sights on something, she never backed off until she reached her goal.

Bree was stubborn that way.

She smiled now and nodded. "I passed their inspections," she confirmed. "And before you think I'm just being noble, I'm not. I love that little girl as if she was my very own and I couldn't begin to picture my life without her. Right now, if some long-lost relative came creeping out of the woodwork and claimed her, I don't know what I'd do," she confessed.

"Other than tie them up and dump them in the river?" he guessed.

"There is that," she acknowledged, managing to keep the grin off for a full fifteen seconds.

And then Sebastian nodded, thinking about what she had just told him. "It must have been very hard on you," he speculated, adding, "when Carrie's father was killed," in case he hadn't been clear in his comment.

Sebastian frowned. He hadn't used her late fiancé's name. He had no idea why he couldn't get himself to say the man's name, but he couldn't.

He was being petty and he knew it. After all, technically Sebastian had given up all claims to Bree when he'd walked out of her life. But though she had physically been out of his life for years now, she hadn't been entirely out of his thoughts.

Never, really.

She lingered in his mind like a song whose melody refused to fade away, as if threaded onto an endless loop.

"It was," she admitted with no fanfare, no dramatic pause. "I began to think that maybe I was jinxed." She looked at him. Did he think about her? After he'd gone off to college, had he spared her the occasional thought, or was she, then and now, being delusional? "Except that you at least didn't die. You just went away."

Sebastian searched for the slightest sound of blame or recrimination, for the accusation that he had just walked out on her when he should have remained at her side, offering his support and help.

But there wasn't any to be found.

Then again, Bree had never been one to throw blame

on anyone, even if they deserved it. She'd always just tried to carry the load on her own, always being the very personification of independence.

"About that," he began, picking his way through the possible minefield spread out ahead of him. "I should have stayed," he began. "After your dad's accident, I should have stayed with you." She'd been, he knew, all alone at the time.

"You should have done exactly what you did," she countered.

He looked at her, surprised.

But to her way of thinking, there was nothing to be gained from blaming him all these years later. It wouldn't get back even a minute of lost time and it certainly wouldn't make her feel vindicated.

"You were supposed to go on to get your degree and do what you love doing—teaching," she insisted.

"That wasn't the only place to get a teaching degree," he pointed out. He could have gone to a local college. Granted, it wouldn't have been as prestigious as the school he'd ultimately attended, but in the end, the knowledge he'd accumulated would have been the same. He was too determined to succeed.

But again, there was no need to rub any of that in.

It seemed to her that they had somehow switched sides on the argument, that he was picking up the banner that by all rights should have been hers and that she was backing what clearly sounded like his side of the argument.

"You're right—it wasn't. But the path you took led

you to your current job, and from what I can gather, that job makes you happy. In the final analysis, that means a great deal," she assured him. Shifting in her seat, she gazed out the window. She'd only been paying moderate attention to the route, but it was looking exceedingly familiar. "Where are we going?"

"I thought maybe we'd stop at Nate's," he said, mentioning the restaurant where they had sat for hours, scribbling their future on napkins and dreaming of the day they could finally get married. "I was surprised to find that the restaurant was still there," he confessed.

Brianna inclined her head. "Not all that much changes in Bedford," she reminded him.

Even as she said it, she couldn't help wondering if going to Nate's was really such a good idea. She hadn't been there since he'd left for college.

There was a reason for that. The place was fraught with memories.

Too many memories.

She had a feeling they would hit her the moment they walked into the place.

Can't be any more difficult facing the restaurant than it was facing Sebastian, Bree. You can do this—you know that.

She gave the mental pep talk her all, but nonetheless she still felt the tsunami gathering again in her stomach as Sebastian brought his car to a stop in the restaurant's parking lot.

Chapter Seven

It hit her the moment she walked in.

The ghosts of memories gone by. Dreams that never had a chance to take hold.

For just a second, Brianna felt herself catapulted back over the sea of years to another, far more innocent time. A time when she had been filled with such great hopes.

As she walked into the dimly lit atmosphere, she could feel anticipation pulsing through her, just as she had all those years ago.

Except that she wasn't that girl anymore. Now she knew better.

"Two?" the brightly dressed hostess in the soft peasant blouse and flowered skirt asked, looking from Sebastian to her.

"Two," Sebastian confirmed.

Why did that sound so lonely to her? Brianna wondered. It was like a promise that had lost its bloom and had been left to die, unfulfilled. "Two" used to sound so intimate, so powerful, like "two against the world."

But again, now she knew better.

"This way, please." Turning on her short, stacked heels, the hostess led the way through an already semi-full dining area.

The restaurant hadn't changed at all, Brianna thought, quickly taking in her surroundings as she walked behind the hostess and just a step in front of Sebastian. Not one little bit. It looked just as if she had walked out of here only yesterday, instead of more than ten years ago.

There were the same eighteenth-century Early American decorations along the wall, including a blunderbuss she'd once admired. Back then, it had appeared real to her. Now she thought of it as all part of the make-believe world she knew that she'd inhabited back then.

"Is this all right?" the hostess asked politely, gesturing to a booth for two located just a shade away from the heart of the dining area.

The booth seemed almost too intimate, despite the fact that there were other tables, filled with patrons, all around that section of the room.

Brianna became aware that Sebastian was watching her. It was obvious that he was leaving up to her the final yea or nay on the seating arrangement.

She would have preferred being out in the middle of the room, but she heard herself saying, "It's fine," even though it really wasn't.

The booth, although not the one that they had usually occupied, was close enough in appearance and location to have passed for it, even upon close scrutiny.

After sliding in, Brianna accepted the menu that the hostess handed her.

Even with a table between them, she was acutely aware of Sebastian's nearness as he took the seat opposite her. The table might as well not have been there, for all the difference it made.

This felt even more intimate to her than when she'd danced with him last night. Why? After all, there was at least some space between them here, while there really hadn't been any last night.

Maybe her resistance against him was weakening, Brianna thought, concerned. Again she told herself that she shouldn't have gone to the reunion, shouldn't have agreed to have dinner with him like this tonight. She'd survived last night and she should have congratulated herself for that and tucked the whole thing away into some faraway box within her mind.

Sebastian studied her face and could almost read the tiny, telltale signs her thoughts left behind in their wake as they crossed her mind. Some things never changed.

"Something wrong?" he asked once the hostess had given him his menu and then retreated into the noisy dining area.

Startled, Brianna looked up. "No, nothing's wrong. Why?" she asked just a little too quickly.

"I don't remember you ever being this quiet," Sebastian told her.

Brianna shrugged, doing her best to look somewhat bored and disinterested. "Just sorting a few things out in my head," she replied rather vaguely.

His eyes never left her face. "Yeah," he said softly, "me, too."

She looked at him sharply when he said that. To her dismay, their eyes met and held for what felt like an endless, unsettling moment. She was tempted to ask just what it was that he was sorting out, but that would have left her open to the same question and, for the life of her, she had no acceptable answer.

The truth was she was just trying to deal with the ghost of a romance that was no longer even on life support. But there was no way she wanted to admit that to him right now.

Or *ever.*

Brianna looked so uncomfortable, he couldn't help noticing. Was that his doing? God, he hoped not. He could remember a time when there was nothing in the world more comfortable for either of them than sharing a conversation, or sharing a dream—or even just sharing the silence.

Back then it was as if Brianna was truly the other half of him. The part, he now realized, that made him better. A better man, a better person.

A better everything.

Sebastian searched for an opening. For something to say that would eventually lead him back to that place that he'd taken for granted because it had seemed so commonplace to him.

Back then he didn't have a real appreciation of just how special that niche actually was.

Sebastian suppressed a sigh. He supposed it went along with that old adage about never knowing what you had until you didn't have it anymore.

And now it was too late. Too late to reclaim anything. Too late to go back and start again.

"So, you became a nurse." He knew the words had to sound incredibly stilted to her, but he pushed on, hoping to somehow work out the kinks, to smooth out the dialogue so that it became more natural sounding.

He wanted, he silently admitted, to get back what they had lost.

What *he* had lost.

If only for a few hours.

"Yes, I did." She was almost certain that she had told him she was a nurse while they were dancing last night.

Dear God, had they run out of conversation already? she thought sadly. There'd been a time when they could literally talk for hours and never come close to running out of words.

But all that was in the past.

Before he had left her to deal with things on her own.

"Do you like it?" he asked. "Being a nurse," he added in case she'd lost the thread of the nearly stillborn conversation.

"Yes," she admitted with a smile, then said for good measure in case he thought she was just paying lip service to the sentiment, "Yes, I do."

"Why?" he prodded, curious about how she felt about

the career that seemingly had found *her* instead of the other way around.

The simple question took her aback and made Brianna think for a second. Back when they'd been together, she'd never had to explain anything to him. More often than not, Sebastian could literally intuit the way she felt about things.

But back then, they could end almost all of each other's sentences.

God, had she ever really been that young and innocent?

"Why?" she repeated, almost in disbelief that he should have to ask the question. "Because I like helping people. I like knowing that because of me, someone feels better, either in general or even just about themselves. That because of me, they've become more determined, or more hopeful." She smiled, more to herself than at him. "I guess working with my dad, bullying him into fighting his way back from despair and getting to a place where he could walk again and do what he did before the accident, showed me what a difference one person can make in another person's life.

"That was," she freely admitted to him, "enough to get me hooked. I really want to make that kind of a difference in other people's lives."

She stopped talking as her words echoed back to her. Brianna flushed ruefully. "I guess I must sound pretty full of myself to you."

After all, they no longer had that connection, that one-on-one way of communicating where each knew what the other was thinking. This man across from her was now a stranger.

"No," he contradicted her, "you sound like just what I need."

Only rigid control kept her mouth from dropping open. "Excuse me?"

He realized what that had to sound like to her. He didn't want her thinking he was trying to pick up where they'd left off years ago—even though he had to admit, if only to himself, that part of him was trying to do just that.

"I mean just what my mother needs," he amended, his eyes on hers to make sure she understood.

"Your mother?" She didn't understand. "Exactly why does your mother need me?"

His mother was a warm, outgoing person, but she was also a private person and he was fairly certain that she didn't want him broadcasting her recent change in condition. But this wasn't exactly the same thing. After all, Brianna was a medical professional as well as a woman of integrity. He knew she could be counted on to be discreet.

And he needed help.

"Well, I told you that my mother had a stroke recently. . . ." His voice trailed off.

When he'd mentioned it last night, she'd just assumed from the way he talked that everything was under control. And since the severity of strokes had such a broad range, from the almost unnoticed to the debilitating, she had thought that his mother had been lucky.

Maybe not.

Brianna was aware of what havoc a bad stroke could cause, how one could ravage a person, reduce her to a shell of her former self. Was that the case, then? Had he just not wanted to talk about it until they were somewhere more private than a high school reunion?

"How bad was it?" she asked in a hushed voice. "Was her vision affected?"

He shook his head. "No, not that she mentioned."

"Thank God for that." And then she thought of another common symptom. "How about her speech? Does she have difficulty speaking?"

He thought for a moment, carefully reviewing their conversations, both over the phone and when he'd arrived. "No, that seems to be fine, actually. She's not slurring her words or anything close to that," he added with relief.

Okay, so far, so good, she thought. "Was there any paralysis? Face, arms, legs?" She recited each part as it occurred to her.

In response to each, Sebastian shook his head. As the gravity of the possible outcomes of his mother's stroke hit him, he realized just how large a bullet his mother had actually dodged. The wave of relief that came over him was enormous.

"I guess my mother was really pretty lucky," he concluded.

"Yes," Brianna agreed with feeling. "Yes, she certainly was." But now that the conversation had taken this route, she still had more questions. "What does the doctor say?"

He thought back to what his mother had said when he'd asked her the same thing. "That she'd had a stroke."

They obviously both already knew that. Brianna was looking for more than just that one terrifying piece of information.

"But you have talked to him, right?" she prodded. Brianna left the question up in the air, as if she took an affirmative answer for granted.

Frustrated, Sebastian was forced to shake his head again. "She doesn't want me fussing over her, or having to bother talking with doctors on what is supposedly my vacation. She told me that having me here for a visit was the best medicine in the world for her." A self-deprecating laugh left his lips. "I really wish I could stay indefinitely—"

She already knew where that sentence was going. "But your job isn't here," she concluded for him, doing her best not to sound dismissive. After all, this wasn't what he'd chosen to do with his life.

The moment she said that, their eyes met and she could see by the look on his face that he remembered when that sort of thing—finishing each other's sentences—happened on a regular basis.

But that was then and this was now, she reminded herself, struggling to maintain strict control over her emotions, because *now* had a completely different set of parameters.

"I'm not a doctor," she prefaced, verbalizing the disclaimer mechanically, "but I could take a look at her for you, talk to her and maybe assess the situation a little further for you if you'd like."

The broad smile on his lips gave her his answer before he even opened his mouth.

"That would be great," he told her. It was the first step in getting someone—preferably her—to stay on as his mother's companion/caretaker. But for now he wasn't going to push her. Instead, he said, "It would go a long way to putting my mind at ease about her condition, as well as helping me make decisions about what to do next."

She didn't want to ask what that meant, afraid that would make her think less of him. These days, so many people treated their parents like toys that had lost their usefulness, their appeal. After years of useful service, they were put out to pasture, so to speak.

"Like I said, I'm not a doctor," Brianna reminded him.

"No, you're not," he agreed. "But you worked a miracle with your father, using nothing more than your sheer determination—"

They'd both gotten lucky there, she couldn't help thinking—she and her father. She knew that he wouldn't have been able to accept facing life from the inside of a wheelchair. He *had* to walk again. There'd been no other alternative.

"But you just said that none of her limbs were affected by the stroke," Brianna pointed out. What kind of a miracle did he need for his mother? Had he omitted telling her something? Or were things worse than he'd initially let on?

"They're not," he agreed. "But anyone who can work the kind of miracle that you did on your dad is the kind of person I'd be more than happy about having around my mother. And don't forget that my mother already likes you."

This was going a little too fast for her liking. Somewhere along the line, she'd lost control of the situation.

"Wait, are we talking about just a plain visit, or is there something more extensive on the table that you forgot to mention?"

He looked at her with the soul of innocence, and she almost laughed out loud at his expression.

"Nothing on the table but just some French bread right now," he told her.

It just so happened that she made her living as a private-duty nurse rather than one who worked long shifts at the hospital, or in a doctor's office. And, as a private-duty nurse, she was on call over the course of the entire day. That was one of the reasons why she generally moved into the home of the person she was taking care of at the time. That way, she was assured of having Carrie with her in the evening.

Her father usually took care of the little girl during the daytime and then he'd drop his granddaughter off where she was staying after six. For now that worked out well for both Carrie and her. When it ceased to work, she would rethink her choice of nursing venue.

But Sebastian didn't know any of this. At least, she

hadn't told him that she was a private-duty nurse. At the moment she just assumed that Sebastian was asking her opinion on things, and that included whether to make use of a private-duty nurse.

Their waitress approached discreetly, waiting for a lull in the conversation. It occurred the moment Sebastian became aware of her presence. Since the menu hadn't really changed in all these years, making up their minds took almost no time at all.

Once the waitress left to give the chef their orders, Brianna asked, "When would you like me to come over to see your mother?"

He refrained from eagerly saying, "Now," and instead diplomatically inquired, "When would you be available?"

As it happened, her last assignment had just ended several days ago. Rather than accept the next assignment that the nursing agency offered, she'd opted to take a little time off. She wanted to spend some quality time with her family, especially the girl who seemed to be harboring feelings of neglect despite the attention Brianna's father was lavishing on her.

In addition, she just needed to have her batteries recharged. She'd been pushing too hard these past few months, doing too much, and it was draining her.

Seeing Sebastian had sufficiently recharged them—and then some.

In all honesty, it was now three days into the self-imposed "vacation" and Brianna was pretty much ready to get back to work. She'd never been one who was able to kick back for long stretches without feeling as if she was in the throes of nursing withdrawals.

Caring for children was an entirely different story, however. In general, she was accustomed to doing at least two, if not three, different things at once.

Even doing just one thing felt as if she was slacking off.

"I could clear some time tomorrow if you'd like," she offered.

"I wouldn't be taking you away from your work?"

"I consider it all part of the job," she told him, "and this would actually be mixing business with pleasure."

Then, in case he thought she was trying to revisit something they'd had in the past, she quickly told him, "I'd love to see your mother again."

"She still talks about you," he told her, leaving off the part about the fact that his mother viewed her as the one he allowed to get away.

"We kind of lost touch when…when my father was hurt," Brianna finally concluded, substituting that for the real reason she and his mother were no longer in communication. They'd lost touch because Brianna had been the one to break contact. Being around his mother had reminded her too much of him, of what she no longer had. Because, even then, she'd known in her heart that he wasn't coming back to Bedford after graduation.

And that had meant that he wasn't coming back to her.

The few conversations she and Sebastian had had after he'd left for college had been short, painful and exceedingly awkward, with far more left unsaid than was said.

And, just like that, the love of her life had become a stranger she had nothing in common with. Maybe they'd never meshed to begin with.

But sitting here opposite him now, she knew that all those things she'd told herself in those long, empty months after they had parted were just so many poor excuses. She *hadn't* stopped caring about him. There were still feelings, still longings pulsating between them. And most likely there always would be, until she was laid to rest six feet under.

And maybe even longer than that.

Chapter Eight

When he looked back on it later, Sebastian felt as if the majority of the evening had been spent in a singular space in time, divorced from any recriminations from past behavior.

Oh, once or twice—possibly even more—he'd caught himself wondering, "What if…?"

What if he hadn't left?

What if her father hadn't been in that accident?

What if she'd come with him and gone to the same college? They'd made plans to move in together and their goal from there had been marriage….

But wondering didn't make it so and didn't answer any of those questions.

At the end of the evening, as he walked Brianna to her door—the way he had walked her so many times in the distant past—he could have sworn they were moving in slow motion. Heaven knew it certainly felt that way to him, felt as if each moment was drawn out, stretched to the absolute limit.

Which might have explained why it seemed to take forever to reach her doorstep.

Yet, conversely, they found themselves there all too soon. Suddenly, there he was, looking down into her face, battling a myriad of emotions, all of which had popped up, dust and all, right out of the past. A past they'd once shared in the belief that it was just the first step toward an incredible future.

And one desire dominated it all.

He wanted to kiss her.

Wanted it so badly that he could all but taste it on his lips.

He knew he could murmur something like "For old times' sake" before he kissed her, but she wasn't a fool. She'd see through that in a heartbeat and more than likely ask him why he felt it was necessary to make an excuse for doing something that had once come so naturally to them.

"I had a very nice time tonight," Brianna said as she turned to face him on her doorstep. "To be honest, I really didn't think I would," she confessed. Not that it had exactly been a walk in the park. There'd been a third companion at the table with them. The ghost of summers past, when things had been so close to perfect and she'd thought that it would always be that way.

"Yeah, me, too," Sebastian responded. Was it his

imagination, or was she even lovelier in moonlight? All he knew was that there was a strong, all but overpowering ache in his gut right now.

"Which part are you agreeing with?" she asked, curious. "That you didn't think you were going to have a nice time, or that you actually *did* had a nice time?"

"Both," he answered.

The temptation to kiss her continued growing and getting stronger. So strong that, without thinking, he reached out to touch her hair, tucking a reddish strand behind her ear just the way he used to.

The tips of his fingers glided ever so lightly along her cheek, sending electric currents zapping along her sensitive skin.

She drew in her breath as her pulse began to beat faster.

Run! her brain pleaded.

If she let him kiss her, Brianna knew that any hope she had of keeping him at arm's length for his short visit would go up in flames.

With shaky knees, Brianna forced herself to turn away from him. She said something along the lines of "I'd better go in before my father sends out search parties to find me. I told him I'd only be gone a couple of hours."

And from where she was standing, it felt as if she'd been gone close to a decade.

Sebastian knew that if he pushed, even just the slightest bit, he could get her to stay out here with him a few moments longer. Knew, too, that if he lowered his mouth to hers, Brianna would be there to return his kiss.

But he also knew that it wasn't fair to either of them—especially to her—if he pressed his advantage. There was no point in starting something that had no hope of a future.

So, even though deep in his soul he didn't want to, Sebastian forced himself to step back. He inclined his head as he did so and said, somewhat amused, "Wouldn't want your dad grounding you on my account."

Was he laughing at her?

Brianna grasped at the feeling of indignation, knowing it was the only thing that might remotely save her from making a serious mistake and kissing *him* goodnight.

"I'm not 'afraid' my father's going to ground me—I'm just being thoughtful. I told him I'd be back by a certain time and I like keeping my word no matter what it's about."

Was that a dig? he wondered. A veiled reference to the fact that he'd once promised her that he would love her forever?

He couldn't fault her for thinking that he'd broken that promise—even though, now that he thought about it, he really hadn't. Because there was still a part of him that cared about her.

Cared a great deal.

So much so that the emotion in question might be

called *love* by those who were still innocent and believed in such things.

"Well, I still wouldn't want to be responsible for that," he told her, then paused before asking, "Are we still on for tomorrow?"

Dazed, relieved to have survived tonight, she looked at Sebastian and echoed quizzically, "Tomorrow?"

"You were going to come over to see my mother and tell me whether or not you thought she needed to have some extra care for a while." He'd ad-libbed the last part, doing his best to inch closer to the real reason he wanted her seeing his mother—to decide whether she could take her on as a patient.

"Oh, of course. Sure. I'll come by," she assured him quickly. "Is two o'clock all right?"

"Any time would be all right," he told her with sincerity. "I'll work my schedule around yours."

Well, *that* was certainly accommodating, she thought. Brianna flashed a neutral smile at him. "Then I'll see you tomorrow at two. At your mother's house. Same address?" she asked at the last moment, realizing that she was taking things for granted. After all, even though she hadn't moved, it didn't mean that other people hadn't.

Sebastian nodded. "Like you said, some things don't change. My mother's still living in the same house," he said. "She loves it far too much to ever consider moving. Believe me, I offered to help her downsize a few years ago by finding a condo for her, but she just wouldn't hear of it."

Brianna hardly heard what he was saying, her attention caught by something he'd said just before he'd told her that folksy story about trying to get his mother to move.

Was that what tonight was *really* all about? Had he set out to press a few of her buttons, make her recall all that they had once been to one another just so that she wouldn't turn him down when he asked her to see his mother?

Had he really turned that cool, that pragmatic? she silently questioned.

She didn't want the answer to be yes.

Maybe it would behoove her to think of Sebastian in that light. Because it just might help turn her into a pragmatist as well.

As she put her key into the lock and turned it, she knew that was not about to happen, not in this lifetime. She had no more of a chance of turning into a pragmatic, practical person than she did of becoming a firefly this fall.

Glancing at Sebastian over her shoulder, Brianna lingered just long enough to say, "Thanks again for dinner."

"No, thank *you* for agreeing to see my mother." He realized that as he said it, he was really already counting on her help, even though he knew he shouldn't. Brianna had every right in the world to give him a few words of assurance and then either move on, or, at most, give him a referral to another nurse.

Initially, after the all but paralyzing fear that his mother had suffered a debilitating stroke had faded, that was all that he'd wanted—to find a competent nurse to look after his mother until she was out of the danger zone.

But the moment he'd realized that Brianna had gone on to become a nurse, he knew that he wouldn't be satisfied with anyone else. Wouldn't be satisfied with anything less than having Brianna sign on as his mother's private-duty nurse for the duration.

He trusted her. Trusted her with his mother's welfare. With his mother's life.

Because he knew Brianna's ethics, knew how determined she could be. Knew that to place his mother's fate in her hands was really the very best thing he could do for his mother.

Don't push too hard, he warned himself now. *At least, not yet.*

He needed to completely win Brianna over first. Since she had always liked his mother, half the battle had already been fought and—as near as he could figure it—won.

"Tomorrow, then," he repeated, then quickly turned on his heel and walked back to his car. He was fearful that he might ruin everything, because just at the last moment, he'd had another quick, strong surge of desire to pull her into his arms and find out if her kiss still made him weak in the knees.

Brianna quickly slipped into her house, incredibly relieved.

And just as incredibly disappointed.

Back in Bedford just a few days, and already he was

making her crazy. Sincerely hoping to dodge her fate at the last moment, she was nonetheless doomed.

Putting on her best face as she braced herself for the onslaught of questions, she went to find her father and get it over with.

"Oh, my sweet Lord, you haven't changed one little bit!" Barbara Hunter cried the moment she saw the woman she'd once thought was going to be her daughter-in-law come walking into her living room.

Entrenched in her role of recovering stroke victim, Barbara was sitting propped up on the sofa, a blanket tucked around her lower half at Sebastian's insistence, and half a dozen small, colorful pillows tucked against her back, also at Sebastian's insistence.

He'd been so thoughtful and considerate from the second he'd rushed to her side that her conscience was making it difficult for her to all but breathe. She didn't like lying to him this way. The whole thing bothered her a great deal.

It would have been bothering her a great deal more if it wasn't for the fact that she knew in her heart of hearts that she was doing this for Sebastian's own good. That she was pulling out all the stops, using everything she had at her disposal, not just to bring together what she'd always considered the perfect couple, but to keep them together until they both realized how very right they were for each other.

And when Sebastian would eventually forgive her—

after the truth had, perforce, come to light—he would understand why she'd done what she had.

But all that was still to come. Right now she had Brianna before her—and a part to play. She had to be on her toes, because Brianna was sharp.

Brianna took the hands that were warmly extended to her, squeezing them affectionately, if ever so lightly. She looked at Sebastian's mother in complete wonder.

She had to admit that she was expecting to see a woman who looked a great deal more frail. For someone who had recently had a stroke, Barbara Hunter appeared amazingly well for her ordeal, almost like the picture of health.

But then, Brianna knew, appearances could be exceptionally deceiving—especially with artfully applied makeup.

Smiling at Barbara as she went to occupy a tiny corner of the sofa beside Sebastian's mother, she said, "I could say the same thing about you, Mrs. Hunter. Your color is amazingly good," she told the older woman in complete awe.

Barbara leaned forward just a tad and confided, "Makeup does wonders," as she dismissed the compliment.

Although she didn't make any sort of regular pilgrimages to the makeup counters in her local malls, Brianna could tell the difference between a face that was only made up to look good, or, as in this case, to look healthy, and a face that actually *was* healthy.

Scrutinizing her, she decided that Barbara Hunter definitely belonged in the second category.

Which, all things considered, seemed rather unusual to Brianna. Something was off.

But she hadn't come to argue—she had come to see if she could offer advice or even a little help. It completely delighted her that Sebastian's mother was not nearly as unwell as Sebastian had first led her to believe.

Was that because the woman had managed to bounce back, making an absolutely astounding recovery, or could he be using his mother to get her to come around, to forgive him and possibly even give them another chance…?

No, she told herself in the next nanosecond. That would mean that Sebastian had turned into a manipulative person, and she didn't want to believe that about him. Didn't want to think of him in that light.

Instead, Brianna preferred to think that his mother was one of the extremely lucky ones whose bodies had issued a warning to them and then just gone back to normal. Back to "business as usual."

"Sebastian told me you had a stroke last week," she said gently.

Was it her imagination, or did the woman's smile suddenly look a little strained?

And if so, why?

Because she didn't want to talk about her ordeal, or because there'd *been* no ordeal?

Brianna's intuition leaned a certain way. Because

this was Sebastian's mother, she decided to dismiss this thought.

"I did," Barbara answered, her voice rather low and somewhat shaky. Was that pain she detected in the older woman's voice?

Or uncertainty?

"I know it's an uncomfortable subject to talk about," Brianna said. "The very thought of it touches on our mortality, but anything you can tell me about the incident—" such a nice, clinical word, she thought, for something so ugly "—would be very helpful."

"Helpful?" the older woman questioned, her thin eyebrows drawing together like an animated line.

"Bree is considering whether or not to take your case, Mom," Sebastian said, interrupting.

Brianna didn't see the hopeful flash in his mother's eyes, but he did.

It made him wonder.

Was the flash there because it made her feel better, having someone she knew looking to help her? Or was there some other reason behind that look?

His life abroad had made him too suspicious, Sebastian thought self-critically. His mother wasn't some conniving schemer—she was a down-to-earth, simple woman who lived alone and who had been understandably frightened by her ordeal. Of course the thought of having someone she knew around to look after her pleased her.

He was searching for hidden meaning where there was none, he thought, chastising himself.

Sebastian rose to his feet. "Why don't I leave the two of you alone to talk?" he suggested, thinking that his presence might make it awkward for his mother to talk about what had happened to her.

"That might not be a bad idea," Brianna agreed.

"Thank you," his mother said to him, looking relieved.

"I'll be in the family room if you need me," he said. And with that, he left the room.

Chapter Nine

"So tell me, what's going on?" Brianna asked Barbara Hunter as soon as her son had left the room. She took a seat on the chair opposite the sofa and focused all her attention on the woman.

Barbara looked at her, doing her best to hide her nervousness. She'd never been good at lying and she knew it. At times, when the truth sounded as if it was a tad suspicious, she'd be nervous that what was coming out of her mouth *sounded* as if she was lying.

And now, given the fact that everything she'd told Sebastian in order to get him to come stateside in time for his high school reunion had been based on a ruse, Barbara felt as if she was knee-deep in falsehoods and bald-faced lies.

Did Brianna suspect?

Could the young nurse tell just by looking at her that she hadn't had a stroke?

By asking what was "going on," was Brianna asking about her symptoms, or the reason behind the fabrications and lies?

Barbara licked her lips to keep them from sticking together. They were bone dry. Even so, she stopped herself before she could moisten them, afraid that the simple act—and the reason for it—would give her away to someone as sharp-eyed as Brianna.

"I'm afraid I don't understand what you mean," Barbara managed to respond quietly, stopping just short of sucking in air as her lungs felt suddenly depleted of oxygen. Lying created the sensation of breathlessness within her.

Maybe she hadn't made herself clear, Brianna thought. His mother looked genuinely uncomfortable and confused. Was that because of the stroke? Or was there some other reason for the woman's discomfort? She certainly hoped that *she* wasn't the cause for the woman's reaction.

Sebastian's mother had always been nothing but warm and friendly toward her, making her feel welcome any time she came over to the house with Sebastian. Making her feel, back then, as if she was already part of the family.

Brianna remembered thinking when she first met his mother that she would have loved, if she were able to pick and choose, to have a mother just like Barbara Hunter.

The very last thing in the world she wanted was to make that woman feel uncomfortable in her presence.

"Are you feeling any physical discomfort right now?" Brianna rephrased. When the other woman shook her head in response, Brianna pressed on. She needed to get her own clear picture of events. "Just what exactly initially alerted you to the fact that you were having a stroke?"

Barbara released the breath that had gotten trapped in her lungs. She felt a little more at ease now. She'd done her homework on this one, looking up on the internet the condition she was feigning. She was rather proud of herself for that, seeing as how navigating on the computer was completely foreign to her.

Admittedly, it had been hard for her at first, but Maizie had shown her how to get around something she referred to as "a search engine," which wasn't an engine at all, just something that allowed her to type in a few key words, in exchange for which she was shown a plethora of things called "websites." And those in turn gave her the information she was looking for—eventually.

It had taken her a while, granted, but now she felt that she was adequately educated regarding the subject matter and ready for any questions that her son might have for her.

Or, in this case, that the young woman she'd hoped her son would someday marry might have for her.

Given the question, Barbara now recited the symptoms chapter and verse, which she'd previously memorized, citing things like "dizziness, nausea and a really rapid heartbeat."

"I thought my heart was going to fly right out of my chest," Barbara told her with just the right touch of earnestness.

"Did you lose consciousness?" Brianna asked.

Barbara paused, trying to remember the right response to that question. She wanted Brianna to think she'd had a mild stroke, one that hadn't resulted in any sort of permanent damage. Other than simplifying her story, it also made it easier for her to have fewer details to keep straight. She knew very well that she couldn't sustain a multilayered performance for an indefinite length of time.

"No," she finally answered with a note of triumph in her voice. "I didn't. I was conscious the entire time."

"Well, that's good," Brianna said with genuine satisfaction. "How did you get to the hospital?"

For a second, the relatively simple question threw her. But after a moment, drawing on her past experiences, Barbara had her alibi in place.

"My friend drove me to the hospital. I called Maizie and told her what I was feeling. She came over right away and whisked me off to the E.R."

Brianna nodded, pleased. She knew that the faster a patient with stroke symptoms received medical attention, the greater the possibility of reversing any damage. Those first crucial minutes made the difference between recovery and all sorts of debilitating effects, ending with paralysis.

That being the case, she needed to get more of a handle on all this. "Would you happen to know how much time passed from the first onset of your symptoms to your arriving at the E.R. and receiving treatment?"

She knew that one, Barbara thought with a tinge of frustration setting in. She really did. So why couldn't she think of it now?

Barbara hesitated for a moment, sifting through the various pieces of information she'd read and absorbed, trying to remember the right answer.

"About an hour altogether. Maybe a few minutes more than that," she added hesitantly. "Maizie's office is close by," she interjected, "and she came the second I called her."

"You're lucky to have a friend like that," she told the other woman.

"In more ways than one," Barbara murmured, then, realizing she'd said that out loud, she flashed a wide smile at the young woman.

Brianna wondered what she meant by that, but there were more important questions to ask Mrs. Hunter at the moment.

"And how are you feeling now?" Brianna asked.

"A lot better—but still rather weak," Barbara quickly added.

Heaven forbid that Brianna thought she didn't need any sort of home medical care. That was the whole point of this, to keep throwing Brianna and her son together until they came to their senses and the spark reignited between them.

The young woman, she recalled, was honest to a fault. That sort of person did not charge for services she felt weren't necessary.

Brianna leaned forward just a tad, her blue eyes peering into the other woman's soft brown ones. "You're not disoriented?" she asked.

Barbara was watching the young woman's face, trying to take her cue from her expression. She decided that she wouldn't want to play poker against Brianna, especially since the younger woman's expression was almost unreadable.

Barbara was left to her own devices as to how to answer, so she replied cautiously. "Maybe a little fuzzy around the edges at times."

"That's all perfectly natural," Brianna told her. "Tell me, were you ever diagnosed as having angina or A-fib?"

Barbara knew what the first condition was and shook her head. "No to angina," she said with confidence. But her confidence tapered off as she asked, "But what's A-fib?"

"Sorry, I shouldn't have just thrown letters at you. It stands for atrial fibrillation." The look on the older woman's face said she was no more enlightened, so she broke it down for Barbara into the simplest terms. "What it means is, have you experienced any rapid heartbeat or skipped beats?"

Until this moment, Barbara had just assumed that everyone had that happen to them on one occasion or another. She still felt relatively safe in her assumption, so she thought it would be all right to answer in the affirmative. "Yes. Sometimes," she qualified.

Brianna went to the next logical question, which in this case involved prescriptions. "Which beta-blocker did the doctor prescribe for you to treat that?"

Barbara's mind went to a terrifying blank. "I'm not sure," Barbara answered evasively.

"That's okay—lots of people forget the name of the pills they're required to take." She rose to her feet. "Where do you keep your medicine?" Brianna asked, perfectly content to do her own legwork. "I'll just take a quick peek at what's there and—"

Barbara panicked. There *was* no heart medication of any kind, because she'd made up the whole thing. She desperately needed a way to distract Brianna.

"Is it hot in here?" Barbara asked suddenly, futilely fanning herself with her hand. "Do you feel warm?" She swayed slightly as she tried to get up. "Oh, I feel so weak, so dizzy…."

Brianna was back beside her in a moment, her arms going around the other woman's girth. Despite its size, she felt she had a good grip on Sebastian's mother. Only then did she ease Barbara back onto the sofa.

"You've got to be careful about making any sudden moves," Brianna gently cautioned her. "Let me check your heart rate," she requested.

Her slender fingers already on the woman's wrist, she searched for Barbara's pulse. Placing two fingers over the quickly vibrating area, Brianna silently counted the rapid beats.

Brianna frowned slightly as she released the wrist. “Certainly feels like A-fib to me.” She took note of Barbara’s expression and misinterpreted its origin. “Don’t look so worried, Mrs. Hunter. I’m sure your doctor told you that the condition is totally controllable. You’ll be back running those literacy courses of yours at the library in no time,” she promised.

As Brianna began to turn away, Barbara caught her hand. She dispensed just the right amount of truth to get what she wanted. “If it’s all the same to you, dear, I’d like to take my time getting better.” Her eyes met the young woman’s. “I had a friend who rushed back into her day-to-day life right after she had a similar incident, and she wound up in the hospital with another stroke, far worse than what she’d had the first time around. I don’t want the same thing happening to me.”

Brianna gave her a reassuring smile. “I understand perfectly and I didn’t mean to make you think anyone’s rushing you to do something you don’t feel ready for. Everyone has their own inner pace,” she added. “And you have to be true to yours.”

“This ‘incident’ has its upside,” Barbara confided. “I mean, it did bring Sebastian rushing back to see me.” Her mouth curved fondly as she spoke about her son. “He wasn’t going to come for a visit until December, if then.” When Brianna raised an eyebrow, she explained. “Things have a habit of coming up at the last minute in his world, and he’s canceled trips to the States before,” she said with a sigh.

“Oh.”

A few things clicked into place in Brianna's head, but she didn't want to say anything out loud just yet. If she was wrong, she'd be guilty of offending Sebastian's mother and she didn't want to do that. She had a feeling, though, that for whatever reason, Barbara wasn't being entirely truthful about what had happened and her condition. Just how much was true and how much wasn't, she didn't know, but Brianna was certain of one thing.

"Sebastian would be relieved to know that you're not standing at death's door with a Now Serving number in your pocket," she pointed out diplomatically. The expression on Barbara's face did not match that of a woman whose mind had been set completely at ease. "What would you *like* me to tell him?" she asked, qualifying the word *like*.

"That I'd feel a great deal better and more confident if I had someone staying with me for a little while."

"You mean him?" Brianna assumed that getting Sebastian to stay for an extended period of time was the woman's ultimate goal.

"Like a nurse," Barbara corrected.

Brianna needed to be perfectly clear on this. She'd initially thought Sebastian was just asking for an evaluation of his mother's condition so he'd know what he needed to do for her.

"Mrs. Hunter, are you asking me to take you on as a patient?" Brianna asked.

Barbara looked at her hopefully, as if she were mentally crossing her fingers. "Could you?" she asked.

Well, her schedule *was* clear, but she needed to get

a few things out in the open and understood first. "I usually move in for the duration of a patient's care."

Barbara nodded. "Even better—I'd feel more secure knowing you were close by," she quickly added.

There was one more very important thing. "Mrs. Hunter—"

Barbara held up her hand, stopping her. "Barbara, please," she requested. "If you're going to be here taking care of me, you should at least be able to call me by my first name," she told the younger woman with a smile.

"I don't move in by myself," Brianna began.

Barbara nodded. "Oh, I'm sure that Sebastian wouldn't mind helping you bring your things over here," she assured Brianna.

Physical logistics was not the problem. She was strong enough to carry her own things. This was far more important than moving suitcases. This was, in essence, the deal breaker if she got the wrong answer.

"No, what I'm trying to tell you is that I'd be bringing my four-year-old daughter, Carrie, with me."

Sebastian had already told her about Brianna's daughter. He'd been so taken aback initially and then just blown away by the scope of the little girl's mind, he'd shared the whole story with her.

After her initial surprise—much like his, she suspected—she'd summoned her courage and gotten on the phone with Brianna's father, a man she'd met briefly at a couple of PTA meetings dating back to when their children were in their last year of high school. After identifying herself, she'd asked him to supply the rest of the answers she needed.

The man had been quite helpful once he understood what she was attempting to do. And he'd been exceedingly charming as well. She'd stayed on the phone quite a while.

"I would insist on it," Barbara told her now. "A child belongs with her mother. Especially a little girl." The soul of innocence, she went on to ask, "Is there anything else?"

"Yes," Brianna replied. "When would you like me to start?"

"The sooner the better," Barbara told her in all honesty. Taught to always seal the bargain, she put her hand out. "So it's a deal?"

Brianna slipped her hand into his mother's, feeling as if she was taking advantage of the other woman. She was sealing a bargain that seemed just far too advantageous for her.

But, for whatever reason, Barbara Hunter truly felt she needed to have her around and to make use of her services. The first rule about nursing was to make the patient feel better, so she was not about to argue the point with the woman.

"It's a deal," Brianna confirmed.

Barbara's grin widened even more.

Brianna stopped moving and just watched her father in uncertain awe.

"You know, if I didn't know any better, I'd say that

you were eager to get rid of me," she told him. For the first time in her recollection, her father was helping her pack her things as well as Carrie's beloved collection of toys and books. Clothes were only incidental to Carrie and not nearly as important as her possessions.

"Eager to get rid of you?" her father echoed, then declared, "Never," in a voice that could have easily belonged to the hero of a melodrama. "I'll be standing by the window, my face pressed against the glass, a candle burning in each hand the entire time that you're going to be gone."

Brianna laughed and resumed selecting and discarding various articles of clothing.

"Very funny. I guess, after all this time, you're probably looking forward to having the house all to yourself," she surmised.

"I promise to keep the wild parties down to a minimum," he quipped.

"How are you going to party?" she asked. "I thought you were going to be standing with your face pressed against the glass, holding a candle in each hand, remember?" she asked, doing her best to sound as if she was at least semiserious.

"Man's gotta eat and take a couple of bathroom breaks occasionally," her father pointed out. "That's why the parties'll be kept to a minimum."

She shook her head. Inside every man was still a wild, spirited teenager, she couldn't help thinking. "Well, you're certainly old enough not to need a lecture."

Her father laughed. "Knew getting old was good for something."

She paused to pat his cheek. "You're not old, Dad, just a little slightly used," she told him fondly.

Looking around the room, she and her father had managed to pack everything she and Carrie were going to need for what she hoped was a short duration. Otherwise, she was going to have to make a few trips back. She supposed that wasn't really a bad thing. It would allow her to look in on her father.

She turned toward him now. "You know where to find me if you need me."

She'd given him the phone number as well as the address the moment she'd walked in. "It's on the refrigerator. You wrote the number in letters big enough for a helicopter pilot to see if he was circling the house."

"If a helicopter pilot is circling the house, we'd have bigger problems than you seeing the phone number I wrote." She grew serious for a moment. He, along with her daughter, had always been her first priority. Time hadn't changed that. "You'll be okay?"

"I'll miss you," he told her. "And the pip-squeak," he added, referring to Carrie. "But I'll muddle through." He kissed the top of her head. "You just go do what you do best. Bully some patient into getting well," he instructed fondly.

"Between you and me," she confided, "I think she's halfway there already."

He looked at her for a moment, wondering just how

much his daughter suspected. Bree had always been a very sharp girl.

"Then this should be a piece of cake for you," he told her. "Speaking of which, I picked one up for you this afternoon when you called to say you were taking on a new case. It's waiting for you in the kitchen whenever you and the pip-squeak want a break."

"Cookies-and-cream?" she asked. It had been her favorite flavor since she was fourteen.

He grinned at her. "Would I get anything else?"

She brushed a quick kiss against his cheek. "You're one in a million, Dad."

"I know." He laughed, putting an arm around each of "his girls." "Let's go break the cake in."

Together, they went to the kitchen to do justice to the cake he'd bought.

Chapter Ten

He was pacing.

Sebastian forced himself to stop. The thing of it was, he hadn't been aware that he was doing it until just now.

This was stupid. Why was he pacing and looking out at the driveway every time he passed the window? He was an adult, not a kid fresh out of puberty. It wasn't supposed to matter to him one way or another if Brianna moved into his house.

His house.

He laughed shortly. After all this time, he still thought of the place where he'd grown up as *his* house. His home. His home even though for the past four years, he'd lived in a sleek, ultramodern apartment in Tokyo.

But *this* was home and Brianna was moving into it. And despite his attempt at a devil-may-care, nonchalant attitude, he kept right on glancing through the window. Moreover, he was listening for the sound of an approaching vehicle.

And when he finally heard it, his damn pulse quickened.

To make matters worse, when he turned, he nearly tripped over his mother's damn cat. Stopping short of just clipping the feline's nose with the tip of his shoe, he managed to catch himself just in time.

He bit back a curse. "Damn it, Marilyn, you're going to wind up flatter than a pancake if you don't stop getting in my way."

Marilyn strolled out of the way, completely unfazed by the fate she'd almost suffered.

When Brianna pulled up into the driveway—at exactly the time she'd told his mother she would arrive—he was at the front door before she had even turned off the CR-V's engine.

Getting out of the vehicle, she looked at Sebastian quizzically. Had there been a change in plans? She couldn't think of another reason for him to have come out to meet her car so quickly.

"Hi," she said a bit uncertainly, waiting for him to say something that would tell her what was going on.

But all Sebastian said in response to her greeting was a more formal "Hello."

Rounding the hood, she made her way over to the passenger side and then opened the rear door.

"We're here, honey," she told Carrie as she leaned in and began removing her daughter from her car seat.

Sparing Sebastian a glance, she gave in and finally asked, "What are you doing here?"

He'd been asking himself that all day. He said, "I used to live here, remember?"

"Yes, I know that. That's not what I meant." *And you know it.* "You came out the minute my tires hit your driveway. Something wrong?" she asked. She scooped Carrie up in her arms and then set her down.

Carrie's attention, like her own, was focused on Sebastian.

"No," he replied, wondering why she would think there was something wrong—other than his having stepped out of her life for the past ten years. "I just thought I'd see if you needed any help moving in."

Something told her that wasn't all, but she let it go. Maybe she was just overthinking things. She'd been doing that since she'd bumped into Sebastian—and all those memories—at the reunion.

"Oh, well, that's nice of you," Brianna acknowledged.

"Despite what you might think, I *can* be a nice guy."

It was on the tip of her tongue to say something that would put the veracity of his statement in doubt, but what was the point of that? Of rehashing everything? The past was gone and there was no going back and fixing it or changing it. She knew that.

So instead, she said, with a complete economy of emotion, "Never said anything else." Then, wanting to change the subject as quickly as possible, Brianna went on to tell him, "And just so you know, I'm not 'moving in.' I'm just in a temporary holding pattern until your mother feels more secure about managing her day-to-day life on her own."

He shifted so that he was directly in front of her just as she was about to open up the vehicle's hatchback door. "You really think she'll be able to?" Sebastian asked.

"No doubt in the world," Brianna answered him honestly. "From our little talk yesterday, I got the feeling that your mother is really a lot better than she thinks she is. She just needs to have her confidence restored and bolstered a little. Once that happens, Carrie and I will be on our way again, riding off into the sunset," she added wryly.

"Like the Lone Ranger," he quipped, amused at the image she used.

Both Brianna and Carrie chimed in together, "Who?"

"Obviously your education has a hole in it," he said, then decided to fill them in. "The Lone Ranger was a lone survivor of an outlaw raid on a company of Texas Rangers. He was nursed back to health by an Indian he'd befriended as a young boy. After he recovered, he put on a mask and rode around the countryside on a white stallion, fighting injustice wherever he found it. He always handed out a silver bullet before he rode away."

"Did he shoot the silver bullet?" Carrie asked.

She'd been so quiet that, for a moment, he'd completely forgotten she was there. "No, I think he just saved them to hand out as souvenirs. Presents," he amended, thinking she wouldn't understand what the other word meant.

Carrie gave him a look that was at once resigned and ever so slightly irritated. "I know what a souvenir is," she told him.

"Sorry." Despite his apology, Sebastian was unable to suppress a grin. The little girl just kept surprising him.

As far back as he could remember, it had been just his mother and him. His father was a soldier who'd perished halfway around the world. Sebastian had grown up always looking for ways to bring in a little money and help his mother. He'd gone through a nostalgic period early in his life, picking through garage sales and the like, looking for old movie and television memorabilia in the hope of stumbling across something rare that would bring in a sizable amount of money. He had wound up getting hooked on old movies and classic TV programs for a while, before deciding his time and effort could be better spent elsewhere.

But the Lone Ranger had always remained one of his favorites. He supposed that was because, at one point in his life, he had identified with the loner who, after having gone through typical—at least for those times—childhood and young adult years, had a life-altering experience that left him with only one friend he felt he could trust.

One friend was all that was necessary when it counted. And his "one friend" had been Brianna.

That, too, was in the past, he reminded himself.

About to comment on the little girl's rather extensive

vocabulary, the remark evaporated from his lips as he looked into the rear of Brianna's car.

From what he could see, it was completely filled.

He glanced back at Brianna, then looked again into the interior of the vehicle. For someone who'd claimed not to be moving in, she'd brought everything with her but the kitchen sink.

"Are all these suitcases filled with clothes?" he asked incredulously, gesturing at the squadron of dark gray cloth suitcases that were packed so tightly together, had they been people, they would have suffocated.

"No, actually they're filled with stuffed animals and books," she corrected. She could tell that he was looking at her to see if she was kidding. She wasn't. "There's just one suitcase with clothes," she told him. "Both of our clothes," she clarified, adding, "Carrie and I don't require much in the way of clothing. She just needs a few changes of play clothes, and I'm in a uniform most of the time."

"You don't have to be if you'd rather not," he told her.

Brianna's mind froze for a moment. Was he telling her she could dress casually, or was he telling her that she didn't need to dress at all?

You're getting too carried away. That's not what he's saying and you know it. For one thing, his mother's here. For another, he wouldn't take a chance on traumatizing Carrie.

Sebastian had always liked children and he could be counted on to be the first to take note if anything was being done to harm a child, even indirectly.

"What do you mean?" she asked.

He'd thought it was obvious, but explained anyway. "You can wear casual clothes if that makes you feel more comfortable. I think my mother wants you to feel right at home here."

"And I want her to feel as if she's being well taken care of and watched over. I think the uniform, however subliminally, might just reinforce that feeling for her. Besides, it's a nurse's uniform, not a suit of armor to be worn during a summer heat wave," she pointed out. "But, thanks," she tagged on, in case he thought she was just being argumentative and difficult. "I do appreciate knowing I have leeway."

Picking up the lightest container, she handed it to Carrie, then took another, far heavier one herself. "If you could point out which bedroom is going to be ours, that would be great."

He picked up two suitcases, one in each hand, then led the way up the driveway to the front door. "Follow me," he told her.

"We will," Carrie piped up with assurance, the voice of a seasoned adult trapped within the body of a small child.

Sebastian pressed his lips together to keep the laugh that rose in his throat right where it was. Turning, he pushed the unlocked front door open with his back and then went to the staircase.

"It's the second room to the right," he told his two-woman entourage.

The first room to the right at the top of the stairs was *his* bedroom, Brianna remembered.

Or at least it had been that one night when they'd discovered each other, and a whole new world had opened up for them.

Or for her, at any rate.

She did her best not to glance toward the room when she reached the landing, but a wave of nostalgia got the better of her. Her eyes darted toward it before she was able to rein herself in.

"Almost there, Carrie," she told her daughter.

It proved unnecessary because the high-pitched voice responded, "I can see that."

Unlike Sebastian, Brianna made no effort to hold back a laugh. "Yes, I'm sure you can. Find a place for that box and we'll go back down for more," she told the little girl. She foresaw *many* trips up and down the stairs today—and possibly an aching back by day's end.

Still holding the box she'd brought up the stairs, Carrie slowly looked around the room, as if seeking just the right spot to house her beloved treasures.

Brianna noticed the curious look on Sebastian's face and guessed at what was going on in his head.

"Location's everything," she explained to him. "Carrie is extremely organized for a four-year-old."

He knew CEOs who subscribed to more chaos than this child apparently did. "She's very organized for *any* age," he corrected.

His observation earned him a wide smile from Carrie that she flashed his way.

Finally making her decision, Carrie walked with determined steps to the area beside the window, then set her box down beneath it.

"It's nice over here. The sun makes it bright. They'll be happy here," she declared.

Brianna glanced toward Sebastian, anticipating his reaction. His eyebrow was raised in a silent query. He was probably asking her the identity of the "they" Carrie was referring to.

"Her stuffed animals," she told him. "She likes to make sure they're comfortable in their new surroundings. It reminds her to think of others before herself," she added.

Carrie was already by the bedroom door. "Can I go down and get some of the others, Mama?"

"Not without me," she reminded Carrie. "You know that."

"I don't want them to get too hot in the car," she explained, trying to give her mother a reason for her sudden break in protocol.

"I think the extra minute or two won't make a difference to them," Brianna assured her daughter.

But even so, she was already leading the way back downstairs. Carrie matched her, step for step, all but leaping to make up for the difference in stride.

Watching the interaction with no small amount of awe, Sebastian brought up the rear.

"Give me the heaviest one," he told Brianna when they'd returned to her car again.

"The heaviest one, huh?" Was he being gallant, or

just macho? Either way, she needed the box out of the car. "That would be the big box in the rear," she told him. "It's packed with her books."

It had taken both her father and her to lift the container and put it into the car. Leaning in now, she pulled the edge of the box over to her a little at a time until she was *finally* able to get it to the edge of the vehicle.

"And it's pretty heavy. Since we're going to be staying on the second floor, maybe we should just unpack the box and bring the books up an armload at a time," she suggested.

"Or I could just take it upstairs for you and save a lot of time," he told her, hefting the large box out of the car.

"It's too heavy," she insisted.

Her words fell on deaf ears.

She should have expected nothing less, she thought. Sebastian could be very stubborn when he wanted to be. Before babies, reality and responsibilities, she could afford the luxury of being reckless and throwing caution to the winds. But no more.

"Careful," she warned, moving out of his way. "Or I'll wind up having to nurse you through the aftermath of a hernia operation."

"If that's supposed to get me to put down the box, it's not working," he told her. "You're going to have to come up with something better than that," he said as he passed her and crossed the threshold leading into his house.

Bracing the contents in his arms as best he could, he made his way up the stairs, moving a tad more slowly than he would have liked. He didn't want the cardboard suddenly to give way and an avalanche of books to come pouring out.

"I forgot how stubborn you could be," she said in a rare display of exasperation.

"Funny, I was going to say the same thing about you," Sebastian answered.

"Mama says it's not nice to be stubborn," Carrie told him, putting her small body in his direction.

"Except at certain times," Brianna felt she had to qualify.

"Is this one of those times?" Carrie asked, turning her face up to her mother.

"I'm afraid it certainly looks that way," she told the little girl, surrendering.

The laugh she heard coming from Sebastian zipped up and down her spine before fading away. Reminding her again that perhaps accepting this assignment was not the wisest thing she'd ever done.

Chapter Eleven

Sebastian had no intention of actually eavesdropping. It just happened.

And it wasn't because he'd actually heard something that involved him, because he hadn't.

At least, not in the traditional sense.

What he wound up witnessing strongly involved him in an emotional sense, causing him to wonder—not for the first time—what if…?

All he'd initially intended was to pass by the living room. He'd been on his way to the kitchen to get himself something to eat. Brianna and her daughter had been in the house for a little more than a week now—long enough, apparently, for Carrie and Marilyn the cat to discover one another; the cat had seemingly "adopted" the four-year-old and followed her everywhere. And while there had been no awkward moments for any of them, he still found himself walking on eggshells, subconsciously wary of dislodging the careful balance of things.

Doing his very best not to stir up old memories, old feelings.

As if he could actually prevent them from finding him....

But Brianna didn't need to know that. Didn't need to know that there was this ache in his chest with her name on it, and every day it got a little bigger, grew a little more unwieldy and challenging.

Feeling this way, he had all the intention in the world to just keep walking by the living room, where he knew that his mother, Brianna and Carrie—with the cat in attendance—currently were. But then his attention was hijacked by the scenario he saw out of the corner of his eye.

A scenario involving his mother, Brianna and her daughter. Three separate generations rabidly involved in what looked like, from where he was standing, some sort of board game. Even the cat appeared to be part of it. Marilyn was kibitzing.

It was an old board game, from what he could actually see. He hadn't thought that anyone, especially children, played board games anymore. In today's sophisticated, high-tech electronic world, a simple board game seemed almost archaic.

Certainly outdated.

Yet there they were, his mother propped up on the

sofa with a mountain of pillows at her back, Brianna and Carrie gathered on the other side of the coffee table, deeply engrossed in something that looked suspiciously reminiscent of his old Monopoly game. The actual game board looked weathered enough to be his—he had no idea that his mother had kept it all these years.

He wouldn't even have looked into the room if it hadn't been for the laughter. That was what had first caught his attention. Not just Carrie's and Brianna's, but his mother's laughter as well.

It wasn't until *after* the sound had sunk in that he recognized it and subsequently realized that he hadn't heard that sound in a very long time.

He'd missed it.

Missed, too, not worrying about his mother, because ever since he'd taken that phone call, he'd been nothing *but* worried about his mother.

At least he'd lucked out by getting Brianna to come stay with her.

Brianna *and* her daughter, he amended.

He wasn't certain who was better for his mother. Brianna had a gentle, soothing way about her, but Carrie—Carrie was a whole different story. As Carrie and the cat had done, his mother and the little girl had hit it off instantly. Now his mother seemed to light up each time that Carrie came into the room.

It made him wonder—and just possibly harbor a sliver of yearning—what it would have been like if he'd married Brianna and started a family with her, giving his mother the grandchild she'd always longed for.

When she'd first mentioned that desire to him years ago, it had just seemed like the standard, humdrum request of every mother with adult children, and he'd just shrugged it off as such.

But now he could see just how strong that desire had to have actually been—and most likely still was—as he witnessed, time and again during this past week, how jubilant his mother became whenever she saw Carrie bounding toward her.

As if she was in the company of her own grandchild.

Sorry, Mom. I guess some things just weren't meant to be.

"Hey, what are you doing hovering over there?" Brianna called to him, breaking into his thoughts.

She'd been watching him beneath hooded eyes for a few minutes now and had given him what she felt was a decent amount of time to sneak away unnoticed if that was what he wanted. But Sebastian had remained where he was, a strange, almost wistful expression on his face.

Maybe he actually wanted to be called over, coaxed a little to join them. She certainly had no problem with that, with pretending that he had to have his arm twisted before he gave in. Having him join them might be great medicine for his mother, who, in her opinion, would really enjoy a nice domestic scene, complete with a family pet, all of them gathered around the coffee table.

So Brianna beckoned him over. "Come join us."

Time to go, Sebastian thought. "No, I'm actually on my way to—"

Although he pointed vaguely in the direction of the front door, which was definitely not the way he'd appeared to be heading, he came up empty. He hadn't counted on being put on the spot and thus had no excuse prepared to use for cover.

"To what?" Brianna challenged. "To go outside and peer in through the window to watch us play your old Monopoly game?"

He waved her off. "No. Really, you just continue doing what you're doing and I'll—"

He didn't get a chance to finish the half-formed excuse because Carrie had already gotten up, quickly crossed the room to get to his side and now had both her small hands wrapped around one of his. She looked as if she had every intention of literally dragging him into the living room and to the coffee table.

"Come," Carrie urged in a voice that sounded more like an order than just a soft plea. "Play Monopoly with us." She flashed a bright smile up at him. "I'm winning."

"Of course you are." He laughed. "I never had any doubts." Still, he tried to hold his ground against the little girl.

It wasn't going to happen, he realized almost immediately.

"But I promise I'll let you win if you come play the game with us," Carrie offered.

"Really, Sebastian, how can you possibly turn an offer like that down?" his mother asked him.

"Carrie hasn't learned how to take no for an answer yet," Brianna warned him, "so she's not about to politely back away or give up easily." She thought of what Sebastian had said to her when she'd first arrived. "And you haven't witnessed stubborn until you've had her wage a campaign against you," she told him, then added, "I'm afraid you're doomed, Sebastian."

Carrie, still holding on to his hand with both of hers and doing it as if she intended to hold on for dear life no matter how long it took, raised her brilliant blue eyes up to his and said what her mother referred to as the magic word. "Please?"

Sebastian knew he was probably just reading things into it, but the little girl made it sound as if her heart would break if he turned her down. And since he honestly had nothing planned and no particular place to go, he gave in.

"Sure, why not?" he said, allowing himself to be urged into the room.

He wasn't prepared for Carrie's enthusiastic cheer greeting his statement, nor was he prepared to see her gleefully leap up and down as if she was a pint-size cheerleader whose team had just scored a winning touchdown.

Neither was he prepared to have her tug on his arm and make him get down to her level.

When he did, she brushed her small lips against his cheek, her touch lighter than a butterfly landing on an orchid petal.

"Thank you," she said in a small, delicate voice that

made her momentarily sound a great deal younger than she normally did.

Sebastian *really* wasn't ready to have his heart utterly melt, just a moment before he served it up to the little girl on a silver platter.

Rising, he found he had to clear his throat. "Don't mention it," he murmured.

He pulled up a chair, taking the fourth side of the game board.

"I don't think I remember how to play," he admitted as he looked down at the board. A quick flash of a memory went by far too quickly for him to grab on to it and attempt to recall anything more.

A wave of nostalgia greeted him. It seemed to Sebastian as if the last time he'd sat just like this, contemplating this very game board, had been several decades ago.

"It'll come back to you," Brianna assured him. Her eyes met his for a brief moment and she added, "It's just like riding a bicycle. Or anything else you learned how to do on a regular basis."

Like love you?

The thought, coming in like a low-flying attack plane, startled him.

Why would it have even crossed his mind? As time had distanced him from his senior year, he had begun to doubt that what he'd felt for her then *had* been love. At least, not the forever kind. Maybe just the puppy-love variety.

That was what he'd told himself.

Seeing her at the reunion that night had stirred up

a lot of old feelings, reminding him of how it used to be. Of how he'd used to feel just being around her. But even so, he hadn't wanted to *actually* put a name to it, preferring that the emotion remain nameless until it had the good sense to fade away.

Obviously his subconscious had other ideas about it, because the nostalgia kept on coming back in insistent waves.

"You're probably right." He picked up one of the remaining pieces on the board. "Okay, let's get to it." He pushed his sleeves up his forearms. "Prepare to be dazzled, ladies." His game piece in his hand, he spared Carrie a glance. "And you don't have to 'let' me win. I can do it on my own, thanks."

Carrie's smile just stopped short of being smug. But the look on her face said she knew better but was so happy to see him play with them that she wasn't going to say anything, other than an enthusiastic "Okay!"

"Let the games begin," he declared, aware that all the markers had gone back to Go for a fresh game.

"I think," Sebastian said to Brianna a great many hours later, "you're raising a pint-size con artist. I can see her in Vegas in another seventeen years, being banned from all the casinos for card counting."

Brianna laughed as she cleaned up what had been an after-dinner round of cards. For such a small number of people, they certainly racked up an awful lot of dirty dishes and cups, she couldn't help thinking, bringing over another pile and putting them in the sink.

"I plan to make sure she only uses her powers for good," she told Sebastian. And then she paused for a moment, looking at Carrie. The powerhouse had finally just dozed off, refusing to miss a moment of what she assumed was an adult conversation: many words, few actual thoughts. "But she really does have a fantastic mind, doesn't she?"

Sebastian laughed and nodded his head. "All I know is that if she were my kid, I'd be studying every night just to try to stay ahead of her."

"I don't know how long I'd be able to keep that up," she told him. "She's already got a mind like a steel trap. It's like she remembers everything she sees, reads, learns—"

Sebastian looked at Brianna in disbelief. "She reads?"

Brianna smiled. It was so common in her life, she forgot that there were many who were fighting illiteracy. She needed to get back in the game.

"Like an old person. My father initially started to teach her. She was reading to *him* in less than two weeks. He's completely crazy about her." Brianna smiled fondly as she gazed down at the sleeping child. "She is rather hard to resist, as I think you might have found out today," she added drolly, referring to the games Carrie had corralled him into playing with them.

"A lot like her mother." Brianna laughed at that and then rolled her eyes. "What?" he asked, not seeing anything particularly funny about what he'd just said.

"Oh, please, don't even go there," she requested. The

man obviously needed a quick summary. "You *so* resisted me," she reminded him, but there was no bitterness or rancor in her voice, no look of recrimination when she glanced in his direction.

"About that..." Sebastian began hesitantly.

She raised her hand to stop whatever he was going to say. "It's okay. I didn't say that to make you feel guilty, or even to get you to apologize, or anything else along those lines. I just wanted to point out that I wasn't irresistible to you, no matter how you 'choose' to remember the past."

Instead of saying anything, Sebastian took hold of her wrist and drew her aside. He didn't want to have Carrie overhear them should she suddenly wake up. Glancing at her now, he wouldn't have put it past the little girl to feign sleeping just so that she could listen to them talk. She seemed to thoroughly enjoy being around adults rather than children her own age.

Brianna began to tug her hand away and found that, although his hold on her wrist felt relaxed, it was really quite strong. Her wrist was staying exactly where it was for the time being.

With a mental shrug, Brianna allowed him to take her over to one side of the room.

"What I 'choose' to remember," he said, keeping his voice low despite the distance now between them and the sleeping child, "is feeling hurt."

Now he wasn't making any sense at all. Brianna blinked, then stared at him, completely confused. What did *he* have to be hurt about? "What?"

"Hurt," he repeated for emphasis. "Because I had this big, romanticized dream, for lack of a better description, of the two of us going off to college and beginning our lives together. You and me against the world, that sort of corny thing," he admitted, growing more uncomfortable, not to mention hot. Who had taken out all the air from around here? "And then suddenly, you weren't part of that—you were telling me you weren't coming with me."

There was a reason for that and he *knew* it, she thought. "It wasn't exactly because I was going off on a month-long holiday touring Europe. I was staying home to take care of my injured father. My injured father who'd *almost died* in a car accident," she underscored, stunned that he had felt and thought that way.

"I know, I know, I was being an idiot. A self-centered, thoughtless, selfish idiot, but I'm just being honest about the way I felt at the time." He broke it down to just a few words. "I felt cheated and abandoned."

"Well, that made two of us," she retorted, doing her best *not* to revisit that time, because it always brought tears to her eyes.

"Yeah," he said, the emotion leaving his voice, "but you were the only one who actually had a right to those feelings. I am really sorry for leaving you to cope with everything on your own back then. I should have stayed to help you, to be supportive of you, and I didn't. I just thought about how you should have been there with me, not vice versa."

That he felt that way, that he was saying all the things

that had, at one time or another, crossed her mind, took the sting out of all the pain that she'd felt over the past ten years. She could be magnanimous now. She couldn't before.

"You had a degree to earn," she pointed out, her tone completely compassionate.

"So did you," he reminded her.

And if she could stay to help her father, he should have stayed to help her. With his mother ill now, he understood every emotion she had to have experienced, every emotion that had chosen to use her body for a battlefield. Since she'd come to them, she'd worked hard at being a pacifist.

"Yes," she agreed, but things had worked out in that area as well. "I was far more flexible about it than you could ever be. If you had stayed here with me, you would have felt I was holding you back, and things might not have gone well for us eventually."

"You mean compared to the way they actually have?" he asked with a touch of sarcasm.

"Compared to the way things actually did turn out," she amended tactfully. "You have a career you love, as do I, and I have a huge bonus on top of that. Had you stayed, then I would have never had Carrie come into my life. That little girl has opened up a brand-new world for me, Sebastian. She's made me a much better person," she confessed.

He looked at her for a long moment, new and old feelings all crowding together in his chest, bringing a host of memories and whispers of the past with them.

He pushed them to one side, not having enough time to sift through them now.

"Not possible," he told Brianna.

"But she did," she insisted. "Carrie has made me a—"

He touched her face then, lightly skimming his fingertips along her cheek. Remembering that old feeling of how his day hadn't actually started until he saw her. "You can't improve on perfection," he whispered.

"Now you're just making fun of me," Brianna protested.

"No," Sebastian told her just before he gave in to the overwhelming yearning that ate him alive from the inside out and brought his mouth down on hers. "I'm not."

Chapter Twelve

Nothing had changed.

And everything had changed.

Sebastian's kiss still had the power to set her pulse racing, to set desire exploding in her veins, swiftly growing and wiping out every thought in her head. *That* part hadn't changed.

But life in general, *their* lives in general, had changed enormously. They had changed in focus, progressed and moved on. Brianna had worked tirelessly to help her father regain the use of his legs, had in effect brought his soul back from the dead. In the interim, she'd gone on to become a nurse as well as kept his store open and running until he was able to resume working there, something that had taken the better part of more than three years.

And, as if that wasn't enough, after that she had also taken on the mind-staggering responsibility of being a single parent and raising her late fiancé's daughter as her own.

As for him, he'd gone on to get his degree, then had restructured his life and moved to Japan, where he was currently putting his skills to use.

Neither one of them was the optimistic and eager teenager on the brink of tomorrow, as they'd been ten years ago. And yet, the essence of those people, those dreamers, was buried deep inside of each of them and had somehow reconnected with this simple, albeit inflaming, pressing of lips.

Unable to pull away, Sebastian tightened his arms around her as he deepened the kiss, deepened it to the point that there was no viable way out for him. Without realizing it, he'd hit the point of no return, at least in this instance, and discovered that Brianna still had a way of speaking to his soul, of making him think of nothing else but her.

Want nothing else but her.

What was to have been just a very simple kiss steeped in nostalgia was anything *but* simple. It made him remember the one night that had, all those years ago, seemed like the beginning of everything. He hadn't realized at the time, a scant few hours before they'd found out about her father's car accident, that it also marked the end of their time together.

Her heart pounding, Brianna threaded her fingers

through his hair. She'd always loved the feel of his thick, silky hair. Her head reeling, she leaned into the kiss.

Leaned into him.

Even as she did, she told herself that this was only going to lead to heartache, but that small voice of logic was getting weaker.

Her desire was blotting out all resistance.

Any moment now, she would throw caution to the winds and allow him to take her to his room. To take her where they were inevitably going.

Where she desperately *wanted* to go.

Everything had changed.

And yet, nothing had changed, because her feelings for him hadn't changed.

"Mama?"

Like a thin, sharp blade, the tiny, almost inaudible voice effectively pierced what had, until just now, felt like an impenetrably thick, clear bubble.

Startled, Brianna practically sprang back, not knowing what she was going to say. Dazed, disoriented, she swiftly tried to clear her head so that she would be able to give Carrie a coherent answer to whatever her daughter was going to ask.

"Yes, honey?"

Dear God, her voice was all but shaking—just like the rest of her. Was that because of her daughter, or because she realized that Sebastian's kiss had opened up the door to a room she had promised herself had been sealed shut?

Carrie looked from her to Sebastian, a puzzled expression on her small, oval-shaped face. "Are we going somewhere again?"

Brianna exchanged glances with Sebastian. He was as mystified as she was.

She turned toward her daughter. "No, honey, we're not going anywhere for a while. What makes you think that we are?"

"Because you're kissing Sebastian goodbye," she said innocently.

"Your mom wasn't kissing me goodbye, Carrie. She was just thanking me," Sebastian told the little girl without hesitating.

Brianna looked at him, amazed at how easily the excuse had flowed from his tongue. Did lying come easily to him these days, or was he just trying to cover for her and set the little girl's mind at ease?

She wasn't sure which it was and it just reminded her that, for the most part, the man standing before her was really a stranger. He'd had the past ten years to become one.

Carrie gazed up at him, clearly confused. Rubbing the sleep from her eyes, she stretched a little, then asked him, "What was Mama thanking you for?"

This time, there was a short pause. Was he waiting for her to come up with something? Because right now, her mind was a complete blank.

And then she heard Sebastian tell Carrie, "Because I told her that I was going to go get a pizza for dinner tomorrow night. Your mom told me how much you like pizza and I do, too." Sebastian sat down beside Carrie on the sofa.

The little girl beamed. "What kind of pizza?" she asked.

Instead of answering, he asked her a question. "What's your favorite?"

"Pepperoni and sausage," Carrie piped up, wiggling her feet in anticipation of sinking her teeth into a slice.

"No kidding," Sebastian marveled. "That's my favorite, too."

His words earned him another wide, all-inclusive grin from the four-year-old.

Brianna knew for a fact that his favorite toppings consisted of four different cheeses and no meat.

Nice save, she mouthed over her daughter's head, impressed with his quick thinking.

She also appreciated his being so thoughtful of Carrie. The little girl had really taken to him. Carrie had been just an infant when her father had died and Brianna always regretted the fact that Carrie was going to grow up with no memory of either of her biological parents. For a short duration, Carrie would see what it was like having a father figure in her life.

Turning toward Carrie, Brianna announced, "It's time to get you to bed, pumpkin."

Carrie appeared crestfallen. "Do I have to go to bed right now, Mama? Can't I stay up for a few more minutes?"

It was hard not giving in to the child. Every day, Brianna had to fight her own inclination to spoil her and let her have her own way. Enforcing a few rules was for her daughter's own good.

"It's already past your bedtime, Carrie," she said as sternly as possible.

"I was asleep before my bedtime, so can I have that time back now?" Carrie asked without even missing a beat.

Sebastian could only stare at her, blown away by her reasoning process. He shook his head as if to clear his own brain.

"I'd start saving up for her college tuition *now* if I were you. This kid has the makings of a really *great* legal mind," he predicted.

Brianna laughed as she gathered Carrie up into her arms. Like a little monkey, Carrie scrambled over to one side, resting against her hip bone. Holding her with one arm, Brianna stroked Carrie's hair with her free hand. "Carrie just likes to argue."

The remark made Sebastian smile. "Like I said, a great legal mind."

"Can Sebastian tuck me in?" Carrie asked suddenly.

Her daughter was just trying to stall, Brianna thought.

"Carrie, you can't just assume someone is at your beck and call just because you want him to be," she pointed out, looking for a way to keep Carrie's feelings from being hurt while extricating Sebastian from what seemed like an awkward situation.

But the one thing Brianna already knew was that you couldn't extricate someone if they really didn't want to be extricated.

And Sebastian obviously didn't.

"I'd love to tuck you in," Sebastian said.

Carrie beamed triumphantly. Her small, sweetheart chin rose up just a tad as she bragged, "See, Mama, Sebastian said he'd love to. That means he's okay with tucking me in."

Sebastian's warm chocolate eyes shifted over to look at Brianna. "I'm sorry. Did I just wind up undoing years of discipline?"

From the dreamy expression in Carrie's eyes, Brianna could only deduce that her daughter had just developed her very first crush. She could only shake her head in response to his question.

"Something like that." She laughed, dismissing the apology. "Don't worry about it. The bottom line is the same as it's always been—that she's happy."

"I think that's safe to assume at the moment," he replied, looking at Carrie.

Because the little girl opened up her arms to him, Sebastian stepped forward to take her from Brianna. "If it's okay with you," he prefaced.

"Sure, be my guest," Brianna told him. "You want to carry her up the stairs, go right ahead."

"She weighs less than a feather," Sebastian said as he took Carrie from her.

"I weigh more than a feather," Carrie protested. "More than a *sack* of feathers," she insisted.

"A *small* sack of feathers," he allowed, easily carrying her up the stairs. "Are you happy, Carrie?" he asked, deliberately keeping a serious expression on his face as he asked.

"Uh-huh," she answered immediately, tightening her small arms around his neck.

He hadn't expected to feel something tugging on his heart just now, hadn't expected to experience a strange, bittersweet feeling in response to the exceedingly simple, uncalculated action. He was beginning to understand what the expression "wrapped around her little finger" was all about. He was wrapped around Carrie's—and he didn't even mind.

"Your bottom line's been met," he told Brianna. "Carrie says she's happy."

"Yes," Brianna acknowledged, "I heard."

Entering the room Carrie shared with her mother, he placed her on the queen-size bed.

"Now tuck me in," Carrie told him, patiently waiting for him to comply.

"Like this?" he asked, taking the edge of the blanket and bringing it to cover her up to her chin.

Carrie wiggled up higher in her bed, moving so that the blanket was a little farther down. "Very good," she pronounced as if she were a teacher and he the student.

"Okay, then, good night," he said to her, beginning to back away.

"What about my story?" she asked, stopping him in his tracks.

"What story?" he wanted to know.

"You're supposed to read me a bedtime story," she informed him. Then, in case he didn't know that she could read, Carrie told him, "I can read it myself, but I fall asleep faster if someone else reads it to me."

This was getting out of hand, Brianna thought, stepping forward. Carrie was stalling. The little girl obviously had a crush. While she could totally understand why Carrie felt that way, she didn't want Sebastian to feel obligated to sit by her bedside and read to her. That went way above and beyond the call of duty.

"I'd run while running is still an option if I were you," she advised. "I'll read to Carrie."

But rather than thank her for coming to his rescue, Sebastian pretended as if he hadn't heard her. Instead, he said to Carrie, "I'd love to read to you. What story would you like to hear?"

Carrie didn't need to hear any more. Scrambling out of bed, she made a beeline for the shelves where her books were housed. After selecting one conveniently located on the bottom shelf, Carrie handed the eight-by-eleven illustrated storybook to Sebastian, then dashed back into bed.

Pulling the covers up to her chin, she happily declared, "Ready!"

Sebastian could feel Brianna looking at him. He wasn't sure if she was waiting for him to begin reading—or to bolt. He wasn't about to do the latter. For reasons he didn't fully comprehend, the idea of reading a bedtime story to an eager audience of one pleased him.

Settling into a chair, he opened the book, then glanced in Brianna's direction.

"Why don't you kick back a little?" he suggested.

There was no reason for her to hang around. He certainly knew how to read a story to a child. "You've more than earned it."

Kick back. Easy for him to say, Brianna thought. She felt so tense right now. The worst part was that she could hardly think straight. But there was no sense in arguing with him about this.

She paused by the doorway. "You're sure you're okay with this?" she asked.

"Very sure," he assured her, then waved her out. "Go. Eat something decadent. Watch something on TV. Read that book you haven't had a chance to crack open. Go," he repeated, motioning her away just before he opened up the book that Carrie had given him. Leaning back in the chair, he began to read.

Brianna forced herself to cross the threshold and walk out of the room. Sebastian was fully capable of tackling the story about the goings-on of one of Carrie's favorite cast of characters. There were seven "Bear" books in the small library that Carrie had amassed. To the best of her recollection, her daughter had selected one from the middle of the pile.

Well, he asked for it, Brianna thought as she made her way down the stairs. She had no idea what to do with the free time she'd been awarded. Every minute of her day had been booked for so long, she was at a loss how to spend unscheduled time.

When in doubt, fall back on your routine, she counseled herself.

So she went to check on Sebastian's mother and

found that the older woman had dozed off watching TV in her room. Brianna's first impulse was to turn off the set, draw the covers over the sleeping woman and shut the light just as she tiptoed out of the room.

But she knew from experience that those simple actions might actually wake up the woman. With that in mind, Brianna lowered the volume on the TV and dimmed the lights only slightly.

She made her way into the kitchen next. She washed the dishes by hand and then tidied up. Finished, she looked around for a moment, regarding the fruits of her labor.

It was at that point that she decided that she'd had enough of "free time." She went back upstairs to check on Carrie and Sebastian in her room.

If nothing else, Brianna was fairly confident that Sebastian was just about ready to be rescued. Granted, he'd volunteered, but that was before he had a clue what he was getting himself into. Carrie was not a child who merely listened docilely.

If a word was skipped, she knew it and asked to have the passage reread. If it was a new story—which this wasn't—there were questions to ask, motivations to explore. Like the inquiring mind that she was, Carrie wanted to understand what she was listening to, no matter how long it took to explain everything.

Brianna quietly approached the room, then very slowly eased open the door that she'd deliberately left ajar. She heard Sebastian's voice, strong and animated, still reading the story to her daughter.

What she *didn't* hear was Carrie questioning anything or offering her comments to Sebastian about the story in general.

That was because, she now saw, the little girl had apparently fallen asleep.

Well, *that* had certainly happened in record time, she silently marveled, easing the door open the rest of the way.

Catching the movement of the door out of the corner of his eye, Sebastian stopped reading and looked up. Seeing Brianna in the doorway, he smiled and mouthed, "Hi."

Then, glancing at Carrie one more time to assure himself that she was really asleep, Sebastian quietly closed the storybook, set it aside on the nightstand and eased himself out of the chair.

Sebastian said nothing as he left the room, afraid that the slightest sound might wake the little girl. But once the door was closed and he'd moved a few feet down the hall, away from the room, he looked at Brianna and smiled.

It was the same kind of slightly crooked smile that had initially captured her heart all those years ago in math class.

"Mission accomplished," he told her with a smart salute. "She's sound asleep."

"I'd give it a little while longer before I said that," Brianna advised. "Carrie has a way of suddenly popping up like toast even if you think she's out like the proverbial light. By the way, your mother is asleep, too."

"That sounds good. The more rest she gets, the faster she'll recover," he reasoned. "Well, I've got nothing planned for the rest of the evening," he told her. "How about you?"

"I've washed the dishes and tidied up, so, no, I don't have anything else planned."

"You *plan* washing dishes?" he asked.

"I don't like going to bed unless everything's cleaned up."

"So you're going to bed?" he asked.

"Eventually," she allowed. "Why? What do you have in mind?"

He thought it best not to share that right now. Instead, he asked, "How about a movie?"

"As long as we can watch it here," she qualified.

"Definitely," he answered. "I'll make the popcorn. You pick the movie," he told her.

Suddenly, she wasn't tired anymore. And the tension she'd been harboring decreased by at least several notches. For now.

"You're on," she told him.

Chapter Thirteen

Brianna realized that she'd been holding her breath through at least half the movie that she'd selected for them to watch. It was an action thriller, but her lack of oxygen intake had nothing to do with the excitement on the screen and everything to do with the untapped excitement sitting fewer than two feet away from her on the sofa.

She kept thinking that Sebastian was just biding his time, waiting to make his move when she was least prepared for it. After all, there'd been blatant signals that he was leaning that way earlier. There'd been definite indications that if Carrie went on sleeping after she had been safely carried off to bed, Brianna and Sebastian would find themselves in his room.

In his bed.

Just the way they had that night when his mother had gone out of town to take care of his sick great-aunt. The night of the prom.

Brianna had to admit that, despite the fact that she had picked the movie, she was only half paying attention to it. But when the credits rolled, the closest she and Sebastian had come to even casually touching one another was when they had both reached for the popcorn at the same time, and she decided that maybe it was time to stop holding her breath.

It was obvious that the long, toe-curling kiss they'd shared earlier was *not* a preview of things to come. Instead, it just happened and was destined to stand apart from anything else that might go on between them.

You're supposed to be relieved, Bree. You don't want to lose your heart to him all over again, remember? This time, you know *there's no future for the two of you. He'll be leaving for Japan again and you'll be staying here, with your child and your father and that career you've hammered out for yourself.*

And then, like an annoying mantra, the voice in her head added, *It never goes well for you when your heart's involved. You know that.*

Brianna blinked. The TV screen in front of them had gone blank. She could feel Sebastian silently looking at her.

"What?" she asked, afraid he'd said something and she'd been so engrossed in her own thoughts that she'd missed it.

"You didn't like the movie." It wasn't a question, but

a verdict, delivered with obvious disappointment. "We could have watched something else."

"No, I liked the movie," Brianna protested, contradicting him.

"You didn't say anything," he pointed out. "Generally, when you watch something, you do a running commentary." At least, she used to, he silently amended.

Brianna laughed quietly. "Not anymore. Carrie doesn't like me to talk while she's watching something, and since she's become my 'viewing buddy,' I've learned to hold my tongue."

"So I have her to thank?" He grinned. "The girl's definitely a genius. I never thought *anything* could get you to hold your tongue and keep from expressing your opinion," he marveled with more fondness than he'd intended.

"I don't know whether to laugh or be insulted," she quipped.

"It wasn't meant to be insulting," he told her. "If anything, it was meant as an affectionate observation." Picking up the remote control, he aimed it toward the set and shut off the TV, then turned so that he was facing her. He found himself hungry for the sound of her voice, to just talk the way they used to. "You've done a terrific job with her. How long have you been raising her?"

"Almost from the beginning. She was thirteen months old when J.T. was killed. I'm the only parent she's ever known." Which struck her as ironic, since she really wasn't Carrie's parent at all, at least not biologically.

"Her mother died in childbirth," she said, aware that she'd already told him that earlier.

"Childbirth?" When she'd initially told him, he hadn't really paid all that much attention to the information, but now he did and he had to admit the thought surprised him. "I didn't think that sort of thing happened anymore."

Unfortunately, the circumstances were against Carrie's mother. "It does if the mother starts hemorrhaging and there's no doctor around."

"No doctor?" he echoed. "What kind of a hospital was she in?"

Brianna laughed shortly, shaking her head. "That was just the problem—she wasn't. Carrie's mother didn't like doctors. Instead, she had a midwife in attendance. Most of the time, that's great and midwives are pretty sharp. But, by some fluke, this one was out of her depth, especially since there were complications right from the beginning."

She could see the whole scenario unfolding in her mind's eye. J.T.'s frantic call to her for help. By the time she'd arrived, the paramedics were already there—and unable to help. The young woman was already dead. She'd stayed the night, taking care of the newborn while trying to keep J.T. calm. He'd been there to help her through her father's blackest days, and she thought it only fair to try to return the favor.

"J.T. blamed himself for her death because he hadn't insisted on a doctor. If his wife had been in a hospital, she might still be alive today. And so would he," she added.

Sebastian wasn't following her logic. "How do you figure the last part?" he asked. "You said he died in a boating accident."

She sighed heavily. She should have been able to get J.T. through his emotional turmoil, but she'd failed. And that would always be on her. "It's way too easy to have an accident if you're driving a craft under the influence."

"He was drinking?"

Brianna raised one shoulder in a vague shrug. "For the most part, he'd stopped. That was part of the conditions of our engagement," she admitted, "that he get his drinking under control. But J.T. couldn't quite put his demons to rest and that weekend was his late wife's birthday. He used to say that he drank to numb the pain and the emptiness."

Her mouth curved in an ironic smile. "The evening we got engaged, he told me that *I* helped numb his pain and fill the emptiness. I guess I just wasn't strong enough for the job that Saturday when he set sail. It was the last time I saw him alive." Brianna looked down at her ring finger on her left hand. It was empty now. She'd switched the engagement ring J.T. had given her to her right hand, a constant reminder of the promise that wasn't fulfilled. "We'd been engaged all of three weeks when he died."

Sebastian was trying to pull the pieces together in an attempt to focus his mind on something other than the fact that he wanted to hold her and make her smile again. A *real* smile this time.

"I thought you said the boating accident occurred a week before the wedding."

"It did," she said. "J.T. was in a hurry to get married. I think he was hoping that I'd make his nightmares go away. Guess I didn't do such a hot job," she concluded quietly.

"Don't you dump this on yourself," Sebastian chided her. He knew she had that tendency. For some reason, she felt it was her job to save the world. For as long as he'd known her, she'd always gravitated toward animals and people who needed saving.

He supposed that, in a way, he fell into that group himself.

"You weren't his keeper," he insisted.

"No," she agreed halfheartedly, "but I was his friend as well as his fiancée. I should have realized that weekend was going to be extra-difficult for him to get through. I should have been there for him instead of opting to keep the store running while he went out."

She shook her head at her own naïveté. "I honestly thought getting away with his friends was going to be good for J.T. You know, a bunch of guys blowing off steam, telling fish stories, things like that." And then she added more softly, "I had a gut feeling, but I didn't pay any attention to it. I thought that if I said anything to him at the last minute about not going, it would have sounded too controlling. So I opted to help Dad in the store and take care of Carrie while he had fun.

"Except that he didn't have fun," she said more to herself than to Sebastian. "The medical examiner said he had twice the legal limit of alcohol in his blood when he died."

"And his friends?" he prodded, wondering why one of them hadn't taken over when they saw that J.T. was in no shape to pilot the craft.

There'd been no help in that quarter, she thought. "According to the M.E., they had all been drinking. The coast guard managed to recover all the bodies," she said, almost as if she was reading an account of the accident out loud.

"No survivors?" Sebastian asked sympathetically.

Brianna shook her head, momentarily unable to answer him. Tears had filled her throat, all but swelling it shut.

Seeing her expression, Sebastian wordlessly slipped his arm around her shoulders and drew her closer to him. His only intent was to offer her some sort of comfort if he could.

"God, but you've had a rough time of it," he told her. A lesser person would have probably crumbled by now, undone by the sheer weight of all the events she'd had to deal with.

Brianna drew in a breath slowly, pulled herself together and then shrugged carelessly in response to his comment.

"People have had it a lot rougher," she told him, refusing to allow herself to slip into a self-pitying mode. She'd been there several times in her life and found that if she gave in to it long enough, it sucked her spirit out of her, leaving her utterly dry. She knew that that would completely destroy her.

So instead, she forced herself to rise above it, to rally as best she could. She'd always been an upbeat person in the long run, and she knew that a positive attitude was the only thing that could see her through the dark times.

"Besides, I've had a lot of good things happen to me, too. My dad survived his accident and he's absolutely fully recovered—"

"Thanks to you," Sebastian pointed out.

She refused to take credit for that. "I couldn't have gotten him to do anything he really didn't want to do." She summarized her part in all this in a few modest words. "I just figured out which of his buttons to press, that's all."

"That wasn't the way I heard the story," Sebastian informed her.

She looked at him, curious. "From who?"

"My mother. She made a point of keeping tabs on you and your father, and then sent me lengthy reports about what was going on."

She had always gotten along with his mother, but when her father was involved in that accident, she'd turned all her attention to making him get well. She'd stopped interacting with anyone else on a regular basis for literally *months*.

"Did you ask her to?" she asked.

He looked at her for a long moment. "I really want to say yes here, but I won't lie to you. She did that all on her own. I think at the time she was still hoping that you and I would…well, you know," he said, not wanting to put either one of them on the spot, or make them uncomfortable by saying the last part out loud.

A sad, resigned smile curved the corners of her mouth. "Yes, I know."

She also knew that if she continued sitting here talking to him about the past, she would wind up giving in to the strong feelings stirring within her, emotions that still belonged to Sebastian alone. It would be a great deal more prudent, not to mention wiser, for her to take her leave now—while she still could.

She began to get up as she made the obligatory excuses. "Well, it's late and I told your mother I wanted to start her on a very light exercise regimen tomorrow, so I'd better be heading up to bed."

Her little speech delivered, she expected to go. But as she turned to leave, Sebastian caught her wrist in his hand.

When she looked at him quizzically, he said, "I'm sorry, Bree."

His words hit her right smack in her chest. She pretended to ignore the sensation vibrating through her. It would only act against her.

"We've already been through this, Sebastian," she told him quietly. "And I said that you've got nothing to be sorry for."

"Yes, I do," he contradicted her. "A whole slew of things to be sorry for. Most of all, I'm sorry that I let you go."

As she recalled, *he* was the one who had gone, not her. "You make it sound as if I was a pet deer you had tethered in a cage and decided to release one morning." His wording left a little something to be desired. "You know, for an English professor, you don't exactly have a way with words sometimes."

Rather than take exception, Sebastian inclined his head, conceding the point. "That's because those are the times when I'm emotionally invested and afraid of saying the wrong thing."

She would have been willing to bet anything that he was anything *but* emotionally invested right now.

"Okay," she allowed, stretching out the word as she tried to understand exactly what he *thought* he was telling her. "In any case, I forgive you."

But as she tried to get up for a second time, she found that Sebastian was still holding on to her wrist. Resigned, she sank back down onto the sofa. "Anything else?"

"As a matter of fact, yes," he answered.

"All right, what?" she asked when he didn't immediately follow up his words with anything further and the moments began to tick away.

"This." He said it so quietly, there was a part of her that thought that maybe they were communicating by telepathy rather than with words. Supposedly, some people in love could do that.

Except that they *weren't* people in love.

Brianna caught her breath as his hand lightly skimmed along her throat. The caress branded her skin.

He tilted her head just a fraction and then, in the next moment, his lips brushed against hers so incredibly softly she was sure she was just imagining it. That she had all but willed it with her mind.

But she hadn't.

And the next moment, the first kiss was followed by another.

And another.

Each flowering kiss was a little more forceful, a little lengthier than the last.

By the fourth kiss, rockets went off in her head and a hunger was suddenly unleashed within her, a hunger that she had never experienced before, even when she'd been on the brink of making love with him that very first time.

The hunger was coupled with fear—fear that he would pull back.

And then he did and she felt a desperation taking hold, interweaving itself with a sense of bereavement.

"You'd better go upstairs," he told her hoarsely. When she merely looked at him as if she didn't understand what he was saying, he repeated the sentence, saying the words more forcefully. "Go. I don't know how much longer I can hold back."

"Maybe I don't want you to hold back," she told him, remaining exactly where she was, her lips hardly moving. The only part moving was her heart, which had gone back to pounding wildly, the way it had initially.

"You don't know what you're saying, Bree."

Her eyes held his as she remembered their past and

remembered, too, what she had once thought would be their future.

"I know *exactly* what I'm saying," she told him, her voice just a hint above a whisper. "Don't worry," she added, never taking her eyes off his. "No strings, no requests for promises. All I want is tonight. Just now," she told him, her breath warm on his lips as she spoke.

Seducing him.

Taking the last of his willpower and breaking it into tiny bits.

"Oh, damn, Bree," he lamented, "you're making it hard to walk away."

"Then don't," she suggested softly. "Don't."

He could feel the last of his resolve being blown to pieces as he pulled her back into his arms. As he kissed her with all the pent-up emotion he had. But now it was out, exploding right before him and ensnaring him just as much as it ensnared her.

It was as if, after years of separation, he'd been allowed to glimpse his soul again.

The intense desire to reunite, to become one, to become whole again, was just too overwhelming to resist.

So he didn't.

Chapter Fourteen

"Wait."

The hoarsely voiced entreaty came from Brianna.

She'd summoned the last of her all but shredded resolve in an attempt to momentarily pause the wild rush that had seized not only her, but she suspected him as well. She needed him to listen to her, provided she could still string a few words together.

Sebastian felt more than heard her asking him to hold off. His pulse hammering against his rib cage, he forced himself to pull back.

It was far from easy, but he wasn't some sort of rutting pig. "You changed your mind."

It wasn't a question but, to him, an agonized statement of fact. At the last minute, her senses had obviously returned to her. The realization created an ache deep in the pit of his stomach.

Paradise lost before it was gained, he thought with a heavy heart, resigned to his fate.

Brianna took his words to be a question and answered him with breathless feeling. "Oh, hell no. I haven't changed my mind, and don't you dare change yours."

He looked at her, confused. "Then why—?"

Brianna didn't expect him to think along the same lines that she did. After all, he hadn't had to constantly place the needs of a little girl above his own for the past three years. She'd been doing it ever since she'd become first Carrie's legal guardian and then her adoptive parent. It was second nature to her.

Even so, it was a struggle to think clearly. All she wanted was to make love with Sebastian. To feel his hands along her body, to finally, *finally* become one with him again.

Her mouth dry, she managed to push out the words and actually sound as if she was making some sort of sense.

"We need to go to your room to do this," she told him. "If either Carrie or your mother comes out of their bedrooms for any reason—"

She didn't need to finish. He understood.

"Right, right," he agreed wholeheartedly, already on his feet. Holding her hand, he drew her up with him as well. Ready to all but sprint up the stairs, Sebastian still paused for a moment. He threaded his fingers through her hair so that he could turn her face up to his. And then he kissed her. Soundly.

Dazed, her head spinning, she looked at Sebastian the moment he drew his lips away from hers.

"What was that for?" she asked breathlessly.

"For not saying no," he told her. The next second, he laced his fingers through hers and was drawing her over to the stairs.

Brianna smiled to herself. How could she say no to him when everything inside her was screaming yes?

The door to Sebastian's bedroom closed.

Finally.

More than ever, she was anxious for his touch, for the feel of his firm, capable hands moving along her skin. Caressing her.

Making love with her.

Clothes flew off their bodies in a flurry of material, falling to the rug, comingling with little to no notice paid to what had fallen where. Clothes didn't matter.

Only *this* mattered.

How had he let this happen? This separation that had kept them apart for so long, that had scissored through their happiness, leaving only rubble and ruin?

The question hammered away at his brain. How could he have allowed hurt feelings to drive a wedge between the two of them?

He needed to know because he'd turned his back on this. He had to have been crazy, he concluded. Crazy to leave her, crazy to maintain distance between them.

Crazy not to attempt to get back in contact with her for all those years.

Years he wasn't going to get back.

Years, despite this frenzy-driven interlude, that he might not be able to trade for something positive on the other side of this night.

Sebastian was no longer a dreamer. He'd long since become grounded in reality and that reality wouldn't allow him to be foolish enough to believe in a different life. He and Brianna had let too much time pass, had too much happen to each of them individually to just murmur, "Never mind," and pick up where they had left off ten years ago.

He knew all this to be true, that it all mattered—but not at this moment.

Now he just needed to immerse himself in her, to absorb her, to drink her in as if she were a tall, frosty glass of water and he had just spent ten years crawling through the desert. He only wanted to feel, think and exist in the moment with her.

And nothing else mattered.

It was a madness in the blood and he knew it, but he didn't care.

As he once again sought her mouth—the very reason for his existence on this earth at this moment—they were suddenly tumbling onto his king-size bed, their limbs tangling, their body parts instantly heating at even the barest hint of contact.

There wasn't a single microinch of his body that didn't throb from wanting her.

Sebastian tried to be as gentle as he could, restraining his all but overwhelming sense of urgency, as he ran his hands all over her body.

Unable to satisfy himself.

Unable to get enough of her.

The quest for more seemed as if it were never ending. And that was the way he wanted it.

Because he didn't want this to end.

His mouth followed the path forged by his hands and he gloried in the fact that Brianna twisted and turned beneath him, arching to absorb every sensation, every delicate nuance.

Brianna felt as if she were running in some endless marathon, unable to catch her breath.

At the same time she was struggling very hard not to emit a cry that would pierce the stillness of the night and quite possibly garner them an unwanted audience of two.

At the very least, it could wake up either his mother or her daughter—if not both—and cause questions to be born full-grown and viable in the wake of the noise.

Brianna was well aware of the danger of crying out, knew that it could very possibly terminate this wild, adrenaline-fueled ride she found herself on. But it was *so* hard to contain the sound of pure, raw, guttural pleasure broken down to its basic components that was throbbing in her throat, begging for release.

She wasn't sure just how much longer she could control herself.

And then it came to her, the only way she knew of to keep from all but shrieking out her enjoyment.

Throwing Sebastian off balance, she deftly switched positions so that suddenly, *she* was the one on top, *she* was the one with the upper hand.

Straddling him now that he was under her, she began to weave a tapestry of soft, openmouthed kisses along his upper torso.

She artfully applied her tongue as well and slowly worked her way down, past his chest, past his waist. Past his navel.

She paused in her impromptu, erotic trail blazing long enough to lightly blow a small cloud of warm air along the lower region of his body.

Just as she'd hoped, she was instantly rewarded with visual evidence that Sebastian was indeed responding to this exquisite torture.

When she heard a strangled groan escape his lips, she knew he was all but at the breaking point.

As was she.

With a triumphant laugh, she hovered a moment longer, seductively teasing him with her tongue just along his hipline. Her heart racing, she slid her way up along the length of his body until their faces were on the same level again.

As she reached down to caress him, he caught her wrist in his hand, holding her still.

"Where did you learn to torture a man this way?" he asked in a barely audible whisper.

"I didn't 'learn' it anywhere," she answered innocently. "It's just creative instinct."

The next moment, raising his head, Sebastian seized her mouth, covering it with his own, and then, as he tasted her surrender, his arms surrounding her, he flipped their positions, reversing them so that once again she found herself under him.

Under him and utterly compliant.

He drew his head back for a second, looked into her eyes and knew—knew she was ready. Knew she was his for the taking.

Which was good, because he didn't think he could hold himself in check even a split second longer.

He took Brianna's mouth again, his pulse racing with each kiss. Echoes of the past tightly surrounded him as he parted her legs with his knee and then drove himself into her as if his very life depended on this union.

Because right now, it did.

They'd been here, just like this, once before. And yet…

And yet it felt all brand-new.

This joining enticed him like a temptress who had been waiting all eternity for this moment.

A wild frenzy rose up in his veins, a frenzy born in the wake of Brianna's frantic movements beneath him.

Born in the barely contained, barely muffled cries of absolute pleasure he tasted as her mouth continued to be sealed to his.

The frenzy continued to grow, feeding on the way her hips were pressed to his, even as they were arching, bucking, moving only slightly less quickly than the wings of a hummingbird hovering in a single position.

He felt her fingers digging into his shoulders, felt her nails scraping against his flesh.

The sharp pain was muted, its edge all but completely blotted out in the wake of the explosions going on inside him.

They reached the very tip of the known universe and then, after hovering there for what seemed like an endless moment, they went into a free fall, their hands, bodies and souls joined.

Sebastian felt that at any second, his heart would crack through his rib cage and make a break for freedom, still pounding insanely.

Instinctively, his arms tightened around Brianna's damp body. At first protectively, and then in fear. Fear that as the moment grew further and further away, so would she.

More exhausted than he'd ever thought humanly possible, Sebastian still managed to turn his head and press a kiss to what he hoped was the top of her forehead.

But he couldn't swear to the accuracy of his delivery, only to the fact that Brianna had stolen not only his breath—and possibly his stamina—but his heart as well.

How can she steal what she already had? his brain taunted him.

In a moment of complete clarity, Sebastian suddenly realized why he'd never been in another relationship after they'd parted company. Because, together or apart, Brianna still retained possession of his heart.

And what good did that do him? he silently demanded. He hadn't had any contact with her after he'd left for college. No contact whatsoever. Instead, he'd allowed his ego, his baseless pride, to dictate his course of action—or lack thereof—and doom him to an existence filled with professional accomplishment yet devoid of any sort of emotional connections.

For all the people that were always around him in Tokyo, he was soul-wrenchingly alone.

"So," he heard her say, invading his thought process, "same time, same place, ten years from now?"

He turned his head to look at her, certain he hadn't heard her correctly. "What?"

"Same time, same place, ten years from now?" she repeated. When the confused expression on his face didn't recede, she patiently pointed out, "We made love here, in your bed like this, the night of the prom."

She didn't have to add what she was leaving unsaid: that they'd made love for the very first time just before the hospital had called on her cell phone to tell her that her father had been involved in a near-fatal accident and that they weren't entirely sure if he would make it through the night.

"Did we?" He asked in such an innocent voice, it was her turn to stare at him.

"You don't remember?" she asked him, trying not to sound as stunned as she felt.

And then he smiled at her, that soft, bone-melting

smile that always got to her. "I don't remember anything that happened before we came up to this room and then went on to systematically destroy the world as we once knew it."

"Oh, you're kidding," she realized, feeling a wave of absolutely stunning relief.

For a second, she'd believed his performance and had actually thought that Sebastian didn't remember their first time the way she did. For her, that first interlude between them was forever embossed on her brain as well as her heart. That it was, in some measure, embossed on his as well meant a great deal to her.

"No," he told her in utter seriousness, "I'm not kidding." He cupped her cheek just before he kissed her softly on the lips. "It *does* feel as if we just forged our own brand-new world."

She smiled up at him, then rested her head on his shoulder as she curled her body up against his.

"That was very poetic," she said with a contented sigh.

She allowed herself just a few more minutes to savor this dreamlike state. All too soon, the peace she was experiencing would break up like the bubbles hovering above a bubble bath. She knew that this contentment's life expectancy was incredibly short. Almost over before it began. That didn't seem very fair.

"Where do we go from here?"

The question suddenly escaped his lips, even though he'd already thought that through logically and knew there was no final satisfactory destination for them.

She raised her head and looked at him. "Do we have to decide that right now?" she asked, lightly grazing his lips with her own.

There it was again, that instant response that only she could arouse from him.

He closed his arms around her, holding her close, taking comfort from the feel of her heart beating against his.

"No, we don't have to decide anything at the moment," he told her.

"Since we're not going to talk, what would you like to do in the interim?" she asked teasingly. They both knew the answer to that question.

He laughed softly, thinking how right all this felt, just as he'd thought the very same thing ten years ago. He'd been right then, as he was right now.

But maybe this time there would be a different outcome.

At least he could hope.

"Guess," he suggested.

"What do I get if I guess right?" she asked, her eyes dancing with barely suppressed mischief.

"Me," he told her.

Her grin was wide as she slid her body up against his again. "Works for me," she whispered.

Chapter Fifteen

And I'm back, Brianna thought with a suppressed sigh as she moved around the kitchen the following morning, doing her best to focus. *Back to the present. Back to reality.*

Last night, she'd gone all the way back to her last days as a high school senior, but now, perforce, she was back. Back to being the diligent nurse, the responsible single parent. Back to being the woman who did her best to be all things to everyone and slept a minimum of hours.

Last night had been about the path not taken, the one she found herself yearning for on those rare occasions when she had more than two minutes to rub together.

Staring into the refrigerator, trying to remember what it was she was looking for, Brianna wished she hadn't gone there, that she had remained firmly entrenched in the present.

As wonderful as last night was, as much as she enjoyed reliving the past, she knew the here and now would be that much more difficult to bear. Because, as full as her life was with her daughter, her father, her work, she had to admit that deep down she was lonely. Not all the time, of course—there were times when she was too exhausted to feel anything at all—but she felt that way just often enough to leave her wanting.

Grow up, for heaven's sake, she ordered herself as she took out a carton of eggs and put it on the counter.

She wasn't the wide-eyed innocent anymore, wasn't on the brink of following her dreams. She *knew* all dreams didn't come true.

All?

Heck, *most* dreams didn't come true. That was because most dreams were just that—dreams, she thought, depositing a large frying pan on the front burner. And while retaining those dreams *did* keep a person going, did give a person purpose, she freely admitted, she had embraced reality enough to know that very few ever came true.

The rest didn't have a prayer of coming true.

Ever.

And by the same token, she knew that there was no future for her with Sebastian. He had his life and she had hers. Moreover, those lives weren't separated by a few blocks or a few counties, or even states, but by half a world.

Idealistic as she once had been, Brianna was *not* so starry-eyed—or so delusional, for that matter—to think that Sebastian would give up everything he had just for her.

The adult thing was to behave as if she accepted that. To behave as if she didn't expect *anything* to change just because, for the space of one night, the earth had moved for her.

Again.

Right. Good luck with that.

It bothered him.

Brianna was acting as if nothing was different, as if last night they *hadn't* both glimpsed what could have been their lives had she not remained in Bedford when he had left.

Last night had wiped out ten years of physical estrangement and let him pick up the dropped thread. Last night had allowed him to see how very *good* it all could be.

Last night had been about beginning again. Except that now it felt as if they hadn't begun anything, just briefly revisited a world that they no longer had access to.

Still, he'd thought *because of last night* that things would be different from here on in.

Granted, he hadn't expected Brianna to slant covert looks his way and act like some love-struck puppy, but he'd expected *some* indication that last night had meant as much to her as it had to him.

Instead, what he got was the impression that it was "business as usual" for Brianna.

To begin with, when he woke up she was gone from his bed. He hadn't thought that she'd sleep in—that didn't mesh with the person she was—but he had hoped that when he opened his eyes she would be the first thing he'd see.

Instead, he saw a vacant spot beside him in his bed.

Then he realized that the pillow and comforter were neatly back in place. So neat that it gave no indication that *anyone* had been there. Had alcohol been involved last night, he might have even thought he'd imagined the whole thing, from the very first kiss to the last wildly erotic surge.

Except that he hadn't imagined it. It had been very, very real. And it had, for that stretch of time—and beyond, as she'd slept beside him and he'd lain there with his arm around her, just listening to her breathe—made him begin to entertain the idea that perhaps there were such things as do-overs.

That once in a while, people did get a second chance to get things right.

But if it all had meant so little to her that she could silently slip out of his bed without a moment's lingering, then maybe he needed to rethink his rethinking.

Two minutes after waking up, he was already in the stall, taking a quick shower rather than the lengthy one with her that he'd fallen asleep anticipating. Within five minutes he was dressed and padding down the stairs in bare feet.

He found Brianna in the kitchen, moving around between the stove and the refrigerator as if she was the one who belonged there and he was the interloper.

As if suddenly sensing his presence, she flashed him a smile. The very same smile she'd been flashing him every morning for the past week and a half. There wasn't even the slightest hint that she was holding back something extra, something special that involved only the two of them. There was no indication whatsoever that they had crossed some magic line, or gone on to a higher plateau.

"Hi," Brianna called out brightly to him. Then, nodding at the frying pan, she asked him, "What's your pleasure?"

It was on the tip of Sebastian's tongue to say, "You" in response, but he managed to keep it back, and Carrie being there, seated at the table, was only part of the reason why he'd refrained.

Carrie was an obstacle easily circumvented if he'd wanted to. The reply could have been tendered in a whisper, with him standing close enough to say the word into her ear. But something told him that the answer would have made her feel uncomfortable, so he told her, "Just coffee, thanks," and then went to the cupboard to get a mug for himself.

Every second of silence felt endless to her.

Brianna searched for something to fill the emptiness. She didn't want Sebastian thinking that she was waiting for him to make some sort of comment or reference to the night they'd shared. She didn't want him to feel on the spot and, more than that, she didn't want to become, by saying the wrong word, the object of his pity.

So, after a moment's internal debate, she went with a topic she deemed to be safe, one that would show him that she had absolutely no expectations because of last night, no demands on him whatsoever.

"So, how much longer is your vacation?" she asked cheerfully as she broke two eggs, depositing them in a bowl and then sending them scrambling about said bowl with a whisk.

"That depends on how my mother is doing," Sebastian told her. "If it looks like she's getting stronger and I feel she's getting better, then I guess I can fly back anytime."

He left his answer open-ended, really curious now to see her reaction. The girl he'd once known would want him to remain and would say as much—passionately. If she didn't, that meant he was in the presence of someone with Brianna's face, someone he didn't know at all.

Brianna chose her words carefully, wanting to convey just the right message, one he could hold on to.

"Well, I'm happy to tell you that your mother's doing remarkably well. As a matter of fact, if I didn't know any better, I would have said that there was a mistake in the initial diagnosis."

But she knew who the woman's cardiologist was and the man had an *excellent* reputation. And even though she hadn't asked to view the E.R. report—that was a matter of privacy between doctor and patient—she was well aware that the cardiologist was at the top of his game.

"Your mother doesn't behave like someone living through the aftermath of a stroke. All in all, I'd say that she's an incredibly strong woman."

She smiled, feeling this was the best possible news she could give him. "She is one of the very lucky ones," she added.

"Right," he murmured, interpreting her words in his own way.

He was right. Brianna *was* trying to get rid of him, to get him to go back to Japan. Otherwise, there would have been something else, something more. Some small attempt with perhaps a white lie to get him to remain a bit longer rather than sending him on his way.

He didn't exactly expect her to pitch herself at him bodily, but he knew her. She would have found something to make the prognosis a little more guarded than it was. After all, he'd indicated that if there was still some sort of uncertainty about his mother's condition, he could stay awhile longer. This cheerful report she'd just rendered was all but ushering him out the door. Quickly. Brianna obviously regretted what had happened between them last night.

Hey, what do you expect? a voice in his head taunted him. After all, he wasn't exactly the same inexperienced kid, either. He'd gone on, made a life for himself—of sorts—and obviously, so had she.

Last night could have very well been just a pleasant interlude for her and nothing further. Certainly not enough to make her rethink things and change her life around.

He had to assume that Brianna was happy with her life, with her daughter and with her career, and that having him around threw a crimp into all that.

Maybe she was even afraid that he would want to change things on her, place demands on her that she wasn't prepared to put up with.

No, it was better just to keep going and not look back. He certainly couldn't allow himself to daydream about building a brand-new life for himself and for her on a foundation that was all but eroding right out from beneath his feet even as he tried to take his very first steps.

Eyeing Brianna covertly to see her reaction, he said, "Well, if she's doing that well, then I guess I'm free to fly back to Tokyo."

"I guess so," she said.

Her smile was rigidly in place and she congratulated herself on not losing a beat despite the very real, very painful ache that she felt was eating up her gut from the inside out.

Brianna was well aware that it wasn't exactly ethical to use his mother as an excuse to stay. She couldn't lie to him about her condition. But wasn't all fair in love and war?

This wasn't war, she reminded herself and then quietly acknowledged that it really wasn't exactly love, either.

At least, not for him. He'd leave the first chance he got.

For her it was a whole different story but it was *not*

a story that she was about to share with Sebastian—or with anyone.

It was *her* story to bear, *her* problem to deal with and resolve. And maybe, if she didn't involve anyone else in it, she might bring about a good conclusion.

Or so she hoped.

"Well, if you're going to be shoving off soon, maybe you'd better spend a little more time with your mother," she suggested brightly, still doing her best to maintain a cheerful countenance. "Otherwise, she's going to feel neglected—and we want her as upbeat as possible, even though, quite honestly, just the thought of you leaving will probably take its toll on her." *As well as on me,* she added silently.

"Right," Sebastian agreed mechanically.

About to leave the room, he turned around to the counter and retrieved the steaming mug of coffee he'd just poured for himself. Without thinking, he paused to take a sip of the hot, inky liquid. As it wound a warm, bracing path through his esophagus, down to his stomach, he looked in Brianna's direction.

"Good coffee," he murmured.

"Thanks. I thought you might like it." She addressed the words to his departing back.

His coffee preference was, even after all this time, one of the things she remembered about him—one of the *many* things she remembered about him, she silently amended. Sebastian took his coffee strong, hot and as black as potting soil—the exact opposite of the way she took hers. She liked her coffee exceedingly pale, with sugar and enough cream to make the cup pass for chocolate milk—light chocolate milk.

Out of the corner of her eye, as she watched Sebastian leave the room—doing her best to prepare for the moment when he would be leaving her life again—she became aware that Carrie had wiggled down off her seat and was now pushing the step stool up against the counter.

The next second, the little girl scrambled up the three steps that allowed her to touch a few things on the counter.

In this case, it was a loaf of bread that had her attention.

"What are you up to?" Brianna asked her daughter, forcing herself to focus on something other than Sebastian and his inevitable departure.

"I'm gonna make some toast," Carrie declared matter-of-factly.

While she was all for encouraging independence in children no matter how young, this was different. She was in no mood to deal with the myriad of difficulties that could come out of the seemingly simple undertaking of making toast.

"That's okay—I've got it," Brianna said.

"No, you don't," Carrie contradicted her, surprising her.

Brianna looked at the little girl quizzically. "Why would you say that?"

"Because you're busy staring at Sebastian." It wasn't an accusation, but a statement of fact.

"No, I'm not," she protested with just enough feeling to sound sincere rather than confused, which she still was regarding Carrie's behavior.

"Yes, you are," Carrie insisted. "You're watching him walk out. Why? Are you afraid he's going to fall down and hurt himself?" She asked the only thing that seemed to make logical sense to her.

"No," Brianna told her patiently.

But I'm afraid that I am. Or have already. I'm afraid that I've fallen in love with him all over again—harder this time—and I shouldn't have.

"Then why are you watching him leave the room, Mama?" Carrie asked.

"I wasn't watching him leave the room," Brianna lied. "I was just thinking."

"About what?" Carrie asked.

"About what to give a little girl who asks so many questions for breakfast," she told her, pointedly looking at her daughter.

"Scrambled eggs, toast and bacon," her daughter recited.

Because she asked for the same thing *every* morning, Brianna's voice blended in with Carrie's, reinforcing the choice.

Carrie broke down in giggles.

And that, Brianna hoped, was the end of the little girl's interrogations.

At least for now.

Chapter Sixteen

Sebastian was upstairs packing.

Which meant that he would be leaving soon, Brianna thought with a heavy heart. Maybe even by tomorrow. She hadn't been able to get herself to ask exactly when. All she knew was that it meant that she'd been right about the other night. It had just happened. It meant nothing to him.

She meant nothing to him.

Despite the fact that she'd told herself that all along, her heart hurt.

When the doorbell rang, she was tempted just to ignore it, but whoever was on the other side of the door might be coming to see Mrs. Hunter. If she let them continue ringing the doorbell, it might make her come down the stairs to answer it herself. Although she was pretty certain that Mrs. Hunter was feeling far better than she pretended, she still didn't want the woman exerting herself.

Still she hurried to answer before the doorbell rang a third time. She did *not* expect to see her father standing on the doorstep. "Dad, what are you doing here?"

Jim MacKenzie looked around as he walked in. "I thought I'd take Carrie home with me for the night," he told her. Still not seeing the little girl, he looked at Brianna and asked, "Where is she?"

Brianna nodded toward the stairs. "Keeping my patient company." A fond smile curved her lips as she thought of the duo. "She and Mrs. Hunter really seem to have hit it off."

"Yes, I know." Her father laughed softly to himself. "She's a pistol, our little girl."

Brianna looked at him, confused. "You know?" she questioned. To the best of her knowledge, she hadn't said anything to her father regarding the situation. "How do you know?"

That was a slip, he thought. Brianna didn't know he'd been in touch with Barbara Hunter, didn't know anything about the nature of what had brought the two of them together in the first place, and he had a feeling that now was not the time to tell her.

"Doesn't matter," he said dismissively. "I thought I'd give you the night off by taking Carrie home with me for the night. I rented some of her favorite animated movies. Thought she might get a kick out of some one-on-one time with her old grandpa."

"How's that giving me the night off?" she asked. "Officially, I'm taking care of Mrs. Hunter. Carrie's good about entertaining herself. She usually hangs out in a corner, reading her books until it's time for her to go to bed."

"Barbara's got to sleep some time," he pointed out. "And then you get the night off—to spend it the way you want," he added, looking at her significantly.

Her suspicions were definitely aroused. Her father did *not* number among the most subtle people on the planet. "And just exactly how would I want to spend it, Dad?" she asked.

His wide shoulders moved up and down in a nonchalant shrug that seemed just a tad too innocent. "Oh, I don't know, maybe with Sebastian. As I recall, you two *were* going together before my accident."

"The operative word here being *were,*" she pointed out. Her eyes narrowed as she looked at her father more intently. "What are you up to, Dad?"

He supposed if he didn't tell her, they were going to dance around the subject all evening, wasting too much time. "All right, Bree, if you want me to be blunt about it—"

"Please, be blunt," she instructed, waiting to hear just what he was plotting.

"I'm trying to give the two of you some alone time—together," he threw in just in case Brianna was going to twist his words around.

A sad smile curved the corners of her mouth.

"That's very sweet of you, Dad, but you could have

saved yourself the trouble of coming here. Sebastian's in his room packing. His mother is doing very well, so he's ready to go back to his life and I really doubt that there's much of a reason for me to be here much longer anyway."

She saw that the last piece of information didn't seem to surprise her father. There was only one reason for that.

"She never really had heart trouble, did she?" She didn't wait for him to answer her. "Dad, if this is some kind of a plot that the two of you cooked up, I'm afraid you've been wasting your time. Sebastian's going back to Japan."

He'd never known his daughter to give up on anything easily. "In the words of the immortal and far-wiser-than-given-credit-for Yogi Berra, 'It ain't over till it's over.'"

Brianna sighed. She was *not* about to knock her head against a stone wall. "Well, it's over. Trust me," she said with finality.

Her father stared at her in complete disbelief. "So that's it?" he asked incredulously. "You're just giving up? You, the girl who kept kicking me in the behind because I said the doctors were right? The girl who said she absolutely refused to let me give up?"

She'd already accepted defeat—why couldn't he? "That was different," she insisted.

"How?" Jim asked. "How was that different from this?"

Why was he making this so hard for her? "Because it

just was. For one thing, you didn't have a life waiting for you in Japan. You were intent on resigning from life."

"But you told me I had a choice. A choice," he repeated. "And Sebastian has a choice. Just like I did," he maintained.

Maybe so, she thought, but he'd picked the wrong one. "Well, he's choosing to leave," she told her father, struggling to keep her voice from quavering.

No matter what she said, Jim found that really difficult to believe. "Did you tell him how you feel?" he prodded.

More than anything, Brianna wanted to deny that she felt anything at all, but that would be lying and she had never lied to her father.

"If he doesn't know by now..." She let her voice trail off, but her meaning was clear.

"So you didn't tell him," her father concluded. He sighed, shaking his head. "Honey, because I love you, I'm going to tell you something that's going to violate the sacred man-code." He leaned into her and said in a stage whisper, "We don't read minds—and when it comes to relationships, we need all the help, all the outright hints we can get." He looked at her pointedly. "For God's sake, *tell* him how you feel. Ask him to stay—unless you don't want him to," he qualified, never taking his eyes off his daughter.

It was a choice between saving face and telling the truth. Since this was her father, she was forced to go with the truth.

"Of course I want him to stay, but wanting him to isn't enough."

He'd always bragged to everyone that his daughter was incredibly bright—but not this time. "I think you're wrong there."

"Dad, what if I ask him to stay…and he tells me he can't? Or he won't?" Which would have been even worse to bear.

"You'll never know unless you put yourself out there, Bree." His eyes, so like hers, held her captive. "And he won't tell you he can't stay." He looked at her and said with conviction, "I know that for a fact."

"How? How do you know that?" she demanded, feeling her heart fluttering in her chest, drawing hope. "Did he say something to you?" Not that she thought that was even remotely possible. When would he be talking to her father? And why?

"No," he told her, "he didn't say anything to me."

She was aware of how carefully he phrased his reply. "Then to who?" she asked, the edge of her temper becoming frayed.

Jim debated not saying anything further. But if he didn't, his daughter would allow the love of her life to leave—for a second time.

Jim made his decision. "Sebastian intimated as much to his mother."

"His mother?" she echoed, stunned. "When did you talk to his mother?" And then she amended her question. "*Why* are you talking to his mother? Dad, what's going on here?"

"Nothing," Jim lamented, "if the two of you continue to insist on remaining in second gear."

"Dad, ten years have gone by since Sebastian and I were 'together,' as you put it," she protested. "We missed our chance."

"Who says you only get one chance?" he pressed, then insisted, "Honey, you *have* been given a second chance. It's up to the two of you to take advantage of it. Look at it this way," he advised. "Maybe everything that happened happened for a reason. If it hadn't, you would have missed out on having Carrie in your life and Carrie would have wound up being swallowed up by the system. You also wouldn't have become the wonderful nurse that you are today.

"And maybe," he speculated, "things were supposed to go this long, roundabout route so that Barbara and I would get together."

A medium-size feather could have easily knocked her over. "You and Barbara," she repeated, utterly stunned by his revelation. "Together?"

"Yes. Me and Barbara. We've been keeping company," he told her quaintly. "And to tell the truth, I've been thinking of asking her to marry me."

Maybe a small feather rather than a medium-size one. "When did all this happen?" she cried. Had she been completely blind and oblivious to everything? Or had they been seeing one another covertly? She was usually far more observant than this.

"I don't run everything past you," Jim told his daughter. "It's enough for you to know it happened—and that

I'm hoping you won't disappoint me and become a bystander in your own life." He looked at her significantly. "Now, go and get your second chance while I go and spend some quality time with my granddaughter—" he smiled broadly "—and my girl."

Because he definitely appeared to be looking past her shoulder, Brianna turned around. What she saw was Carrie walking into the room. She was holding on to Barbara's hand. A very hale-and-hearty-looking Barbara, she noted.

There was a glow about the older woman when she looked at her father. They definitely had a connection, Brianna thought.

"Grandpa is going to make dinner for Mrs. Hunter and me," Carrie announced cheerfully. "And then we're going to watch *Little People,*" she added, referring to a popular children's movie that had just hit the DVD market.

Carrie seemed so excited, Brianna didn't have the heart to say anything except, "Well, have a good time, honey." Bending down to her level, she gave the little girl a warm hug and kissed her. Carrie dutifully stood still for it, even though it looked as if she wanted to wiggle free.

"You, too, dear," Barbara told her significantly as Brianna rose back to her feet.

Her father offered Sebastian's mother his arm, which the older woman readily accepted, slipping her own through his.

"Don't wait up," her father told her with a wink.

And then just like that, he, Carrie and Sebastian's mother were gone.

Brianna stood there for a moment in the silent house, staring at the closed door and mulling over her father's words. She debated whether to ignore them—or act on them.

She chewed on her lower lip nervously. What if her father was wrong?

What if he was right and she did nothing?

Torn, Brianna decided that if she didn't confront Sebastian about her feelings, if she let this moment just slide by and slip into oblivion, she would never forgive herself.

Bracing her shoulders, she took a deep breath and went up the stairs. She felt as if she was walking up to his door in slow motion. Even so, she couldn't get herself to knock right away.

Instead, she stood there for a moment—maybe even several minutes—arguing with herself in silence.

This was getting her nowhere. Since when was she such a coward? Brianna silently demanded.

Biting off a choice word, she knocked on the door.

The moment she did, the door flew open and she found herself looking up into Sebastian's soul-melting brown eyes.

How was she going to face not seeing him again?

The sudden sharp ache in her abdomen answered the question for her. She wasn't going to face it. She couldn't. Not without a fight.

"Something wrong, Bree?" he asked her. "Is it my

mother?" he asked, suddenly thinking the worst. That was where his thoughts were going as he packed, to the worst scenarios. He realized that what he was really trying to do was talk himself into staying a little longer.

And not just because of his mother…

"No, she's fine. Really," she assured him. *Okay, then what are you going to tell him about why you're standing in his doorway?* She searched for an answer. "I just thought I'd pop in for a second…to see if you needed any help packing," she concluded, looking at the open suitcase on the bed.

Turning, Sebastian followed her line of vision and then shrugged. He'd been at it for a while, moving in slow motion.

"I was never very good at packing," he confessed.

"Maybe that's because you don't want to go," she suggested matter-of-factly. Brianna held her breath, waiting for his reaction—knowing she was going out on a long, shaky limb.

Sebastian eyed her sharply. Was he that transparent? "What makes you say that?"

Brianna sighed, wavering. She debated backtracking. But she'd come this far, so she might as well go the distance.

"Wishful thinking," she answered quietly.

Sebastian realized he was holding his breath. "By wishful thinking you mean—"

"That I don't want you to go, okay?" she finally blurted out.

Her answer made him laugh. "That's funny, because

I really don't want to go," he heard himself confessing. Once the words were out, he felt a huge sense of relief.

She didn't understand. This whole day, he'd seemed so focused on leaving. "But then why are you packing?" she asked.

"Because if I stay, I might get used to it, used to being here with you—"

She was still waiting to hear something convincing. "And that would be bad because…?"

Pacing now, Sebastian blew out a breath. "Because I have no right to think that you could forgive me for allowing us to drift apart the way I did."

The fault wasn't his alone, she thought now. "It takes two to drift," Brianna pointed out. "And if you forgive me, I'll forgive you," she told him, still holding her breath, still waiting to see if she'd made a mistake by being so honest with him.

"That easy?" he asked, amused despite himself.

Brianna watched him for a long moment. She wasn't sure if he was being serious or not, but she knew that she was, at least about the forgiving part. She wanted no more stumbling blocks, no more obstacles in their way. They'd already lost too much time. To lose more would only be compounding the sin, adding insult to injury.

"That easy," she assured him with a smile.

Overwhelmed, relieved, Sebastian impulsively took her into his arms and kissed her.

And then stopped abruptly.

He couldn't afford to let himself get carried away, no matter how much he wanted to. It was too early in the evening. He was certain that both Carrie and his mother were still awake.

"Something on your mind?" she asked, mentally crossing her fingers that, whatever it was, it wasn't going to make him back away from her.

His grin seemed positively wicked and instantly got to her, speeding up her pulse even more than his kiss just had.

"Lots," Sebastian confessed. "But it's going to have to wait for a few hours."

She had a feeling she knew exactly what he was thinking, so she told him with confidence, "No, it doesn't."

"Oh?" And then he noticed that, although his bedroom door was now open, he didn't hear any noise coming from outside his room.

Curious, he stepped out into the hallway. The sound of the TV, the hum of voices, a radio on somewhere—none of those typical noises were audible to him tonight.

He looked at Brianna and asked, "Where is everyone?"

"Out," she answered simply, unable to suppress the smile that insisted on playing on her lips.

"Carrie and my mother are both out?" he questioned. His mother was recovering from a stroke. Why had Brianna let her go out by herself? Or worse, with Carrie?

"Carrie and your mother are both out," she repeated. Then, to set his mind at ease, she explained, "My father came by and took Carrie and your mother back to his house for dinner and an animated movie."

He could see her father taking Carrie home for that, but his mother as well? It didn't make any sense.

"He took my mother?" he asked incredulously. "You're sure?"

"I'm sure," she answered glibly, then let him in on the rest of it. "It seems that the two of them have been 'keeping company,' to use my father's words."

For a second, Sebastian's mouth dropped open. He hadn't thought that the two even knew one another. "Since when?"

"Since a while, apparently," she told him. "Actually, I think my dad's getting ready to ask you for your blessings."

His brow furrowed as he tried to make sense out of what she'd just told him. "Exactly what is it that I'm blessing?"

"What do you think?" she teased. Then, to make sure that there was no misunderstanding, she added, "I think those two crazy kids want to get married."

"Now you're kidding me."

The next moment, he was surprised to see Brianna shaking her head. "Nope. I'm being serious. They're being serious," she specified. "It looks like you're the only one here who isn't serious."

As if taking his cue, Sebastian pulled her back into his arms, this time with the reassuring knowledge that they were alone and would remain that way for at least several hours to come.

"Who says?" he challenged.

She could feel her body heating up already. "Well then, why don't you put your money where your mouth is?"

The expression on Sebastian's face sent her pulse scrambling in heated anticipation. "I'd rather put my mouth where yours is."

"That, too," she encouraged seductively.

He began to lower his mouth, then stopped one more time. "Oh, by the way—"

"Yes?" she asked, trying hard not to sound as impatient as she felt.

"Will you finally marry me?"

"Any time, any place," she told him without the slightest hesitation. "Now, shut up and make love with me before I jump you."

"Promises, promises." He laughed, then said far more seriously, "Gladly."

It was the last word either one of them said for a very long, satisfying time.

* * * * *

"I've yet to meet a surgeon who isn't full of himself, a total control freak."

"So says the hospital controller," her friend Ryleigh pointed out.

"That's my job title, not personality." She got mad every time she thought about the pressure Spencer Stone had put on her. "What part of *no* doesn't he understand?"

"Now's not the time—"

"Yeah, it is." Avery was warming to her subject. Even her friend's weird eye-rolling and nodding her head toward the doorway didn't penetrate the tirade. "I swear, if I ever meet a nice doctor, I'd have sex with him at that moment—"

"Avery—" Ryleigh was dragging her hand across her throat, the universal cut-off sign.

She felt her stomach drop and heat spread through her. "He's behind me, isn't he?"

HOLDING OUT FOR DOCTOR PERFECT

BY

TERESA SOUTHWICK

First published in Great Britain 2013
by Mills & Boon, an imprint of Harlequin (UK) Limited,
Eton House, 18-24 Paradise Road, Richmond, Surrey TW9 1SR

ISBN: 978 0 263 90118 4
ebook ISBN: 978 1 472 00494 9

23-0613

Harlequin (UK) policy is to use papers that are natural, renewable and recyclable products and made from wood grown in sustainable forests. The logging and manufacturing processes conform to the legal environmental regulations of the country of origin.

Printed and bound in Spain
by Blackprint CPI, Barcelona

Teresa Southwick lives with her husband in Las Vegas, the city that reinvents itself every day. An avid fan of romance novels, she is delighted to be living out her dream of writing for Mills & Boon.

To Neel V. Dhudshia, MD, the right doctor
in the right place at the right time. Thank you
from the bottom of my heart for giving it one more try.

Chapter One

Avery O'Neill had guilty secrets, but her attitude toward a certain cardiothoracic surgeon wasn't one of them.

She stopped pacing long enough to look at Ryleigh Evans, her best friend. "It's bad enough that I have to put up with Spencer Stone at your wedding. Far be it from me to question your future husband's taste in a best man. But I just found out I have to go to Dallas with him."

This was Ryleigh's office and she was behind the desk, watching Avery walk back and forth to work off her frustration. Her brown eyes sparkled with more than bridal happiness. She was also rocking a pregnancy glow with a baby due in four months. She was a beautiful brunette and happiness made her more beautiful than ever.

"Why do you have to go with him?" she asked.

"For months I've been telling Stone that the surgical robotic system he's lusting after—just like he lusts after every attractive single female employee at Mercy Medical Center is not in the budget. He went over my head to my boss, who pointed out that Doctor Heartthrob brings patients, publicity and revenue to Mercy Medical Center. In short, he's the golden boy and we need to keep him happy."

"And just how are you going to do that?" Her friend Ryleigh's tone dripped with double entendre.

"Don't go there."

Avery certainly wasn't planning to. Spencer Stone was only interested in casual sex—and that didn't interest her. She knew his type—big man on campus. The guy that girls couldn't say no to. In high school she'd learned the hard way that there were consequences for not saying no and sleeping with that guy. Hers were an unplanned pregnancy and a newborn daughter she'd had to give up for adoption.

Her gaze dropped to her friend's baby bump and the way she absently and protectively rubbed her hand over the swell of the growing child. A familiar envy, longing and sadness rolled through her. Avery covered it the way she always did, by being prickly. Ryleigh teased that it was one of her best qualities, but she'd never confided her guilty secret, not even to her best friend.

"I have to go with Stone to talk to the financial people and find out if this Star Wars technology is fiscally feasible."

"And what will he be doing while you're playing with numbers?"

"He'll be playing with the really expensive Star Wars technology."

Ryleigh nodded sagely. "Well, I can see their point. Hospital administration doesn't want him to contract his considerable skills to another facility. But he's officially really good at fixing hearts."

"Good thing because he breaks so many. He's a pain in the butt."

Ryleigh slid her a look of exaggerated patience. "You'll

get to know him better at the wedding. I promise not to say I told you so when you find out you're wrong about Spencer. If he were as bad as you think, Nick wouldn't like him or ask him to be his wingman for vow-taking."

The day after tomorrow her best friend was remarrying Dr. Nick Damian, the love of her life and father of her unborn child. Avery was the maid of honor, which meant she'd have to play nice. But that was two days away and now, she was annoyed. "Stone's a jerk."

"Not true. He's a really nice guy."

"Right." Avery folded her arms over her chest and faced the desk with her back to the open office door. "I've yet to meet a surgeon who isn't full of himself, a total control freak."

"So says the hospital controller," Ryleigh pointed out.

"Job title not personality." She got mad every time she thought about the pressure Spencer Stone had put on her. He buried her in emails with a subject line of 9-1-1, or stat, or Code Red. When that didn't work he tracked her down in the hospital wherever she happened to be, although so far he hadn't breached the sanctity of the ladies' room. "What part of no doesn't he understand?"

"Now's not the time—"

"Yeah, it is." Avery was warming to her subject. Even her friend's weird eye-rolling and nodding her head toward the doorway didn't penetrate the tirade. "I swear if I ever meet a nice doctor, I'd have sex with him at that moment—"

"Avery—" Ryleigh was dragging her hand across her throat, the universal cutoff sign.

She felt her stomach drop and heat spread through her. "He's behind me, isn't he?"

"I understand we're traveling together. Hello, Avery." Heart-of-Stone himself walked up beside her. His grin was wicked. The expression on his face was full of the devil.

"And since I'm a really nice surgeon and dressed appropriately, it looks like we'll be having sex, too."

"Don't be mean, Spencer," Ryleigh scolded. "I defended you. I'd appreciate it if you didn't make a liar out of me."

Avery didn't know what to say. She'd just insulted the brilliant doctor that hospital administration was jumping through hoops to keep happy. They were traveling together because he wanted a robot and she had to crunch the numbers to make it happen. If Stone said take a flying leap, her boss would ask how high and how many times. If Stone said fire Avery O'Neill, they would have her severance ready faster than you could say "may the force be with you."

She looked at her friend because she couldn't look at *him.* "You need to give me a bigger shut-the-heck-up motion next time."

"Next time?" Spencer rested a hip on the corner of Ryleigh's desk. His piercing green eyes snapped with intelligence. Dark blond hair was cut military short and suited his square-jawed face. It just wasn't fair that he made the green scrubs he wore hot as a sexy kiss under a full moon. "You have plans to trash talk me again, Tinker Bell?"

She winced, but didn't say anything. He called her that because she was five feet tall, barely weighed a hundred pounds and her blond hair was cut in a short pixie style. Ryleigh had said the look suited her but the nickname didn't do a whole lot for her professional image.

"Was there something you wanted, Spencer?" Ryleigh asked. She reached into a desk drawer and pulled out her purse before standing.

"Just wanted to double check on the wedding rehearsal time," he said.

"Tomorrow. Six-thirty at the house. We're taking the wedding party to dinner after."

"Who's in the wedding party again?" he asked, the sinful sparkle in his eyes aimed directly at Avery.

"Oh, please, Spencer. You have a mind like a steel trap and never forget anything. You know it's just you and Avery. She's my best friend and maid of honor. Don't pick on her."

They were the only attendants for the small intimate wedding and the next two days were going to be like a never ending double date. Karma was having a good laugh at her expense.

"Okay." He nodded to Ryleigh. "And you're feeling okay?"

"Great." She smiled and rubbed a hand over her belly. "Morning sickness is gone. Although why they call debilitating nausea that lasts twenty-four hours a day 'morning' is beyond me. But currently all is well."

"Good."

"Okay, you two, I have to go meet Nick. But feel free to use my office for restoring diplomatic relations."

"You don't want to play referee?" Spencer asked.

"Not even a little. Be excellent to each other," she added sternly on her way out the door.

When she left Avery and Spencer eyed each other. His expression was challenging but he didn't say anything. The silence was making her nervous and she needed to fill it. Partly because there would be no massive wedding party to buffer them during the rehearsal festivities and ceremony. And partly because she also had to work with him. And travel with him, which was worse than working with him.

"About the jerk comment…" She took a deep breath and met his gaze without flinching. "I was simply stating an opinion. I'm sorry if it hurt your feelings."

"You don't look sorry," he said.

That's because she was only sorry he'd overheard. "It's all on the inside."

"Unlike your stated viewpoint, which you put right out

there. One that didn't allow for the fact that I *have* any feelings."

From where she was standing, he didn't. "Do you?"

"Of course."

The teasing tone and gleam in his eyes didn't convince her but the combination made her pulse pick up more than she liked or even wanted to acknowledge. He was too handsome, too sexy, too confident, too smooth. Too much of everything that left her too little peace of mind. Filling the silence had only made her nerves more nervous.

Now what?

"So, it's good we talked." Avery slid her hands into the pockets of her black slacks. "I should be going now."

"It's quitting time, right? Is there somewhere you have to be? Do you have plans?"

"No."

"We should go get a drink," he said.

No, they shouldn't. "Why would you want to do that?"

The words just popped out of her mouth. She didn't mean to be rude, but definitely could have been more tactful.

Surprisingly he laughed. "It never occurred to me I needed a reason to ask a woman to go for a drink."

"Well, you asking just came out of the blue for me. We don't have what you'd call a going-for-drinks kind of relationship. It sort of took me by surprise."

"So, you're saying I *do* need a reason?"

She could feel the skepticism and suspicion on her face, but tried to suppress it. "Not exactly."

"That's okay. I can come up with more than one."

"Such as?"

The way he folded his arms over his broad chest made his shoulders look even wider. Her mouth went dry and there was a hitch in her breathing. It was okay with her if he thought she was unreasonable and not worth the trouble, but that could put a speed bump in her career.

"If we had a drink together, we'd get to know each other better."

"Good luck with that." She resisted the urge to put her hand over her mouth and simply mumbled, "Sorry."

He grinned. "It would ease tension and make the wedding festivities more fun and the trip to Dallas more relaxed."

On what planet? "Look, Dr. Stone—"

"Call me Spencer. It'll be easier that way. Especially at the rehearsal dinner."

Nothing about it was going to be easy. "Whatever I think about you, I'd never do anything to spoil my best friend's wedding day. And I'm a professional businesswoman. My personal feelings, whatever they are, will not affect my ability to do my job well."

"So, you're opposed to getting to know me?"

"It's not really necessary," she hedged.

"And that's a no to a drink?"

"Yes, that's a no," she said.

"Okay." He stood and looked down at her before saying, "See you later, Tinker Bell."

Avery stared after him for several moments. Over the years she'd spent a lot of time by herself but for some reason *alone* was bigger after sharing space with Spencer Stone. Probably because he'd taken up so much of her space and now it was emptier. Plus, she felt a little guilty for speaking her mind, which was weird. The guilt, not the speaking her mind.

Even though he was the same type as her first love, it wasn't fair to cast him in the same mold as the guy who'd gotten her pregnant and then joined the army to avoid her and any responsibility for his child. She wasn't normally a person who judged someone else based on rumors, hearsay and innuendo. But she had a weakness for guys like Spencer Stone and in her experience it didn't end well. Avoiding him altogether was the wisest course of action.

Fixing hearts might be his medical specialty, and by all accounts he was very good at it. But he was also good at breaking them—and she wasn't about to make hers an easy target.

It was a perfect evening for a wedding, but Spencer Stone was incredibly grateful he wasn't the one getting married. He held beating hearts in his hands and performed life and death procedures every day without breaking a sweat but the pressure of committing to another person forever made him want to poke a sharp stick in his eye.

But if Nick was determined to go through with it at least Mother Nature had given him perfect weather. April in Las Vegas was worth tolerating summer months when the temperature was hotter than the face of the sun. In the groom's backyard the air was somewhere in the low seventies. A sky with wisps of clouds was changing from blue to brilliant shades of orange, pink and purple as day faded to twilight. He supposed it was romantic if one was into that sort of thing.

Not his job right now. He was standing in the groom's backyard doing his best man duties. Several years ago he and Nick had met in the doctors' dining room at Mercy Medical Center and hit it off right away. Spencer had missed the first wedding because it had all happened so fast, but he hadn't missed the changes in his friend when the marriage fell apart. As if Spencer hadn't already been overthinking commitment, the negative impact on Nick from that experience really gave Spencer pause.

But now his buddy was tying the knot again with the same woman. And having a baby. It all looked perfect and Spencer envied them. He wasn't brave enough or dumb enough to take the step unless he knew it was the absolute right thing to do. In his life mistakes, both professional and personal, weren't allowed.

Nick stood beside him under a flower-covered arbor that had been set up and decorated for the festivities. Invited guests were talking quietly, waiting for the ceremony to start.

The bride and groom were having a small service—no tuxes, thank God, just dark, tasteful suits. Fifteen or twenty people he recognized from Mercy Medical Center sat in chairs set up on the patio beside the pool. Nick and Ryleigh had no extended family as far as he knew. Unlike himself, Spencer suspected they were blissfully unaware of how a family could complicate events like this in one's life.

"Do you have the rings?" Nick nervously brushed a hand over his dark, wavy hair.

Spencer felt for the jeweler's box in the pocket of his suit slacks. He faked an omigod expression when he asked, "Was I supposed to bring them?"

"Nice try, Stone. Even if you weren't kidding, nothing could rattle me today."

"Why?" Spencer was curious because he'd be sweating bullets if he was in Nick's shoes.

"Because no matter what happens, regardless of any technical glitches, Ryleigh is going to be my wife. Again."

"You're not worried that it won't work out?"

"Been there, done that," Nick said, blue eyes going intense for a moment. "I screwed up letting her walk out of my life once. It won't happen again."

"How can you be so sure?"

"Hey, aren't you supposed to be keeping me calm? Questions like that could send a nervous groom sprinting for the nearest exit."

"That's the thing." Spencer shook his head in amazement.

"You're rock solid. This is a life-altering move. I've seen you in the E.R. working on a kid with constricted airways and struggling for the next breath and you were nothing but nerves of steel. It's creeping me out that you're even more cool now. This is huge, man."

"And it's right."

"But how do you *know?*" Spencer insisted.

"I just do. When you know, you know." Nick gave him a warning look. "Don't ask."

Before Spencer could ignore the warning and ask anyway, the sliding glass door into the family room opened and Reverend White, the hospital chaplain, walked outside. He was a fit man, about sixty years old with a full, thick head of gray hair. Warm brown eyes surveyed the gathering.

"Ladies and gentlemen we're about to begin. If you'll all please rise to greet the bride."

As the chaplain moved up the aisle created by the two groups of separated chairs, everyone stood up. Moments later Avery walked out of the house. She was carrying a bouquet of lavender roses that matched the color of her dress. The full, swirly, sexy silky hem stopped at her knees and the high, matching pumps made her legs look a lot longer than he knew they were.

For just a second he'd have sworn his heart actually stopped. Not a comfortable feeling for a cardiotheracic surgeon, or any guy for that matter.

Then Ryleigh, holding a single white rose, appeared behind her maid of honor. In a floor-length flowing strapless gown she looked gorgeous and radiant, just as cool and collected as her groom. Spencer glanced at Nick's face and knew his friend was going through the heart-stopping sensation. He didn't even want to know why he knew that.

Avery stopped, took her place across from him, and for just a moment their eyes met. Probably it was just the spirit of the occasion, but for once she didn't look like she wanted to choke him.

Speaking of necks, hers drew his full attention in a big way. More specifically the see-through lavender material that covered her arms and the expanse of chest just above her small breasts. There were no visible bra straps, which made him far too curious about the lingerie under her dress, or lack thereof. Technically the skin wasn't bare, but for the life of him he could not understand why that was about the sexiest thing he'd ever seen.

Then Spencer snapped out of it when Nick moved and held his arm out to his bride. Ryleigh slipped her hand into the crook of his elbow, smiling with the same serene certainty her groom had demonstrated. Behind them everyone sat down again.

The reverend opened the book in his hands, then looked out at the guests. "Who gives this woman to be married to this man?"

"I give myself to Nick, freely and with love."

"I give myself to Ryleigh and our child, freely and with love." Nick put his palm on her stomach and the intensity of the feelings behind the words was there in his eyes.

Spencer knew the personal and profound promises following this public declaration had been written by Nick and Ryleigh. But it was the look on their faces that struck him. They only had eyes for each other. Then the reverend was asking for the rings, which he handed over, after a wink to his friend.

Nick kissed his bride while the guests cheered and clapped. At this point in the festivities it was time for bride and groom, best man and maid of honor to sign the wedding license and take a few minutes for private congratulations. Spencer held out his arm to escort Avery, who almost hid her hesitation. But she put her hand in the crook of his elbow and they walked into the house.

Spencer Stone was normally attracted to tall women with legs that went on forever. Blond, blue-eyed little bits of nothing who looked out of a fairy tale—even if they didn't act that way—were not his cup of tea. But there was something about Avery O'Neill that unsettled him, maybe because she'd told him no. But that didn't explain why the scent of her skin slipped inside him and made his head spin like a centrifuge. At least he hid it better than Avery did her aversion to him.

After the legalities were squared away, the four of them gathered around the coffee table where two silver buckets of ice held a bottle of champagne and apple cider—in deference to the bride's delicate condition.

She held up her flute with the nonalcoholic drink. "You two are welcome to have something stronger. Nick said if I couldn't drink champagne he wouldn't, either."

He slid his arm around his new bride and pulled her close. "In the spirit of solidarity. We're pregnant."

Avery laughed. "You'll be singing a different tune when her ankles swell up."

"If I could share that, I would," he declared, laughter in his eyes.

"Right," Avery and Spencer said together.

He met her astonished gaze, then cleared his throat. "As best man it's my honor to make a toast to the happy couple."

"Please," Ryleigh said.

"First of all, congratulations. To my friend, Nick, health and happiness." He clinked his glass to the groom's. "And Ryleigh. You look happier than I've ever seen you and more beautiful. All brides should be pregnant."

Spencer glanced at Avery and saw a frown in her eyes for just a fraction of a second. So quick he wondered if he'd imagined it. Except he'd been on the receiving end of numerous O'Neill frowns and knew he wasn't mistaken. She'd looked the same way during the ceremony, when Nick and Ryleigh pledged their love to each other and their child. That wasn't a frown-worthy moment. Which made it another in a growing list of questions about the mysterious, yet intriguing Miss Avery O'Neill.

"Thank you, Spencer. That was lovely." Ryleigh picked up the single white rose she'd held during the ceremony and handed it to her maid of honor.

Avery looked surprised as she took the flower. "You're giving this to me?"

"Yes. It's simple, beautiful and pure. A symbol of my love for Nick. Traditionally whoever catches the bridal bouquet will be the next to get married, but I didn't want a bouquet."

"Good, because I don't want to get married." But she held the rose to her nose and breathed in the fragrance.

"This represents nothing more than my hope that you'll find a love as enduring and perfect as Nick's and mine."

"Thank you." Avery's voice trembled with emotion just before she leaned over and hugged her friend.

"Okay, Mrs. Damian, now it's time to mingle with the other guests," Nick said.

"Lead the way, Dr. Damian."

Hand in hand the newlyweds went outside. Avery started to follow and Spencer stopped her with a hand on her arm.

"Wait a second."

"Why?"

"I'd like to clear the air while we have a minute."

"There's no air to clear."

"Come on," he said. "This is me. I know you're not very good at hiding your feelings. And I mean that as a compliment."

"Look, Dr.…Spencer," she said. "There's nothing to

say. After today, any personal obligations that we have in common are fulfilled."

"But there's still our mutual business trip," he reminded her.

"Mutual, meaning shared. But that's not the case with us. You'll do your thing. I'll do mine. Our paths may be parallel, but won't necessarily cross. So, again, no air to clear."

"So, you don't want to meet my family?"

"Excuse me?"

"My parents live in Dallas. My sister and her family will be there on vacation at the same time."

"Is that why you were so—" She stopped for a moment, searching for the right adjective. "So *aggressive* in your pursuit of robotic technology?"

"If I wanted to visit, I'm perfectly capable of doing that on my own. Combining objectives is better time management. My schedule is complicated and it can be a challenge to work in a vacation. Surgery can't always be put on hold. Emergencies happen. You get my point."

"I do," she agreed. "But, I have a budget meeting with the regional VP and you're seeing family. As I said, we won't be joined at the hip. So, still no air to clear."

There was no animosity in her expression, just a matter-of-fact resignation. Usually women *wanted* to cross his path. They went out of their way to stand smack in the center of his path so there was no way on earth he could possibly miss them.

Not this woman.

He couldn't swear that there wasn't just a little ego involved in his curiosity to figure out how she rolled, what was going on with her. Why she wasn't interested.

"Why do you dislike me?"

"I don't." Her eyes didn't quite meet his.

"I'm the first to admit that sometimes my determination can be off-putting—"

"Really? That's the best description you've got?" She smiled, but it was brittle around the edges.

"Okay. My standards are high. I can be a real pain."

"You'll get no argument from me."

"I'm told determination is a good quality."

"Unless you're going after something you can't have," she said.

He had a feeling they were no longer talking about surgical technology.

"So, you don't like me."

"Let's just say you remind me of someone."

"And you don't like him?"

"No, I don't." That signature O'Neill frown darkened her eyes again. "Now, if that's it, I'm going to join the celebration on the patio."

That wasn't all, but he didn't stop her from leaving. Spencer knew he was paying the price for whatever the jerk she didn't like had done to put the twist in her panties. He would be happy to *un*twist and remove said panties, but it was going to take some effort.

He was nothing if not a high achiever, and determination was his middle name. However long it took, he was going to show her that he was a nice doctor who more than met her criteria for having sex.

Chapter Two

Bright and early Monday morning, Avery walked into her office at Mercy Medical Center where her assistant was waiting. Chloe Castillo was a brown-eyed, curly-haired brunette in her mid-twenties. She was pretty, smart, funny and, right now, quivering with anticipation.

"I want to hear all about the wedding," she said. "Don't leave anything out."

"Good morning to you, too."

"Yeah, yeah. Blah, blah." She followed from the outer reception area into Avery's office and rested a hip on the desk.

"The weather was absolutely perfect. There were just enough clouds to put pink, purple and gold in the sky."

"You just love torturing me, don't you?" Chloe sighed. "I guess my questions need to be more specific. How did Ryleigh look?"

"If she weren't my best friend, I could really dislike that woman. She couldn't look bad after mud wrestling a pig.

But a pregnant bride? In a word? Awesome." Avery smiled at the memory. "She was completely stunning in a simple, strapless, satin floor-length gown. I thought Nick was going to swallow his tongue when he first saw her. And Spencer said—"

Now she'd done it. Opened a can of worms. The last thing she wanted to talk about was *him,* but she knew that gleam in Chloe's dark eyes. Fat chance her assistant had missed the slip, let alone allow her to slam that particular door shut. Although in a very committed relationship, she had a notorious crush on the hospital's exceptional heart surgeon.

"What did Doctor Hottie say?" she prompted. "Spill it, girl."

Avery sighed. "He said he'd never seen Ryleigh look more beautiful."

"And?"

"How do you know there's an 'and'?"

"I can tell by the way your mouth is all pinchy and tight." Chloe folded her arms over an impressive bosom. "Your body language couldn't be more closed if you were wearing a straightjacket."

The downside of this woman's intelligence and friendship was that she didn't miss anything and wasn't afraid to ask about what you'd left out. Avery met her gaze. "He told her that all brides should be pregnant."

"Oh. My. God." Chloe's expression was rapturous as she made each individual word a complete sentence. "Silver tongue devil. How sweet is that?"

Avery couldn't agree more, but didn't allow the envy she felt for her friend to get in the way of wanting more than anything for her to be happy. Spencer's lovely words had crossed her mind more than once during Ryleigh and Nick's reception. Avery had been pregnant once and thought she was going to be a bride, but Fate stepped in and said, not so fast.

"Ryleigh ate it up," she said to her assistant.

"Of course she did. What woman overflowing with estrogen wouldn't?"

Avery resisted the urge to raise her hand. Spencer Stone definitely had a way with words, but talk was cheap. Actions spoke louder and nothing he'd done had changed her mind about him being a scalpel-wielding, stethoscope-wearing Lothario.

"So..." She looked at her assistant. "Nick and Ryleigh are married again. Now we have work—"

Chloe held up a hand. "That pathetically small amount of information didn't even begin to take the edge off my curiosity."

That's what Avery was afraid of. It was too much to hope she'd get off that easily. Chloe wasn't the only one fascinated with him. Most of the female population at Mercy Medical Center acted like twits when the heartthrob heart doctor sashayed down the hall. Avery was the only exception as far as she knew, but maybe she was the only one who'd been so profoundly and personally burned in the past by someone she'd trusted.

Someone just like Spencer.

"What else do you want to know?" Her assistant wouldn't give up until all the pertinent facts were out there. It was best to know what facts she considered pertinent and keep the rest to herself.

"Tell me about your dress."

She smiled, cutting through her tension. "It's gorgeous. Lavender with the most feminine skirt that swirled like silk heaven when I walked. The sleeves and bodice are sheer and—"

"What?" Chloe said eagerly.

"Nothing. Just that I found a pair of four-inch heels that matched perfectly."

There was no point in sharing that Spencer had looked her up and down as if he liked what he saw. His gaze had lingered for a while on her chest and there was a shade of curiosity in his expression as he'd studied her. At that moment she'd been dying to know what was going through his mind, then reality reasserted itself and she let the question go. The saying that curiosity killed the cat was a saying for a reason.

"Tell me what the doc was wearing."

"Nick had on a dark suit and—"

"Not that doc. He's spoken for." Chloe rolled her eyes. "The other doc."

"Also a dark suit. Crisp cream-colored dress shirt and matching satin tie."

Chloe fluttered her hand in front of her chest. "Be still my heart."

No kidding. Avery had seen him in scrubs, jeans and slacks with sports shirt. The wedding was the first time she'd ever seen him in a suit and tie. It was memorable, and that was an understatement. If he wasn't so good at what he did, a career in modeling wasn't out of the question. That was a sentiment Avery would take to her grave and now it was time to change the subject.

"Pretty is as pretty does," she said.

"I don't even know what that means."

"Just that it's not smart to judge a book by its cover."

One of Chloe's dark eyebrows lifted questioningly. "You're just full of clichés today. That man is fine and friendly."

"Does your boyfriend know you have a crush on Dr. Stone?"

"Admiring a good-looking man is not cheating. My heart belongs to Sean, but I'm not blind."

"So he doesn't know your secret?"

"No. And speaking of secrets, I want to know how Dr. Stone somehow manages to stay friends with all of his exes."

"You think that's an admirable quality?"

"Yes. You don't?" Chloe shook her head. "Why do you dislike him, Avery?"

"Think about what you just said. *All* his exes being the key phrase. Doesn't the sheer quantity of women give you any pause at all?"

"Not when a man is that charming," Chloe said. "You could take lessons from him."

Spencer had implied as much when he'd asked why she disliked him. That wasn't a detail she chose to share—or the fact that he'd wanted to clear the air between them. What was that about? Or asking her to meet his family in Dallas? And what was the point? She'd all but told him he was barking up the wrong tree. A personal relationship wasn't a prerequisite for working together.

She looked at her assistant. "Charming is as charming does."

"I cannot even believe you said that to me." Chloe sighed dramatically. "How about this? One picture is worth a thousand words. Throw me a bone here. Tell me you've got at least one."

"Okay. Yes, I've got one." Avery pulled her cell phone from her pocket, pushed some buttons until she found a snapshot of the bride, groom, best man and maid of honor. "Knock yourself out."

"What a beautiful couple." Chloe took the phone and her dark eyes went dreamy just before that damn gleam returned. "You and Dr. Stone aren't too bad, either."

"There is no me and Dr. Stone."

"Uh-huh. This picture tells a different story."

"What are you talking about?"

Chloe handed back the phone. "It's all there in living

color. The way he's looking at you. Like he could just eat you up."

Avery saw what the other woman meant. It was hard to miss the determination Spencer had been peddling, up to and during the wedding festivities. The intensity in his eyes as he looked at her had tingles dancing up her spine and unleashed the always lurking shivers of awareness. The feeling of not being in control unleashed her inner prickliness.

"He might try to take a bite out of me, Chloe, but I'm awfully tough to chew. Better men than him have tried." She put her phone in her pocket. "Now, we've got work to do."

Chloe tapped her lip. "Speaking of work, I just got a memo from administration authorizing your trip to Dallas with Doctor Hottie."

"I wish you wouldn't call him that." Even though truer words were never spoken.

"Be that as it may, do you want me to make reservations?"

"Yes. But coordinate with Dr. Stone's office manager on dates, flight arrangements and hotel rooms. Also, my meeting with the Regional Vice President the Friday before we get into the robotics technology on Monday. And before you ask, that was definitely plural on the room thing."

"Will do, boss. A lot of women would love to be in your high-heeled pumps."

"Chloe, it's business."

"Just saying—"

She pointed to the doorway. "Back to work before we both get in trouble."

Her assistant saluted and left without another word.

Avery sat down behind her desk and turned on the computer. She knew Chloe was right about a lot of women who'd like to be walking in her shoes, but a lot of women hadn't been through hell and had their trust stomped out of them.

Spencer Stone was just a little too perfect for someone like her, someone who had a secret she didn't talk about. And there was a good reason.

It was a painful lesson, but she'd learned it well. When everything looks like it's falling into place, it's actually falling apart.

Still in his scrubs after an emergency surgery to open up a blocked vessel in a patient's heart, Spencer Stone took the elevator to Mercy Medical Center's administration offices located on the second floor. It had been two weeks since the wedding and that was the last time he'd seen Avery O'Neill. The memory of her in that sexy, see-through lavender dress had never been far from his mind and he was looking forward to seeing her again. No matter what she was wearing.

There was a flash of adrenaline as he wondered what she'd say to get his blood pumping this time. How would she surprise him?

When the elevator opened, he stepped out and walked down the carpeted hall. Her door was the third one on the right and he went inside. Her assistant, Chloe Castillo, was on guard duty behind a desk in the reception area. She did a double take when she recognized him.

"Hi, Dr. Stone."

"Chloe. How are you?"

"Great. Yourself?"

"Never better." Couldn't hurt to get the controller's assistant on his side. "Have you done something different with your hair?"

She automatically touched the dark curls by her cheek. "No. Same as always."

"And, as always, you're looking beautiful."

"Thanks. It's not true, but very charming of you to say so."

"I'm a charming guy."

"Preaching to the choir, Doctor." With her thumb, she indicated the closed door of the office behind her. "I'm not the one you have to convince."

"Yeah. I sort of picked up on the fact that I'm not her favorite person."

"You want my opinion?" she asked.

"Yes." He needed all the help possible to loosen the purse strings and this woman knew the crabby controller better than him.

Chloe glanced over her shoulder. "All that cool reserve of hers and that abrasive streak she rocks? It's a layer of self-protection. I think some guy dumped on her pretty badly and she watches her back."

"Avery said that?"

"Not in so many words." She shrugged. "I just connected the dots from remarks she's made in passing."

"I see."

Normally, it wouldn't occur to him to ask for details, but in Avery's case the thought crossed his mind. Since inquiring wasn't appropriate, he didn't. Still, he wanted to know more about the mysterious controller and not just because knowledge could help get her on board with the outrageously expensive equipment he wanted.

"Is she free? Can I talk to her for a few minutes?" he asked instead.

"There's no one in with her now. Let me check her schedule." Chloe changed screens on the monitor and looked it over. "No more appointments for today and it's almost quitting time so there shouldn't be a problem."

Her boss probably wouldn't agree because she didn't try to hide the fact that every time she saw him was a problem. Now he was determined to change that.

"Thanks."

"Don't mention it." She clicked the computer mouse a couple times and shut down her system. "And it's time for me to go home."

"Plans tonight?"

"Yes." Instantly she smiled.

"Someone special?"

"The best guy in the whole world."

"He's a lucky guy," Spencer said.

"There's that charm again." She nodded her head toward the closed door. "You shouldn't be wasting it on me. You'll need every ounce of it in there."

"I've got some to spare."

"I just bet you do." She grabbed her purse, then said, "I'll let her know you're here and say goodbye."

"How about if I announce myself and let her know you're gone?"

"That works. 'Night, Dr. Stone."

"Have a good evening."

Spencer watched her walk out and, for some vague reason, envied the fact that she wouldn't be alone tonight. He couldn't say the same.

With a sigh, he walked past the desk, knocked once on the door then opened it and poked his head inside. "You didn't get the message that it's time to go home?"

"What are you doing here?" Avery looked first surprised, then annoyed.

He preferred surprised. "Chloe's gone for the day. I told her I'd let you know."

"Okay." She looked down at the papers on her desk, then back at him when he didn't leave. "Was there something else?"

"We're leaving tomorrow for Dallas. I thought we should discuss our trip."

"Thanks, but it's not necessary. Between your office manager and Chloe, arrangements have been made and I have all the information."

Spencer moved farther into the room and invaded her space when he parked a hip on the corner of her desk. Avery's big blue eyes narrowed in disapproval and it felt like he'd stepped into a Deepfreeze. Oddly enough, the look made her even more intriguing. Sort of like a kitten bracing for battle with a pit bull.

Her short blond hair highlighted her killer cheekbones and a mouth that a stronger man than him would have trouble resisting. That thought exposed how he'd been lying to himself. He'd been so sure time and distance would blunt his reaction to the cute-as-a-button controller, but he'd been wrong. On some level he'd believed not seeing her for the past two weeks would mellow her attitude and his fascination, thereby canceling out any feeling. But apparently he'd been wrong about that, too. It was like a force shield went up whenever she saw him and he wanted to bring it down.

And that's when he realized what it was about her that sucked him in. It was the challenge of melting the ice cube on her ass. You didn't grow up the first-born son of Catherine and William Stone and ever consider turning your back on a challenge.

"So, why do you dislike me?" he asked. No point in beating around the bush.

"We've been through this," she said, skillfully not answering the question again.

"And yet, I'm not satisfied."

During that last conversation the implication had been that he reminded her of someone. If Chloe was right, he brought to mind the guy who'd dumped her.

Avery folded her hands on the desk and didn't look away. "That's your problem, not mine."

"You indicated that our wedding obligation was fulfilled and therefore any reason to play nice was over."

"You disagree?"

"We'll be spending a lot of time together over the next couple days," he answered.

"On business," she clarified.

"Even so, the trip will be easier if we can be cordial."

"I'm always friendly." She looked away for just a second. "Mostly."

"Here's the thing, Avery. I know I pushed you hard for this equipment."

"Yes. Determination you said. And it paid off. You got your way."

The "aha" light went on. "Are you still annoyed that I went over your head to your boss?"

"Among other things."

The journey of a thousand miles starts with a single step and he'd worry about "other things" later. "It's cutting edge technology."

"No pun intended."

When the corners of her mouth went up his pulse did, too. "Actually that's part of the appeal. The robot makes a perfect incision every time."

"I'm sure you make a perfectly fine incision, Spencer, or your reputation wouldn't be what it is."

"I do my best and I'm damn good."

"Modest, too," she said, smiling.

"Just stating the facts. But this surgery system brings a level of precision that I can't duplicate. No human can."

"So you want to be perfect."

That wasn't necessary. Not really. He just didn't want to make a mistake, professionally and personally. In his family nothing short of excellence was tolerated. That's how he'd been brought up and why he was the best now at what he did.

"I'd like to know why you're so dead set against this surgery system. All I want," he said, "is every advantage available to achieve the best outcome for my patients."

She nodded approvingly and earning the victory of her good opinion was sweet. And short. "My problem is that what you want is a capital expenditure."

"Robots don't come cheap."

"I'm all too aware of that. But there's only so much money in the budget. Spending it on what you want means that something else equally as important doesn't get funded."

"Such as?"

"Ventilators for babies. Don't you think it's vital to give children the best possible start in life?"

"That's a loaded question."

"It's my job to ask the hard ones. Make the tough choices. And I wish there was an unlimited supply of funds, but that's not how it is."

"You're right. And a good start for every child is imperative." He stood and folded his arms over his chest. "In a perfect world there would be enough money for everything. But hearts are my business. With cardiovascular disease on the rise it's also important to use the latest innovations to improve and prolong the life of parents so they can use the benefit of their experience and wisdom to guide those children into adulthood."

She sighed. "It doesn't hurt that this surgery system is flashy and newsworthy. Not unlike yourself, Doctor."

"You think I'm newsworthy?" He'd take it if that was the best she could do.

"My boss does. I'm still not convinced it's the best use of money."

"And we'll have several days together to debate the pros and cons." He put his palms flat on her desk and met her gaze. Her eyes went wide and the pulse at the base of her neck fluttered wildly. It made him pretty happy that he affected her that way. "I think when we get back to Las Vegas you will see the fiscal practicality of this expenditure."

"It's going to be an uphill battle," she informed him.

"And that's not all."

"What else could there possibly be?" She leaned back in her chair.

"I intend to change your mind about me while we're gone."

"In Dallas." Her tone put it on a par with having a bad case of the flu.

"Yes." He pointed his finger at her. "You've been warned, Miss O'Neill."

"Good to know. I'll see you there."

"Actually, that's why I stopped by your office in the first place."

She frowned. "I don't understand."

"We should carpool to the airport tomorrow." When she opened her mouth to argue, he held up his hand. "We're on the same flight. Going in the same car will save money on transportation and parking. I thought that would appeal to a budget-conscious lady like yourself."

For the first time since he'd known her Avery O'Neill was speechless and he used the silence to best advantage.

"I'll pick you up bright and early in the morning."

Chapter Three

Under normal circumstances Avery loved going to McCarran International Airport, but nothing about this scenario was normal. For one thing, it involved Spencer Stone and he pushed all her buttons. None of them good. She still wasn't sure how he'd talked her into this carpool. That wasn't exactly true—he'd talked and when he stopped there'd been no room to maneuver. A negative response had been impossible so she'd given him her address.

Now she was waiting for him on the front porch of her small, three-bedroom house in the Green Valley Ranch area of Henderson. She'd bought it new a year and a half ago, a symbol of starting with a clean slate. Moving forward. It was important to leave behind her polluted past and the stigma of a pregnant teen who didn't keep her baby.

Just then a sporty blue BMW pulled up to the curb. Since she didn't know anyone with a luxury car she assumed it was Spencer. That was confirmed when he got out. Oh, boy, was it confirmed, she thought, as he walked toward her up the stone path. In a navy blazer with gold buttons, tan slacks, white shirt and tasseled loafers with his swagger set on stun, he quite literally stole the breath from her lungs. The dark sunglasses added more dazzle to his dashing look.

"You're early," she managed to say.

"And you're ready."

"Yup." There'd been lots of time to make sure of that, what with not sleeping much. And for good reason. There'd been no way to prepare for the fact that he smelled as good as he looked. She was such a sucker for a good-smelling man, but was doing her best to get over it. "Let's go."

He glanced at her small weekend suitcase on wheels with carry-on bag attached, then met her gaze. "Where's the rest of your stuff?"

"That's all there is."

"You do realize we'll be gone several days. Visiting several hospitals in the Dallas Metroplex?"

She nodded. "It's all business meetings. Coordinate right, travel light."

"Sounds like a marketing slogan." The words were teasing, but his expression was puzzled. He lifted his sunglasses and hung them from his jacket pocket. Piercing green eyes grew intense as he studied her. "You're not like other women, are you?"

"I'm not sure whether to be insulted or flattered, but… why do you say that?"

"It's definitely a compliment. And I say it because, until now, I've never met a woman who could take a trip of this duration with only one small bag."

"Considering the sheer number of your women—"

"My women?" One light brown eyebrow lifted.

"Hospital talk." She shrugged. "There's no way to stop it."

"Ah." He slid his hands into his slacks pockets. "The

rumor network at Mercy Medical Center is as intricate as the capillaries, veins and vessels that comprise the body's complex circulatory system."

"News does travel fast." She couldn't help smiling because the comparison he'd made was accurate but leaned toward the brainy geek side. That was contradictory to his playboy image and oddly endearing.

He stared at her. "Wow."

"What?"

"You smiled."

"I do it quite often." She knew where he was going with this.

"Not with me," he said. "When I'm around, your good humor is as rare as rain in Las Vegas."

And for good reason. He was brash, confident and just her type. The type who promised everything she'd always wanted then left without a word.

He glanced at the Rolex on his wrist. "We better go. There could be traffic."

"Okay." She pushed the handle of her suitcase down and started to lift it but he brushed her fingers aside.

"I'll get that." He settled his sunglasses over his eyes, hiding any expression that might be there. "And for the record…I do date, but the number of women I go out with is greatly exaggerated by the hospital's rumor network."

There was no response she could make to that, which was becoming an annoying pattern where he was concerned.

He opened the car door and handed her into the passenger seat. When he was behind the wheel, that sexy masculine smell surrounded her, even more potent than before. It felt like he'd wrapped her in his arms and overwhelmed her senses. Then he fit the key into the ignition and the car glided forward. It was like riding on a cloud.

Avery knew her best defense was to push back this out-of-control feeling with words but so far that hadn't worked very well with him. Still, conversation was better than awkward silence. So she came up with a topic as innocuous and close to a man's heart as she could.

"Nice car."

"Thanks. It's a terrific machine." He glanced her way for a second. "And before you get your panties in a twist about boys and their toys, I'm going to again request that you be as objective as possible when we gather information about the surgery system."

"I will," she promised.

Whatever flaws Spencer might have personally, as a doctor he was beyond reproach. Objectivity wasn't plentiful where his personal life was concerned, but without a doubt she knew that saving lives was profoundly important to him.

Avery remembered their conversation in her office less than twenty-four hours ago. They'd both agreed that kids deserve the best start in life. Part of her wasn't talking about it in a medical way. She was a product of divorce and didn't see her father after he left. At seventeen she'd gotten pregnant and her baby's father disappeared. It broke her heart that her mother had refused to give her a home if she kept her infant daughter. Only with time had she gained the wisdom to realize that the baby was better off in a stable home with two parents. Still, a trauma like that left an indelible mark on the soul.

"You're uncharacteristically quiet." Spencer's voice cut through her dark thoughts.

"I hate flying." She loved the airport but dreaded getting on a plane. "I can't wait for technology that can beam us where we want to go."

"It will no doubt be expensive to demolecularize someone, transport them to another location and remolecularize them." His tone was wry.

"In a perfect world there will be plenty of money."

Spencer guided the BMW onto the 215 Beltway going west then took the Sunset exit toward McCarran. In minutes there were signs directing them toward Arriving or Departing flights and short- or long-term parking with blue, green and yellow triangles on the roadway. He went to valet, of course, which was the priciest option. So much for his soapbox stand on sticking to a budget and keeping expenses down.

After unloading their luggage, he handed the keys to the attendant and they wheeled the bags into the building and past the classic red Thunderbird on display, a nod to the fact that it was flashier and more fun in Vegas. After passing shops and slot machines, the escalator was on their right and went down to the next floor for check-in. Preferred, of course, where there was no waiting.

Since the two of them were traveling on the same reservation confirmation number, they walked up together. There was a very attractive blonde behind the high counter who was only too happy to help Spencer.

She looked at the computer printout and her smile grew wider. "So, you're going to Dallas, Dr. Stone?"

"We both are," he said.

"May I see your ID?"

"Of course." He handed over his and Avery's, which got a cursory look, as compared to a long perusal for his.

"Your flight is on time, Doctor, and leaving from Gate D14. If there's anything I can do to make it more pleasant, please don't hesitate to let me know."

"Thank you."

They followed signs for their gate and Avery said, "Doctor Awesome strikes again."

"Oh, please," he scoffed.

Before she could rebut, they joined the line to pass through security. After again presenting IDs and boarding passes, they fell in with people removing shoes, belts and watches as carry-on luggage went on the conveyor belt and into the screening process.

Spencer was waved through the metal detector by a—what else?—female uniformed agent. Naturally, she gave him a big, flirtatious smile as he went through. After gathering up everything, they proceeded to the waiting area and found seats side by side.

Avery looked at him in awe. "Being you must be extraordinarily wonderful."

His expression oozed amusement. "What are you talking about?"

"Every woman you encounter falls in worship at your feet."

"Every woman?" he said, giving her a pointed look. "I can think of one notable exception."

"Does it ever get old?"

"I think you're exaggerating."

"You think wrong. Take the TSA lady." She folded her hands in her lap. "Normally they're cold, efficient, abrasive even. Not only was she pleasant, the most vigilance she showed was checking out your butt."

"As flattering as that is—"

"I could see she was wishing you'd opt out of a scan and give her an excuse to pat you down."

"I didn't notice."

"Of course you didn't. Why should you? It's probably always like that."

He grinned. "Was anyone rude to you? I could beat them up."

"No. But compared to the way you were treated, I could

have been the third asterisk at the bottom of security rules and regulations."

He laughed. "I think you're making it up."

"I swear." She held up her hand in a solemnly sincere gesture. "Does being perfect ever get old?"

"You wouldn't say that if you knew me better."

Clearly she'd been teasing him and it was by far one of the most harmless things she'd ever said to him, but all traces of amusement disappeared from his face. The contrast was so obvious and striking that she wondered what nerve she'd stepped on.

Not even her comment about all his women had made him look like that. Was it possible Doctor Heartthrob actually had a heart? Intriguing and, darn it all, the realization made her want to know more.

Spencer sat on the chrome and black faux-leather connected chair beside Avery and waited for their flight. Since her question about whether or not being perfect ever got old, they hadn't exchanged any words.

His fault.

Apparently this visit to see his family was stirring up a whole pile of psychological crap, although he shouldn't be surprised. Trips home usually did that, what with the pressure on the Stone kids to achieve. His sister, Becky, had performed every aspect of her life to William and Catherine Stone's expectations. Her twin, Adam, was a doctor and didn't care that the folks disapproved of his area of specialization. But Spencer was the firstborn son and hadn't been cut any slack, couldn't get to a place where he was neutral. He still cared deeply whether or not he made a mistake and disappointed them. His reaction to Avery's teasing words proved that.

Just then there was an announcement in the terminal informing everyone waiting for the flight to Dallas that their aircraft would be landing soon. After the passengers deplaned, boarding would begin.

"That's my cue." Avery stood and settled the strap of her purse securely on her shoulder. Then she pulled out the handle of her carry-on to take it with her. "I'm going to the ladies' room."

"I'll watch your bag," he offered.

"That's okay."

"You don't trust me." His eyes narrowed on her, but a smile threatened.

"Not exactly. But I wouldn't put it past you to tell a security guard it was left unattended."

"That would never have crossed my mind," he said. "Thanks for the idea."

"No problem."

He grinned and it felt good. She was a welcome distraction from his dark thoughts. "Seriously, won't it be faster and easier if you don't have to drag it with you? Since I need your cooperation to get my way with the robotic surgery system, would it really be smart to play a practical joke?"

"Now that you mention it…" She looked thoughtful. "And no one ever said you didn't have a high IQ."

"So it's settled. I'll watch your bag."

She studied him for a moment. "You really don't mind?"

"No."

"Okay. Thanks." She pushed the handle back in and left it beside him.

Spencer studied her as she walked away. No, study was the wrong word. He checked out her butt. Dynamite. The white collar of her silky blouse was neatly folded over the jacket of her black crepe suit. Trim shoulders narrowed to a slim waist and curvy hips covered by the matching skirt. Sheer black pantyhose sheathed her shapely legs and high heels made those legs look longer, sexier. And then he saw it.

Red on the soles of her shoes.

The flash of color was like finding out her secret. A hint that she wasn't as proper as she pretended. That there was a playful and passionate woman beneath that business suit and prim exterior. This was both good news and bad.

The red-soled shoes turned him on in a very big way. But she'd made it clear that trying anything personal was a hanging offense and he really did need her help to convince the powers that be at Mercy Medical Center that what he wanted was a good idea. About ten minutes later, through a break in the airport crowd, he spotted her walking toward him. This time he missed seeing the red-hot soles of her sky-high shoes. But the front view made up for it. Normally he liked a woman's hair long, falling past her shoulders, because running his fingers through it was about the most erotic thing in the world.

But Avery was different. The pixie haircut suited her delicate features and highlighted the slightly tilted shape of her big eyes. And sexy? He could imagine himself cupping that small face in his hands while kissing her until she begged for more. As far as the sexy scale went, that visual buried the needle in the hot zone.

"Hi." She stood in front of him and glanced at the flight information displayed at their gate. "Looks like our plane is here. People are getting off."

Her tone said she'd rather they stay on and go somewhere else so she wouldn't have to.

Spencer stood and looked down at her. "Flying is absolutely the safest way to travel."

"So I've heard."

"But you don't believe it." That wasn't a question.

"I much prefer my feet firmly on the ground, thank you very much."

"Imagine that," he said. "A controller who's a control freak."

"Not with everything."

Uh-huh, he thought. "Just money and transportation."

"Possibly a few other things."

"Well, I appreciate that you stepped out of your comfort zone to come along," he said.

"Like I had a choice."

"You did."

She shook her head. "When my boss got involved there really weren't a lot of options. Saying no without a better excuse than aversion to being in a flimsy long white tube that climbs to over thirty thousand feet and hurtles through the sky at over five hundred miles an hour could be a career ender."

"There's my brave little soldier," he said.

When she met his gaze, her expression was wry. "If that's the bedside manner your patients get, you should know it could use work."

"I can do better."

Her eyes widened slightly. "Is that a threat?"

"No. A promise."

Before she could question that further, a voice came over the loudspeaker and said that they were ready to start boarding the flight to Dallas. Anyone needing assistance or flying with small children should step forward. A few minutes later first class passengers were called.

"That's us," he said.

She grabbed the handle of her rolling carry-on and fell into step with him. "How did you pull that off? Getting the hospital to cough up a more expensive ticket."

"I like more leg room. I can afford it. I paid the difference between first class and coach."

"Then I'll wait until they announce boarding for the peasants," she said.

"Not necessary. We're sitting together."

"But I didn't pay—"

"Don't worry about it. All taken care of." He carried his briefcase in one hand, then curved his other around her arm and urged her to the opening where the Jetway waited. The airline employee took and scanned their boarding passes and wished them a good flight.

"Fat chance," she mumbled.

Their seats were in the third row—hers by the window, his on the aisle. He set his briefcase down, then took her bag and stashed it in the overhead bin.

"Thanks," she said.

"No problem."

He stepped back so she could precede him into the row, where she sat and immediately secured her lap belt. He slid into the seat beside her and watched her face as all the color disappeared. Anxiety turned her eyes darker blue and her leg moved as her heel tapped a nervous staccato. He wanted to put his fingers on her knee. Partly because he just wanted very much to touch her there, but mostly to soothe the nerves. He was fine with breaching the line between personal and professional to distract her, but was ninety-nine point nine percent sure Avery would have a problem with it.

"So, you're pretty nervous."

"What gave me away?" At least she was trying to joke.

"Mostly that woodpecker imitation you're doing with the heel of your shoe."

Her leg stopped. "Now you know I didn't lie. Love the airport, don't like getting on a plane. I hate flying and officially, I hate you for making me do it."

"Maybe I can help."

"You're going without me?" she asked hopefully.

"No. But I'll let you ask me anything you want."

"Professional?"

"Or personal. Nothing is off-limits."

A gleam stole into her eyes. "That could be more dangerous than a cruising altitude of thirty-nine thousand feet."

"Maybe." He rested his elbows on the arms of the seats then linked his fingers. "So, hit me."

The bustle of passengers boarding had subsided and the flight attendants secured the cabin, then closed the door to the Jetway. As the plane started to move slowly backward, the aircraft safety precautions were reviewed.

Avery gripped the armrests and her knuckles turned as white as her face. When he took her left hand and held it, his only motivation was to make her feel safe. He should feel guilty about taking advantage of the opportunity to touch her, but he couldn't manage it.

"I'm serious, Tinker Bell. Ask me anything."

She looked at him and said, "Okay. Did you decide to become a doctor to help people?"

"Of course not. I did it for the women and sex," he answered without missing a beat.

She laughed as he'd hoped. "So you didn't choose the profession because all arrogant jerks become doctors?"

"I didn't really have a choice."

"How so?" She looked interested instead of anxious.

"My parents are the walking, talking, breathing definition of high achievers. In their eyes I fall short on an annoyingly regular basis."

"You're joking."

"Swear." He held up his hand just as the pilot announced they'd been cleared for takeoff.

"But you're a famous and in-demand gifted cardiothoracic surgeon."

"Tell me about it." He felt the plane make a turn, then pick up speed.

"What the heck could your mother or father possibly do that's more prestigious than that?"

"Dad is a Nobel Prize winning economist. Mom is a biomedical engineer whose work has revolutionized diagnostic equipment that helps people all over the world. My younger sister, Becky, is a rocket scientist and works for NASA."

"Good grief." Her voice raised to be heard over the whine and noise of the jet engines.

"Actually, in the Stone family, I'm something of a slacker. Only my brother, Adam, takes more heat than me about his career."

"What does he do?"

"Doctor," Spencer informed her.

"Of course he is."

"Family practice. But the folks don't see that as living up to his potential."

"And you seriously want me to meet them? They probably won't let me in the house and if they do, I'll be politely asked not to touch anything."

"No way," he scoffed. "They're really great people."

"Who set a very high bar."

"And speaking of high…" He looked across her and out the airplane window. "We're in the air and picking up altitude. The flight attendants are moving about the cabin and preparing for in-flight service. I draw your attention to this because we've successfully taken off and you have yet to freak out."

"You're right." She laughed. "Now you can add 'distracting fearful flyers' to your impressive resume and list of accomplishments."

"When are you going to admit I'm a nice man who happens to be a doctor?"

The look on her face told him she remembered her words that day in Ryleigh's office.

If I ever meet a nice doctor, I'd have sex with him at that moment.

A red-hot memory of the scarlet soles of her sky-high shoes made him even more acutely aware of how much he hoped that she'd sincerely meant those words.

Chapter Four

Avery was amazed that she forgot to be afraid at a cruising altitude of twenty-nine thousand feet.

The flight to Texas took just under three hours and she chatted the whole way with Spencer. Who'd have thought such a thing was possible?

Spencer was so charming and funny and interesting that when she remembered her feet were not on the ground, it had very little to do with the fact that she was in an airplane and a whole lot to do with her traveling companion.

As if that weren't bad enough, he was also a gentleman. He'd put her carry-on bag up and he took it down. Then he carried it off the plane. She wasn't used to this kind of treatment from a man, which kind of made sense since she pretty much avoided men. But for the next few days she couldn't avoid this one, not completely. At least she'd have her own space at the hotel. After checking in she'd spend the afternoon preparing for her meeting with the regional VP of the Mercy Medical Corporation.

Spencer walked up the Jetway beside her. "Have you ever been to Texas before?"

"No."

"I'll have to show you the sights."

"That's okay. There probably won't be time." Not if she was lucky.

For the first time, keeping her distance from Spencer Stone didn't come easily. Apparently he'd weakened her emotional defense system as easily as he'd managed her fear of flying.

They exited the Jetway and walked through the waiting area at the gate, then followed the signs to baggage claim. There was a revolving door and after negotiating it, the next step was to find the carousel that corresponded to their flight number. That didn't take long, but the little elves who unloaded the luggage from the plane took their sweet time. Finally, the warning buzzer and light signaled that the conveyor belt was starting up and spit out suitcases, backpacks and boxes.

Spencer grabbed her bag and before she could process the fact that he'd recognized it, he snagged his own.

"We have to catch the shuttle for the rental car lot," he said.

"Is it that far?"

He laughed ruefully. "Like everything else in the Lone Star state, DFW airport is big. There's a centrally located rental car facility about ten minutes away, not counting stops at the other four terminals to pick up passengers."

"Okay, then." She connected her carry-on bag to the bigger suitcase, leaving just one handle to pull. "I'll follow you."

They went down the escalator to the first floor where

ground transportation was located. Their shuttle was waiting, which was lucky. As it turned out, that was all the luck she got for the rest of the day. She turned on her cell phone and listened to a message from Chloe. Her Friday meeting had been canceled.

When they were settled the van moved forward, out into the sunlight, as it negotiated the curving and intricate roads onto the main highway. That's when Avery could see the airport and signs directing cars to terminals A, B, C, D and E.

She could only see out one side of the vehicle, but it was enough to get an impression. "Texas is really flat."

"Around here," he agreed. "There are hilly parts that we natives call—wait for it—Hill Country."

"No way," she teased. "How original. Must be named by a man."

"Are you saying that men have no imagination?"

"Yes. And a distinct lack of poetry. They just name it what it is."

"And that's bad—why?" he asked. "There's nothing wrong with straightforward."

She couldn't argue with that. The problem was that in her experience men weren't always up front and honest, her first lesson being when she was a pregnant seventeen-year-old. It was a good thing she didn't have to meet Spencer's folks. Apparently they had no tolerance for flaws and she had too many to count. One look at her and she'd be outted as unworthy.

"What's wrong?" Spencer's deep voice snapped her to attention.

"Nothing." She had to figure out what she was doing tomorrow. "I'm just trying to take it all in."

"Don't bother. There's not much to see until we get out of the airport."

She nodded and just watched buildings go by. There were

planes parked here and there, which indicated maintenance facilities. Then the shuttle exited the highway, turned left and followed the road for a few miles where it pulled into a lot. After grabbing their luggage, they walked into the air-conditioned building and found a spot in the line that formed.

"Since the reservation's in my name," Spencer said, "I can handle the paperwork."

"Okay. I'll keep an eye on your bag."

She stood out of the way and watched him work his way closer to the counter. More than one woman did a double-take after noticing tall, handsome, hunky Spencer Stone. So, the women in Texas weren't immune to his charisma any more than the females in Las Vegas. It wasn't a comforting thought. He had the trifecta of temptation—above average good looks, charm and sense of humor.

After a brief exchange with a rental car representative, he was lacking the last of the three. The expression on his face as he walked toward her was distinctly annoyed, if not downright angry.

"What's wrong?" she asked.

"The reservation's screwed up. They're not expecting us until Sunday."

"But today is Thursday."

"That's what I said," he told her grimly. "It's not like Laura to make a mistake like this."

"Is that your office manager?" Stupid question, but she wasn't at her best when thrown a curve.

He nodded. "She's been a little distracted lately. A rebellious teenager and she's a single mom. Personal problems."

And now they had problems. "Can we take a taxi to the hotel?"

"Not necessary. There was a car available. I just wanted to fill you in."

She nodded. What was there to say? Then something occurred to her. “Laura made all the arrangements, right?”

“Yeah.”

“Maybe I should check on the hotel. If one date was wrong that might be, too.”

“Good idea.”

After he walked back to the counter, Avery pulled the file with paperwork from her carry-on bag, then used her cell phone to make the call to the number listed. Her stomach dropped when the worst was confirmed. They were in Texas three days before the hotel expected them and had nowhere to stay.

When Spencer returned with car keys in hand she broke the news. “The hotel has us coming in on Sunday, too.”

“So, did you tell them we’re here now?”

“Yes. And, we’ve got a problem.”

“Oh, good. Another one.”

“There’s a convention in town and no rooms available,” she informed him.

“Great.” He rested his hands on lean hips.

“We need to find another hotel. Maybe we can ask the car rental agent for a recommendation. I can make some calls and find rooms.”

“No.” He shook his head. “I’ve got a better idea.”

“Better than a room?” She didn’t like the sound of that. “I hope you’re not planning to pitch a tent somewhere. If so, you should know that I’ve become pretty attached to things like beds, running water and that lovely little thing called electricity.”

“Not to worry.”

A gleam stole into his eyes and his mouth curved into a mischievous smile that snarled her senses and stole her breath. That reaction gave her a really bad feeling about his better idea.

"Worrying is what I do best," she said.

"The place I have in mind has beds, indoor plumbing and juice for your blow dryer."

"What do you have in mind?" she asked warily.

"My family will put us up."

His parents? The people who set such a high bar that being a doctor wasn't good enough?

"I couldn't possibly impose on them," she said quickly. "But you go ahead. I'll find a room somewhere. It will be fine."

"You won't be imposing. They'd love it."

"You can't just drop in and bring a friend." A Nobel Prize winning economist and biomedical engineer didn't sound like your average go-with-the-flow couple. "It's too much trouble. They'd have to make room—"

"My parents' house is like Buckingham Palace."

"Really?" The comparison to royalty did nothing to anesthetize her nerves.

"Not quite the palace, but it's got more square footage than they know what do with."

"Spencer, I can't."

"Sure you can. Live dangerously."

"That's not my style." Not anymore. The one time she'd done that her life had fallen apart.

"Then your style needs to loosen up."

"I like my style just fine, thank you very much. Fending for myself isn't a problem. We don't have to be joined at the hip. I've got your number."

And how. This was probably a blessing in disguise. Alternative housing would give her even more distance and that would be a good thing after he'd been so nice to her on the plane.

"Really, you go see your family," she urged him.

"Not without you. Come on." He curved his fingers around her upper arm and tugged her along.

Her head was spinning. That was the only reason she didn't put up more protest. So, not only was she going to meet the overachievers, she'd be staying with them.

Wouldn't that be fun?

About as much as a root canal without pain meds.

Spencer loved his folks, but visits were always a challenge. He was a nationally respected cardiothoracic surgeon, for God's sake, but all it took was walking through the front door of their house and he instantly became the boy he'd once been, always trying to prove himself. The child who worked so hard to be as good as they were and more. The kid who brought home flawless report cards and heard nothing unless one was less than perfect. Silent disappointment was the worst.

He pulled the rented Mercedes to a stop in front of the impressive brick house. This suburb of Dallas was home to a former president, chief executives of global companies worth billions, and Catherine and William Stone.

Without saying a word, Avery gaped at the sprawling, red brick structure with a portico supported by four white columns. The estate was set back from the street by a large, perfectly landscaped yard. When she looked back at him he saw that her jaw dropped and her mouth was open but no words came out.

"It's not often you're speechless." He rested his wrist on the steering wheel of the sporty car.

"It's not often a girl like me gets to see a house like this." She glanced at him, then turned back and stared some more. "I'm waiting for the riffraff police to show up and escort me back to the poor side of town."

"There's the bright, shiny optimist I've come to know."

"This is a joke, right? Your parents don't really live here, do they?"

"Come on. I'll show you."

Spencer got out of the car and went to the passenger side, then opened the door for Avery. She didn't get out right away and he was afraid it would take a shoehorn to dislodge her.

"You look like you're expecting a psycho killer to jump out of the bushes with a knife. What are you afraid of?"

"I told you. The riffraff police. Seriously."

"Stick with me, Tinker Bell. I'll protect you." Spencer took her hand in his and was surprised at how small it felt. How delicate. Not to mention how cold her fingers were. "Trust me. Catherine and William Stone don't bite."

Unless you performed below their expectations. The Stone children, especially the oldest son, were held to the highest possible standards. And those standards were perilously close to perfection, which meant no mistakes tolerated.

He tugged her up the front steps, past the columns and to the white front door. Then he took out his key and fit it into the lock.

"Aren't you going to knock?" Avery asked, clearly horrified.

"I grew up here."

"No way."

"'Fraid so." He unlocked the door and the alarm beeped. After punching in the code on the keypad to disarm it, he said, "Welcome to the Stone family home. Be it ever so humble and all that."

She walked inside and turned in a circle to take it all in. "This entryway is as big as my house."

"You're exaggerating." But he looked at the place where he'd spent his youth and tried to see it through her eyes.

On either side of the foyer were twin staircases with cherrywood spindles and banisters that led to the second story.

Marble tiles covered the floor right up to the thick beige carpet of the massive living room on one side and a formal parlor on the other. Straight ahead was the kitchen.

But Avery wasn't looking there. She was still in awe of the entry. "You could play roller hockey in here."

"In this house," he said wryly, "that would be like landing a 747 on water."

"What does that mean?"

"You'd only do it once."

"The butler was pretty strict?" she asked.

"No. He was a teddy bear. Mom didn't tolerate insubordination."

Avery was quiet a moment, listening. "Is anyone here?"

"Doesn't look like it. They're either at work or playing golf."

There was a pleading expression in her eyes. "Let's make a run for it. There's still time. I'll go to a hotel."

"No." His mother had hinted that they didn't see much of him and with his sister driving up from Houston it would be a good time to visit. Originally he'd given his office manager the dates for a quick trip to see the robot, one that included a dinner with his folks. But after he convinced Avery's boss to send her along, the trip got longer. Spencer was pleased, for some reason wanting her here, and surprised the reservation was screwed up. "The folks will be home soon and I'm sure would like to meet you. Want a guided tour?"

"This place looks like a museum, which would make you a docent."

"Used to be." That was as good a way as any to describe his childhood. He took her hand. Again he felt the delicacy. But this time it came with an instinct to protect her. It was unfamiliar because he never stayed with a woman long enough for anything that intimate to take hold. "Come on."

He led her into the kitchen with its white cupboards and

black granite countertops. His parents were nothing if not dramatic. The appliances were stainless steel. And spotless.

Avery's eyes were wide. "This is the biggest kitchen I've ever seen. Love the pots and pans hanging from the rack over the island. Which is big enough for a jumbo jet to taxi for takeoff."

His right eyebrow rose. "That's a curious metaphor given your aversion to planes."

"But appropriate." She walked to the doorway and glanced into the dining room with its formal cherrywood table and twelve cream-colored, brocade-covered chairs. The matching breakfront and buffet lined the room with enough space left over for a touch football game.

"Love the white crown molding and chair rail against the yellow walls."

"My mother did the decorating."

"She has excellent taste."

He walked her upstairs and through the six bedrooms, two that shared a bath and the others with their own. There was more crown molding, chair rail, matching furniture and coordinating window coverings. Avery oohed and aahed at everything.

"It's not that big a deal," he protested.

"Maybe not to you. But to a girl who grew up in a rundown north Las Vegas trailer park, this is a *very* big deal."

That was the first time she'd shared anything about herself, but what really got Spencer's attention were the shadows in her eyes after saying it, the same shadows he noticed at the wedding. Just like then, he wondered what she was thinking. "It's just a roof over our heads."

She made a scoffing noise. "As roofs go, it's perfect."

His parents wouldn't have it any other way. And just as they reached the downstairs entryway, in walked his father and mother.

"Oh—" Tall, blonde Catherine Stone smiled. "Mystery solved. Now we know who belongs to the car out front. What are you doing here, Spencer?"

"I have business in Dallas and just stopped by."

"You didn't say a word. And I thought you were going to miss your sister's visit. Isn't this a wonderful surprise, Will?" She smiled warmly and gave him a hug.

"The best." His father was the same height as Spencer. Trim and silver-haired.

"Hi, Dad."

"Good to see you, son." Blue eyes that missed nothing settled on Avery. "Who's this?"

"Avery O'Neill. She's the controller at Mercy Medical Center." He met her gaze. "This is my mother and father. Catherine and William Stone."

"It's a pleasure to meet you both." She shook their hands.

"You should have told us you were coming," Catherine said. "We could have put off our golf game and been here to meet you."

"I wanted it to be a surprise." Always better that way, he'd learned. Catching them off guard gave them less opportunity to do a mental bullet point presentation of how to make his life perfect.

"You definitely did that. What business brings you to Dallas?" Will asked.

"We're looking into the robotic surgical systems at Baylor and Dallas Medical Center. I want to see it in action and Avery's job is to figure out how to pay for it."

"Ah, numbers. A girl after my own heart." His father smiled.

"So it really is business?" His mother looked let down.

Only a minute into the visit and Spencer had already disappointed her. "Yeah. Why?"

She shrugged. "It's just that we never get a chance to meet—your friends."

She'd hesitated just long enough so that he knew she meant *girlfriends.* The only time he'd brought home a girl to meet the folks it had been a disaster.

"It really is just business." He looked at Avery and saw disapproval in her eyes. Apparently he was disappointing all females today. "But there was a glitch in our travel arrangements and the hotel isn't expecting us until Sunday night. I was hoping—"

"The thing is—" Avery cut him off. "Spencer wanted me to see the house. And it's really lovely. But now he's taking me to find a hotel."

"Absolutely not. You'll stay here with us." Will put a hand on her shoulder. "And what kind of hosts are we? Let's go into the family room."

"I don't want to impose, sir," she protested.

"The name is Will and you're not imposing." There was actually a twinkle in his father's blue eyes. That was a first. "Did you see the size of this place? A person could wander around for weeks and not run into another living soul."

"Will is right." His mother slipped her arm through Avery's and urged her toward the other room. "We'll just go get comfortable and visit. Then we'll have cocktails and figure out something for dinner."

"I don't want you to go to any trouble." Avery glanced over her shoulder and the look she shot him promised retribution. "It's not okay to drop in without warning. I'll just find—"

"I absolutely won't hear of it," Catherine said. "Any friend of Spencer's and all that. Now sit. Relax. Will and I will put together a tray of refreshments. We don't see nearly enough of Spencer."

Zinger. But they were really being gracious and welcoming to Avery. He was grateful for it. "Thanks, Mom. Dad."

Catherine stopped on her way to the kitchen. "As you know, Becky, Dan and the twins are driving up from Houston this weekend. So Adam is planning to come by. It's an unofficial family reunion. Too bad your grandmother isn't in town. She's on a cruise to Greece."

When they were alone Avery plopped on the sofa and glared. "And who are Becky, Dan and the twins?"

"My sister. Her husband. And my niece and nephew. And I already told you about my brother, Adam. He lives here in Dallas."

"So it really is a family reunion."

"Not officially. Gram isn't here. And thank your lucky stars for that."

"Why?"

"How can I put this in terms you'll understand?" He thought for a moment and remembered her first words. "My paternal grandmother, Eugenia Stone, *is* the riffraff police."

"Ah. My stars truly are lucky." She linked her fingers in her lap.

"Yes, indeed." Spencer had managed to choose a medical specialty that impressed his not-easy-to-impress grandmother. But Adam hadn't escaped the scrutiny and continued to take a ration of crap over his career choice. "She's a domineering old bat."

"Wow, I feel much better now." There was steel in her voice although even that didn't disguise the anxiety in her eyes. "You are in so much trouble, Doctor."

"Why? The folks are happy to meet you. Any friend of Spencer's…"

"We're not friends."

"No?" He sat down beside her. "That hurts. And after I

bared my soul on the plane just to take your mind off taking off."

"Yeah." She blew out a breath. "And all you gave me was that becoming a doctor to have sex with women was your motivation."

He covered her cold hands with one of his. "There's no need to be nervous."

"Easy for you to say."

Not really. He was in for a private grilling on what he'd done recently that was noteworthy. Awards. Commendations. Articles published in the Journal of the American Medical Association. It's just how his folks were and Spencer hoped he measured up because they were a very tough act to follow.

"If I can't talk you out of being anxious, I'll let you ask me more personal questions to distract you."

There was grudging gratitude on her face. "There you go being nice again. Just stop. It's out of character for you. And I have to say that it's freaking me out."

He laughed and draped an arm around her shoulders for a quick hug. "That's my girl."

The words came naturally, but she wasn't his girl and the thought nicked a vein of regret. Having someone be his girl would require crossing a line he didn't want to cross. It was bad enough that Avery had him flirting with that line, but a smart guy like him wouldn't go there again.

Chapter Five

The next morning Avery walked downstairs and followed the smell of coffee which led her to the kitchen. Spencer was already there, his back to her as she walked in the room.

The click of her low-heeled shoes sounded on the marble tile and he turned. "Good morning. Did you sleep well? Was the room comfy? Running water? Electricity?"

"It's like a hotel suite." And she'd slept as well as could be expected what with knowing he wasn't far away in a bed under the very same perfect roof.

Letting his gaze wander over her navy crepe jacket and slacks, he said, "You got some place to be?"

"Actually, as you know, my meeting was canceled. I have nowhere to be until Monday morning."

"And yet you look like you're dressed for work."

It would be easier that way. The longer she spent with Spencer Stone, the more the line between personal and professional blurred. Dressing for work was like putting on armor for a medieval joust. Plus… "This is all I brought with me."

He put his mug on the granite countertop as if even holding it skewered his concentration. "You didn't plan to do anything but work on this trip?"

"You make it sound like an offense punishable by death."

"It kind of is." He folded his arms over his chest, drawing attention to the way his casual T-shirt outlined the muscular contours. The shorts he had on showed off equally muscular calves with a dusting of hair that was incredibly masculine and appealing. "Life is about more than business and work. No one, including your boss, expects you to only attend meetings or be in a hotel room."

"So, you're saying I should have brought sporty clothes?" she asked.

"Yes."

"Wow."

"What?"

"You're probably the only man on the planet giving a woman grief for *under* packing."

"Excuse me? Was that a compliment?"

"Did it sound like one? Hope not, because I wasn't being nice."

His grin and the gleam in his green eyes tilted her world, a world that was already spinning sideways. He'd been nothing but funny and sweet since picking her up yesterday morning. On top of that she'd spent the night in his parents' home and they couldn't have been more hospitable to her. That's because they didn't know her past, her secret, her badness. And there was no reason why they ever should. Or Spencer, either.

"Speaking of nice," she said, "where are your folks?"

"Working. Both had things to take care of."

If they'd known he was coming would those things have

been put on hold? Is that why he hadn't given them advanced warning? "It was nice of you to surprise them."

"It's better that way." His tone was light, but the humor faded from his eyes. "Then there's no disappointment if it doesn't work out."

An interesting reaction that made her wonder how a busy, brilliant and successful son like Spencer could possibly let down his family. He was the best in his field and highly respected across the country. She was about to ask, then thought better of it. Whatever his issues, they had nothing to do with her. Yesterday he'd implied they were friends, but she wasn't so sure.

"It would appear the stars and planets are aligned since this unplanned Stone family reunion is coming together." She remembered his mother saying that they didn't see enough of him. Must be nice to have family that cared whether or not you visited. Avery wouldn't know.

"Since the rest of the family isn't due until tomorrow," he said, "you and I are on our own today."

"I've got work. Things I need to look at before Monday—"

He shook his head. "You've got bigger problems than that."

"I do?"

"The folks are planning a barbecue tomorrow. Around the pool. What are you going to wear?"

She looked down at her pricey pants and the matching jacket. The white silk blouse was one of her favorites. "I don't have much choice unless you want to do surgery on this outfit. You could take your scalpel to these expensive slacks and turn them into cutoffs."

"Although it looks lovely on you, that suit is a little conservative for my taste. I had something else in mind."

"Going naked isn't an option."

"As appealing as that would be," he said, green eyes instantly intense, "I was thinking of something else."

"What?"

"A trip to the mall," he said.

She gaped at him. "Now you're starting to scare me."

"I don't know why." He picked up the mug beside him. "The last time I checked, it was a good place to pick up non-professional clothes to get you through the weekend."

"I could find some things at a discount store. There's no need to jump into organized and sustained shopping with both feet."

"Why not? I don't mind it."

"I can see how you managed to stay friends with all your women."

"Oh? And how do you know I do that?"

"It's a rumor."

"And why does shopping explain it?"

She shrugged. "A man who's not afraid of the mall is an incredibly brave and appealing man. But since I'm not one of your women, a full-on retail fling to impress me really isn't necessary."

"True." He sipped his coffee. "But would you turn down the opportunity to compare and contrast Dallas stores with Fashion Show Mall in Las Vegas?"

She stared at him, knowing he'd backed her into a corner. He'd taken away every possible out for her except the excuse that she was a quart low on estrogen. Or admitting the truth—which was that she was doing her best to avoid him.

That had been her plan when getting out of this trip became impossible. He'd play with the high-tech toys and she'd play with the numbers. Their paths would be parallel but not intersecting, giving his charisma little or no chance to work on her.

She'd been so wrong about everything, including her immunity to the effects of his charm. But she was nothing if not a realist. There was no choice but to take him up on his offer and go shopping. If only to show him his flirting was a waste of time and energy.

"Thank you, Spencer, I'd love to go to the mall with you."

"Excellent."

After a quick breakfast of coffee and toast, they were in the rental car on the way to Galleria Dallas. Spencer drove confidently, as if he knew the streets like the back of his hand, which he probably did.

"So, you grew up in Dallas?" she asked.

He glanced at her and nodded, his eyes hidden by dark aviator sunglasses. "I was born in that house. Actually at a hospital, but you get the drift."

"Wow. So your parents didn't go through the poor-as-church-mice stage of marriage?"

"No. My dad's family is pretty well off."

Duh. Eugenia Stone. His father came from the side of the family with old money.

"In some ways that makes your success in the medical profession even more remarkable." She kept to herself the fact that it also made her like him even more.

He guided the car onto the freeway, or tollway, or a multiple-lane road with a number that clearly meant something to him. "Why remarkable?"

"You didn't need the money, but still made something of yourself." She'd made something of herself because she needed the money. When you don't have any, a profession working with it makes perfect sense.

His mouth pulled tight for a moment. "So, you think I could have rested on my laurels and lived off the family money?"

"Yes."

"Clearly you don't know my family." There was an edge to his voice.

Avery studied his profile and realized she didn't need a full-on expression to know this topic wasn't his favorite. "You don't want to talk about this, do you?"

"Not particularly."

"Okay." She looked at the lush landscape whizzing by. The stately architecture made even older buildings look graceful and elegant. "Why is everything made out of bricks?"

"It's not, actually. That's a facade. But the material is easily accessible which makes it cheap."

"And pretty." She looked out at the flat land and felt as if she could see for miles. "It's so green here. Trees, grass, shrubs, flowers. So different from Las Vegas."

"Texas gets a lot of rain when there's not a drought. It's humid, not a desert."

"So, unlike native Nevadans or transplants like yourself, Texans don't look at a pile of rocks and immediately think landscaping?"

"No." He laughed and the tension eased out of his jaw.

Avery couldn't see his eyes, but somehow knew the gleam would be back. It would spoil her day to examine exactly why that pleased her, so she didn't. He was taking her to the mall and she refused to analyze or think about anything that would ruin shopping.

Spencer had expected to grit his teeth and get through the retail experience, but it was actually fun. He looked down at Avery's happy smile and knew she was the reason. He realized something else, too. Keeping the smile on her face was more and more something he wanted to do.

"So, where to now?" He fell into step beside her as they walked out of Nordstrom where she'd purchased a pair of jeans on sale.

The price had made her sweat, but the upscale store offered free alterations and the pants needed shortening. She'd joked that they could make shorts out of what they cut off, but saving money made her feel a little better. After what she'd said about growing up in a trailer park, he understood why that was important. Clearly, she'd made something of herself without having advantages. Getting an education is easy if you don't have to worry about how to pay for it. He would bet she'd had to worry. There were many reasons he respected her, but that was at the top of the list.

"We have at least an hour until your jeans are ready. And you'll need a few more things for the weekend."

Her shoulder brushed his arm as they strolled down the main mall corridor. It was bright and very mall-like with stores on either side.

"Saks Fifth Avenue is out of the question. Too pricey." She was focused on storefronts passing by and didn't look up at him.

Just as well. He was fairly certain the fact that he was charmed by her would show in his expression. It never would have occurred to him that beneath her feisty and frugal exterior beat the heart of a retail marathoner and he liked that about her, too.

"I follow the sale signs," she said, explaining her strategy. "Ooh, look." She pointed to the Ann Taylor shop. "They have sizes for petites."

That she was, he thought. Tiny and tough and too guarded for her own good.

"Speaking of small," he said, following her into the shop. "I'm having trouble grasping the concept of a size zero."

"Why?" She was already browsing through a rack of shorts in her size and every time she pulled one out, he took it from her.

"Because zero is nothing. How can it be a legitimate size?"

"It's smaller than the next size up, that's how." She apparently thought that made it crystal-clear.

"If someone is too small to wear it, does the size designation go into negative territory?"

Her hand stilled on the hangers and she looked up, her lips twitching. "In that scenario one would have two choices."

"And they are?"

"Custom-made clothes or shopping in the children's section of a department store."

"Okay."

He stood behind her, studying the particularly tantalizing column of her throat. His fingers ached to move that prim white silk collar aside and have his way with the skin on her neck, to see how she tasted. Feel the moment his touch made her shiver.

To distract himself from the erotic thoughts he said, "I had no idea how complicated women's clothes are."

"You act like this is your first time, Doctor. I got the impression you've done a lot of shopping."

"No. I just said that I didn't mind shopping. And this is my first time checking out the Tinker Bell rack. Where's the fairy dust glitter?"

She ignored that. "So, your type of woman doesn't need to have several inches taken off the hem of her jeans?"

"There is no 'my type.'" Not completely true since he'd thought the same thing at the wedding. Avery wasn't what he considered his type, but the fact that there was something fascinating about her hadn't changed.

"Oh, you definitely have a type, Spencer. And your women don't need to have the hems taken up on their jeans." She smiled mysteriously before saying, "I'm going to try on this stuff."

"Okay."

Spencer watched the sway of her hips as she walked to the dressing room in the back of the store. At some point he would have to set her straight on the record of "his women." She made it sound like he dated every tall, eligible bachelorette in the Las Vegas Valley, which wasn't true. Although he also wasn't a monk.

The thing was no one would accuse him of being especially intuitive where feelings were concerned. But he couldn't shake the impression that Avery used "his women" remarks to create a barrier between them. Two days ago that would have been okay, but now it wasn't and he couldn't define why.

He wandered around the store for about ten minutes before finally spotting her at the cash register with several pairs of shorts and a couple shirts. This woman made up her mind quickly and knew what she wanted. The thought popped into his mind before he could stop it.

He hoped she wanted him.

And that was just stupid. Not because dating a woman from Mercy Medical Center was frowned upon. He'd done that before without causing friction in the workplace. It was because Avery wasn't a casual fling. He'd worked hard to take the wary expression out of her eyes and was making progress on that front. But he wasn't sure how far he wanted it to go. A guy had hurt her and he didn't want to be a repeat. If he was a betting man, he'd put money on the fact that she was attracted to him, too. The best plan he had was one step at a time, taking his cues from her.

She met him in the doorway with her bag and he took it from her.

"I can carry that," she protested.

"I'm a guy. It's what we do."

"Not in my world." Just like that her wary look was back.

Damn it.

Time to change the subject. "Did you bring sneakers?"

"Didn't think I'd need them," she said.

"You will for what I have in mind next."

"And what would that be?"

"It's a surprise."

"I don't like surprises." Tension tightened her voice and that got his attention.

Spencer looked down and saw that her happy smile was gone. "That's just wrong, Miss O'Neill. It's a bad attitude and one I intend to change."

"Good luck with that."

By the time she picked out sneakers, socks and sandals, her jeans were ready. She changed out of her suit and the salesperson put it on a hanger with clear plastic. Avery was now dressed for fun and he planned to make sure that happened. It was time to show her around.

He drove to the West End of Dallas and passed the Sixth Floor Museum where the memorabilia and pictures of the Kennedy assassination were displayed. Then he got on the freeway.

"Am I being kidnapped?" Avery said after almost an hour. "You're starting to scare me."

"So you keep saying. This is just another side to my personality."

"I'm not sure I like this side that keeps promising a surprise."

"Trust me."

"Famous last words. That's what all the serial killers say."

"We're almost there." He saw his exit and took it.

She saw the signs, too. "This is Fort Worth."

"I know. We're going to the Stockyards. It's a big tourist attraction."

He followed directions to the nonpaved parking area,

pulled in and took a ticket for payment. After finding a space and turning off the car, they got out and walked through the lot. Souvenir, clothing stores and restaurants with Western facades lined the street. Before they could cross, he noticed the spectators gathering on both sides of the road.

Avery started to move, but he put a hand out to stop her. "Wait."

"Why?"

"You'll see."

A few minutes later men dressed like cowboys in worn jeans, boots, hats and chaps herded a couple of bored long-horn steers past where they were standing.

"In the 1800s this is where ranchers from the southwest brought their stock to be shipped to market," he said.

"Very cool." She pointed across the street. "That cowboy parked his steer over there by the hitching post. Look at the sharp horns on that thing. And people are taking pictures of kids sitting on its back."

"Do you want one?" he asked.

"A picture?" She looked up, eyes wide. "I'm not sitting on a wild animal. If he turns his head too fast someone could lose an eye."

"Coward. I think they're old, tired and probably on Prozac." He took her elbow as they moved with the crowd to the opposite side of the street. "How about something to eat?"

"I'm starving."

"Barbecue ribs okay? There's a place here that has the best anywhere, in my humble opinion." When she nodded, he escorted her to Riske's. It was past lunchtime so there was no wait for a table. After ordering two beers, beef ribs with fries and corn on the cob, he watched Avery look around.

"I can see why you made me buy sneakers and change

into jeans. Very Old West," she said. "Just the opposite of Dallas."

"Dallas and Fort Worth are two sides of the Texas coin. One sophisticated, the other laid back. It's a unique juxtaposition." From the expression on her face he could tell she was impressed by the wooden floors. Red-and-white-checkered cloths covered the tables. The decor was Western—ropes, saddles, wagons, wood.

She met his gaze and smiled. "Thanks for bringing me here, Spencer."

"You're welcome." He saw hesitation and knew there was something else. "What?"

She glanced down for a moment before adding, "I wanted to tell you that I might have misjudged you."

"Might have—how?"

She rubbed a finger over the plastic tablecloth, tracing a red square. "You're not what I expected."

"And what was that?"

"A jerk."

"Thanks, I think."

"I'm not saying this very well," she apologized. "I didn't expect that you'd be fun and funny. You're so difficult and demanding at the hospital."

"I like to think of it more as having perseverance and high standards."

"You say potato, I say po-tah-to." She shrugged. "But you're a lot more likable than I thought you'd be."

"Did you just say I'm a nice doctor?"

The pink that colored her cheeks clearly indicated she remembered her comments when she didn't know he was standing behind her. "Don't push your luck, Doctor."

He couldn't help it. That was a cue if he'd ever heard one. She'd told her friend that if she ever met a nice doctor, she'd have sex with him right there. Obviously she hadn't meant at the Fort Worth Stockyards, but he intended to find somewhere private.

Very soon.

Chapter Six

The next day Avery met the rest of Spencer's family. His younger sister, Becky Stone Markham, her husband, Dan, and their six-year-old twins, Kendrick and Melanie, drove in from Houston, arriving midmorning. Adam showed up about an hour later. Introductions and explanations of her presence were made and now Dan and the twins were in the pool. Everyone else was sitting outside on the covered patio.

This backyard was the biggest Avery had ever seen, but things were bigger in Texas, right? Beyond the brick-trimmed cement was an Olympic-size pool. On the other side of it, the expanse of grass stopped at a creek that surrounded a small area of earth, shrubs and trees. These people owned an island, for goodness' sake. So far no one had accused her of being a fraud and asked her to leave.

Catherine bustled around setting out snacks and refilling ice chests with water, soda and beer. Finally, she joined the group and asked her daughter, "What's new at NASA, dear?"

That's not a question Avery had ever heard before in polite, casual conversation. She was sitting on a plush, cushion-covered love seat beside Spencer and she was successfully hiding her tension. Other than her feeling like a failing student in the Advanced Placement class, it was a beautiful late-April day and she was glad to have shorts and a cotton shirt from the mall.

"Not much new at NASA. Same old, same old. Not enough money and too many politicians butting in." Becky had light brown hair and beautiful blue eyes. She had to be in her early thirties, but looked too young to be a rocket scientist. There must have been skipped grades along the way. She was sitting on the arm of her father's chair, her hand on his shoulder. "We're in transition, what with the shuttle program ended."

"I can't believe you haven't perfected wormhole technology to facilitate nonvehicle travel to other planets," Will said.

"But no pressure," his daughter teased.

"Just saying." Will shrugged. "A discovery like that would put us way ahead of other countries in terms of technology, discovery and military defense strategy."

"I'll work on it, Dad. On one condition." She patted his shoulder. "You stop watching old episodes of *Stargate SG-1*."

Adam laughed. His coloring was the same as his twin sister, but in a masculine way. He bore a striking resemblance to the actor who'd played Captain Kirk in the most recent *Star Trek* movie. "You got him there, Becks."

Will didn't deny it. "I find the show relaxing after a stressful day."

"More soothing than golf?" Spencer asked.

"Yes. No one keeps score," his father said. "Except the characters who count how many times *SG-1* has saved the world."

Avery wondered if they kept score for their children. From

what Spencer had said, he felt a lot of pressure to perform. Did Becky and Adam, too?

Adam studied his parents. "When are you two going to retire?"

"Never." Catherine looked at her husband. "What would we do with ourselves?"

"We still have a lot to offer the world." Will winked at his wife.

Avery was in awe of the global scope their areas of expertise involved. They cast a large shadow and had three extraordinary children, too.

"Still, Dad, stress takes a toll," Spencer pointed out. "It can compromise organ function and is a proven risk factor for heart attacks."

"There's nothing wrong with my heart."

"So you've had your annual physical?" Adam asked.

"I've been busy."

"Don't put it off, Dad." Adam leaned forward, resting his elbows on his knees.

"Since when did you become a cardiac specialist?" There was a twinkle in Will's eyes as he deflected attention from himself. It didn't take a rocket scientist to see he didn't want to answer the question.

"Ah." Adam's nod said he was accustomed to this conversation. "Here we go. Avery, just so you know, I'm the Stone clan's slacker. It's a dirty job, but someone had to do it."

"Spencer said you're a family practice physician."

"Is that even a medical specialty?" Becky taunted.

"For your information, twinner, it's a focus of medicine that provides continuing and comprehensive health care for individuals and families across all ages, sexes, diseases and parts of the body. Medical intervention is based on knowledge of the patient in the context of family and community, emphasizing disease prevention and health promotion."

"So you know a little bit about a lot of stuff?" Spencer joked.

"The good of the many outweighs the good of the one," Adam said to defend himself. "Everything has to work together efficiently. And there are an infinite number of factors that influence the whole. Specializing in, say, cardiothoracic surgery is like teaching a child math without reading. Or reading without math. Balance is the key."

"I see your point," Avery said. "And I bet Spencer doesn't need a robot. He just wants a new, expensive toy."

"Traitor," Spencer said. "I thought you were on my side."

"I have yet to form an opinion about your surgery system." Tingles marched down her spine when his breath tickled her ear. It was difficult to form a rational thought but she did her best to pull everything together. This was not a group prone to tolerating an idiot. "I'm not taking sides. Merely acknowledging the practicality of the field."

"I like her." Adam grinned and looked at his brother. "She's a keeper."

"I'll pass that along to the powers-that-be at Mercy Medical Center."

"I appreciate that." Avery felt a slight stab of disappointment that he'd flipped a personal remark back to the professional, and how crazy was that? That was the comfort zone she'd been struggling to achieve.

"Speaking of Mercy Medical," Adam said. "The corporation funds small clinics all over the country."

In her position as controller, she saw a lot of financial information regarding the company's different operations. "I knew that," Avery said.

"I didn't." Spencer stared at his brother.

"You would if you looked at the big picture instead of just one small part." Adam hesitated for a half second, then said to his parents, "I've applied for a job at a clinic in Blackwater Lake."

"Montana?" Will asked.

"Yes. It's a challenge to retain a doctor there and the community needs one."

"It's a challenge because the community is so small. And rural," his mother said, clearly not happy. "What about your career? That's a step backward—"

"Not if it's what you want, and I do." Adam's tone didn't allow for argument and his jaw tightened.

There was an awkward silence until Becky said, "Grandmother will not be happy."

"The heck with Eugenia," Catherine said. "I'm not happy."

Spencer leaned down and whispered, "Riffraff police."

"I heard that," Adam said. "And while Grandmother is less than diplomatic a good portion of the time, she always tells it like it is. And I think you all know that I'm her favorite grandchild."

"There's no accounting for taste," Becky countered, not denying the statement.

The uncomfortable banter continued, but eventually passed, and Avery enjoyed watching Spencer interact with his family. It was a side of him she'd never seen before. However competitive the Stones were, each of them had a place to belong and the love they shared was obvious.

Growing up, Avery had only her mother and after the pressure to give up her baby, that bond had all but disappeared. A couple of years ago her mom died of cancer and she felt the familiar twinge of pain and regret that they never truly reconciled. Avery knew now that letting her baby be adopted had been the only choice. She just hoped, and said a little prayer every day, that her daughter's mother and father loved her as much as Will and Catherine Stone did their kids.

"Penny for your thoughts." The deep voice pulled her back

from the dark reflections. Spencer was still sitting beside her on the love seat.

She met his gaze. “Hmm?”

Spencer frowned. “You have the strangest look on your face. Where did you go?”

The bad place, she wanted to say. To the emptiness inside her that, because it would never be filled, she tried to close off. Sometimes she was successful and sometimes the memory came back unexpectedly and brought with it a sharp pain. But the shame wasn’t something she talked about. Not even to Ryleigh who was her best friend. And she barely knew these people.

Avery looked at the bustle around her. Becky and Catherine wrapped fluffy towels around the twins, who were wet from the pool and hungry after swimming. Their dad was air-drying as he chatted with Will and Adam.

“I was just thinking what a wonderful family you have. Your folks did a great job with you guys.” That wasn’t a lie. It’s what had been going through her mind. Among other things.

Spencer’s gaze skittered away to his folks, but darkness mixed with pride on his face. “They are great, but it wasn’t easy to grow up in this family.”

“Because they expected a lot?” On the plane he’d taken her mind off her fear of flying with teasers about himself.

“If I screwed up,” he confirmed, “I heard about it big-time.”

“Oh, please. This is you we’re talking about. Make a mistake? *The* Spencer Stone, M.D.?” She shook her head. “Never.”

“Boy are you wrong.” He wasn’t kidding.

“Okay. Tell me one time you messed up.”

“I asked the wrong girl to marry me.”

Had she heard right? Mercy Medical Center's most eligible bachelor? "I didn't know you were married."

"I'm not—now or ever."

"Then I don't get it."

He blew out a long breath. "In college I fell in love with an art major. That was mistake number one. Math and science gave her hives. Imagine that in this family. But she was beautiful, outgoing and free-spirited. A breath of fresh air and so different from anyone I'd ever known before."

"And you asked her to marry you."

He nodded. "I was going to med school and wanted her to come with me."

That was so romantic. Something she'd never expected from him. "What happened?"

"I didn't expect her to say thanks for asking, but no."

Avery couldn't believe she'd heard him right. "She turned you down?"

"Yes." There wasn't the slightest hint of amusement in his tone or expression. "My first mistake, no, make it the second after proposing, was telling my sister. She blabbed everything. Then the folks weighed in about how shocked they were at my choice. The girl was completely wrong and inappropriate. They never liked her and wondered what I saw in 'that woman.'"

"Throw salt in the wound," she muttered.

"Yeah." His voice was grim, as if the memory still stung. "No sugarcoating how they felt. In fact, they said straight out that wasting my time with her was a blunder of major proportions. So, even without actually making the mistake of marrying her, I royally messed up. An art major was wrong for me in every way and on top of that, she'd never have fit into the family."

Avery put her hand on his, a gesture to convey her empathy because somehow she knew he wouldn't want to hear words of sympathy. "Tough crowd."

There was a wry expression on his face. "You have no idea."

And there was no chance she ever would. If any of them found out her secret, Spencer would get an earful about setting a low bar by associating with the likes of her, let alone dating. Or falling in love. She was certainly a waste of his time. The Stone family would frown on their firstborn getting involved with a woman who got pregnant and gave up her baby. And it was the last part that would be unforgivable because facing up to mistakes was a responsibility. The thing was, Avery couldn't forgive herself. How could she expect anyone else to?

But Spencer's confession made him seem more human, more likable even than yesterday at the Stockyards. Or the day before that on the plane. If she'd stayed safely tucked away in her Mercy Medical Center Las Vegas comfort zone, she would never have known that the man who had so many women had once been hurt by one. That explained a lot about why, by virtue of sheer numbers, his relationships were so superficial. He did that on purpose.

It would be so much easier if he was the jerk she'd thought. And better still if she'd kept to herself the fact that she thought he was a nice doctor. One who'd overheard her say if she found one, she would have sex with him. How she wished she didn't want to.

Later that evening Adam had gone home and his twin sister took her tired family upstairs to settle in for the night. Avery sat on the patio with the rest of the Stones and Spencer was beside her on the love seat. Again. That was becoming a pattern and the jury was out on whether or not it was a good one.

Every time their arms bumped or thighs brushed, she felt a pop, snap and crackle, then immediately looked for the sparks to show up in the dark night. She'd tried a couple of times to excuse herself and go inside, but each attempt resulted in either Spencer or one of his parents deliberately drawing her back into the conversation. She kept waiting for them to realize she was a fraud.

"Seriously, Avery, I can't thank you enough for all your help getting dinner on the table." Catherine was on the love seat across from them, beside her husband. "I'm so grateful. Everything went like clockwork. The extra pair of hands made a huge difference, what with children around. And I don't just mean Becky's kids."

"I didn't do that much," Avery protested.

"That's not what I saw." Spencer shifted to look down at her and his leg touched hers, then stayed put. "My mother, better known as Maleficent, kept you in the kitchen for hours."

Avery hoped the glare she shot him was visible in the moonlight and he would move his thigh away. The contact was distracting.

"Don't say that to your mother. It's the least I could do to thank your folks for their hospitality."

Catherine smiled and ignored her son's teasing. "It wasn't necessary to earn your keep, sweetheart, but very much appreciated."

"I was happy to help." She looked at Spencer. "And you were less useful than a bump on a pickle."

"Excuse me?"

"There were vegetables to cut up. Fruit to slice and dice. You were nowhere to be found."

He folded his arms over his chest and his shoulder grazed hers. "I was deeply involved in a very competitive game of

Marco Polo with my niece and nephew. The stakes were very high."

"Oh?" Her tone conveyed the sarcasm of her raised eyebrow that he might not notice in the dim light on the patio. "And what was that?"

"We were going for king of the pool."

"Who won?" Catherine asked.

"I did."

"That's funny," she said. "Much like the Queen of England, a title with no power. You were unable to exert any influence over peace around here tonight."

"Your skills," Avery agreed, "would have been better served in the kitchen."

"Really?" Now *his* tone conveyed the sarcasm of a raised eyebrow.

"You're a surgeon," Avery pointed out. "Cutting the celery sticks in just the right diagonal lines is right up your alley. And scooping out the watermelon without getting too close to the rind would not have been a challenge for you."

"No," he said, "but, alas, these hands must be protected at all costs."

"No excuses, Doctor." She shook her head emphatically. "What with your superior IQ, I expected you to think those carrots into slices and take the tops off those strawberries with sheer mental power."

Will and Catherine thought that was hilarious and laughed until they cried.

"Oh, Avery," his mother said, wiping her eyes, "you are the most refreshing young woman he's ever brought around."

"No scraping and bowing from you." Will nodded approvingly. "I like her, son. She keeps your hat size in check."

"Come to think of it," Catherine said, "you haven't brought anyone home for quite some time. How long has it been?"

With their bodies touching, Avery felt Spencer tense and knew why. She figured right around the time he went to medical school was when he'd introduced the wrong woman to his folks and he still had the marks from that experience. The thing was, he hadn't brought anyone home now, not the way they meant. And if the truth about her came out, there was no question in her mind that they would be pretty vocal about his mistake.

Oddly enough, she felt an impulse to protect him. "Spencer doesn't have time for women."

"You don't date, son?" His father sounded just the slightest bit concerned.

"Too many people depend on him. He's busy saving lives and has no interest in meaningless, time-consuming personal pursuits."

"Really?" his mother said.

"Avery is exaggerating." There was a barely concealed trace of amusement in Spencer's voice. "I go out."

"When he can," Avery added. "And believe me, it's not easy being Dr. Spencer Stone, dedicated to fixing hearts. But it's a good thing he's so gifted because when he walks down the hall in the hospital you can almost hear hearts breaking."

Will playfully shook his finger at her. "You're teasing us."

"I'd never do that," Avery promised. "It's his chops I'm busting."

"Well done." Catherine applauded.

"Hey, you guys," Spencer protested, "I'm sitting right here."

Avery teasingly punched him in the shoulder. "Imagine what I say behind your back."

"Actually," he mused, "I don't have to imagine. I walked in on you telling Ryleigh Damian what you really thought of me."

"I remember."

Was the erotic gruffness in his voice only obvious to her? Thank goodness it was dark out here, Avery thought. His parents couldn't see that her face was bright red, although Spencer could probably feel the heat radiating. She only had herself to blame for the sex-with-a-nice-doctor remark. Saying it wasn't a problem. His overhearing it was.

"So, don't keep us in suspense," Will prodded. "What did you say behind his back?"

"Oh, wow," she stalled. "It's been a while. I think it had something to do with how determined he is."

Spencer leaned down and whispered in her ear, "Liar, liar, pants on fire."

It was true, and she felt the fire of her attraction inside and out.

"He always did have a lot of perseverance," his mother said. "Before he was a year old, he was determined to walk. When he fell, there was no crying. He just got up and tried again."

Not with relationships, Avery thought. He admitted being in love, but that didn't work out. Now all she'd seen was quantity over quality. One would have to assume it knocked him down and he had no intention of getting up to try again.

Will chuckled at the memory of his son learning to walk. "Strong willed, that's Spencer. If he set his mind to something, look out. He'd go after it with a vengeance."

Avery embraced that warning although she knew from firsthand experience that Spencer Stone didn't give up. If he had, she wouldn't be here now.

"You don't get to be one of the top cardiothoracic surgeons in the country without motivation. And the goal should be getting to number one," Will added.

Motivation was a good thing, Avery thought, but couldn't help wondering about Spencer's. He'd opened up to her and she knew his parents' approval was important to him. *She* could see that he already had that, but got the feeling he was still trying to cancel out that one mistake.

"Speaking of motivation," Catherine said, "it's getting late and I'm tired."

"Me, too." Will stood and held out his hand to pull his wife to her feet. "See you in the morning, you two."

"Good night," Avery and Spencer said together.

Then they were alone.

It could have been romantic except that she was who she was. And Spencer was who he was. None of that, however, stopped her heart from beating too fast. All of a sudden breathing became tough to pull off. Spencer was like a fire that sucked the oxygen out of the space he occupied. The best remedy was to exit his space. Stat.

"I think I'll turn in, too," she said.

"What's your hurry?"

"No hurry. Just tired. Tomorrow is going to be another busy day."

"Why? We're just hanging out," he said.

"Right. I like your family, but just for the record, the Stones are exhausting."

"Point taken. You need your rest." His quick agreement was surprising. "Just give me a chance to thank you."

"For what?"

"Coming to my rescue. About dating," he added. "Why did you?"

"That's a good question." She shrugged. "But I don't have an answer."

"Champion of the underdog?"

Avery laughed because that was so not the way she thought of him. "You are many things, but underdog isn't one of them."

"Sometimes it doesn't feel that way."

The edge in his voice confirmed her guess that he didn't

see the approval. "You gotta love family. Can't live with 'em, can't drag 'em behind the camper."

He laughed. "That statement has an oddly redneck sort of Zen wisdom."

"And on that note, I'm going to say good night." She stood quickly before he could do something to change her mind. Not that he would, but still.

He unfolded himself from the love seat and looked down at her. "Okay."

As they walked through the house, he turned off lights. Then he followed her upstairs and to the door of her room, just down the hall from his.

"See you in the morning." She put her hand on the knob.

He didn't move, just looked down at her. "There's a tradition in the Stone family that includes a good-night kiss for guests."

Interesting. "You're making that up."

"Yes, I am." There was a deliciously wicked expression in his green eyes. "What gave me away?"

"There was no tradition last night." And last night the pulse in her neck wasn't throbbing in anticipation the way it was now.

"Because I didn't know then how much my parents like you. A good-night kiss seems appropriate."

"Do you always do what authority figures want?"

"Always."

"That makes one of us." Her voice was husky and her hands shook.

Then he touched his mouth to hers and all she could think about was how soft his lips were. And warm and… In a heartbeat the gentle contact turned demanding in a way that had nothing to do with her saying good-night and everything to do with begging him to take her now. He cupped her cheek in his palm and made the touch more firm as he kissed her over and over again. The fingers of his other hand trailed down her neck and over her shoulder until the backs of his knuckles rested against her breast.

She ached for his touch on her bare skin and throbbed in places that would welcome his attention. Fire licked through her and sucked the air from her lungs until her breath came in quick gasps.

She moaned against his mouth and it sounded loud in the quiet house. His parents' house.

She pulled back and frantically whispered, "Spencer, someone will hear us—"

"Do you know how big this place is?"

She nodded. "But there are a lot of people here. The kids could wander down the hall. Someone could get lost…"

"Then we shouldn't stand here." He was breathing hard and there was a dark intensity in his expression. "Invite me in."

She shook her head. "I can't."

"But you want to." He must have seen the regret.

"Good night." She turned and opened the door, then slipped inside and closed it.

She leaned back, every part of her aching for more. How did this happen? When did things change so that she had skin in the game? Skin that was now tingling for his touch.

And his folks had confirmed what she already knew about his legendary determination. If he decided to go after her with a vengeance, her willpower didn't stand a chance.

Chapter Seven

The next morning Avery walked outside, coffee in hand, to sit in the shade on the patio and watch a spirited game of soccer already in progress on the huge lawn. Spencer and his niece took on Adam and their nephew. If this was what he defined as "hanging out," she wouldn't survive any organized Stone family activities.

Kissing Spencer last night probably didn't qualify as an activity, but she had survived it. Just barely. If they hadn't been under his parents' roof, she wasn't sure the words "good night" would have come out of her mouth.

When Adam kicked the ball out of bounds, Spencer held up his hands to form a T and pulled rank to convince the kids a time-out was necessary. There was a pitcher of sweet tea on the table, but the doctors explained to the boy and girl that water was better for hydration. Four bottles came out of the restocked ice chest and were handed out. Adam talked game strategy with the kids and Spencer sat down beside her.

"Good morning."

"Same to you," she said.

He took a long drink from his bottle of water and the sight of his strong neck working as he swallowed was strangely sexy, erotically masculine, endlessly fascinating. "It's hot out already."

"I noticed."

He looked at her. "Did you sleep okay?"

"Great." And she had slept fine, in between all the hours she *couldn't* sleep because of thinking about kissing him. The expression on his face told her he knew she was stretching the truth. "How about you? Did you sleep well?"

"Great," he echoed.

The thing about being a liar herself was that spotting another one was easy. And she was going to hell. Not just for bending the truth, but for being so happy she wasn't the only one affected by that kiss.

"Uncle Spencer—" Melanie marched over to them. She was a beautiful child, in spite of the pout on her pretty little face. Her long, light brown hair was pulled up into a ponytail and swung from side to side. "Ken says I don't dribble good."

"I assume she's not talking about drooling," Avery said.

"No. Ballhandling skills," he confirmed. He turned his attention to the little girl in front of him. "Your brother is trying to psych you out."

"What does that mean?" Green eyes the same shade as his own drilled him.

"It means he wants to make you think too much so you'll slow down."

"Because I'm faster than him. I knew it." She smiled, then turned away and ran back to her brother. "Uncle Spencer said I'm the fastest."

Uncle Spencer's expression was wry. "That's not exactly what I said. You're my witness."

"I am."

Avery glanced over at the boy and girl who were now debating the issues of speed and skill. The baby daughter she'd given up would be ten years old now, older than the twins. Was her little girl happy? Could she stand up for herself? Did she feel wanted, and most important, loved? She always thought about her child, but even more lately, because it was becoming more important that Spencer not know and despise her.

"Don't look so serious." His deep voice had just a hint of confusion. "I was only kidding. They always try to one-up each other. Wanting to be the best is a Stone family trait."

"She's got to hold her own against the boys." Avery wasn't only thinking about Melanie.

"Don't worry. I'll take care of her."

Avery could only hope that her daughter had an uncle like him in her life.

He turned at the sound of his name. "I think I'm being paged."

Melanie was waving him over. "I'm ready to play again. We have to score a goal, Uncle Spencer."

He jogged off and followed the other three out into the yard that was as big as some parks. She could hear squeals of laughter and chatter, but not what they were saying. Avery didn't know the first thing about soccer, but she could tell that Spencer was working overtime to steal the ball and pass it to Mel. Adam was doing his best for her brother. Teach and have fun—those were goals that had nothing to do with scoring and everything to do with a couple of pretty special uncles.

"Good morning." Will sat down in the chair next to hers.

"Hi." She took a sip of her coffee.

"Did you sleep well?"

"Yes." And the lies just kept on coming. She felt a flush burn up her neck even though he didn't know what happened between her and his son in the hall. "You?"

"Great." He looked at the quartet on the grass, then back at her. "How come you're not out there?"

"Besides the fact that I know nothing about the game and my participation would make the teams lopsided in a bad way, it's too darn hot."

He laughed. "Actually, the temperature isn't that bad, but the humidity is high."

"I can really feel the difference between Dallas and Las Vegas."

"You have a dry heat." There was a twinkle in his eyes.

"We have a saying where I come from—it's not hot until the thermostat hits a hundred and five."

He whistled. "I'll take the humidity."

"I have to admit," she said, "in July and August, sometimes September and October, I'm glad I have an indoor job."

"Smart girl."

"I try, but I'm pretty much nowhere in your league Mr. Nobel Prize for Economics." She knew there was hero worship in her eyes. "Your analysis of search markets and the application of it to the labor pool has shaped official thinking and generated government initiatives to help get people back in the job market after long stretches of unemployment."

Amusement made his eyes crinkle at the corners. "So you know my work?"

"I aspire to understand it." She laughed self-consciously. "I researched you on Google."

"Ah. That's a relief."

"How so?"

"I was afraid that a pretty girl like you was all work and no play."

Busted, but she didn't plan to share that tidbit of information. "Are you still teaching?"

"Some. A semester here and there. Mostly I do consulting work. These days the economy is about doing more with less. Recession taught us lessons that aren't necessarily all bad. We're learning to minimize waste. Companies are putting their capital where it will do the most good."

"That I *do* understand. It's why I'm here. To see if the surgery system Spencer wants is worth the cost. Long-term."

"That's important for fiscal health. Your job is very important."

"Not on the scale of what you do." She glanced at him and saw the pride on his face as he watched his two sons entertain his grandchildren. "I'm completely in awe of your accomplishments."

"As the kids would say, it's no big whoop."

She laughed. "I disagree. If it wasn't a big deal, the Bank of Sweden wouldn't have created a Nobel Prize for economics in 1969." At his wry look, she added, "I looked that up in Google, too."

"I'm proud of that award," he admitted. "But it pales in comparison to the challenge of being a father. It's not just a biological distinction, you know."

"I really don't." For reasons she didn't understand, confiding in this man was something she wanted to do. "My father wasn't involved much with me even before my parents divorced. After that, he just disappeared altogether."

There was an intensely disapproving expression on his face. "How old were you?"

"Twelve."

"My congratulations to your mother. Against the odds you turned out well." He patted her hand. "When Becky was twelve I actually felt my role in her life expanding. There was that whole pesky, inconvenient interest in the opposite sex starting to surface. As much as her mother and I wanted her in a convent until she turned thirty-five, my daughter was having none of it. All we could do was hope the boys who came around were gay. Not exactly realistic! When hanging out with the opposite sex stopped being cute and turned into relationships, being good with economics models wasn't much help."

"What about Spencer? And Adam," she added.

"Different personalities, unique challenges."

She'd always wondered about the nature versus nurture debate and how it affected an adopted child. But the choice to relinquish hers had been based on practical things that Avery wasn't in a position to give her. Without a high school diploma she couldn't get a decent job to put a roof over their heads, food on the table or clothes to keep her warm. She'd never thought about parenting worries.

"What kinds of challenges?" she asked.

"A father walks a fine line. Unlike mathematics, there's no formula to determine a workable ratio between what your children are capable of and how much pressure to exert in the interest of getting them to achieve their potential."

"In other words, to ground them or not to ground them for grades?"

"Precisely." His smile vanished as quickly as it appeared. "I'm still not certain that we did our best."

"For what it's worth, Will, I think you did a great job with your kids."

"That's nice of you to say, but—I wonder."

And those two words were more mysterious than his economic theories. He and his wife had raised a rocket scientist and two physicians. It didn't get much better than that.

She gave up her baby and still believed in her heart that it was the right thing to do. But she also wondered: Was her baby girl paying too high an emotional price for being adopted? Were the parents who took her putting too much pressure on her? Or not enough?

And then there was the problem of her temptation to sleep with Spencer last night. Thank goodness she hadn't. It's all fun and games until you have sex and realize there are feelings involved. And she would never be good enough to fit in with these people because the brilliant and exceptional Stone family would never understand why someone could give away their flesh and blood.

She knew that because if Spencer was a slacker who was one heartbeat from failure, she wasn't worthy to breathe the same air.

Spencer looked out the kitchen window at the kids playing in the pool with his folks. The soccer game earlier had been fun, but he was going to be sore. At home he stayed in shape with pickup games of basketball and used his treadmill for more than a clothes rack, but Mel and Ken had so much energy.

"Spencer?"

He turned around at the sound of his sister's voice. In a bathing suit cover-up and carrying towels in her arms, it appeared she was on her way out to the pool.

"Hey, Beck."

She moved closer and set the stack of towels down on the kitchen island's black granite. "We haven't really had a chance to talk."

"It's always hectic." There was a look in her eyes, a tension in her tone that warned him something was up. But he knew she'd get to it in her own way, her own time, if she wanted to talk about whatever it was.

For just a moment his sister's grin chased away the shadows. "You brought a friend to the family reunion."

"And that's noteworthy—why?"

"I didn't think you had any friends."

Is that what Avery was to him? That kiss last night felt a lot more than friendly. The power of it spooked him at the same time he wanted more. A lot more.

"Avery is a colleague. From Mercy Medical Center."

"Okay."

"She's here because there was a mix-up in dates and reservations for a business trip."

"If you say so." Becky studied him with the same intensity she brought to her work, a fire in the belly that was moving her to the top of her profession. "I hope she's not just another fling."

He didn't do permanent, so Becky was doomed to disappointment. Curiosity made him ask, "Why do you say that?"

"She seems really nice. Sweet."

That made him smile. It wasn't the first descriptive word he thought of where Avery O'Neill was concerned. Sexy. Sassy. Smart. But she was sweet, too. "Avery is one of a kind."

"Well, she's really cute. Love her name, by the way."

"I'm sure she had nothing to do with it." He'd never asked how she got the name. Whether it was from someone in her family. In fact, he didn't know all that much about her, except that she'd grown up in a trailer park. The only fact clear in his mind was that the attraction he felt wouldn't go away. That hadn't happened to him since college and should have been enough to cool his jets. Somehow it didn't.

"Where is she, by the way?"

"Upstairs. Packing. We're going to the hotel in a little while to settle in. It's closer to our meetings and we have to be at the hospital early."

"Separate rooms?" Becky was naturally inquisitive and didn't hold back. Even with personal questions.

"Yes."

"And how long have you known her?"

"A few months." Since he'd started his campaign for the robotic surgery system and Avery told him no. "She's intriguing."

"So, you've been dating for a while."

"Actually, we've never gone out." No had been her answer to having a drink together. Part of what got his attention in the first place was her negative attitude, the unreasonable stubbornness. And the fact that she put him in the same category as a jerk in her past. "The closest we've come to a date was standing up for mutual friends at their second wedding."

Becky's eyebrows rose. "Second?"

"Long story. Suffice it to say that their love rekindled and there is a child involved."

"Happy ever after." Her tone was wistful. "I'd like to hear about it sometime."

"I know we haven't had much of a chance to talk, but I noticed you're not your perky self. You're down about something." Spencer rested his forearms on the granite and met her gaze. "What's wrong, Beck?"

"What makes you think there is something?"

"This is me. I know we don't talk as often as we should, but no one knows that everything's-not-right face like your big brother. So spill it."

"How perceptive of you." Her smile was small and fleeting and sad. "My life is in the toilet."

"Is this hormones talking? That time of the month?" If it was, that would be a first. Becky Stone Markham was too disciplined, too focused, to let something like premenstrual tension get to her.

"If only." The scorn in her voice confirmed his instinct that there was more to it.

When she didn't elaborate, he said, "I don't talk to mom and dad as much as I should, either, but they never miss an opportunity to make sure I feel like a deadbeat compared to you."

"Oh, please." Becky rolled her eyes. "This coming from the hotshot cardiothoracic surgeon."

"Seriously." Fixing things was what he did. He wanted to fix the pain she was valiantly trying to hide, but couldn't unless she told him what it was. "They're so proud of you. You've got a successful career in a traditionally male profession. You're a wife, mother of twins—"

"Nothing our mother hasn't already done."

"It's a different world now. Arguably more pressure on women. But you've done it all, and got it all." He envied her more than she could possibly know. "Beck, you got it right. Unlike me."

"No." Vehemently she shook her head. "You're the smart one."

"Because I'm alone?" God, that sounded pathetic.

"If you don't make a commitment," she argued, "you can't make a mistake."

That was his motto and someday he'd get the saying done in needlepoint for his wall. But he zeroed in on the word "mistake." "Are you saying you made a mistake with Dan?" he asked sharply.

"Technically, the mistake is his for cheating on me."

All his big-brother testosterone fueled an anger that roared through him like an F5 hurricane. "I'm going to punch his lights out."

"No, you're not."

"Give me a good reason—"

"It will make things worse."

"But I'll feel better. How did you find out?" he demanded.

"What you're asking is whether or not he confessed voluntarily. And that would be no. I caught him." She folded her arms over her chest. "I found emails. Text messages."

"Where is he?"

"Why?" she asked warily. "Are you still going to beat him up?"

"You don't think I can do it?"

"No. I'd just rather you didn't. For one thing, you're a surgeon and you have to think about your hands. I'm pretty sure breaking one would make it impossible to use the robot."

He knew she had a point. "Give me another reason why I shouldn't deck him."

"I think he wanted me to find out about the affair."

"Because…"

"Think about it. We're both pretty smart and he's a genius with computers."

"I could cite statistics about technically smart men who make stupid personal mistakes."

"Me, too. But I truly believe he could have easily kept me from seeing those messages." She sighed. "And I have to bear some of the blame."

"I don't think so," he said angrily.

"It's so sweet that you want to look at this so one-dimensionally and protect me. But I'm the one living it. My work is demanding and full of stress. As is Dan's. Then there's the twins and their school, plus activities. Dance class for Mel. Karate for Ken. Sports for both of them. Dan and I are running in different directions to keep up. Even if we could carve out time for us, we're tired."

"Apparently he's not too tired to see someone else."

"I think it was a cry for attention."

"Then you're a nicer person than me." Spencer stared at her. "He couldn't just ask for attention?"

"That would be too easy. We're complicated people."

"Too smart and driven for your own good?"

"Back at you, big brother."

This wasn't about him and he wasn't going there. "Do the folks know?"

"I'm afraid to tell them," she admitted.

He understood how she felt, but still asked, "Why?"

"Because I don't want to shatter their image of me. Seeing disappointment in their eyes—" Her voice broke and she put a hand over her trembling mouth.

Spencer moved then and gathered her into his arms. "You have to tell them or at least give me a shot at Dan."

"No to both. I can work this out."

"How?"

She sniffled. "I'm still trying to come up with a plan."

"Do you love him?" He wasn't sure how that was relevant after what the bastard had done, but figured he should ask.

"Yes."

"You're sure?"

"It's the only thing I am sure of." She smiled up at him and stepped away.

"Does he love you?" Once upon a time he'd planned to spend the rest of his life with a woman and thought his feelings were reciprocated. Boy had he been wrong. It hurt a lot. He didn't want his sister to feel that kind of pain.

"I intend to find out what his feelings are."

Spencer wondered how she planned to do that, but didn't ask. "If there's anything I can do, don't hesitate…"

"Thanks. It's a great relief just to tell someone."

"Anytime."

"I better get outside or the folks might suspect something's wrong." She gathered up the towels. "Thanks for listening."

"Mom and Dad will listen. They'll understand."

"Do you really believe that? You of all people? I'll never hear the end of the mistakes I've made."

"Right." He kissed her forehead. "Let me know how it goes. And if there's anything I can do."

"I will."

She walked outside and Spencer felt helpless because just listening didn't seem to be enough. But Becky was right about one thing. He'd never forget the disappointment in his folks when he'd confessed his romantic fiasco, then his mother's outburst about how wrong for him "that girl" was and the disdain in her voice when she'd said everything. It wasn't painful enough that he'd had his feelings handed back to him. He had to hear how foolish his choice had been and how much no one had liked her.

It wasn't an experience he wanted to repeat.

Never again. Spencer Stone would never allow himself any flaws for public consumption. If that wasn't his core belief, he wouldn't be a perfect boyfriend to a lot of women.

Avery's pixie face popped into his mind and desire trickled through him as it always did. She was intriguing and he would unravel her secrets. But that was all.

No commitment.

Chapter Eight

Sunday afternoon, with mixed feelings of relief and regret, Avery said goodbye to the Stone family. Then it was on to the hotel and getting ready for business meetings in the morning. Fortunately, Spencer knew where he was going and didn't seem inclined to conversation. In fact, he looked an awful lot like a man seriously brooding about something.

If it had anything to do with her, he would say so. When he didn't, she watched the big blue sky filled with puffy white clouds and the scenery streaking by as the sporty luxury car raced down the freeway.

When he finally exited, it was obvious they were in an upscale part of Dallas but she was completely unprepared for the elegance when they turned onto Turtle Creek Boulevard.

Spencer stopped by the gracefully arched awning and a sign that said Rosewood Mansion on Turtle Creek. This couldn't be right.

She'd called to check the reservation at the airport's off-site rental car area but the connection had cut in and out. At the time, reservation dates were more important than property names. She should have paid more attention.

"We're in the wrong place." She met Spencer's amused gaze.

"No. This is it."

"You can't be serious."

"Yes, I can."

"I thought we'd be staying at Harry's Hotel. There's no possible way this place is in the hospital budget."

"First of all, I don't stay at anything resembling a Harry's Hotel."

Of course he didn't. Because no matter what he claimed about not being perfect, he was so close it was scary. Before he could tell her the second of all, a valet opened the driver's door for him and a bellman did the same on the passenger side for her.

Spencer came around and took her hand, then slipped it into the crook of his elbow. Truthfully, she was grateful for the support as they went inside.

The hotel entrance was all marble, high ceilings and tall curved windows. A sitting area in the lobby looked just like a living room with couches, chairs and a fireplace for casual, cozy conversation. Every detail was extraordinarily gorgeous.

Avery knew she was gawking but just couldn't manage to wipe the awe off her face. There were too many details and she couldn't look at all of them hard enough.

"No offense to your parents. Their house is wonderful. But *this* is Buckingham Palace."

"I'm glad you like it."

"And aren't I the lucky one that the riffraff police have the afternoon off. If not, I never would have made it this far inside." She looked at him in his gray slacks and black sport coat with the crisp, white shirt beneath. "You should have warned me when I had the chance to shop for better stuff."

He let his gaze wander over her wedge sandals, white capris and black, rhinestone embellished T-shirt. "You look beautiful."

"I bet you say that to all the girls."

To his credit, he didn't have a smooth response at the ready. He looked at her for several moments before answering.

"If I say this time I really mean it, you'll have a snarky comeback about me being shallow as a cookie sheet. But I'm going to say it, anyway. You look beautiful. And I really mean it."

"Good one," she said. "And spoken with just the right amount of sincerity."

"Go ahead and scoff. But let me just say that I've never meant those words more than I do right now. With you."

His green eyes glowed with intensity, convincing her to believe, and the belief made her heart pound so hard it tripped all her warning signals.

"Look, Spencer, clearly the price of a room here is going to implode my financial statement for this trip." She should have paid more attention, but when Spencer was involved it was hard to keep one's mind on the facts. The fact was she'd buried her head in the sand and her backside was exposed. Now she was in a pickle. "I'm going to have to make other arrangements."

"No. The planning was done at my direction, by my office manager. The mistakes are mine and not your responsibility. When receipts are calculated, I will pay the difference."

Avery shook her head. "I can't let you do that."

"Your permission isn't required."

"Spencer—" She twisted her fingers together and met his

gaze. Of course he could afford it. In the world of Spencer Stone, M.D., the price of living the good life was insignificant. For her the cost could be high and she didn't just mean this hotel. "It's awfully nice of you to offer, but—"

He gently pressed his index finger to her lips, stopping the words. "This is my way of apologizing for being so, let's call it resolute, in pursuing this new technology for Mercy Medical Center."

"You were a pain in the neck. It was nearly impossible to hide from you."

"Aha, so you were trying to dodge me. That's why I couldn't track you down."

"The ladies' restroom was my best refuge," she admitted.

He held his hand out, indicating the breathtaking lobby. "So this is an improvement over the bathroom at work and my way of making up to you that you had to take cover there."

She frowned as a thought occurred to her. "Is this a bribe to get me on board with the robot you want?"

"That's what I love about you, Avery." He grinned and shook his head. "You don't have a suspicious bone in your body. Always willing to give a guy the benefit of the doubt."

She had good reason. Guys had an annoying habit of letting her down. Sooner or later a girl stopped giving them the opportunity.

"Am I wrong?"

"Yes. I don't need to buy you off. I'm confident that when we leave Texas you'll be convinced of the fiscal as well as the medical merits of this technology." He slid his hands into the pockets of his slacks. "I have no ulterior motive for picking this five star, five diamond hotel. The only one of that distinction in Dallas, by the way. I just want you to stand down. Relax. Enjoy yourself."

A few days ago she might have doubted Spencer's sincerity, but not so much now. She'd seen him with his family, watched him with the kids and knew why he was a favorite uncle, and he'd opened up to her in a personal way.

Before getting on that plane a few days ago she would have told him no without a moment's hesitation. Knowing him better now, she knew he was sweet and genuine. That's probably the reason he'd been able to maintain friendships with the numerous women he dated and dumped. She just didn't want to be president of the Spencer Stone exes club.

Before Dallas she'd have been certain that wouldn't happen, but now she knew what kissing him was like. It probably wasn't heaven, but close enough to see a glimpse. Accepting his offer wasn't just walking on the wild side, it was like leading the race down Rowdy Road. But when he was this charming, telling him no wasn't a viable option.

She nodded. "I've never stayed anywhere as beautiful as this."

"You haven't even seen your room yet."

No, but it was seeing *his* room that made her nervous. Although it shouldn't be a problem since she had no intention of going there.

"I'm sure it will be the perfect place to prepare for our meetings—or even relax."

Relaxing in this perfect deluxe patio room was going to take some time and effort. The king-size bed was covered with a comforter encased in a white duvet and had a tufted bench at the foot. French doors led to a patio and just inside the opening was a tangerine-colored love seat with an ottoman and brocade throw pillows. On the other side was a work desk. Crown molding was an elegant touch on walls painted a serene beige.

All her business clothes were hung in the closet and her new casual things tucked away in drawers. Before heading to his room, Spencer had escorted her here and said he'd be by at six-fifteen to pick her up for dinner. Then he disappeared before she could say no.

Scary but true, she was looking forward to dinner and had primped more than she'd ever admit to him. The yellow sundress, white shrug and low-heeled gold sandals she had on were impulse buys from that shopping day at the Galleria, when she'd realized Spencer was not the jerk she'd thought. Today she'd realized that traveling in Dr. Spencer Stone's orbit required a certain dress code. Her budget probably couldn't sustain the code, but given his love 'em and leave 'em history, that shouldn't be an issue.

She checked her lipstick and makeup in the mirror by the door, then fussed with the short wisps of hair around her face. The pixie style wasn't time-consuming, but she wasn't sure if it added sophistication or just made her look about twelve.

A knock on the door made her jump, then she took a deep breath, nodded at her reflection and opened the door. Spencer was standing there looking as handsome as sin and her heart skipped.

"Wow." A tinge of surprise mixed with the approval in his tone.

"Hello to you, too."

"Sorry." He didn't look it and continued to stare at her. "Hello," he finally said. "You look beautiful."

"You said that earlier and swore it was the truth, though I didn't believe you."

"I sincerely meant it then," he vowed. "But now, as my nephew would say, you look beautifuller."

She laughed. "He's a heartbreaker in training. And his sister is pretty awesome, too. In fact, your whole family is quite something."

"Most of them." For just an instant there was an angry expression in his eyes, then it was gone. "Shall we go?"

"I'll get my purse." The thing was so big practically everything she owned would fit inside. Her key card was on the entryway table beside it.

"You don't need it," he said.

"How nice it would be not to lug that thing around, but I don't have pockets. Nowhere to put my room key."

"I'll hold it for you." He had on tan slacks and a navy-blue jacket, this time with a light yellow shirt. It was almost as if they'd coordinated outfits. "I've got pockets."

"Okay. Thanks."

He took it, then held out his hand. "After you."

"Where are we going?" she asked, letting the door close behind her.

"The Mansion Restaurant, right here on the property. You're going to love it."

She didn't know about the food, but Spencer was definitely growing on her. That was both good news and bad. Good because this trip was a lot more pleasant than she'd thought it would be. Bad because this trip was pleasant. But it wasn't the real world. And once the decision was made about the equipment he wanted, there was no reason for him to be in her world. Her eyes were wide-open and she had no expectations. There wasn't anything to lose if she let down her guard and had fun for the next couple of days.

They found the restaurant lobby and, like the rest of the property, it was unique. Black-and-white tiles covered the floor and an elaborate wrought-iron railing curved to an upper level. The hostess checked the reservation he'd made, then escorted them to a table beside an ornately carved white fireplace. For a restaurant that was nearly full, the place was remarkably quiet. Staff efficiently bustled around and the murmur of subdued voices floated in the air. As if this was a church, Avery wanted to whisper.

Within seconds, someone appeared with Perrier to fill water glasses and the waiter greeted them with menus.

She glanced at the appetizers and slid a wry look across the table. "Goat cheese tortellini? Lobster risotto? Foie Gras? Fancy schmancy."

"What sounds good?" he asked, scanning the choices.

"That would be easier to answer if I could identify some of this stuff." She studied the choices again. "I'm not sure what shaved manchego is, but Mansion baby greens, date and pine nuts are within my scope of the familiar, so I'll go with that."

"No caviar parfait? Or East Coast oysters? It's rumored they're an aphrodisiac." His tone was teasing, but there was a gleam in his eyes that brought back memories of that KISS.

In her mind all the letters were capitalized because of how good his mouth felt on hers. Staring at his handsome face across the table was hard enough without eating some kind of food that might make her throw caution to the wind and do it again.

"Oysters are slimy and not very attractive."

"Got it." He nodded. "Only pretty food."

When the waiter returned, they both ordered salads and fish—grilled Columbia River salmon for him, wild striped bass for her. She refused to believe that you are what you eat and that she'd turn wild. They decided to share an order of black truffle-ham macaroni and cheese. Spencer ordered a bottle of Chardonnay. The waiter opened it with a flourish, then poured each of them a glass before drifting away.

When they were alone Avery said, "I wish they had a sample plate, just a bite of everything. I'd love to taste Texas grit fries. And what the heck is chipotle aioli, anyway?"

"Probably not pretty," he jokingly warned.

"By definition fries can't be slimy, no matter what the ingredients are."

He laughed, then held up his wine glass. "To you."

That was a surprise. "Me? Why?"

"You survived a weekend with the Stone family."

"That was easy." She touched her glass to his. "I liked them all."

"They're okay." Spencer took a sip of wine, then frowned. "With one exception."

Avery waited for him to elaborate, but he was silent and clearly angry. "What's bugging you?" He opened his mouth with the look of a man intending to deny it, so she held up her hand. "Don't waste your breath. On the drive here you were in a snit."

One eyebrow rose. "I've been described as a jerk, an egotistical jerk, a pompous ass and other names I can't repeat in mixed company. I've been justifiably angry in the performance of my job and these episodes have been described as tantrums, meltdowns and other things I also can't repeat. But I'm pretty sure no one has ever accused me of engaging in a snit."

She shrugged. "First time for everything. And I'm not wrong. You had a scowl on your face while driving that sweet car. As behavior goes, yours had snit written all over it."

He finished the wine in his glass and the waiter appeared to refill it and top off hers, then discreetly backed off.

"So, what has your boxers in a bunch?"

One corner of his mouth quirked up. "It's too bad your career involves numbers and spreadsheets, because you certainly have a way with words."

She refused to let him distract her from whatever it was he didn't want to discuss. "You're not the only one with a stubborn streak, Doctor. I'm not changing the subject until you answer the question."

"Did you ever think about being a lawyer?" He correctly interpreted the "oh, please" look she leveled at him. "Okay. You win. This afternoon Becky told me Dan is cheating on her."

"Right now?"

"Probably not this minute. But he had an affair."

"I don't know what to say." She blinked at him. "Scratch that. One word should do it. Pig."

"Unlike you, not even a single word did it for me. I wanted to punch his lights out, but she wouldn't let me."

"Worried about the magic hands."

"Not her words, but yes." All traces of humor vanished. "And she refused to let him take all the blame which is just nuts."

"I don't understand," Avery said.

"She claimed his sleeping with another woman was a cry for help to work on their marriage instead of a mistake of major proportions."

"You clearly think she's wrong."

"I've never been married and don't get an opinion."

"Your parents probably do," she said.

"I'm sure they would. If they knew." He sighed. "Becky's afraid to say anything and risk disappointing them."

"What is it with you Stone siblings?" she blurted out.

"I'm not sure how to respond to that." Surprise chased the scowl off his face.

"Not everyone has parents like yours who give a darn whether or not their kids turn into productive adults. Adults who are just like every other adult on the planet. Stuff happens." She stopped to take a breath. "And from a parent's perspective, they can't be a best friend, but they are a role model. But you and Adam and Becky are grown-ups now.

She might want to share her problems with them just because it would make her feel better to tell someone who loves her. Besides you."

"Okay."

"And one more thing while I'm at it. As an impartial observer I can say something without a doubt."

"And that is?"

"Your folks love their kids and grandkids. They would do anything for you guys."

"So noted."

The subject was dropped as their salads arrived with shaved manchego that looked a lot like cheese. It was served with all the pomp and performance of a Broadway show. After that Spencer seemed more lighthearted, as if the responsibility of angry big brother had lifted from him. He was always charming and funny, but now the charm and humor came at warp speed. It turned a girl's head for sure and Avery was not immune.

After dinner they stopped at the bar and he ordered two snifters of brandy which they took outside to the garden terrace.

"There's a fire," she said, sitting on the padded love seat in front of it. "In a fireplace."

"Just where it's supposed to be." Spencer sat beside her. "Are you cold?"

"Not with you here."

The wine had mellowed her out and a sip of brandy burned down her throat then all the way through her. The thing was, alcohol wasn't necessary to make her burn. All she needed was Spencer.

She rested her head on his shoulder. "This is nice."

"I couldn't agree more."

Avery heard something in his voice, a sort of intense, hoarse quality. Her hormones whimpered and she wanted him with every fiber of her being. Apparently she'd relaxed too much, a chronic hazard when Spencer spread his charm on so thick she could see, smell, touch and taste it.

She sat up and drank the rest of her brandy, letting it burn some sense into her before there was no turning back. "I have to go now."

"So soon?"

She set her snifter on the table. "Early day tomorrow. Places to go. People to meet. Can't have you saying I gave your robot a thumbs-down just because of being crabby and tired."

"I'd never say that. I've known you to be crabby, and lack of sleep had nothing to do with it." Amusement laced his voice.

"Thank you, I think." She stood. "Anyway, thanks for dinner. See you in the morning. Good night, Spencer."

He grabbed her hand before she could go. "Let me walk you to your room."

"You don't have to do that. I'll be fine. Five star, five diamond mansions on Turtle Creek don't let serial killers in."

She tried to be as teasing and witty as possible, but the touch of his fingers was shorting out her mental faculties. All she could think was, *if I only had a brain.*

Spencer stood and put his hand at the small of her back, gently, temptingly nudging her forward. "Resistance is futile. And besides—"

"What?" Dear God, did that breathless voice really belong to no-nonsense Avery O'Neill?

"I've got your room key."

She could demand he hand it over, but that would require an explanation. The only one she had was the need to be by herself as soon as possible to keep from doing something stupid, something she'd regret. Or maybe something she wouldn't regret that would come back to bite her in the butt. Something stupid might start with kissing him. Or letting him kiss her.

The thing about kisses was that they were dangerous. A doorway to promises. Hope. A future. But Avery knew better than to put her faith in any of those things. She had believed once upon a time and it all blew up in her face. She was a lot smarter now, unless Spencer made her stupid.

There was no way she could explain any of that to him, so she forced a smile. "You're nothing if not a gentleman."

The time it took to get back to her room was both too long and too short. They stood in the hall by her door and Spencer inserted the key card, waited for the go-ahead green light, then turned the knob. He pushed and left his palm on the door, holding it open.

"You know, Tinker Bell, the Stone family good-night tradition is still in force even though we're at a hotel. In fact, *because* we're not under my parents' roof, it's practically mandatory."

She stood in the doorway looking up at his handsome, smiling face, but there was a fire in his eyes that tempted her beyond any reasonable boundaries of willpower.

"Oh, Spencer—"

That was all the encouragement necessary. He lowered his mouth to hers and just like before, the sparks sizzling between them ignited into flames. She'd never be sure whether or not he backed her into the room or she pulled him inside, but in less time than it took a heart to beat they were alone behind a closed door.

There was a moan trapped in her throat and Avery couldn't make it stay there. The feel of his arms was too good. It had been so long since a man held her, wanted her. He pressed his lips to hers as if he planned to consume her and she gloried in the sensation. Her response was immediate and explosive. Fire raced through her and his harsh breathing indicated she wasn't the only one feeling it. He dished out passion and she gave it right back to him.

His mouth was open on hers, his tongue aggressive, teasing, taking her higher. She slipped her fingers through his thick hair as he pressed his palm to her thigh and slid her skirt up. Their bodies were touching from chest to knee and she could feel the hardness of him through the thin cotton of her sundress.

And he never stopped kissing her.

There was no time to think and she didn't really want to.

Then both of his hands were under her skirt, cupping her butt. He lifted and she tightened her arms around his neck, her legs circling his waist. Her sandals slid onto the carpet and she was glad. One less thing to get off.

"Housekeeping turned down the covers." His voice was a husky vibration that made her neck tingle. "Someone's getting a really big tip."

"That works for me," she whispered as he carried her to the bed.

He gently set her on the edge, then backed away and yanked off his coat, then pulled his shirt over his head without undoing the buttons. She tugged the hem of her skirt up and off came her dress. After dropping it beside the bed, her gaze lifted to his and she watched his green eyes darken with desire, indicating he liked what he saw.

Her heart pounded and every nerve ending in her body was throbbing. She hadn't worn a bra. All that stood between her and what she wanted more than her next breath was a pair of bikini panties.

Chapter Nine

In seconds Spencer was naked and Avery returned his bold, assessing look with one of her own. His shoulders were broad, his chest wide with just the right amount of hair dusting the contours. His flat belly and long, muscular legs gave him the lean look of a runner.

And then there was that part of him that was all male and made her female parts quiver.

"Is everything all right?" he asked, gravel wrapping around every word.

"Perfect."

When she reached out for him, he joined her on the bed and gathered her close. In spite of her conflict and resistance, she slipped into his arms as easily as anything she'd ever done in her life. He brushed his palm over her bare breast and down her side until he hooked a thumb in the elastic of her panties and dragged them down her legs for her to kick off.

And then he kissed her, firing up her senses and her wanting. She couldn't seem to draw enough air into her lungs and her hips arched against him. He knew what she was asking for and settled his body over hers. His knee nudged her thighs apart before he gently pushed inside, filling her, thrusting deeply. She picked up his rhythm effortlessly, as if they'd done this before.

The sensations that rushed through her were more powerful than anything she'd ever felt in her life. Like a tornado. A tsunami. The tension inside her coiled and curled, twisted and tangled until she prayed to come apart. He slid his hand between their bodies and with his thumb found the knot of femininity where they were joined. One touch sent her over the edge, tumbling into a chasm of pleasure so powerful she reveled in the aftershocks and held on to him for all she was worth. He murmured words she didn't comprehend but knew were absolutely right.

And then he began to move again. One thrust. Then another. Until he went completely still and groaned out his own release. Struggling to catch his breath, he rested his forehead against hers and she felt more than saw his grin.

"Definitely perfect," he said.

Euphoria lasted just until rational thought returned and that wasn't nearly long enough. On the plus side, at least she'd kept her promise not to go to his room. The minus part was how idiotic she'd been to think that promise would protect her from herself.

And that was the worst of all. They'd been so caught up in the passion that neither of them had thought about protection.

The next morning while driving to Mercy Medical Center Dallas, Spencer decided that the silence in the car could appropriately be described as pregnant. As in, what the hell had he been thinking last night not using a condom?

The short answer was he hadn't been thinking, at least not with his head. He'd wanted Avery in his bed pretty much from the first moment he saw her, but the acute factor had gone up ever since that kiss outside her door at his parents' house. Hell, the intensity had been there since that day in Ryleigh's office when Avery promised to sleep with the first nice doctor she met. Spencer was far too happy he'd been that nice doctor.

There was no easy way to ask, but he really had to know. Without looking at her he said, "Are you on the pill?"

"No." She didn't ask which pill, an indication the subject was on her mind, too. "There's been no need for birth control. And I didn't think that would change."

"Because you don't like me."

"I didn't."

Past tense. That was something, anyway. He was glad she didn't hate his guts. "Meaning you do like me now?"

She glanced at him and her expression was uneasy. Instead of responding to the question she said, "I should have said something last night. To put a stop to things. I know better than that."

"Don't." With his eyes still on the road, he reached over and squeezed the hands clenched in her lap. "There were two of us in that room."

"I can't argue with that."

"Look," he said, "if you're worried about— There's something—"

"Of course I'm concerned. And I know what you're talking about, the morning-after solution. I did some research on it and there are concerns for me. Besides, the timing was all wrong."

"You're sure?"

"Not as much as if we'd taken precautions, but cautiously optimistic."

Her tone lacked conviction, but he'd take whatever he could get.

Spencer pulled into the hospital parking lot, braked at the stop sign, then slid a look at his pensive passenger. "Are you having regrets?"

"Only that a couple glasses of wine and after dinner brandy took my IQ down a couple of notches." One corner of her mouth quirked up. "But don't worry. It was nice."

Nice?

That was the absolute best adjective she could come up with for sex that was fantastic? On a scale of one to ten it was a fifteen and possibly pushing twenty. Stupendous came to mind. And, although personally he thought the word overused, it was pretty awesome.

Spencer heard a car horn and in the rearview mirror saw that there was someone behind him. Damn. She'd been a distraction for a while now and after last night it was worse. And once in his bed wasn't enough, he realized.

After parking, they walked side by side into the hospital lobby, with its tile floor and signs on the wall with arrows to the medical and administrative offices. This was where each of them went their separate ways.

"I'll see you later," he said.

"Have fun with your robot. Maybe it comes with a light saber and a direct line of communication to the force." Her full lips curved up.

"That probably costs extra," he reminded her. "Rumor has it that the controller squeezes a penny till it screams for mercy."

"I'm almost positive you meant to say frugal," she said before turning down the hallway that led to the business office.

Spencer went in the opposite direction, toward the medical wing. His friend, Dr. Carter Hackett, met him at the double doors to the surgical area, wearing his usual green scrubs with a white lab coat over them. The man was about his age, height and build, with salt-and-pepper hair and piercing blue eyes. They'd met at this hospital while both were surgical residents.

"Good to see you, Hack." Spencer liked the irony of the nickname, although it was a misnomer. Carter was one of the finest cardiothoracic surgeons he knew.

The other doctor shook his hand. "How long has it been?"

"About a year. Since the last time I was here to see what's new."

"The da Vinci robotic-assisted surgical system isn't brand-new technology. It was actually developed by the military, a way to help wounded battlefield soldiers from a safe distance." Carter never missed an opportunity to instruct. "There are constant advances in the field. Just like TV, computers or even cars, it's almost obsolete when you drive it off the lot."

"Preaching to the choir, buddy. Show me what you've got."

Carter nodded. "I've arranged to have a robot free to demonstrate and we'll look at some film footage so you can see it in action."

Spencer followed him into a surgical suite that was familiar territory but the four-armed machine was different and special. Carter slid his hands into the gloves and demonstrated how the arms moved.

"Every surgical maneuver is under the direct control of the surgeon," he explained, showing off by using the levers.

Spencer watched, fascinated by the dexterity of the tiny robotic fingers' precise movements and pictured them fixing a valve or blocked blood vessel in a human heart.

"It reduces wound site trauma," Carter explained. "The

invasion of the chest wall is only as big as the circumference of the arm. There's no need for the surgeon to get hands and wrists into the surgical field."

"Very impressive."

One of the first things taught to a medical student was to do no harm. If intervention was necessary to save a life, there was an obligation to do as little damage as possible. A surgeon learned that manipulating internal organs caused discomfort to the patient. Don't touch unless absolutely necessary.

The thought of touching reminded him of Avery. In the heat of the moment last night it had felt absolutely necessary to touch her. She was like a fire in the blood, an ache in his gut, an itch that had to be scratched. And again he knew once wasn't enough.

"Spencer?"

"Hmm?" He blinked at his friend.

"Something wrong?"

"No." Only that the woman had managed to distract him yet again. "Why?"

"It's like your mind is somewhere else. Are your folks okay?"

"Yeah."

Carter studied him, that clinical expression doctors had when evaluating a situation. "You said on the phone that Mercy Medical Center's controller was going to be here with you."

"Yeah. She's with the numbers geeks as we speak."

"She?" His friend's blue eyes sharpened with interest.

"Avery O'Neill. She's skeptical about spending money for a robot when that could go to other things, including but not limited to vents for babies."

"I see." Carter nodded. "Financial concerns in practicing

medicine are always a juggling act. Is that the only thing on your mind?"

"What else would there be?" Another round of sex with said controller, complete with the feel of her skin and the scent of it flooding his senses, tying him in knots. He'd really been looking forward to seeing this machine and all he could think about was Avery. Tinker Bell won out over technology and that had never happened to him before. "Wasn't there something else you wanted to show me?"

"Oh. Right."

Spencer followed the other doctor who had a TV in his office. After sliding a DVD into the player, Carter pressed a button on the remote and images flashed on the screen. There was a human heart and blood vessels being manipulated by the metallic fingers in a valve replacement procedure.

"With da Vinci," Carter explained, "you get a 3-D tissue plane to better see the anatomy of muscle and vessels. With a high-definition magnified view of the field you're working in and precision control of your instrument, the patient's outcome is going to be far superior. The results transcend the limitations of traditional surgery."

"So it's perfect?" Spencer asked.

"Pretty much." Carter settled his hands on his hips. "Nice to know some things don't change."

"Like what?"

"You." There was that clinical expression again. "Still an incurable perfectionist."

Spencer shrugged. "I'm an old dog. Not even the great and powerful Carter Hackett can teach me new tricks."

Even if he wanted to learn.

Mistakes were costly. As far as his career that meant a patient's survival. Personally an error involved his soul and was a price he refused to pay again. In his work there were unknowns and factors that were unforeseen. In his life, all he had to do was walk away before anyone got hurt.

It concerned him that he wasn't ready to walk away from Avery yet.

Avery was having dinner with Spencer in the Terrace at the hotel. It was a lounge area with a fireplace where food from the on-site restaurant also was served. They were sitting at a right angle to each other eating their salads. He was having a beer because she'd declined sharing a bottle of wine, determined to keep her wits about her this time.

She chewed a bite of lettuce, the flavor mixed with delicious cheese and pine nuts. They hadn't been able to compare notes after leaving the hospital to return to the hotel because one or the other had taken cell phone calls from work back in Las Vegas.

"So, tell me what happened with Dr. Hackett." She winced after realizing that came awfully close to a how-was-your-day-dear remark. It was a business question and business was the subject she planned to focus on for the rest of this trip.

"First I want to know what you found out from the money people." He took a forkful of salad and watched her expectantly as he chewed.

"Reimbursement for the procedure is generous and fast. Medical insurance companies are enthusiastic and encourage it because hospitalization time is less and costs go down accordingly."

"So you're on board with purchasing the system?"

"It appears that the expenditure can be paid off fairly quickly allowing eventual profits to be channeled to the programs and projects that are postponed." She met his gaze. "Assuming the other hospitals we're visiting give me similar information, I'll recommend purchasing the surgical system."

"You have no idea how happy I am to hear you say that." His voice hummed with excitement.

"Why? What did you find out?"

"Carter confirmed all the research I've done, but seeing it in action was—" He shook his head, struggling for a description. "Way cool."

She couldn't help smiling at his enthusiasm. "That's the official medical terminology?"

"There are no words. The thing practically feeds you and wipes the crumbs off your face."

"Tell me everything." It was inconvenient how appealing he was in his passion for his work. She'd blamed wine for lowering her willpower, but that had nothing to do with it. Seeing him like this completely neutralized her resistance.

"The important thing to remember is robot-assisted. It's actually the surgeon who manipulates the metal hands."

"Metal hands?" She frowned. "That sounds kind of sci-fi creepy."

"Not at all. It's a machine assisting a doctor. The incision is exactly the same every time. Perfect. We're talking tiny robotic fingers moving precisely around the heart at the end of a small tube. It doesn't need nearly as broad a field as you would for two human hands." He rested his forearms on the table and eagerly leaned forward. "That means it's a minimally invasive procedure. There's no need to crack the chest, cut the bone or wire it all back together."

"Ouch." Involuntarily her hand rested on her heart. "Vivid description."

"Sorry. But necessary to explain why the hospital stay is shorter and so is recovery. The patient is back to normal activities, including work, in a matter of weeks not months. There's less pain and scarring. No more incision line from sternum to belly."

"Sounds like a miracle for cardiac patients."

"And doctors," he added.

"How so?"

He took a sip from his longneck bottle of beer and held his hand out, steady as a rock. "Even the most gifted, steadiest surgeon has minor vibrations in his hands. This system eliminates that. It corrects for the shaking and allows for more precision than is humanly possible, making that part of the surgery perfect."

She realized he put a lot of pressure on himself to not make a mistake. It was extraordinarily admirable, but she felt sorry for him, too. The robot wasn't human and didn't have the capacity to love. Spencer was all man but wouldn't let himself love.

"Do you realize how many times you just used the word perfect?" she asked.

He grinned. "Carter said the same thing. He called me an incurable perfectionist."

Avery knew Spencer was talking about medicine, but his partiality to perfection extended to the bedroom. He'd made perfect love to her last night. She shivered, although it was far from cold in this room. Memories of his hands on her body produced powerful sensations even now, and a profound longing for more.

"Is something wrong, Avery?"

"Hmm?" The sound of her name snapped her back to attention. "No. I guess Dr. Hackett correctly diagnosed that being perfect is important to you."

"Have you met my folks?" He stopped as the waiter left fresh rolls and removed their salad plates.

"I liked your mother and father very much."

"Don't get me wrong," he said quickly. "They're good people who love their kids, and the three of us put them on a pedestal. But as the oldest and first, the demand for excellence was focused on me."

She ran her finger through the condensation on the outside of her water glass. "I suspect their expectations were high for you growing up. You didn't mention your grandfather, but just from what you said about his wife, imagine what your father went through being a boy in her house."

He thought that over for a moment, then shuddered. "And Eugenia was the fun one."

"I rest my case."

Just then the waiter brought her steak, his scallops and an order of Texas grit fries with chipotle aioli. She tried one and it was delicious. Regular fries would never be the same again, which was probably a metaphor for life after this trip with Spencer.

The beef was delicious, too, and she wondered if everything familiar in her life would pale in comparison to this time of learning about Spencer. The pressure he put on himself as a kid must have been enormous because it was a weight on him even now.

She put her fork down. "Spencer, I think most kids want to please their parents. That's probably universal. I certainly understand how difficult it is to deal with parental disapproval."

"You know—" He stared at her intently. "It occurs to me that all of my dark secrets have been aired ad nauseam and your life is a complete mystery to me."

"It's unremarkable." Except for that one huge mistake and all the heartbreak, fear and pain that followed.

"That's hard to believe because you're such a remarkable woman." He pointed at her. "And don't tell me I say that to all the girls because it's not true."

She couldn't say anything because her heart was hammering too hard. Finally she just whispered, "Thank you."

"That's it? No sharing?"

"I'd bore you into a coma."

"I'll take my chances."

Oh, please don't push, she thought. Lately the past had weighed even more heavily on her and things she hadn't told even her best friend could so easily slip out.

"I don't want to talk about it."

He frowned. "Because you're in the witness protection program?"

"No, of course not."

"On the run from Russian mobsters," he persisted.

"Oh, please. My last name is O'Neill."

"Could be an alias," he pointed out.

"It's not."

"I'll take your word for it. I know," he said, snapping his fingers. "You're a spy. You could tell me, but then you'd have to kill me."

"Right. Because there's so much financial information on the Mercy Medical Center database that is of interest to our enemies."

"Right." He grinned. "Give me something."

"You're not going to drop this, are you?"

"That's not my current plan, no."

"I could get up and walk out," she threatened.

"I'm really hoping you won't." Questions mixed with sympathy in his eyes. "So, how bad could your past be?"

"I got pregnant when I was a senior in high school."

He looked shocked. "I have to say that's not what I expected."

The burden of her secret had been heavy for so long that she wanted to tell him all of it. "I was scared and told my mother right away. My dad walked out on us when I was twelve, so it was only her and me."

"How did she take it?"

"Not well. She was a cocktail waitress at one of the downtown resorts and money was tight. She never missed a chance to tell me that if *she* hadn't gotten pregnant with me in high school, she'd have had a good life. But now she was a single mom with too much responsibility and never missed a chance to warn me not to even think about getting pregnant."

"And?" he asked gently.

"Let's just say that's not what I was thinking about in the backseat of football quarterback Dave Gibson's car the night of the homecoming game when I lost my virginity." Or last night, either, with Spencer. Oh, God… Surely history wouldn't repeat itself.

"What did she say when you told her?"

"Not much to me, but apparently a lot to his family. Next thing I knew Dave proposed and I thought it was all going to be okay. We'd make a family."

"But it wasn't okay," he guessed.

"He didn't show up for the wedding."

"Bastard." His voice was harsh and angry.

"I found out later that he joined the army."

"I say again—bastard." Spencer took her hand. "I'll find him and beat him up."

His fingers felt strong and safe. And the gesture was unexpected. Even so her smile was sad around the edges. "I thought you doctors took an oath to do no harm. Between your sister's husband and my jerk, that's an awful lot of fighting you're talking about, Doctor. Not good for these surgeon's hands, no matter how much assist you get from the robot."

"What happened to the baby?"

She should have expected the question. Automatically she tried to pull her hand from his but he squeezed her fingers reassuringly. His expression held nothing but sympathy and encouraged her to say it all.

"My mother gave me an ultimatum. She said another mouth to feed wasn't an option. If I kept the baby, the two of us could just get out." To her horror, tears blurred her vision. After all this time the memory still tore her apart. Her voice broke when she said, "There was no way I could take care of her."

"Her?"

"I had a baby girl and gave her up for adoption."

A tear rolled from the corner of her eye and he brushed it away with his thumb. "I knew you were a remarkable woman."

Shocked, she met his gaze. "Did you hear what I said? I gave her away."

"I heard." He linked his fingers with hers.

His grip was so tight, she had the feeling that if they'd been anywhere but a very public restaurant she'd be in his arms. From experience she knew it was an awfully nice place to be. "I signed the legal papers so that two strangers could take her home with them."

"It was an extraordinarily generous thing you did. You gave her life times two. Not only did you bring her into the world, you were unselfish enough to make sure she had a life with a mother and father who would love her."

Was that just lip service or did he really understand? "You make it sound noble, but it felt so wrong. And my punishment is to always wonder whether or not she's okay."

"If she's anything like you, she'll be just fine. She'll grow into a remarkable woman, too."

Avery never expected this level of understanding from Doctor Perfect. Maybe it was because he'd taken so much heat from his family. Speaking of family, he might not judge her, but not everyone would share his point of view. She slipped her hand out of his because of how desperately she wanted to leave it there. So much for keeping focus on business. She'd never told anyone about this achingly personal part of her past and couldn't help wondering why now. Why him?

All the pain of that time overwhelmed her now. She wasn't sure why she'd spilled her guts, except maybe to give him an excuse to leave before she was in too deep. But Spencer had said all the right things and was behaving more perfectly than she would ever have imagined. That just made it all worse. Her odds of returning to Las Vegas with her heart unscathed were not good.

She desperately hoped the odds of a pregnancy were just as slim.

Chapter Ten

Spencer sat beside Avery on the plane for their return flight to Las Vegas. They rested in the wide leather seats of the first-class section while the other passengers boarded and stowed carry-ons in the overhead bins. The process was nearly complete and they'd be leaving in a few minutes. On this trip time had gone quickly and yet it felt as if he hadn't been home in years.

He glanced at Avery who was looking out the window. Her knee was bouncing, her fingers plucking at the denim covering her thigh and she was chewing on her lower lip. It was time to distract her and he wasn't sure whether or not to use sex, work or weather.

He decided to start with an innocuous topic and work up to the specific.

"So, what did you think of Texas?" When she didn't answer he said, "Avery?"

"Hmm?" She looked at him. "What?"

"Did you like Texas?"

"It was fine."

"Wow. There's high praise. I'll be sure to pass along your boundless enthusiasm to the Chamber of Commerce and the Department of Tourism. It will make great advertising copy. I can see the headline in the brochure now—Texas is fine."

"What do you want me to say?"

"Tell me your favorite part of the trip." He knew what his was, but this wasn't about him. He wanted to hear from her and in the process take her mind off being nervous.

She thought about the question for a moment. "I'd have to say a highlight for me was meeting your family."

"Really?" That was unexpected. "Not shopping? Or sight-seeing?"

"I can shop at home, although your sacrifice in taking me was much appreciated. And the Stockyards was a lot of fun. There's nothing like it in Las Vegas." Her knee had stopped moving. "But I really enjoyed your folks. And your siblings. Although they made me feel stupid."

"You're one of the brightest women I know. But why did you enjoy Adam and Becky?"

"You take them for granted and that's normal. But I grew up by myself. No one to take the heat off with my mom. I was the focus—good or bad." She sighed. "My favorite thing was watching Adam and Becky put you in your place."

"Don't get used to it. Remember, at Mercy Medical Center I'm a god." The plane moved and Spencer could see that they were pulling away from the gate. It didn't look as if Avery noticed because she was laughing.

"Pretty soon you'll be a god with a robot that doesn't have feelings to hurt."

"Oh, please. I'm a swell guy."

"Swell? Who even says that?"

"It's a special word specifically reserved for doctors with the best people skills."

"That's what you call it?" She gave him a wry look. "The word 'people' implies both genders and your skills lean toward swell mostly with the ladies. Plural."

That's because there was safety in numbers, he thought. There was only a problem if you narrowed the field to one. Although, while he was trapped on a plane with that one and her scent tempted him unmercifully, he was doing his damnedest to treat her the way he treated other "people." But she tugged at him like no one other woman ever had.

"Ladies like me and I like them," he said.

"Why do you suppose that is?" Eyes narrowed, she stared at him.

"I don't suppose. I know why it is and so do you. I'm a nice doctor."

The pink in her cheeks and the self-conscious way she rubbed a finger under her nose indicated she recalled what she'd said about sleeping with the first nice doctor she met, then following through in Texas. He would never be sorry she'd proven to be a woman of her word.

Spencer had been all in favor of another go at proving her word, baring her body, but then she'd told him about her past and bared her soul. She'd once told him he reminded her of a guy she didn't like and now he knew why. Afterward, his goal had been to prove he was nothing like that guy. That included being sensitive enough to back off, not push her.

The silence between them dragged on. He stared at her, waiting for her to confirm a good opinion of him but she stared right back, not giving an inch.

He could feel the plane making the turn onto the runway and revving the engines for imminent takeoff. "What is it with you, Avery?"

"I have no idea what you're talking about."

"When are you going to admit that you were wrong about me? That you made a snap judgment then put on stubborn like white on rice and refused to take it off."

One of her dark blond eyebrows rose. "You're not by any chance referring to the irrational rant you overheard in Ryleigh's office, are you?"

"The very one."

She lifted one shoulder in a shrug. "That was just me venting."

"I think we both know now that if you hadn't changed your assessment of me, that very *fine* interlude at the Mansion on Turtle Creek never would have happened."

"Why are you pushing this?" she demanded. "Why is it so important that I take back what I said?"

"Because it distracted you from the fact that we took off and are very close to cruising altitude without you white-knuckling anything."

She looked out the window where big, fluffy white clouds dotted the view, then glanced at the flight attendants just leaving their seats to move about the cabin. Meeting his gaze, she grinned. "You are one sneaky surgeon."

"I prefer to think of it more as Doctor Dashing to the rescue."

"Tell me, Dashing…" She tapped her lip thoughtfully. "Is the surgical cap you wear in the O.R. big enough for that swelled head? Can the inflated ego be surgically reduced?"

"Mocking me will not distract me from getting a retraction out of you."

"What will?"

A kiss. Biting his ear. Leaning close and brushing her soft breasts against his arm. He was almost positive any of the above would make him forget that he was after an admission of guilt and an act of contrition. They were, however, on an airplane and activities of the intimate kind required privacy.

"Just tell me I'm a nice doctor," he suggested.

"Why don't you tell me your favorite thing about Texas," she countered.

Besides sex with her? Her expression didn't change so he was pretty sure he hadn't said that out loud.

"My favorite thing," he mused. "It was so eventful. But, I'd have to say playing with the robot and getting you on my side. To buy it," he added.

"The other hospitals confirmed everything said at Mercy Medical Center Dallas. It was really a no-brainer."

"So, let me get this straight." He shifted in his seat to look at her. "I was right to pester you about the robot. You like my family. The mall excursion and my part in getting you there was appreciated. And I was your friendly and informative Dallas/Fort Worth Metroplex tour guide but—"

"What?"

At the Stockyards she'd confessed that he was nicer than she'd thought, but he wanted her to take out the qualifier. "You refuse to admit that I'm a nice doctor?"

"Yes."

"Well, I've got you all to myself for a couple of hours until we get back to Las Vegas. Plenty of time to change your mind. Consider that a warning."

But when their arms brushed, he needed to take his own advice. Just the touch of her bare skin released a desire that slammed through him like a sledgehammer. It was a pretty forceful reminder that he wasn't finished wanting her.

The screwup in dates had made this trip just long enough for him to get used to seeing her cute little pixie face every morning for breakfast. She jump-started his day. He was starting to read her mood from the way her mouth turned up or down, the sparkle or absence of it in her eyes. All of that was disconcerting to a man like him.

On top of that, she'd told him her secret and clearly had

expected him to judge her for giving up her child. Instead, he respected her more. It had taken strength of character to make that choice. Her selfish mother had barely been there and was looking for an excuse to throw her out. In spite of it all, Avery O'Neill had grown into a beautiful, courageous woman brimming with intelligence and character. He admired her very much.

And that was incredibly inconvenient.

He'd been carefree and content before going away with her and he would do everything possible to be that way again. Obviously they were going home in the nick of time.

He wasn't finished wanting her, but returning to reality would let him have her on his terms.

"We're beginning our descent into Las Vegas and the captain has turned on the fasten seat belt sign so everyone should take their seats and buckle up. Winds are out of the south with gusts up to forty miles an hour so there may be some bumps. We should have you to the gate pretty close to on time."

Avery gripped the armrests. It was the only way to control an uncontrollable situation. Spencer might have successfully distracted her leaving Dallas, but there was no way he could make her un-hear that announcement and prevent white knuckles now. She wasn't sure whether it was better to know about rough air and work up a really serious case of apprehension, or be surprised when the turbulence hit and risk a massive adrenaline rush that might stop her heart. There were many advantages to flying with a heart surgeon and she'd list them in alphabetical order as soon as the plane was on the ground.

Spencer pried her fingers from the armrest and wrapped his big warm hand around them. "It's safer than driving a car."

"Until it's not." She met his gaze. "You do realize that logic is no match for irrational terror?"

"Yes, but I had to try."

"And I appreciate it." Not only that, she left her hand in his because it felt really good and reassuring not to be alone. This was the first time she hadn't gone through the anxiety of a round-trip flight by herself.

"I'm a nice guy." He was still trying to get her to say it.

"Prove it. Say something right now to distract me."

"But no pressure—" He thought for a moment. "What's your favorite movie?"

She didn't have to think very hard about that one. *"Terminator."*

His expression was full of disbelief. "You're joking."

"Nope. Ninety percent of my mental faculties are occupied with being terrified. Ten percent isn't nearly enough juice to joke." She took satisfaction in having surprised him so completely.

"I'd never have guessed. If there was a bet riding on it, I would have said *Pride and Prejudice.* Maybe *The Hangover.*"

His timing was perfect because she laughed when the plane bounced. "Obviously you'd have pegged me as a chick-flick kind of girl. And I am. But *Terminator is* a love story."

"The movie I saw had shooting, running, screaming, robot eyeballs plucked out and stuff blowing up."

"Ah. The male point of view."

"What does that mean?"

The plane shook again and her stomach dropped, but he squeezed her hand reassuringly. "It means," she said, "that there's no romance in your soul."

"I have as much romance as the next guy."

"My point exactly. If we ask the next guy about the movie he'd say truck explosions, car chases and shoot-outs."

"So?" He shrugged. "What's wrong with that?"

"None of it would have happened except for the love story."

"Who had time to fall in love?"

"Kyle Reese." The flight attendants made a last pass through the cabin to pick up cups, napkins and check seat belts and tray tables. Avery looked at the man beside her. "In the future, he fell in love with a picture. That's why he comes to the past to save the life of the woman who will give birth to the man who saves mankind from the machines." She sighed. "I defy any woman not to swoon at the words, 'I came across time for you, Sarah.'"

"I think I dozed off during that part," he teased.

"Why am I not surprised?" She shook her head. "But think about it. If not for love, there wouldn't have been a story."

He nodded slowly. "Your theory has merit."

"Thank you." She glanced out the window just as the plane banked into a wide turn. She felt her stomach shimmy, and not in a good way.

"What's your second favorite movie?" he asked.

"*Star Wars*—all six. And *Indiana Jones.* All of them."

"A girl who likes action-adventure."

"Yeah. As long as I don't have to watch while riding in an airplane." There was a sensation of dropping and floating with moments of shuddering and jolting in between. "I always wonder whether or not all that shaking will make the wings fall off."

"We're almost there," he said reassuringly.

Then the plane descended and sort of floated lower and lower until she felt the wheels touch the ground once, bounce, then touch again before brakes were applied to slow the aircraft.

"Now it's like a big, expensive bus," Spencer said.

Relief flooded her. "Thank you, Spencer."

"For what?"

"Talking me down. Literally."

"It was my pleasure," he said graciously.

"Seriously, you *are* a nice man."

His eyes widened. "Did I just get a retraction?"

"You did and this is very much on the record. I was wrong about you."

"So, all it took to get the truth out of you was a plane ride with mild turbulence."

"Whatever works." She smiled. "I can be a little stubborn."

"No? Really?" he said, teasing her. "I hadn't noticed."

She laughed, but the smile faded as the plane pulled up to the Jetway. It hit her suddenly that she was home and had to face the fact that life would go back to the way it was before Spencer had started harassing her. He'd gotten his robotic surgery system and had no reason now to track her down at work. So this was it. Over and out. Wow, what a downer that was, like sudden turbulence to the heart.

When they were parked and the plane door opened, Spencer stepped into the aisle so Avery could precede him off the plane and into the terminal. The smell of sugar from a candy kiosk and the ringing of slot machines was proof positive that this was definitely Las Vegas and not Cleveland.

"And we're home."

Avery glanced up at his tone and was surprised that he didn't look especially relieved to be here, either. Probably because he was anxious for the awkward parting to be over. No doubt he was sorry about not having separate cars here at the airport in order to make a clean break. Now it would be impossible on the way to her house to avoid tension.

So she'd slept with him. Big deal. Actually it was to her but she had no illusions about anything more. He'd wanted his robot and sex. His expectations had no doubt been met.

She hadn't realized she had any except getting through the whole thing unscathed. At least one of them had met a goal.

Side by side they walked through the airport, taking two moving walkways and an escalator down to baggage claim on the ground floor. After locating the correct carousel for their flight, they waited until luggage moved down the ramp and retrieved the bags. Then it was another trip up in the elevator to the parking garage.

Spencer handed the claim ticket to the valet and a few minutes later his car arrived. The last step in leaving was a stop to pay for parking. After that he concentrated on driving, getting on the 215 Beltway going toward Henderson.

They hadn't exchanged more than a word or two since she told him he was a nice man. If he wasn't, he wouldn't care that this was it and the quiet spoke volumes about the level of awkward he obviously felt. She desperately wanted the drive to be over, to deal with this sadness alone.

And finally her wish was granted when Spencer pulled up in front of her house. "Home again," he said.

"Thanks for the ride." Avery smiled as brightly as possible. "If you'll just pop the trunk, I'll grab my bag and you can be on your way."

"I'll get it."

She wanted to scream. As much as she wanted it over, she also wanted this moment to last forever. How was that for internal conflict? But he hefted her suitcase to the front door and she was digging in her purse for house keys.

"Well, that's it, then," she said.

Spencer rubbed a hand across the back of his neck. "I don't quite know how to say this—"

"I know what you're going to say." She interrupted because she couldn't bear to hear him make excuses about why it was best they didn't see each other again. "And don't worry about it. All's well that ends well. The trip started out rocky, but was a success. You were a great traveling companion, so let's leave it at that. Now everything goes back to the way it was before we left."

He looked surprised. "Are you saying that you don't want to see me again?"

"No." Avery stared at him, knowing she couldn't have heard right. Apparently her ears were still plugged from the pressure of flying. "I mean—what?"

"I was wondering if you'd go out to dinner with me."

"You were?"

He wanted to see her again? Here in the real world? A giddy sort of excitement escaped and spilled through her, so powerful there was no way to cram it back inside.

"I'd like to call you," he said.

"Okay."

"Okay, then." He smiled, then turned and walked back to his car.

Avery let herself into the house, then leaned her back against the door. Doctor Dashing didn't brush her off. She couldn't believe it and the feeling was like flying.

The problem with going up was that sooner or later you had to come back down. And the contrast between her misery at the airport and her happiness now told her that the coming down part wouldn't be a controlled landing. It would be more like a crash and burn.

But that was a problem for another day. Her new motto was to live in the moment.

She would enjoy whatever this was until the end. And it would end—because that's how Spencer Stone operated.

Chapter Eleven

The morning after returning from Dallas, Avery walked into the hospital and headed to her office with a somewhat weird and foreign sensation drifting through her. If she had to pick a word, she would call it happiness. And she was happy because there was something to look forward to. Her path might cross Spencer's here at work and the thought made her heart skip and put a spring in her step. She loved her job, but the change in her attitude about Spencer Stone was the icing on the cake. It was so much better than hiding in the ladies' room to avoid him.

Or she might not see him at all. He was on the medical/surgical side of the hospital and she was administration, pretty far apart in terms of job description and geography, but there was always a chance. And even if there was no Spencer sighting it didn't matter because he'd said he would call. That was the coolest part of all.

After turning in to her office, she saw her assistant at the desk. "Hi, Chloe. Beautiful morning, isn't it?"

The young woman looked up from her computer monitor, a humiliated expression in her dark eyes. She buried her face in her hands and dark, curly hair fell forward. "I am so incredibly sorry."

"For what?" Avery moved closer to the desk.

"The mix-up in your reservations."

It seemed so long since that day in Dallas, maybe because so much had happened in between. She'd gotten to know Spencer better, much better if you counted sleeping with him, and she did. But she'd also learned there were chinks in his armor and that leveled the playing field for mortals like herself.

"No big deal," she said to her assistant.

"The thing is Dr. Stone's office manager set everything up," Chloe went on as if she hadn't heard. "When she phoned and got the first date wrong, I should have double-checked everything, but I had that big project due for the administrator. Besides I figured Doctor Hottie had the most skin in the game and considering how you felt about spending money on a robot, well, I just thought the travel details would be all right coming from his side. I can't tell you—"

"Stop." Avery held up her hand to put an end to the soliloquy of shame. "Take a breath."

Frowning, Chloe studied her. "Your mouth isn't all pinchy and tight, so you don't look like you plan to fire me, but I wouldn't blame you if you did."

"No one's getting fired."

"But it was a mess."

"Not a big deal. My meeting was canceled. Truthfully, it was nice to have a day to acclimate." And get to know Spencer better. "It all fell into place, so stop working yourself up."

"You're sure?"

"Positive. And for the record? You discussed all this with me on the phone. Let it go."

"I'll try."

"We all make mistakes."

Well, she amended, everyone except Spencer. He was Doctor Perfect and held himself to a higher standard which she now understood. Oddly enough, another thing she'd learned was that he seemed to cut everyone else some slack. He couldn't have been more supportive when she told him about giving up her baby girl. It was a hollow in her heart that would never be filled although there was no question in her mind that it was the right thing to do at that time in her life. The best thing for her child.

"I'm glad we're okay," Chloe said.

"Definitely." The happiness she'd been rocking this morning made her smile now. "I think I'll get my emails out of the way first. I only got halfway through in Dallas, and there must be a bazillion."

Her assistant looked surprised. "You sure you're okay?"

"Yeah. Why?"

"That was the first time you mentioned an accumulation of email without using a colorful adjective in front of it. And you smiled when you said it."

"I'm just in a good mood." She shrugged.

"Well, then," Chloe said, her sass factor restored. "Next time I screw up, I hope Doctor Hottie returns you from another trip with the same forgiving attitude."

"Time to get to work," was all she said.

Several hours later Avery's mood was still good, but her eyes were threatening to cross from looking at her computer monitor for so long. When Ryleigh stood in her doorway it was a welcome relief and a good excuse to take a break.

"Hi, you." Avery stood, came around the desk and hugged the other woman.

"Hi, yourself. I just have a few minutes, but wanted to stop by and welcome you home. See how the trip went."

She rubbed her friend's growing baby bump. "Wow, Ry, you're really starting to pop out."

"I so am. And thanks for not saying something like 'you've really gotten big.'"

"You're my best friend. I'd never say anything like 'if they broke a bottle of champagne on your bow and put a flag in your hair you could take your place in the Pacific fleet.'"

"With friends like you..." But she laughed.

"Seriously, you look beautiful, Ry." She sat down behind the desk and her friend took one of the chairs in front. "You're glowing."

"I feel great." Like all pregnant women with a belly, she was losing her lap and rested her hands on said belly. "The baby is fine, too. We found out the sex."

"I thought you and Nick were going to be surprised."

"He changed his mind and there was no way he was going to know by himself."

"So, are you going to tell?"

"Girl." She grinned.

Avery didn't think anything could perforate her happy balloon, but a sharp shaft of envy did a fine job. It was involuntary. She'd been prepared to feel nothing but good for her friend who had the man she loved and now would have his daughter. It was everything Avery had once thought would be hers until the guy split and she lost everything.

"Congratulations." She managed to pull herself together and put a smile she hoped was the right wattage on her face. "Have you picked out a name yet?"

Ryleigh nodded. "Nicole Avery."

Now she felt even more shallow and selfish for her feelings. "It's beautiful. Thanks."

"The names of my two favorite people in the world. Of course we want you to be her godmother."

"It would be my honor." Avery said the words automatically even as guilt swirled.

If Ryleigh knew what she'd done, would she be trusted with this new little girl?

"So," she said, "how was your trip? Did you like Dallas?"

"I did. We accomplished everything on the agenda." And then some. "And I have to say that you were right about Spencer."

"Oh?"

"He is a nice man."

The other woman looked concerned. "So you slept with him."

Avery blinked at her. Was it tattooed on her forehead? "How did you know?"

"This is me."

"Okay. Right."

"And because this is me I'm going to tell you something."

Avery's happy deflated a little more at the somber tone. "What?"

"He is nice. And he's fun. But don't make the mistake of falling in love with him."

"Who said anything about love?"

"No one. But you're attracted to him and have been for a long time."

"How in the world would you know that?" Avery demanded.

"The way you complained about him. Have you ever heard that love and hate are really close? You didn't want to, but you like him."

"Okay. You're right."

"I worry about you, Avery. It's clear to me that you take things hard. That you don't let go."

"What have I ever—" Avery stopped when her friend put up a hand.

"I just know. There's something sad in your past. You've never talked about it and I'm not asking now. But I can see it in your eyes sometimes. If you want to tell me, I'll always listen. You know that. But I can't just stand by and say nothing and let Spencer be another sad thing in your past. I promised not to say 'I told you so' when you found out you were wrong about him, but I really hoped you wouldn't sleep with him." She stood. "Just, whatever you do, don't make the mistake of falling in love. He keeps it all about fun. You do the same."

"Don't worry," Avery promised.

"I can't help it. I love you. And, on that note, I have to go."

Avery hugged her friend again, then sank down in the chair behind her desk. Ryleigh's warning really shook her. She'd known getting involved with Spencer was a bad idea. Hadn't she been the one who teased him about all his women?

Then he'd said he wanted to see her again. Better than anyone she knew guys promised stuff all the time and never came through. Now she was back to reality and not just because of returning to Las Vegas. Ryleigh had just delivered a verbal head smack.

Don't count on anything with Spencer Stone—not a phone call or anything more—no matter what he said.

"I knew that," Avery whispered to herself.

In spite of the warning, happiness and hope died a little more every day Avery was home from Dallas and there was no contact with Spencer. It had been over a week.

In spite of Ryleigh's warning, Avery hadn't been able to stop herself from walking the halls of Mercy Medical Center closest to surgery on the second floor. She'd never "accidentally" bumped into Spencer by the waiting room there. Probably because she wasn't anxiously waiting for an update on a loved one.

Except she sort of was.

Where Spencer was concerned, she was afraid she felt something perilously close to love. Ryleigh had been right to warn her not to let her feelings go too far, but the warning was one trip to Dallas too late. Now Avery was slinking around the halls like a besotted high school girl looking to run into the object of her crush. She'd been an idiot and it was time to face that.

After one incredible night in his arms, he'd never made another move to touch her. She wasn't sure why the promise to call, but no doubt he'd had a chance to think it over and decided he didn't want a girl who could do what she'd done. She wasn't perfect and only perfection would do for Spencer Stone.

She got home from work on Wednesday and realized she'd lost count of how many days had passed without seeing him. Hope had been clinging to life support but now it was pretty much time to pull the plug. She went straight to her bedroom, stepped out of her suit pants and jacket, then hung them up and slipped on a pair of cut-off denim shorts and a black tank top. The death of hope didn't deserve a chic outfit. Something sloppy would do just fine.

It also didn't deserve a nice dinner. Feeling hurt and used the way she did, frozen little square microwavable mystery meat, rubbery green beans and reconstituted mashed potatoes with facsimile sauce masquerading as gravy was all she could manage.

She opened the white microwave door and shoved in the food, then hit three-minute express cook. Barefoot, she walked around assembling napkin, fork, knife and a bottle of water. There was an unopened bottle of wine in the fridge, but having a glass would be a painful reminder of that lovely interlude in Dallas. Opening that bottle of wine would be like letting the memories escape and would only allow in the pain she was desperately holding off.

Leaning against the black granite counter topping the oak cupboards, she listened to the oven hum and watched the light inside. Usually being in her charming kitchen with the cute little knickknacks arranged above the cupboards cheered her up no matter what. Tonight there was only one thing that could cheer her up and she'd been a fool to hope for him.

The oven beeped and there was another simultaneous noise that sounded a lot like the doorbell, but hope had played cruel tricks on her before. With mitts, she took her dinner out of the oven and set it on her small round oak table for two. Then she heard it again.

Definitely the doorbell, and the ring of it tripped up her heart.

It was hard not rushing to peek out the peephole, and she couldn't control her pounding heart as she opened the door. "Spencer. I didn't think I'd… I wasn't expecting…"

Without a word, he moved close and pulled her against him. He wrapped his arms around her and buried his face in her neck. Without a word, he just stood there and she felt the tension in him.

The words popped out of her mouth before fully forming in her head. "Do you want to come inside?"

"I thought you'd never ask." He let her go, but his fingers slid down her arm before finally breaking contact to walk in and look around. "Nice place."

She realized he'd never been inside her house. "I like it," she said. "Small. Just right for one person."

"Avery—" He must have heard the edge in her voice because he reached out a hand.

She backed away. "I was just about to eat a frozen dinner. Didn't expect you'd be coming by."

"Sorry. I should have called—"

"You don't owe me an explanation."

"Yeah. I do. It's been crazy since I got back. Getting up to speed on my patients. Paperwork. Emergency surgeries. By the time I could even think about calling it was late and I didn't want to wake you."

When the haze of angry hurt cleared she realized he did look tired. She'd worked in the hospital long enough to know that any time off for a doctor made quadruple the work when he returned. That didn't mean he couldn't pick up the phone. But then his words sank in. He got calls at all hours for surgical procedures and it wasn't unusual for him to walk out of the O.R. in the middle of the night. She wouldn't have cared about the time if he woke her, but he wouldn't know that.

Her heart softened. It wasn't smart. It wasn't good. It just was and she couldn't stop herself.

"Would you like a glass of wine?"

Wine rhymed with spine and apparently she didn't have one where he was concerned.

"I'd love one," he answered.

"Follow me."

She felt him behind her and wished she had dressed better. Death-of-hope clothes weren't her best look and since he was here, the requiem might have been premature. But she so didn't need to go there. She'd gone from the gutter to the balcony of a luxury high rise and if she fell again it could leave a mark.

She went to the refrigerator and pulled out the wine, got two glasses from the upper cupboard, then busied herself opening and pouring.

"Would you like a frozen dinner? They're adequate if you

need some food. Or I can put together some crackers and cheese. Grapes and strawberries."

"I'm not hungry." His voice was angry and cold.

It chilled her. When she turned he was leaning against the countertop, arms folded over his chest, staring at the floor. He was still wearing scrubs and there were lines of fatigue on his face. She saw something in his eyes, too.

Anguish. Desperation. Guilt.

"What's wrong, Spencer?" He shook his head but she wasn't going to let him blow her off. "Don't even try to tell me it's nothing because I can see that's not true. What's wrong?"

His eyes were dark with self-loathing. "I lost a patient tonight."

"Oh, Spencer—" She moved closer but he sidestepped her touch. "What happened?"

"Aortic aneurysm." His mouth pulled tight. "A bubble in the blood vessel near the heart. It started to leak into the chest cavity. The guy is Director of Laboratory Services at Mercy Medical. One of our own."

"A hospital employee," she echoed.

He nodded. "He was at work and had chest pain then walked himself to the E.R. EKG and blood tests ruled out a heart attack but they were thinking gall bladder because of radiating pain. Aneurysms get overlooked too much unless you're having a CT scan for something else and it just gets picked up."

"But you did find it?"

He nodded. "He wasn't a candidate for a chest repair. Would have bled out as soon as we went in."

"So there was nothing you could do?"

"There's a relatively new procedure. Threading a graft and stent through the femoral artery up to the leak to stop the blood flow." He rubbed his hand over his face and the anger returned. Anger clearly directed at himself.

"What happened?"

"He was a smoker. Quit a couple years ago, but a lot of damage was already done. The arteries were full of plaque. They crunched to the touch. Threading the stent through was practically impossible. At one point I perforated the vessel because it was so hard. Tried one more time and got it. Blood stopped instantly."

"That's good."

He shook his head. "Just as I was thinking we had it, his heart stopped and we couldn't get him back. The repair was too delicate for chest compressions or defibrillation. That didn't leave us much to work with and I lost him."

"I'm so sorry, Spencer."

"Sorry doesn't mean squat when you don't get the job done."

"It's not your fault." But she knew he was blaming himself. It's what he did, how he grew up. Moving closer, she took his hand to keep him from retreating. "What about the family?"

"They knew all the risks. Ten percent chance of stroke. Fifteen for paralysis because of where the leak was in relation to the spinal cord. They still trusted me to save him."

"Did you do your best?" She put her hand on his cheek and gently turned his gaze to hers even though she already knew the answer.

"Of course."

"That's what I thought. Because you're you and can't do less than that." She threaded her fingers through his. "If you hadn't done everything possible, you'd get my permission to kick your ass from here to next Tuesday. But it's not your fault that he picked up a cigarette and got hooked, probably when he was a rebellious teenager. You did everything humanly possible to save his life. You're a brilliant and skilled doctor but you're not God. You don't get to decide when it's someone's time to go."

He didn't answer, just continued to shake his head.

Avery had never seen a man more desperately in need of a hug. She hesitated a fraction of a second, her finely tuned self-protective instincts kicking in. Then she brushed them aside. Whatever "this" was between them didn't matter right now; whatever pain might be hers later wasn't important. She just couldn't *not* put her arms around a man so clearly requiring comfort.

"I'm here." She held him close and rested her cheek against his chest, reassured by the strong, steady beat of his heart.

"Avery—" Her name was a sigh as he tightened his hold. "I've missed you."

Intensity was etched into every line and angle of his face. He lowered his mouth to hers and the touch made her burst into flame. The hunger for him was instantaneous as memories of a night in Dallas heated her blood. When she pulled back they were both breathing hard.

"It's time you saw my bedroom." Her voice was a wanton whisper.

"That's the best offer I've had all day."

She led him down the hall to her bedroom with its green-and-plum-colored floral spread and matching fluffy shams. The walls were olive-green with white baseboards and crown molding. Everything about it was feminine, yet Spencer didn't look at all out of place. He was one of those masculine men who dominated the room no matter the decoration. For right here, right now he was hers.

He tossed pillows and yanked off the blanket and comforter, leaving the pink sheets bare. Then he took out his wallet and put a condom on her nightstand.

Avery couldn't resist the way his wide shoulders moved, the muscles bunching and flexing beneath his scrubs top. She came up to him and wrapped her arms around his middle, fitting herself behind him, resting her cheek on his back.

He put his big hand on hers and sighed deeply, as if letting go of the burden weighing him down. Then he turned and took the hem of her tank top and drew it up and over her head.

"You're not wearing a bra." A small, mischievous grin turned up the corners of his mouth.

"I'm sorry."

"Don't be. Not on my account." He held her bare breasts in his hands and brushed his thumbs across her nipples, turning them hard as pebbles.

The touch set off an electric shock that shot straight through her, settling in the bundle of nerve endings between her thighs. She moaned and her head dropped back, exposing her throat. He touched her and kissed her until her legs went weak and she dropped onto the bed, reaching her arms out to him.

He didn't waste any time pulling off his scrubs. She was grateful that besides freedom of movement for his work there was a lot to be said for easy removal of pajama-like attire. In three seconds flat he was naked and beside her, stretching out on the cool pink sheets. With his left hand he removed her shorts and panties, then held her—bare skin to bare skin. He slid his hand down her back and cupped her butt, squeezing as he pressed her closer to his hardness.

"I need you. Now," she breathed, as urgency surged through her.

"Not as much as I need you."

He moved away for a second and then ripped open the square foil packet before covering himself. In the next moment, he settled himself over her and thrust inside. The coiled tension there exploded and pleasure poured through her. The next instant he joined her in release and she felt his shudders as an extension of her own. They held each other until their bodies went limp and he tucked her against his side.

A short while later, he made love to her again. And again after that, all through the night. Her body was tired and satisfied, but her head wouldn't shut off because she'd realized something.

Ryleigh's warning about not getting involved with Spencer was wise. When he showed up at her door tonight, a smart girl would have told him no. Avery considered herself a smart girl, but saying no to the tempting Dr. Stone had been a challenge she'd failed. She'd seen him cocky, arrogant, determined and charming, but never vulnerable. It made her weak.

She couldn't be that way again.

Chapter Twelve

For the first time in his life Spencer didn't feel alone and it had nothing to do with his brother, Adam, sitting next to him in the passenger seat of the car. He'd arrived that day for an interview at Mercy Medical corporate headquarters for the Blackwater Lake job. He'd said it went well and now the two of them were headed to Avery's house for dinner.

She was the reason he didn't feel alone and Spencer wasn't comfortable about it. He'd been brought up to be independent and never let himself need anyone. There had only been that one college slipup where he'd been kicked in the teeth. He was a quick learner though and once was enough. No one had ever gotten close again.

Until Avery.

Something inside him had shifted that night he'd lost a patient. A compulsion too strong to fight had sent him to her. That had been rocky and unfamiliar ground. Yet he'd seen her every night since unless an emergency prevented him.

Now Adam was in Las Vegas and she'd invited them to dinner, claimed she was looking forward to seeing his brother again. For some reason she seemed to like his geeky, pushy, overbearing family.

"You're different with Avery." Adam's comment came out of nowhere but was disconcertingly right on.

Spencer took his time to think about what to say as he navigated the curving street from his big house on the hill overlooking a golf course and the Las Vegas Strip. He continued down Eastern Avenue headed toward the 215 Beltway east and Avery's house in Green Valley Ranch. His brother was so right on with his observation Spencer figured his response should be firmly anchored in nonchalance.

Finally he said, "What do you mean different with Avery?"

"You took her home to meet Mom and Dad."

"No." Spencer glanced over at the passenger seat. "We had a travel glitch."

"One that could have been resolved at a hotel," Adam pointed out. "But I think you were after the family's approval."

"A—I don't need approval. B—there's nothing to approve of. And I have to ask, do you have a psych degree to go with that family practice specialty of yours?"

Adam laughed. "Just the reaction I expected."

"What the hell does that mean?" he asked irritably.

"And a bonus reaction."

"Oh, for God's sake, stop with the cryptic comments so I can tell you you're wrong about all of it."

"You can tell me that but it doesn't mean you're right."

"Adam, I swear, if you don't stop with the babble I'll pull this car over and—"

"What? Leave me on the freeway?"

"Maybe." Spencer negotiated a soft right turn onto the 215 Beltway and merged with traffic, heavy on Saturday night.

Now that he thought about it, Avery lived farther from the airport than he did so pickup and drop-off for their business trip had been out of his way. For the purposes of this conversation, that realization didn't sweeten his temper.

"Here's my professional opinion as a health care practitioner who specializes in the entire person, not just body part trauma management." Adam paused dramatically. "Your eyes are only on her when she's in a room full of people."

"You did not just say such a chick thing to me."

"I study human behavior. I watch, observe, make assessments. It's what I do."

Spencer glanced at him. "That's like something I might hear from Becky."

"Or mom."

He glanced over and they both said at the same time, "Maybe not mom."

"Seriously, little brother, Avery is a beautiful woman. What man doesn't stare at her?"

"Seriously, big brother, you know as well as I do that there's just looking to appreciate a woman and then there's *looking* and not being able to take your eyes off her mouth."

Spencer was used to being the smartest guy in the room and it was annoying to be bested by his younger brother. But not even under threat of torture would he admit that Avery's mouth had fascinated him from their very first introduction and turned him on even more now that he knew how good she felt, how sweet she tasted.

He only said, "For the record, bro, you're full of it."

"Not the first time you've told me that and definitely not the first time you've been wrong." Adam's voice was annoyingly cheerful.

"This time I'm not."

His brother was full of it even if he wasn't wrong about Spencer being fixated on kissing Avery. And he'd done a whole lot more than kiss her. He couldn't seem to get enough of her.

But that was just for now. This relationship, or whatever, would run its course. They always did.

"Not to change the subject, but I'm changing the subject," Spencer announced. "You're sure about this Blackwater Lake move?"

"Very."

"It's a pretty small place compared to the Dallas/Fort Worth Metroplex."

"That's what makes me sure."

"You're not running away?" Spencer glanced over.

"Coming from you that's the pot calling the kettle black, to utilize a cliché." Adam's expression was wry.

"Here we go again."

"Just saying, Spence, at least I took a chance on marriage."

"And it turned out to be a disaster," Spencer reminded him.

Ignoring the comment, Adam went on. "You've been on the dating treadmill and won't get off ever since that art major in college."

Call him nuts for not wanting to make another mistake. "In a word it's caution. I'm not running."

"Let's call it walking fast and consistently in the opposite direction of anything that even has a whiff of commitment."

"Oh, dear God—" Spencer stopped in front of Avery's house. "Here we are. And not a second too soon."

After he turned off the ignition, they exited the car and walked up to the front door. Avery must have been watching because she answered right away.

"Hi." She smiled, but it was a little off. "Welcome to Vegas, Adam."

He bent down to kiss her cheek. "Nice to see you again."

"And in my natural habitat. Come on in. It's hot out here."

They walked inside and the temperature was cooler but Spencer was still hot and that was all about Avery. This happened every time he was with her. And yes, damn it, he always looked at her mouth. If Adam hadn't been there he would have taken her in his arms, kissed the living daylights out of her, then taken her to bed. Instead, he did a friendly peck on the cheek like his brother had. Which, by the way, he wasn't especially happy about.

After a short tour of her place they ended up in the kitchen. The first time he'd seen it Spencer had thought the warmth and charm suited her. Nothing had changed his mind about that.

"Can I get you guys something to drink?" she asked. "Wine for Spencer. Adam?"

"That's fine. Unless you happen to have a beer."

"As it happens, I do. Sierra Nevada okay?"

"Perfect."

She poured one glass of wine, then grabbed a longneck from the refrigerator. After handing them out she opened a bottle of water for herself.

"You're not having one?" Spencer held up his long-stemmed glass.

"I have to get dinner on the table and part of the preparation involves fire."

"You're barbecuing," Adam said.

"Yes. Fire good," she said. "But not when one is a little tipsy."

"Can I help?"

Spencer felt like a Neanderthal for not offering. "Yeah. Tell us what to do."

"It's all pretty easy. Already microwaved the potatoes and they're in foil to warm on the grill. Salad's made and only needs tossing. I'm marinating chicken breasts. Keeping it healthy. Hiding my junk food fetish from the health care professionals." She sipped her water. "Adam, I hear you're interviewing for the job in Blackwater Lake?"

"Yeah. Final meeting's on Monday."

"So you're visiting with Spencer?"

"Don't ask me why. He's got the personality of a rottweiler, pit bull mix."

She laughed. "He'd tell you I do, too."

"Good thing," Adam said. "Who else could stand him?"

"Hey," Spencer protested.

"I didn't think so." Avery's tone and word choice indicated past tense.

"That was before you got to know I'm a sweetheart of a guy."

"Interesting." Adam was leaning back against the kitchen island, keenly watching the back and forth. "Usually people get to know him and decide they were right not to like him."

Avery settled her gaze on Spencer's. "I can see that about him. But how can you not like a man who takes you to the mall and helps you shop for casual clothes because you'll be sightseeing and all you brought was business suits?"

"You don't say?" Adam shot a look that said "and you gave *me* a hard time about a sensitive side."

"It was the least I could do. My office screwed up the reservations."

"So," she said. "Are you guys hungry?"

"Starved." But Spencer was looking at her mouth again. And his brother's throat clearing said he didn't miss it.

"I'll fire up the grill and put the potatoes on."

"Can I do anything to help?" Adam asked.

"Put the salad on the table. Oil and vinegar okay with everyone?"

"Fine," both said.

Twenty minutes later the three of them were sitting around the table, plates filled. While they'd dug in to the food, she'd refreshed his wine and Adam had another beer. She got another bottle of water for herself.

"Can I pour you some Chardonnay?" Spencer asked her.

"Thanks, but I'll stick to water. Have to hydrate when it's hot. Don't want to look like a boneheaded tourist who consumes alcohol then collapses because what you really need is good old H2O."

"Maybe later," he said.

Without saying one way or the other she turned to Adam. "So, how long are you here for?"

"A week. Maybe longer if necessary. I expect an offer and can take care of the paperwork in person."

"You seem very sure this is what you want."

"I am."

"Then I hope everything works out."

"I have a feeling it's the beginning of a new and exciting adventure." He watched her for a moment. "Are you feeling all right, Avery?"

"Yes." She looked up quickly. "Why?"

"You look a little pale."

"I do?" she asked, pressing her palms to her cheeks.

"You said there was a lot piled up at the hospital after the Dallas trip." Spencer studied her and realized she didn't have the usual Tinker Bell glow. "Are you working too hard?"

"No. I think I'm just not ready for the triple digit weather yet. Heat takes a lot out of you." She shrugged.

"You're not eating much, either." Adam was looking at her nearly untouched food.

Spencer just realized he and Adam had nearly finished and she'd taken about four bites of chicken. Her baked potato was still in the foil. And she'd been moving the greens around her plate but not much went into her mouth.

"I'm just not very hungry. The heat affects me that way." Avery jumped up and cleared plates from the table. "Who's up for dessert? Strawberry shortcake."

Spencer watched her gather small plates and forks. Then he met his brother's concerned gaze and remembered what Adam had said about the value of observing as a tool for gathering medical information. This was a smack-the-forehead-moment because he, Spencer, had not picked up on the signs. His brother was a hell of a good physician and Blackwater Lake, Montana, would be crazy not to grab him before someone else did.

Spencer could learn from him and he would. But first he wanted answers and Avery was the only one who could give them to him.

After the brothers Stone left, Avery collapsed on her living room sofa and practically curled into the fetal position. And wasn't that ironic considering. She was sitting knees to chest, forehead on knees, still upright but not quite sure how she managed to stay that way.

All she wanted to do was cry or throw up. Or both. She'd thought she'd held it together pretty well until Spencer's brother started asking questions. He was far too perceptive but seemed to accept her explanation and didn't push. Spencer's expression grew guarded and clearly he hustled the two of them out of here as quickly as possible. It was a relief to be by herself.

Spencer had to know what was going on but she wanted to pick the time and place to tell him.

The soft knock on her door startled her. It wasn't very late, but not the hour someone normally came by. At least no one besides Spencer. She jumped up and looked through the peephole. Her heart hammered and she wasn't sure if that was because of being so happy to see him. Partly dreading to see him. Or the fact that he'd chosen for her the time and place to hear what she had to tell him.

She unlocked the door and opened it. "Hi. Come in."

"I took Adam back to the house and came back because we need to talk." He stared at her. "You don't seem surprised to see me."

"Besides the fact that it's not unusual for you to stop by unannounced and at odd hours, you're right. We do need to talk."

His face was grim as he walked inside. Turning he said, "What's really wrong, Avery? And don't tell me you're overworked and hot."

"Have a seat, Spencer." She passed him and stood in front of the sofa, stomach churning. Feeling pretty vulnerable and hating it, she didn't want to sit until he did. She didn't want him looking down at her. If nothing else it was symbolic of the fact that she wasn't a powerless teenager, but a woman in charge of her life.

"I don't want to sit. Tell me why you didn't eat and avoided having wine. We both know you do have a glass on occasion." The words could have been teasing except for the gravel in the tone and the grimness in his eyes. "What's going on?"

"I'm pregnant." Two simple words that would change everything.

He had the oddest expression on his face, stunned yet not completely surprised. "Are you sure?"

"I did a pregnancy test. It was positive. You're the doctor. How sure is that?"

"Not my field of expertise."

"According to what I read in the instructions, it's pretty close to one hundred percent. We've been back from Dallas two weeks. And my symptoms are exactly the same as—" She couldn't look at him.

"What symptoms?"

She met his gaze and hoped for a grin, not necessarily a proud-I'm-going-to-be-a-father one. Just a crack in the Stone facade, a small hint that he didn't hate her. But his expression didn't change.

"I'm nauseous and eating is a problem. Emotional." And her breasts were sore, but she wasn't sharing that with him.

"And you felt like this when you were pregnant before?"

"Yes." Although it was a lot of years ago, the emotional trauma of being pregnant at seventeen had seared the memories into her heart forever.

"Have you seen a doctor?"

"No."

"You need to," he said.

"I will." Legs shaking, she lowered herself to the sofa. If he looked down on her, so be it. She covered her face with her hands and felt the cushion dip when he sat beside her.

"Are you okay?"

You tell me, she wanted to say. So far he hadn't smiled or touched her. Ever since that night he'd lost a patient in the O.R., he hadn't walked into her house without pulling her into his arms and kissing her until she could hardly drag air into her lungs. Now she needed a hug more than she had ever needed one in her life.

"Avery?"

She sighed and lowered her hands. "I can't believe I made the same mistake."

"There were two of us," he said quietly.

"Still—one unplanned pregnancy is a mistake. People would say two is a lifestyle choice. But it had been such a long time since a man held me—"

"Don't—"

"I can't help it." In Dallas, when he'd touched her the need had been overwhelming. All she could think about was being with him. It was the most wonderful experience of her life. But this serious Spencer, so different from the charming, caring man she'd come to like, possibly more than like, was quickly turning into the worst thing ever.

She met his gaze. "Birth control wasn't my first thought that night."

"It wasn't mine, either, but it should have been." There was anger in his eyes and no way to tell if it was directed at her or himself. "I've got more experience."

Avery felt the lump form in her throat and prayed tears weren't in her eyes. Hoped he couldn't see how those words cut. Damn hormones made everything feel worse. She'd teased him about "all his women." This was not something she wanted to think about, let alone hear his confirmation that it was true.

"Can I get you something to drink?" she asked.

"Do you have scotch?"

She shook her head. "Beer or wine. Water."

"No, thanks."

From his perspective something stronger to deal with this news made sense. But she hated being a problem that needed a stiff drink.

"Avery, just so you know, we'll handle this together."

Handle? This?

She had a sort of spacey, surreal sensation going on, but knew it would pass. Reality would set in. The nausea, emotional rollercoaster and tenderness would turn into water retention, fatigue, then feeling a new life move inside her. The love and instinct to protect was intense and unwavering. At seventeen she'd done her best and every day for as long as she lived she would hope the decision had been the right one. That she'd protected her baby girl by giving her two parents who really wanted her and loved her.

This might be the same mistake but the outcome wouldn't be.

"And just so *you* know, Spencer, I'm keeping this baby."

"Okay." There wasn't the slightest trace of feeling in his voice.

Was he angry? Scared? Disapproving?

She sighed. "I have no expectations. It's my decision. You don't have to be involved. It's not your responsibility."

"The hell it's not." His eyes blazed green fire.

She tried to tell herself that anger was better than the robot he'd been since walking into her living room. "I can take care of myself and my child."

He stood and looked down at her. "This is my child, too."

"That doesn't matter to some men." She had the scars to prove the truth of those words.

"I'm not some men. I'm not him." He started pacing the floor. "Let me screw up before you start throwing blame around."

"Okay."

Part of her wanted to jump to her defense. The rest was too tired. There was no energy to explain that it was easier to go to the bad place and know she could handle the worst than to hope for everything and be completely crushed when she didn't get it.

She stood and met his gaze. He was still looking down at her but that was only because he was taller, not because she was less than his equal in this situation. "I just didn't want you to think I intended to make this any harder for you than it already is."

"Don't worry about me. I can take care of myself. But I can't believe you'd think I would walk away from my responsibilities."

So, that's all this was. The zinger hit its mark and she barely suppressed the wince.

"Okay, then," she said. "Guess there's nothing more to talk about."

"There's plenty more, but not tonight." He walked to the door and settled his hand on the knob. "Call the obstetrician. I can recommend one—"

"I'll do it."

"Make an appointment and let me know when."

"All right."

"I'll be there."

Because he felt obligated.

After he left she leaned against the door and settled her palms protectively over her still flat abdomen. She was nothing more than a responsibility and it broke her heart because she wanted to be so much more.

Chapter Thirteen

A week later Avery went to work even though she'd never been so tired in her life. Lately sleep was hard to come by, a direct result of being pregnant, telling Spencer he was going to be a father and the carefully blank look on his face afterward. When she'd slept at all the dreams were more like nightmares. She was exhausted, but job security was even more important now and she couldn't afford to not show up. She wouldn't be anyone's responsibility. Taking care of herself was second nature and that was just fine with her. *She* wouldn't let herself down.

Finally it was almost quitting time and she was worn out. She set her cell phone on the desk, checked her email and inbox to make sure nothing needed her attention until tomorrow, then shut down her computer. There was a soft knock on her office door before it opened and Ryleigh walked in.

"Hey, A, what's going on?" Her beautiful brunette friend was wearing a high waisted royal-blue maternity dress. She instinctively rubbed her hands over the bigger-every-day belly.

That's when Avery burst into tears. Dear God she hated the hormones.

"Oh, my God. What is it?" Ryleigh was beside her in seconds.

On some level, Avery wondered how a pregnant lady could move so fast, but she was sobbing too hard to get the words out.

"It's okay, sweetie," she said.

Avery buried her face in her hands and shook her head.

Ryleigh leaned down and pulled her close, at least as close as she could with the baby bump. "Whatever it is you can tell me. You know that. But you've got to stop crying."

"I c-can't." She felt something move against her arm, a ripple and wriggle that she remembered from a long time ago. It was all baby and brought on a fresh wave of tears.

The other woman pulled a chair from the front of the desk and sat down so they were face to face. "Okay, it's tough love time. Stop it right now. Stop crying and tell me what's going on."

"It's all so horrible."

"Did you kill anyone?"

"Of course not." Finally she lifted her face.

Ryleigh nodded calmly. "And you're not sick?"

"No."

"Okay. Good. And you're not bleeding or on fire." She looked expectantly, then added, "I can't help without more information. Out with it. I've never been a mom before but this must be how it feels."

Avery met her gaze and blinked back a fresh wave of tears at the mom reference. "I'm pregnant, Ry."

"Okay. All right. Now we're getting somewhere." Her

friend's voice was deliberately calm but there was no way to hide the shock in her eyes. "Does Spencer know?"

"What makes you think he's the father?"

"Unless you've secretly been seeing a trapeze artist from Le Reve or a magician from the Hard Rock, I'd put my money on the doctor who took you to Dallas. Am I wrong?"

Miserable, Avery shook her head. "I don't know how it happened."

Ryleigh's expression was mocking in a best friend kind of way. "I could get out my graphs, charts and ovulation information, but for me and Nick it was nothing more than well-timed chemistry."

"It just happened one night." Avery sat back in her chair and heaved a sigh. "After a couple days with his family he just didn't seem like such a pain in the neck. A nice doctor, just like you told me."

"That opinion might be premature. And you really didn't have to sleep with the first nice doctor you met." There was an edge to her tone.

"You were right about him, though. He is a nice man. One who went out of his way to take me to the mall because I only brought professional clothes. Then he gave me a tour of the Metroplex. His parents are wonderful and people like that don't raise a toad."

"He took advantage of you."

"No."

"You're an innocent and he manipulated you into a vulnerable situation."

"I don't think so." Avery shook her head. "He could have steered me to an alternative hotel for manipulation and seduction, but he took me to meet his family."

"Where he could charm you and lower your defenses."

Avery sniffled, then reached for a tissue from the square, flowered box on her desk. "He's not a premeditated charmer.

It comes naturally to him. I don't believe he set out to seduce me. I just made it particularly easy for him to."

"Was liquor involved?" Ryleigh's mother lion protective face looked adorably fierce.

"Yes." Avery smiled. "But neither of us had too much. We both knew what we were doing."

"Still, he has way more experience than you."

So Spencer had reminded her. "Thanks for pointing that out, Ry."

"I'm not being mean. Just stating a fact."

"Okay." She couldn't look at her friend for this. "But I'm not as innocent as you think."

"What are you saying?"

"I might have been naive once upon a time, but not since I got pregnant at seventeen."

"Avery—" There was shock in her friend's voice and questions in her eyes. This time she didn't try to hide it. "I can't believe you never said anything to me."

"I just couldn't. Too painful. Didn't want you to judge."

"You know me better than that," Ryleigh scolded.

"Now I do. But in the beginning—" A lump in her throat stopped the words.

"I always felt there was a part of your life you didn't talk about. Something you wouldn't share even with me."

"I'm not proud of it. Burying the whole thing seemed best, but apparently I should have stitched a sampler and hung it on the wall as a reminder."

"For Pete's sake," Ryleigh said, "it takes two for that particular mistake to happen."

Again her friend quoted Spencer. "Still, it's what I get for not being able to say no." But only to him. "It's just that it had been so long and I was out of practice. And…"

"Spencer doesn't have that excuse." Ryleigh's voice softened when she asked, “Did you have the baby when you were a teenager?”

She nodded. “It never crossed my mind not to.”

“And the father?”

“Captain of the football team. Heat of passion. My first time. Backseat of his car.” But at least this time the setting had been elegant and comfortable. Doesn’t get much better than the Mansion on Turtle Creek. Or the perfect Dr. Stone.

“What happened to the big man on campus? I guess he supported your decision?”

“That was probably the most humiliating part.” Avery twisted her fingers together in her lap. “He proposed.”

“You’re married?” Now Ryleigh didn’t hide the shock.

“No. A civil wedding was arranged but he didn’t show. I think his parents insisted, but he joined the army to get away from me and the baby.”

“Bastard.” There was loathing wrapped around the two syllables. “What happened to the baby?”

“My mother said that she couldn’t handle another mouth to feed. If I insisted on keeping my baby I could do it somewhere other than under her roof.”

“Oh, sweetie—” Ryleigh leaned over and gave her a hug. “What did you do?”

“There really wasn’t a choice if my little girl was going to have any chance for a good life. I gave her up for adoption.” She lowered her gaze. “It wasn’t even about food, clothes, toys. I wanted her to be loved and protected, things money couldn’t buy. I had enough love, but no way to give her security and stability.”

Ryleigh nudged her chin up until their gazes locked. “You’re the most caring and courageous woman it’s ever been my privilege to know.”

“I’m not—”

“No way.” She held up a finger. “No argument.”

"Okay." Her lips curved up but it lasted only a second. "I'm not going through that again, Ry. I want this baby so much and I can take care of it now."

"Of course you can." Ryleigh's smile was brimming with encouragement. "Have you told Spencer?"

"Yes. Although I didn't plan to quite so soon." She tugged at the tissue in her hands. "His brother's in town on business. I made dinner for them and Adam noticed I wasn't eating much. His specialty is family practice and he asked if I was feeling okay."

"Spencer didn't notice?"

"He did after that. And I knew he knew. When he came back later he'd already connected the dots. I'd never planned not to tell him, but I'd hoped for a little more time to prepare a speech." She looked at her friend. "He knows about my past."

"Good."

"All I could get out was that I'm keeping this baby and he doesn't have to be involved."

"Yes, he does." Ryleigh was adamant.

"That's what he said." More precisely that he didn't run away from responsibility. That still smarted.

"Anything else?"

Avery shrugged. "He's still processing the information."

"What's to process? He's going to be a father. You're the mother of his child."

"It was a shock to him, Ry. He's a busy doctor."

"It was a shock to you and everyone is busy. That doesn't mean he gets a pass on being there for you. Your body, your baby, doesn't mean he gets to turn his back. He needs to be there to support you. If he doesn't, he's not the Spencer Stone I know and will get a stern talking-to. And Nick will have something manly to say, as well."

Avery knew she wanted Spencer involved in her life

whether or not she was having his baby. She wanted that so much it hurt. But she'd rather hurt than have him involved out of obligation. He'd said the right things, but the look in his eyes was so emotionless, so disconnected. She had no experience with someone who stayed for her, someone who cared for her. There was no reason to believe Spencer would react any differently and she couldn't afford to let herself believe he might.

"It's okay, Ry. I don't need him."

"He better do the right thing."

Avery held up her hand. "Don't go there. Two wrongs and all that."

"I just meant financial and emotional support. Who said anything about marriage?"

"No one." But clearly Avery had thought about it on some level or *she* wouldn't have gone there. And she knew why. She'd never felt for any man what she did for him, but… Yeah, there was always a but.

"He had a right to know about his child and I'd never keep that child from him. I have no intention of asking him for anything."

Ryleigh nodded. "If you didn't say something that fierce and independent, I'd think you were taken over by aliens."

"I have been," she answered, settling her palm on her tummy.

"No matter what, sweetie, you won't be alone. Nick and I are there for you."

"I know—" Her voice cracked but she swallowed. "Damn hormones. You're going to make me cry again."

"I'm right there with you." She gasped. "I just thought of something. Our babies will be less than a year apart. They can grow up together and be best friends. Like us."

"I hadn't thought about that yet." Avery smiled. "How cool will that be?"

"I know, right?"

Avery's cell phone rang and she looked at the caller ID. Spencer. Part of her wanted to ignore him. Part felt a surge of pure joy. She wanted so badly to talk to him. Together the two parts made her heart pound.

She picked up the phone and pushed Talk. "Hi, Spencer." Ryleigh gave her a big thumbs up.

"How are you feeling?"

The deep voice made her shiver and long to be in his arms. "The same."

"Are you eating?"

"Some. Food isn't very appealing right now."

"You've got to eat. I've checked around and Rebecca Hamilton is the best obstetrician on staff at Mercy Medical."

"That's what I hear." When Ryleigh stood and indicated she was leaving, Avery waved goodbye and nodded at the talk later gesture her friend gave her. Then she was alone. "I'm going to contact her office."

"Already did. I called in a favor and you have an appointment tomorrow at three. Do you know where the office is?"

"Medical building on Horizon Ridge Parkway, not far from the hospital."

"Okay. I've got a surgery in the morning, so I'll have to meet you there."

"If you can't, don't worry about it," she said.

"I do worry. And I'll be there." After a short silence he spoke and his voice was deeper. Tense. "Take care of yourself, Avery."

"I always do."

Because no one else ever had. Spencer was doing all the right things for all the wrong reasons.

At two-fifteen the next day Avery left her office at the hospital and walked to her designated parking place. It was almost June and in the nineties. Nights cooled off and were beautiful, but soon it would be hot twenty-four hours a day. At least she wouldn't be too huge with child during Las Vegas's brutal summer months.

Her daughter had been born the end of September and Avery pictured her at different ages. Maybe there was a pool in her backyard. Or she went to friends' houses to play in the water and cool off. Hopefully she was healthy and happy but there was no way to know for sure.

That was the hardest part.

After starting her car she pulled out of the lot and onto Eastern Avenue, then turned right on Horizon Ridge Parkway. Five minutes later she was at the medical building and easily found Rebecca Hamilton's office on the first floor, facing the rock and plant landscaped courtyard.

There was no sign of Spencer but she'd arrived early to fill out paperwork. He'd arrive after insurance information was obtained and consents were signed—that was his role. The action hero. People willingly put themselves in his hands, but she wasn't one of them.

In front of the obstetrician's door she took a deep breath and whispered, "Here we go, little one."

Inside, the office was cool and it took a moment for her eyes to adjust from being out in the sun. After checking in with the receptionist, she handed over her Nevada driver's license and insurance card, then received a stack of paperwork as thick as *War and Peace*. Personal information, medical history, patient privacy laws, permission to release information for billing purposes. No wonder they requested that a patient arrive early. One latecomer could send the schedule into chaos.

At five minutes to three, she had writer's cramp and a chance to check out the waiting room. It was cheerful and elegant with powder-blue paint and a coordinating geometric chocolate-brown paper accenting one wall. Brown tweed chairs and sofas lined the room with tables and a leather ottoman in the center that added flat space for magazines and children's toys.

There were five or six women waiting, some obviously pregnant, others with infants in carriers here for a post-birth follow-up visit. When she'd had that last checkup, her baby belonged to another woman. The memory made her eyes sting with tears just as the door opened and Spencer walked in.

He slid his aviator sunglasses to the top of his head, blinked once, then saw her and walked over, taking the open seat.

Frowning, he said, "What's wrong?"

She almost laughed and said, "Duh." They were sitting in the obstetrician's office because she was pregnant and it wasn't planned. Wasn't that enough wrong for him?

"Everything's fine," she assured him.

"Then why do you look like you're going to cry?"

"Hormones." And a pain in her heart for the little girl she would never know. But this baby was hers. "The state of pregnancy makes a woman emotional. No matter how smart a man is, he'll never understand. I'll do my best to keep it in check."

"Not on my account. All I need is a second or two of warning when it's time to duck. My reflexes are pretty good."

Just the hint of his grin had her smiling. "You have my word."

The door beside them opened and a young woman in maroon scrubs stood there with a chart in her hands. "Avery O'Neill?"

She slid to the edge of the sofa and looked at Spencer. "I'll see you in a few."

"I'm going with you." He started to get up.

"No." She shook her head, but didn't touch him. "I'd rather you didn't."

"Don't shut me out. This is—"

"I know. Your baby, too." She glanced around and several women looked up, then away. She wasn't even showing yet and felt like the elephant in the room. "But this is very personal. An *exam*."

Comprehension dawned. "Okay."

"At the appropriate time, I'll ask you to come in. If you want."

"I want."

There was fierce intensity in his eyes and it was tempting to cling to that as a sign that he cared but she wasn't foolish enough to go there.

"Okay." She nodded. "I'll have someone come and get you."

Avery followed the young woman down the hall and into the exam room with the tissue-covered table and stirrups that every woman loathed. Posters on the wall depicted the female form with labeled organs and pictures of embryo and fetus in various stages of development.

"Miss O'Neill, it's nice to meet you." The assistant was in her late twenties or early thirties, a pretty brown-eyed brunette. "We need to get your height and weight."

"That's harsh," she teased.

"You don't look like you need to be concerned. I'm Karen, by the way. You'll be seeing a lot of me over the next months." She indicated the tall scale in the corner of the room. "During pregnancy it's important to make sure you're gaining enough weight, but not too much."

"No pressure." Avery had been through this once and had noted a first pregnancy in her medical history. No doubt to keep the schedule running smoothly, Karen hadn't seen that yet.

"It's not hard if you're already eating a healthy diet. And you look like you do. Just keep it up. Sometimes there's a tendency to retain water in the last trimester and you could have weight gain, even though you haven't significantly altered your way of eating."

"Okay." Avery knew that.

She stepped on the scale and Karen wrote something down on the chart, then raised the ruler and noted her height.

"You're a very petite person."

Probably why Spencer called her Tinker Bell. "It's an advantage on an airplane. Top shelf of the grocery store?" She shrugged. "Not so much."

Karen laughed. "There's a gown and drape on the table. Everything off and the doctor will be in shortly."

"Thanks."

Avery did as directed and the paper crinkled when she hauled herself up on the table. A few minutes later there was a knock on the door just before a beautiful blue-eyed blonde walked in. She looked like a teenager dressed up for Halloween in blue scrubs.

"Hi, Avery. I'm Rebecca Hamilton."

After shaking hands, she studied the doctor. "No offense, but I'd like to see your driver's license. You don't look old enough to be out of college let alone completed medical school."

The other woman laughed. "That happens a lot. I skipped grades in school, but I assure you I took all the classes and went through the appropriate training. If you want to check out my credentials, you wouldn't be the first."

"No. Your reputation is stellar. My best friend, Ryleigh Damian, is one of your patients."

"Ah." Understanding swept into her blue eyes. "My office

manager mentioned that Dr. Stone, the cardiothoracic surgeon, insisted on you being seen right away."

"He's the baby's father." No reason to hold back; it would be out there, anyway. "I'm sorry if he—"

"Don't be. I'm happy to help a colleague. He's the guy I'd want if my heart ever needs fixing."

Avery's was on the verge of breaking and he was the only one who could fix it. "He's in the waiting room right now."

The doctor nodded her understanding. "I'll talk to you both when we're finished."

A few minutes later the physical exam was over and Avery got dressed. Then she was directed to an office where Dr. Hamilton sat behind her flat oak desk. Spencer filled one of the visitor chairs and for the first time she noticed he was in scrubs. Obviously he'd come from the hospital, too. She sat next to him and wished he'd reach for her hand. He didn't.

Rebecca smiled at them. "Congratulations. You two are going to have a baby. You're about four weeks, Avery. Your health appears to be excellent and everything looks fine."

Avery still felt surreal about it, but hearing confirmation that all was well relieved her mind. "Good."

"I have informational materials about what's happening over the next months. The changes in your body. What to expect."

"I took anatomy," Spencer said dryly.

"But obstetrics is not your specialty. Would you want me working on your heart?" The tone was firm, but faintly amused. "And it's different when someone you love is going through the experience."

Avery glanced at him but he didn't meet her gaze. Love? Not so much. Responsibility? Now there was something he understood.

The doctor looked at Avery. "You need to take prenatal vitamins, schedule regular checkups. As you approach full term the appointments will be more frequent. There's initial blood work you need to have done. At five months we'll schedule a routine ultrasound. And you'll probably want to tour the hospital's OB facilities." She met Spencer's gaze. "Have you ever done that, Doctor?"

He had the good grace to grin sheepishly. "No. This is my first. And I'm pretty much confined to the O.R."

Dr. Hamilton smiled back as she handed him a manila envelope. "Read this. My cards are inside. If you have any questions please call. My goal is to ensure that you have a smooth pregnancy, a healthy baby and peace of mind."

If Rebecca could pull off that last part she was the smartest person in this room. Avery didn't think there was a pill or treatment on the planet that could erase her uneasiness.

They shook hands with the doctor, stopped at the reception desk to schedule the next appointment, then walked outside. Both of them slid on sunglasses and Avery couldn't help thinking they were both putting up shields.

"Are you going back to the hospital?" he asked.

"No. I took the afternoon off. Thanks for coming, Spencer." When she started to walk away, he reached for her hand to stop her. Looking up, she saw her face reflected in his sunglasses. She wondered if he saw the anxiety there. "What?"

"I'm going to follow you home."

"That's not necessary."

"Argue if you have to, but there's no changing my mind."

As if he thought she needed to see he was telling the truth, he slid his glasses off. The look was anything but reassuring. In the doctor's waiting room pregnant patients were glowing with anticipation of the experience, but Avery wasn't one of them. She couldn't be happy because the baby's father didn't look happy. She knew that not-happy look was the one right before the man you love disappeared.

It was darned inconvenient to know she loved him while constantly bracing for the moment she realized he was never going to show up again.

Chapter Fourteen

On the drive home Avery glanced in her rearview mirror and saw Spencer following closely behind. If she suddenly hit her brakes there was a good possibility he would run into her back bumper. This level of paying special attention would warm her heart and soul except she knew it was all about doing the right thing, the perfect thing. Making sure she got home without incident to avoid a guilty conscience or risk disappointing anyone.

She so didn't want to be a stepping stone to sainthood. She was a flesh-and-blood woman who'd just realized her warm feelings had escalated into head-over-heels love. And the recognition of that fact still had her reeling.

She arrived home and hit the remote button for the garage door, watched it go all the way up, then turned off the ignition, leaving the car in the driveway. After exiting, she weaved through all the stored boxes and into the house through the door that led into her laundry room and the kitchen beyond. Spencer parked behind her and followed her inside.

After setting her purse and Dr. Hamilton's manila envelope of information on the island, she turned and forced a carefree smile. "Okay. I'm home in one piece. Thanks, Spencer. I can take it from here."

Without responding to the dismissal he said, "Are you okay?"

"Fine. I don't need a babysitter."

"In about nine months you will." It should have been a light comment, but he didn't smile. Dragging his fingers through his hair, he exhaled slowly. "So. A baby."

"Yeah. I know the over-the-counter test is pretty accurate, but somehow seeing the doctor makes it more real."

He leaned back against the counter across from her and folded his arms over his chest. "What do you think of Rebecca Hamilton?"

"I like her."

He nodded solemnly. "Nick would do his homework and not go along with the choice if Hamilton wasn't the best."

"I know." She couldn't stop a small smile. "And more important, she didn't let you intimidate her."

"Can you believe the mouth on that woman?"

"It was classic. Beautiful. Blonde. You pegged her for a pushover and she set you straight," Avery said. "The smackdown was so smooth, one hardly realized she'd done it."

His eyes narrowed. "So you like seeing me put in my place?"

"It happens so seldom. I took notes."

"Pregnancy has given you a mean streak. What kind of example is that for this baby?"

Just starting to relax and get sucked into his charm, Avery felt her own smackdown. *This* baby. Not *our* baby.

"I think I need to sit," she said, turning her back.

Spencer followed her into the living room. "Are you all right?"

"Fine." Just pregnant, hormonal and sad. "I'm tired. Having no regard for the fact that it's not morning right now the nausea comes and goes at will." Just like men, including him. "Please go, Spencer. Don't you have hearts to fix? Lives to save?"

"Yes, as a matter of fact. But not until you're settled and comfortable."

Then you'll be here awhile, she thought. Comfort was hard to come by these days. He was doing all the right things, yet it all felt so wrong. She sat on the sofa and tucked her legs up beside her.

Looking down at her he said, "Have you eaten lunch?"

"Couldn't." She shuddered at the suggestion. Even now there was a lump in her throat as she remembered the cafeteria's steam table cuisine. "The mystery meat made me want to gag. The thought of a hamburger turned my stomach. Looking at it all made me want to run screaming from the room but I held back." She shrugged. "Didn't want to hurt the chef's feelings."

"I'm sure he can take it. The best adjective the hospital employees can come up with for it is nasty. Probably wouldn't have been the first time the cafeteria had a runner." He sat on the sofa, a foot away, and rested his elbows on his knees. "What about ginger ale and crackers? That might make you feel better."

"Oddly enough, that sounds good. How did you know?" Maybe one of his women had been pregnant. "As we established in Dr. Hamilton's office, obstetrics is a little out of your field of expertise."

He shrugged those broad shoulders. "Sometimes it's just common sense. An upset stomach needs something in it to calm down. Ginger is good for that—hence ginger ale. Saltine crackers are bland. You don't need to make things worse with hard to digest stuff." He stood. "I'll go to the store and get you a few things."

She swung her legs off the couch and stood. "No. I'll take care of it. Your patients need you."

"There's no emergency. It's nothing that can't wait. I'll be right back. Sit tight." He stopped with his hand on the front doorknob, classic pose of a man who couldn't wait to escape. "Is there anything else you need?"

"No."

"Okay. I'll be back in a few minutes. This won't take long."

When he was gone, she whispered to the emptiness surrounding her, "The only thing I need isn't anything you can buy in the supermarket or anywhere else."

She needed him. His love.

Nick and Ryleigh's wedding seemed a lifetime ago, but she remembered as if it were yesterday. Spencer had told Ryleigh how beautiful she looked, that all brides should be pregnant. Now Avery was going to have his baby. On top of that she was in love with him.

It would have been perfect if he'd asked her to marry him after the doctor confirmed they were having a baby, but he'd only proposed crackers and ginger ale.

The worst part was he hadn't touched her. Not once. No hug. No ecstatic taking her in his arms to lift her off her feet and swing her around. She was nothing more than a duty, like a patient who needed him.

He was looking for perfect. She and this situation were anything but.

It was almost midnight on the same day Spencer had found out for sure he was going to be a father.

He was sitting out by his pool and listening to the soothing sounds of the waterfall cascading over rocks in the far corner of his huge yard. Adam was in the chair beside him, leaving soon for Montana and a major lifestyle change. What he wanted, so good for him.

That was the most complex thought he could manage since all he thought about was how pale and tired Avery looked when he'd had to leave her earlier this afternoon.

He was going to be a father and that was his own damn fault. All he'd been able to think about was having Avery every way possible. In his arms; in his bed. He would never deliberately hurt her, but the thought of protecting her from pregnancy hadn't gotten through how desperately he'd wanted her. It had been a stupid, rookie mistake, but every step of the way with her he'd acted like a rookie.

So now he was going to be a father. It was a concept he was still trying to wrap his head around.

"It's a good thing Smith is taking call for you." Adam sipped his beer and stared out over the valley in the distance and the lights on the golf course below.

"Yeah. I can have a couple beers."

"So far you haven't consumed enough alcohol to talk about what's on your mind. Talking would do you good." Adam could often be sarcastic, but he wasn't now.

Maybe a deflection would work. "What makes you think I have something to talk about?"

Pool and backyard lighting revealed his brother's expression which clearly said don't-even-try-to-B.S.-me. "Come on, Spence. I saw the signs before you did. It's not your fault you didn't get it right away. Cracking chests and threading grafts through arteries barely wider than a piece of string requires a very high level of concentration. But you need to balance that important work with a satisfying personal life. You'll be much happier when work and love are symbiotic."

Spencer looked sideways at his brother and drank the

last of his beer. "Who are you? Guru Bob the spiritual life coach?"

"Maybe." Adam grinned, completely unfazed. "Look, you've got to talk to someone."

"No, I don't."

"Stubborn can be a double-edged sword when you're arrogant *and* smart. One bad experience in love and you never go there again? If that happened to your career, a lot of your patients wouldn't survive because they wouldn't have the benefit of your skills."

"Okay. Guru Bob it is. Just throw me a warning before you pull out the crystals and astrological charts. I'll be leaving then."

"Don't knock it, Spence. The stars and planets could probably run your life better than you are right now."

"Says who?" Spencer squeezed his beer bottle so tight it crossed his mind that shattering it in his hand was a possibility and not a good one for a surgeon. Avery had warned him about protecting his assets.

God, he missed her right now.

"Look, I don't have the patience for this." His brother's voice was laced with irritation. "I'm pretty sure Avery is having your baby. Tell me I'm wrong and the subject will never cross my lips again."

"I wish I could, but you're too damn smart for your own good," he said grudgingly. "And observant. As far as I'm concerned it's not one of your best qualities."

"Nobody's perfect. Not even you, although no one can say you haven't tried."

"Avery is having my baby." There, he'd said it out loud. "We had an appointment today and it was confirmed."

"Who's the doc?"

"Rebecca Hamilton. By reputation she was my first choice."

Adam's eyes narrowed. "How did Avery take that?"

"That was her choice, too. She'd already made up her mind. Her best friend is pregnant and seeing Rebecca, too."

"So, there's consensus and harmony." Adam grinned. "I'm channeling Guru Bob tonight."

"Stop."

"The greatness of the guru can't be silenced when the stars and planets are aligned—"

"Maybe throwing *you* in the pool would short-circuit some of that greatness."

"Possible." Adam's expression grew serious. "But first I want to talk about what you're going to do."

"About what?"

"Maybe if I throw you in the pool it would loosen your tongue."

"You mean about the baby." Spencer leaned back in the patio chair and linked his fingers over his abdomen. "No brainer. I already did it and I'm going to be a father."

"Actually I was talking about Avery, the baby's mother."

"What about her?"

"Are you going to marry her?"

Now it was out there in the universe that he was facing a scenario that he'd sworn never to face again. Marriage. Not a sure thing. A gamble he never wanted to take because of all the potential for screwing up.

Risks were inherent in his work but only when there was no other option to save a life. In those cases he didn't make the final decision. After being informed of every possible complication, a patient or family member signed a consent. But that was professional and this was personal.

"Am I going to marry her?" he repeated.

"Surely the thought crossed your mind."

"Why surely? Taking that step isn't a requirement for fatherhood. You know how I feel about marriage."

"And I've seen you with Avery." Adam shook his head. I also know what happened to you and why committing is retty scary—"

"I'm not scared."

Adam huffed out an exasperated breath. "This is not the ime for macho bull. If you're not sure of Avery's answer ou won't ask the question. I get it. College girlfriend broke our heart and made you look like a fool. Mom thought she vas wrong for you and didn't hold back when she said so. 'ou felt foolish *and* humiliated. It's an experience you don't vant to repeat."

"As much fun as it is reliving my youthful indiscretions, an we get to the point? Or change the subject?"

"It doesn't take my unique powers of observation to see ou and Avery are good together."

If he meant missing her when she wasn't there and wantng to be with her all the time, then Spencer would agree vith his brother's diagnosis. But between him and Avery, here was so much personal baggage they could fit enough tuff for a trip around the world. Twice.

"Adam?"

"Hmm?"

Spencer stared at the lights across the Vegas valley and he clear, midnight blue sky. "I wish she'd quit looking at me ike she's surprised I showed up. Or that I'm going to disapear any second."

"The lady got dumped on."

"Pretty much." There was no need to talk about the baby he gave up for adoption. It was no one's business but hers. and now his. Along with the determination to make sure no ne ever hurt her again. Including himself.

Adam sat up straighter and rested one ankle on the oppoite knee. "So you both have commitment issues."

"That's fair to say."

"It's a lot like rebuilding muscle. Positive action over an over until trust happens and gets stronger. You have to kee showing up. Don't disappear. Eventually she'll stop lookin as if that's what she expects."

Spencer glanced over. "As easy as that?"

"Yeah." Adam smiled, but it faded almost instantly. "S I'm glad we talked it over now because we might not hav another chance."

"Why?"

"The folks will be here tomorrow."

"Because of the baby?"

His brother chuckled. "It's not always about you."

"Says who?"

Adam continued, "I talked to mom yesterday and they'r coming to see me off to Blackwater Lake."

"What?" Spencer sat up. "You're not going back to Dalla first?"

"No need. There's not much in the apartment because never settled in. Always felt it was temporary."

"But there are still loose ends to tie up."

"All done by phone," his brother said. "I hired a movin company to pack up and ship it all to Montana."

"Isn't that awfully fast?"

"I'm anxious to start putting down roots. I think the folks trip here is a last ditch effort to talk me out of ruining m life. So, I would very much appreciate you breaking you news first. That will definitely take the heat off me abou wasting my skill and talents in the frozen backwoods tundr of that state up north, as mom calls it."

Wasn't it convenient, Spencer thought, that Catherine an William Stone would be there tomorrow. They could kill tw Stones with one trip. Two sons who didn't meet their expec tations.

Spencer had no choice but to tell them the truth, face t

face. He was going to be a father out of wedlock. There was no way to brace himself for the disappointment he'd see in his mother's eyes after that bombshell.

It was the best of days; it was the worst of days.

Spencer's work day had clicked along like a well-oiled machine. He'd seen patients in the office and never ran behind because they all showed up on time and there were no emergency calls. Hospital rounds had gone smoothly; all his surgery patients were doing well.

His evening was in front of him and he wanted to see Avery so bad he could taste it. He'd never in a million years admit it to his brother, but Adam was right. Calling and showing up every day would convince her that he planned to call and show up every day. Prove he wouldn't walk out on her or his child.

When he passed his large, desert-landscaped yard and pulled into the driveway, it turned into the worst of days. Adam's rental car was there, meaning he was back with the folks from McCarran Airport. It was time to confess his sins, and take the consequences. He'd rather take a beating but silent, disapproving disappointment was more their style.

He parked and got out, then muttered to himself, "Time to get this over with."

After opening the front door, he heard voices in the family room and headed that way through the large entryway with curved stairways on both sides. Catherine and Will were sitting on the leather corner group facing the fireplace with flat-screen TV above. Adam was in the kitchen making cocktails, per the plan they'd discussed.

He stopped in the doorway and smiled. "Hey. How was your flight?"

"Spencer." Catherine got up to give him a hug. "We were on time, thank goodness. All was perfectly smooth until we came over the mountains into Las Vegas and heat thermals from the valley made it turbulent."

Hang on, he thought. There would be more bumps even though they were safely on the ground. But that news could wait until they all had a drink.

"I'm glad everything went okay."

Will shook his hand then pulled him into a quick embrace. "It always surprises me to see the slot machines at the airport."

"This is Vegas, Dad." Adam walked over with two vodka tonics, handing one to each of them.

Spencer hoped he'd made them stronger than usual. "Not long ago someone won a couple million on a machine at the airport."

"That's why they call it luck." Will sipped his drink then nodded approval to Adam. "Good, son."

"Do you have some cheese and crackers, Spencer?" Catherine set her drink on the coffee table coaster then started for the kitchen. Apparently the question was merely a formality. She was a force of nature and would make it happen.

"I'll get it, Mom." He followed her and found a cutting board and knife. Where was the surgical robot when you needed everything to be perfectly sliced? "There's a new cheese store in Tivoli Village near Boca Park. They said this stuff is good."

"I took a peek around your house while we were waiting." Catherine looked up from arranging different shaped crackers on a plate. "It has so much space and lovely graceful arches and ceilings."

"Yeah. I like it."

"When are you going to redecorate?"

"It hasn't been a priority." He moved beside her and she took the cheese, artfully assembling it.

"Maybe a woman's touch is required."

Spencer's gaze jumped to hers. "What's wrong with my couch? I have taste."

"Of course you do. It comes from my side of the family."

When Will and Adam joined them, Spencer was grateful that this kitchen was big enough to hold a convention of cardiologists. It gave each member of his family adequate personal space for their larger than life personalities. And again he thought of Avery. She was such a little thing, yet her big heart, warmth and sass kept her from getting lost among the strong Stone men and women. She fit in with them.

He'd bought this place because it was big and flashy, but Avery's house was a home with sweetness and charm. Maybe that was all about her being there and he wished he was with her right now. That feeling wasn't just because of the news he had for his folks. It was something that got stronger every day, the need to see her, talk to her.

Hold her.

"How's Avery?" Catherine asked.

Spencer had wondered more than once in his life whether this woman could read his mind. "Why do you ask?"

"It's not a trick question. We met her a short time ago and she stayed in our home. She's a friend of yours and we became fond of her."

"Okay."

Adam leaned back against the counter, a beer in his hand. "So, I'm looking forward to moving to Blackwater Lake."

Spencer met his brother's gaze and gave a slight nod, thanking him for taking the heat off.

"Delicious," Catherine said after putting a piece of cheese on a cracker and taking a bite. "I think, Adam, that if working in a small town is something you want to try for a while, you should do it. Get it out of your system."

Adam sent him a look that clearly said you owe me big for this. "It's not a phase, Mom, like skateboarding, baseball or baggy shorts. This is my life and something about Montana fills up my soul."

"Poetically said." She finished her cracker. "You do realize there are probably wild moose, bears and mountain lions as well as no direct flights from there to Dallas?"

"Don't worry. The wild animals probably don't come to the clinic for their health care needs. And I'll still come to visit you."

"You better." She smiled, then looked at Spencer. "I noticed you made some changes in the backyard."

"Yeah. Landscaping. Added the waterfall. A built-in barbecue."

"There's a great view out there of the Strip and a golf course," Adam said. "I'll show you guys."

"Take your father. Spencer and I will meet you out there," Catherine said. "We'll bring out the drinks and snacks on a tray."

Now was his chance, Spencer thought. One parent at a time. Divide and conquer. "I don't have a tray, Mom."

"Didn't think so. But you do have something to tell me."

"What makes you think that?"

"I'm your mother." She shrugged as if that said it all, which it probably did.

He wasn't a parent yet and couldn't relate. But he did brace himself because putting it off wasn't smart. "Well, you're right. There is something and it involves Avery. But she's not to blame. It's my fault." Rip off the bandage quick. "She's pregnant and I'm the father."

"I see—"

"I'm sorry if I'm a disappointment to you."

"A new grandchild?" Catherine smiled. "A baby. How wonderful."

"It just happened. I didn't plan this. It's not the way you

raised me. I take the steps in the right order but this time I messed up. I'm sorry this situation isn't perfect."

"What are you talking about?"

"I let you and Dad down. I made a mistake. It's not my finest hour and I didn't get it perfect. I haven't messed up for a really long time, not since before med school—"

Suddenly his mother's eyes were full of understanding.

"Oh, Spencer—" She moved closer and hugged him. "You thought your dad and I expected you to be perfect?"

"Well…yes," he finally said. "You and Dad never screw up."

"I can't believe you believe that." She reached up and gently smacked the back of his head. "Maybe you're not bright enough to be a Stone and we were given the wrong child to take home from the hospital."

"Excuse me?"

"The best way I can explain it is that you were our first and you didn't come with an instruction manual. We wanted you to be the best you can be. To do that there's a delicate balance between motivation and pressure to succeed. And then the twins came along and we were so tired taking care of two babies, we sort of left you on your own. But you were so independent." She stared at him for a few moments, waiting for him to comment. "I'm a biomedical engineer so communication isn't my strong suit. It's time for you to contribute."

He thought back, feelings running together between the child he'd been and the man he was now. It was hard to put it into words. "You and Dad are so successful, I guess I always wanted to do at least as well, maybe better. But you're a tough act to follow. Only perfection would qualify as success."

"Oh, son…" Her brown eyes filled with regret and a sheen of tears. "If that's the lesson you learned, then we failed you.

A parent's instinct is to protect their children. Shield them from things. Try to provide a safe, stable environment. But imperfect people fall in love and there are bumps in the road."

He didn't remember anything but smooth waters. "You and dad?"

"Of course." She ran her finger around the edge of the cheese plate. "Did you ever wonder why there were so many years between you and the twins?"

"No. You always had a plan and if I thought about it at all, I figured that was it."

"Men plan, God laughs." There was pain in her voice. "I had trouble conceiving again, but finally it happened. We were so ecstatic until I miscarried. Even though we had you and loved you so much, it was devastating to lose that baby. I was depressed and your dad withdrew. We separated for a while."

Vaguely Spencer remembered his father being gone, coming for visits. Then he was back. "I didn't know what was going on."

"Because we messed up." She sighed. "We had problems and didn't handle it well with you or each other. By the way, every marriage has its ups and downs. I know what Becky is going through right now."

"She told you?"

"Uh-huh. She said you told her we'd understand and you were right. We did our best. I told her and I'm telling you that marriage takes work but if you have love there's a lot to work with."

"I don't know what to say."

"Good because I'm not finished talking yet." She smiled. "Love and marriage are messy and real and not perfect which makes life all the more exciting and wonderful. You've got to live, Spencer. Take a chance. Let yourself go. You're not going to get it perfect all the time, only some of the time. But in between is good, too. I've been so worried about you being alone."

"I haven't been." Sort of. He dated, but until Avery he'd been alone. Lonely.

"You're lying to yourself if you're choosing quantity over quality. Trust me on this, if you're looking for a sign from God that you're making a perfect choice, you'll be waiting for a long time. And I would hate to see you lose out on something wonderful because you think your father and I expect perfection."

"You just expect perfect judgment. It was clear you weren't too pleased with mine in college."

"What are you talking about?"

"The message came through loud and clear to anyone within earshot that you never liked her, no one in the family liked her and she never would have fit in. I was an idiot for loving her."

"Sweetheart—" Catherine's mouth trembled and she pressed her lips together for a moment. "You're my baby no matter how old you are. That girl broke my baby's heart and I hated her for it. I thought it would help you get over her if we told you she wasn't right. Instead, it made you not want to try again."

"That's the message I got." Until Avery made him ignore it. Being with her was more important than worrying about whether or not his judgment was flawed.

"Well, it's the wrong one," she said firmly. "I couldn't stand to see you so hurt and it was all I could think to do. I'm so sorry, Spencer. Your judgment was never in question. That girl was stupid for rejecting you."

"I think so, too."

"But Avery isn't stupid." Catherine touched his arm. "And she's good for you."

"She's a special woman." He kissed his mother's cheek and felt a weight lift from his soul. "Not unlike another woman I know. Are we okay, Mom?"

"You tell me." She sniffled. "Your father and I love you unconditionally. Never doubt it."

"Okay. You and dad are the best ever."

"Spencer, I want you to do something for me."

"Anything."

"Don't be sorry about this baby. Your father and I are thrilled, or he will be when you tell him. This is a new life."

"Maybe two lives," he teased.

"Don't start competing with Becky. This is a new life. A gift. Yours and Avery's child is special and unique. Don't commit to her if you don't love her. But if you do, letting her get away because you're afraid of making a mistake would be stupid."

"Who's getting away?" Will walked in the kitchen and set his cocktail glass on the granite.

"Avery and Spencer are going to have a baby," Catherine said. She looked at her son. "Sorry. I'm just too excited to keep it to myself. Isn't that wonderful news?"

"Congratulations, son." There was a huge grin on his father's face. "I like that girl."

"Me, too," he said.

"What are you going to do?" Catherine asked.

"Good question." Spencer wasn't sure.

He'd let Avery down because he was afraid of making a mistake and that was the biggest mistake of all. Now he needed to figure out how to fix the mess he'd made of everything.

Chapter Fifteen

Avery cleaned up her kitchen after making a dinner of grilled chicken and salad. It had been a struggle to finish, what with feeling like roadkill, but she was eating for two and took that responsibility very seriously. That almost made her smile; she was starting to sound like Spencer. It all felt surreal, even though he'd been shoulder to shoulder with her when this pregnancy was confirmed. Afterward there'd been no contact with him since he'd followed her home from the doctor.

The definition of leaving was no contact and she'd thought she knew how to prepare herself for this. After all, the disappearing man experience wasn't new to her. But it was like trying to brace for blindness, for never seeing blue sky and sunlight ever again. There was no way to skip over all the steps of shock, grief, loneliness and go right to the part where a dark existence without pain is the norm. A state of mind where you can move forward even though you know you'll never be truly the same again.

She was just wiping down the kitchen countertops when her doorbell rang. Her glance automatically jumped to the digital microwave clock that said it was after eight. No one stopped by at this time of night. Except…

Her heart automatically said it was Spencer, even though she'd talked herself down from the hope ledge moments ago. But who else could it be?

She hurried to the front door and peeked out the window. Her recoil had more to do with surprise and shock than anything else. There was a Stone family member standing there all right, but not the one she'd expected, not the man her heart ached for.

Catherine Stone was standing on her front porch and there was no way that could be good.

Maybe the riffraff police baton had been passed from his grandmother to the next generation of women and she was here to do the Stone dirty work.

Avery knew her car was in the driveway and made a mental note to clean out the boxes in the garage so she could park out of sight. That way if someone she didn't want to see dropped by she could pretend to not be home.

The bell rang again and made her jump. Avery had a sneaking suspicion that Catherine Stone wasn't going away until she'd said what she came here to say. Might as well get it over with. She opened the door and faked surprise. What with being a bad actress the act probably fooled no one.

"Catherine! What are you doing here?"

"Avery." She looked friendly enough, even bent down to give her a hug that felt warm and genuine. "It's nice to see you."

"I didn't know you were coming to Las Vegas."

Because Spencer hadn't said a word. Mostly because she

hadn't seen or heard from him. And it hurt even more to think she'd fallen so hard for the sort of man who'd send his mother to deliver the news that he was never going to be part of her life. Or the baby's.

Again she felt stupid for not thinking this could happen. Apparently her learning curve wasn't as highly developed as she'd thought.

"May I come in?"

"Of course. I'm sorry." Nothing that had happened was this woman's fault. She'd been genuinely gracious in Dallas and didn't deserve less than graciousness here in Las Vegas. "Please come in."

Catherine glanced around and Avery found she really wanted this woman's good opinion. Then she decided if Spencer wasn't going to be part of her life, neither would his family. If she never saw any of the Stones again, why should she care what they thought about her or her home?

"Your house is very lovely," Catherine said with a smile. "Very much you."

Lovely? Like her? That was okay, right? "It's small compared to yours."

"It's not the square-footage, but what you do with it that counts. And you've made it a home filled with comfort and warmth. If your living room is anything to go by."

Spencer seemed to like the bedroom, too, but that was TMI for his mother.

She simply said, "Thank you." Speaking of comfort and warmth… "Can I get you something? Iced tea? Water? I could make lemonade. I don't have any wine."

"Because of the baby?" There was no anger or disapproval in her blue eyes, only understanding. "Spencer told me."

"I didn't really think this was a social visit."

"On the contrary…" Catherine looked at the sofa. "May I sit?"

"Of course. Apparently my manners are missing in action along with my appetite and energy level."

The older woman sat and patted the cushion beside her, indicating Avery should take a load off. She did, but tried to maintain a safe comfort zone.

Catherine sighed. "I know what you mean about nausea, fatigue, bloating and baby weight. Those aren't the best parts of being pregnant, but it's well worth the discomfort when you hold that baby in your arms."

Avery could never forget her first pregnancy for more reasons than the toll it had taken on her body, but she had no intention of sharing any of it with Spencer's mother. "Does he know you're here?"

Without asking who "he" was, Catherine shook her head. "It's male bonding ritual time. Spencer is out with his father and brother doing whatever men do to become closer, something that doesn't require sharing their feelings, I'm sure. They can act like Neanderthals. Probably a facsimile of hunting and gathering that involves sharp projectiles and sticks of some sort."

Avery was tense, really wound tight, but couldn't help laughing at the description. It seemed he'd inherited charm and wit from his mother. "Aha, caveman stuff. You just described a Las Vegas buffet, darts and playing pool."

"That's exactly what they were talking about." The older woman smiled as if Avery was the smartest kid in class. "They hired a car for the evening."

"Smart," she agreed, then her smile faded. "But I'm still wondering why you're in town. Is it about my pregnancy?"

"Adam is taking the job at the Mercy Medical clinic in Blackwater Lake. He's moving there right away."

"That's fast. But it's what he wanted."

Catherine sighed. "When he was a tantrum-throwing two-year-old, I always said his determination would be a good quality in an adult. Now I want those words back."

"You don't want him to go?"

"It's not Dallas and we'll miss him. Mostly his father and I hope he's making the right decision. But our youngest son is convinced this is what he wants." She shook her head. "His father and I like having him close by. Letting go isn't easy no matter what age your children are."

"I can imagine." The words were automatic because Avery didn't have to imagine. She remembered the ache in her heart when the nurse took her infant daughter away for another woman to raise. The only thing worse would be if that baby girl wasn't on this earth at all.

No way would she ever give up the child she carried now.

The older woman's expression grew serious. "But I think you know I didn't come here to talk about Adam's career choice."

"No. I don't imagine you did." The knots in Avery's stomach, just starting to unravel, pulled a little tighter.

"I wanted you to know that Will and I are very excited about another grandchild."

Even though this baby had been conceived outside of marriage? That was unexpected from Doctor Perfect's flawless parents. "You are?"

"Absolutely." The smile on her face was real and warm, exactly how a prospective grandmother should look.

It was the expression Avery had longed to see on her own mother's face when told she was going to have a grandson or granddaughter but it never happened. And that's when Avery's eyes filled with tears.

Sniffling, she muttered, "Darn it."

Catherine moved closer and pulled her into a hug. "Don't cry."

"I'm not. Not really. I think it's just hormones leaking out of my eyes."

"I don't know whether to smile or say yuck." But her body shook with laughter.

Avery pulled away, wiped her eyes, and made a spontaneous decision. Spencer knew about her past and it was bound to come out because secrets never stayed secret. The information should come from her.

"Catherine, before you're any nicer to me, I need to tell you something."

"Anything, sweetheart."

She took a deep breath and let the words spill. "When I was seventeen, I got pregnant."

"Okay." The woman's expression could have been either sympathy or shock, but it was hard to tell.

"My mom wasn't supportive and I had no way to take care of a baby. The father was pressured to marry me, but he didn't show up because he'd joined the army."

"Jerk ran away from his responsibilities." Her eyes grew wide. "And you thought I was here to tell you Spencer had gone off to join Doctors Without Borders?"

"It crossed my mind." Avery shrugged. "Anyway, I had no choice. I gave the baby up for adoption. It was the best thing for her. Judge me if you want, but given the same circumstances, I'd make the same decision."

"First of all, my son wasn't raised that way. He would never send me to deliver a message like that and if he even tried, I'd tell him to stuff a sock in it. He would tell you the truth, face to face." Spencer's mother took her hand and held it between her own. "Second, I am judging, sweetheart, but not in a bad way. Doing what you did for your baby is one of the most courageous things I've ever heard."

"It wasn't perfect—"

Catherine frowned, clearly irritated. "What is with you

and Spencer and the quest for perfection? I told him, and I'll tell you, it's an impossible goal and no one expects it. All you can do is your best. No one can ask more of you than that."

Avery nodded, emotion choking off words for a moment. "I just wanted you to know that I didn't plan for this to happen, but my situation is different this time. I have a career. I can take care of myself and this baby. And I will be a good mother to him or her."

"And I want you to know that Will and I are there for you if you need anything."

"Thank you, Catherine."

"There's nothing to thank me for. You're part of the family. We love you and this is our grandchild."

At least some of the Stones loved her, just not the one she wanted most. But it was probably for the best that Spencer hadn't proposed out of obligation because she didn't want a man who didn't want her.

Tough talk that didn't even begin to stop the hurt. She believed Catherine was sincere in her offer of help and her baby would have grandparents. That was nice, but what Avery had always wanted was to be part of a family, one with a father, mother and child.

She tried to convince herself that what Spencer's mother offered was almost as good, but her heart wasn't buying it.

Spencer sat on a chair at the low counter by the nurse's station in Mercy Medical Center's Intensive Care Unit. He needed to do chart notes on the open heart surgery patient just moved from the recovery room to the cardiac care unit, but all he wanted to write was "wife driving everyone nuts." She was clueless and demanding. Fluff husband's pillow. Straighten his sheets. Someone needed to tell her the man was on a ventilator, sedated to keep him calm and didn't give a damn about pillows and sheets.

Julie Carnes, one of the best critical care nurses in the cardiac unit walked up beside him. She was a pretty blonde, one of the few he hadn't asked out, meaning Avery couldn't call her "one of his women." There were no women, not anymore.

Avery was the only one on his mind.

But Julie had a smirk on her face and a twinkle in her blue eyes that meant trouble. "Mrs. Benedict wants to see you right away."

"Oh?"

"It's about her husband."

"Really? Not cell phone restrictions in ICU?"

"I explained to her that in critical care rooms we're attuned to the equipment and every beep. When we hear a different sound it's a distraction."

"So, does she want to talk to me about catered lunch or the bridge club on Tuesday?"

"No. She wants to know when housekeeping is going to clean his room and change his bed."

"You're making that up," he accused her.

"Yes." Then her blue eyes turned serious. "There's no question that she's a demanding woman. But she needs reassurance, Dr. Stone. She loves the man and wants to know he'll be all right. Forget about the fact that it feels like she's hounding you."

Spencer suddenly got his own demanding behavior. No wonder Avery had been annoyed with him when he'd badgered her unmercifully about the robot surgery system. It was a miracle she hadn't clobbered him with her laptop or choked him with his own stethoscope. Part of his determination had to do with the fact that she had always fascinated him, but Dallas had turned that into so much more.

Now Avery was all he could think about. Her and the baby. He'd been busy with his family in town and his brother eaving for Montana. He hadn't seen her at the hospital, but new she was good at avoiding him when she wanted and ad probably taken to hiding out in the ladies' room again ecause she didn't trust him not to disappear.

Then he'd had this emergency bypass. He'd called her ffice, home and cell numbers, but she wasn't picking up, t least not for him. Before heading back to Dallas, his parnts had told him they had every confidence he would do the ight thing with Avery and their grandchild. And he would, s soon as he could get her to talk to him.

"Dr. Stone?"

That voice. Mrs. Benedict. But Julie's words went through is mind. *She loves him and needs reassurance.* If Avery had procedure this serious, words wouldn't be nearly enough ntil he could see for himself that she was okay.

He stood up. "Mrs. Benedict. How can I help you?"

The dark-haired woman was in her sixties, short and ound. When she started to cry, he put his arm around her. I know ICU is scary. There are all kinds of machines beepng and flashing numbers."

She nodded, then pulled away and brushed at the moisure beneath her eyes. "That tower of stuff with all the tubes utting things into him, and taking stuff out. I—"

"Everything he has is helping him to get well."

"It doesn't feel like he'll ever be the same again." Her lips rembled, but she got control. "I just want to talk and laugh nd have him tell me what to do when we get your bill."

Spencer laughed, impressed by her strength and sense of umor under difficult circumstances. He pictured Avery that vay. "He's strong. A fighter. And he's got you."

Spencer hoped he had Avery.

A look of determination replaced the tears on Mrs. Beneict's face. "Then I'll give him everything I've got."

He realized the pillow fluffing and sheet changing were

just her way of controlling an uncontrollable situation. An again he thought of Avery. "Are you taking care of your self?"

"I know it's hard to believe looking at me, but I can't ea Sleeping is hard, too."

"You have to do both. Getting him back on his feet wil be a long haul and that's all going to be on you."

There were tears in her eyes again, but she said, "I'll d whatever it takes to get him well. Sweet talk, tears and wha I do best. Nagging."

"Good." Spencer nodded. "It will be up and down, goo days and bad." Exactly what his mother had said about mar riage. Not perfect, but worth it. "Right now I don't see an reason medically why he won't recover. When friends offe let them help." He gave her his card. "Call me anytime if yo have any questions."

"Thank you, Doctor."

He put his arm across her shoulders and gave her a squeeze. "I'll keep checking on him. And you."

She walked away and Spencer finished up his chart note then sat for a few minutes thinking. He'd always concen trated on surgical perfection. Until now the patient an family point of view had been off his radar but he was seein life through eyes opened by loving Avery O'Neill.

He'd worked so hard at not making a mistake that he' missed out on the best part of life. But maybe he'd just bee waiting for a sassy, sexy blonde Tinker Bell to show him playing it safe was the biggest mistake of all.

Seeing her was always the best part of his day. She wa the toughest, most tender, sweet, beautiful-inside-and-ou woman he'd ever known and he couldn't imagine his lif without her in it. Her and the baby. He loved them both an had never been more sure of anything in his life.

Suddenly it was vitally important to tell her. He looked a

the clock on the wall. It was three-thirty and she would still be at work.

Not even the ladies' room could hide her from him now. He'd definitely made a mess of things, but thanks to his brother, Adam, he knew what to do to fix it.

Avery looked across her desk at Ben Carson, her boss. He was over six feet tall, with dark hair and brown eyes. Handsome, she supposed, and a bachelor. Because he wasn't attached, someone was always trying to set him up. Chloe often said Avery should flirt with him a little, but she'd never been interested. Now Spencer had spoiled her for any other man. Darn him.

This meeting in her office was to discuss Spencer's robot and approve her shuffling funds from different programs, trying to minimize the impact on each one. The goal was to acquire cutting-edge technology, no pun intended, without losing quality care in any other area of the hospital.

"Good job." Ben handed back the report. "I can't think of anything you didn't already cover. This is very thorough and well thought out, Avery. Now we need to talk about—"

The door to her office opened without warning and Spencer stood there. "I need to talk to you."

There was no doubt he meant her. "I'm in a meeting—"

"Avery—" Chloe was hot on Doctor Hottie's heels. "I tried to tell him you were busy, but he just blew right by me."

Spencer never looked at anyone but her. "Nothing is as important as what I have to say to you."

"It never is," Avery said. "Don't worry, Chloe. You're not in trouble."

Her assistant nodded, then backed out of the room.

Avery forced herself to look at Spencer. Seeing him made her heart hurt but looking away was impossible. She memorized the stubborn tilt of his head, the arrogant curve of his mouth that turned soft and tender when he kissed her. Used to kiss her, she corrected.

She also knew how intractable he was when he wanted something. Then he got what he wanted and lost interest. At least he had with her. She wouldn't take his calls because she didn't want to hear him say he was breaking it off. He would think that was the right thing, but it would only hurt her more.

"Spencer," she said. "When Ben and I are finished I'll be happy to brief you on the time frame for your robot, but right now I'm busy."

"Nice to see you again, Dr. Stone." Ben stood and held out his hand.

Spencer took it grudgingly. "Carson."

"Avery has been telling me about this remarkable surgery system. It's a pretty impressive piece of equipment and got us to wondering if we're successfully serving the cardiac care needs of the community. We're in regional talks to implement a state-of-the-art cardiology center. Would you be interested in being the medical director?"

"Right this minute I'm only interested in talking to Avery."

"Spencer—" She was sure her cheeks turned red and didn't need him jeopardizing her job by slipping from the professional to the personal. "Dr. Stone, I'm working. When Ben and I have finished, I'll be happy to discuss whatever you want."

Big, fat lie. She knew he wanted to be finished with her and hearing him say so straight out was going to be horrible.

"If it will get Ben out of here faster," Spencer said, intensity making his narrowed eyes look like green flames, "I'll agree to be the cardiology medical director, but I need to talk to you alone."

"I'm going to hold you to that, Doctor." Ben walked to the

door. "We can finish up later, Avery. I'll have my secretary set up a time."

He was out of there before Avery could plead with him not to leave. Spencer had already cracked her heart and now he was going to break it.

"Situation normal," she said. "You're the golden boy of Mercy Medical Center and you always get what you want. So make it quick. I've got work to do."

Spencer moved closer. "You have every right to not trust me. I haven't been there for you, not really since we got back from Dallas. So, I just want to straighten things out. Tell you how I feel—"

"Stop. Let's cut to the chase." What an appropriate choice of words. He'd chased until she surrendered. Now he'd lost interest as she'd expected. It was her fault for not being strong enough to resist him. "Look, Spencer, your robot is not only approved, it's taking Mercy Medical Center to a new level of cardiac care. You can stand down and quit bugging me. Mission accomplished. You got everything you wanted."

"Not yet." He was so close now only her desk separated them. "But I will if you agree to marry me."

Avery was sure she hadn't heard right. "Excuse me?"

"It's a simple question," he snapped. "Will you marry me?"

That's what she'd thought he said. "No."

"What?"

"I understand you're not accustomed to hearing that. Let me repeat. N-o."

"Why?"

"I don't really have to give you a reason." Her legs were shaking so badly she could hardly stand, but she'd never needed to be strong more than she did right now. "But here it is. You don't really want to marry me."

"The hell I don't," he snapped again.

"You think you have to be perfect and do the right thing because I'm pregnant with your child. But that's not the right thing for me. So the answer is no." She shrugged. "I want more."

"You want more? I'll give you more." He stared at her, raw emotion smoldering in his eyes. "I'm in love with you. I want you, to spend the rest of my life with you. I want our baby and you should know before you say yes that I want more kids. I know you and words aren't enough. So I'll keep showing up every day until it sinks into that stubborn head of yours that I am not going to disappear. I would never walk out on you or our child. I couldn't leave you even if there wasn't a child. I love you more than anything. If you know me as well as you think, you know I'd never lie."

Avery believed him. Doctor Perfect *wouldn't* tell a lie. To her complete horror and humiliation she started to cry and buried her face in her hands.

In a heartbeat Spencer was around the desk and holding her. "I thought you'd push back and fight me every step of the way, but I never expected this. Please don't cry, Tinker Bell."

"Damn hormones," she choked out, resting her cheek on his chest.

"You're going to have to help me out here. Is this happy or sad crying?"

His heart was beating strong and steady beneath her cheek and she smiled through her tears. "And they say you're the smartest person in the room."

"Not when you're in the same room. I've been the biggest idiot on the planet but you have to understand this is new territory. I've never been in love before. Just say you'll marry me."

"Okay." She pulled away and he brushed the moisture from her cheeks with his thumbs. "I'll marry you."

"Why?" But the single word had his mouth curving up in a grin that was so very Spencer it made her completely happy.

"I love you," she said simply. "But my yes has one condition."

"Anything."

"Don't expect me to be perfect."

"It's highly overrated." His smile widened. "And boring. All I want is you. Just the way you are."

Dr. Spencer Stone fixed broken hearts and knowing he loved her had just worked a miracle with hers. Loving him and being loved in return made it worth holding out for Doctor Perfect.

* * * * *